As they stoo[illegible]
a bulky [illegible]
came chuffing
down the trail.

■ ■ ■

"'Tis horrible to look upon." Weegee turned her face to Jon-Tom. "Where have you brought us, spellsinger?"

The monster was the size of several elephants. It had eighteen legs, all of them round, and as it thundered southward Jon-Tom could just make out the legend inscribed on its flank.

PIGGLY WIGGLY

"Out with it, mate. You know where we are, don't you?" Jon-Tom didn't reply. Mudge turned away from him.

There was no sea to be seen; only mile upon square mile of dense forest broken by a single wide, paved trail. Weegee waddled over to a wooden square that topped a post. She couldn't make out the alien hieroglyphics on it but Jon-Tom could.

"I didn't think Hell would have quite so many trees." Weegee was examining a pair of acorns.

"We're not in Hell," Jon-Tom assured her. "Just Texas."

BOOKS BY ALAN DEAN FOSTER

Alien
Aliens
The I Inside
Into the Out Of
Krull
The Man Who Used the Universe
Pale Rider
Shadowkeep
Starman

THE SPELLSINGER SERIES:

Spellsinger
The Hour of the Gate
The Day of the Dissonance
The Moment of the Magician
The Paths of the Perambulator
The Time of the Transference

Published by
WARNER BOOKS

ALAN DEAN FOSTER

THE TIME OF THE TRANSFERENCE

A Warner Communications Company

WARNER BOOKS EDITION

Cover art by Tim Hildebrandt

Warner Books, Inc.
666 Fifth Avenue
New York, N.Y. 10103

 A Warner Communications Company

Printed in the United States of America

First Printing: January, 1987

10 9 8 7 6 5 4 3 2 1

For Richard and Karen and
Michele and Dawn Hirschhorn,
A small detour down the byways of life.

From cousin A, D, & F.

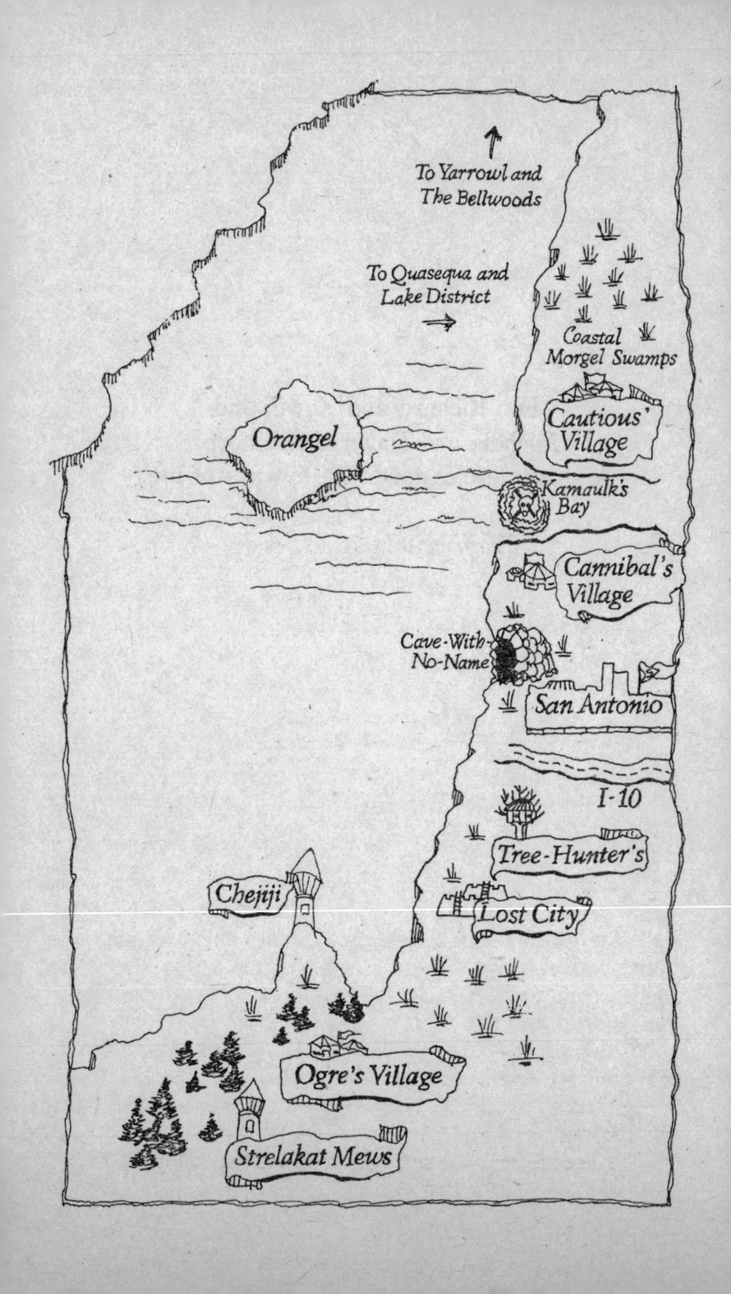
To Yarrowl and
The Bellwoods
To Quasequa and
Lake District
Coastal
Morgel Swamps
Cautious'
Village
Orangel
Kamaulk's
Bay
Cannibal's
Village
Cave-With-
No-Name
San Antonio
I-10
Tree-Hunter's
Chejiji
Lost City
Ogre's Village
Strelakat Mews

I

''Jon-Tom, there's someone in the tree.''

From the abyss of deep rest he replied. ''Huh—what?''

Feminine fingers imprinted themselves on the flesh of his shoulder. ''I said *there's someone in the tree*.'' The voice was sharp, melodious, familiar, as well it should have been.

Extending himself mightily, he opened one eye. Moonlight gilded the branches of his home and those of the belltrees that surrounded the glade of oaks. Morning was conspicuous by its absence, nor was there any indication that the sun intended to put in an appearance any time soon. He listened intently.

''Go back to sleep, Talea.'' He turned over slowly. ''There's no one in the tree.''

''Not our tree, idiot!''she whispered huskily. ''Old hardshell's tree.''

''Of course there's someone inside Clothahump's tree.''

He told his mind to go back to sleep. His subconscious laughed at him. "Clothahump and Sorbl."

"The wizard sleeps the sleep of the dead and I know what Sorbl sounds like when he's drunk. This is different, Jon-Tom. Trust me, I know sounds in the night."

He sat up, rubbed his eyes. "From stalking innocent citizens in dark alleys, no doubt."

She punched him in the ribs. "Don't be funny. I've put those days behind me. I'm serious, Jon-Tom." She looked toward the window that punctured the tree wall. "I don't know how you can sleep through that racket anyway. They've been screaming and shouting over there for half an hour. Naturally now that you're awake they've stopped."

In the silence that followed, the sound of breaking crockery and muffled oaths drifted across the flowerbed. Talea's face whipped 'round to stare at him.

"Don't tell me you didn't hear *that*."

Still half asleep, he frowned and pushed the covers forward. "I won't, because I did hear it. So they're having a party over there or something. Wouldn't be the first time Clothahump's entertained out-of-town visitors. Some sorcerors can get pretty wild when they've had a few."

"If it's a party, why weren't we invited? You know how old shelldrawers likes to show off your music."

"So it isn't a party. What if they're friends of Clothahump's from far away and they don't want to be disturbed?"

"I don't care if they're visiting from another planet. I've got a busy day tomorrow and I need my beauty sleep." Angrily she put her fists on her hips. This did wonderful things to the rest of her body. He stared at her, sitting there next to him in bed, the moonlight highlighting the shadows and secret places of her body, and his thoughts drifted from the continuing commotion next door.

"You don't need any beauty sleep. You're perfect already." He reached for her.

"Oh no." She skittered away from his hands and smiled determinedly at him. "I didn't wake you up for that. At least, not right now." Her expression softened. "Can't you go over there and tell them to keep it down? Even if they are wizards.'' Another burst of noise from the turtle's tree punctuated her request.

He eyed her longingly for another moment, then turned and slipped from beneath the covers. Winter was loosening its grip reluctantly this year, so he stepped into slippers and a heavy robe. While Clothahump could dimensionally expand the interior of a tree to provide its occupants with spacious living quarters, he had yet to figure out a practical way to heat one without burning the tree itself to the ground.

Walking to the single bedroom window, he gazed across the sleeping flowers toward the immense ancient oak that the wizard called home. He thought he saw lights flickering inside, but that could be an illusion cast by the dimension spell. If it *was* a torch or glow bulb, it probably meant that Clothahump had caught his famulus in the chemicals again and was chasing him around the tree. He said as much to Talea without turning to face her. If he saw her sitting there naked on the bed he wouldn't be able to concentrate on anything else.

They had been living together for several months. Time enough to discover that she was as adept at making love as she had been at picking pockets, the latter a distressing habit he was having a hard time breaking her from. The dimensionally expanded tree had been a present from Clothahump. Designed, she'd noted sardonically, to make sure Jon-Tom stayed close to his mentor. Clothahump wanted Jon-Tom close at hand in case he had any more potentially lethal errands to be run. But that hadn't been reason enough for her to turn the gift down.

''Clothahump's the world's greatest wizard. It's not my place to tell him how to behave.''

She yanked the heavy quilts back up to her neck. ''You need an excuse to stand up to him? Okay—tell him that your sweet, demure little Talea badgered you unmercifully until you had no choice but to stumble over and pretty-please ask him to shut his exalted self up. For the rest of the night, at least. As the greatest wizard in the world I'm sure he can decapitate Sorbl silently. And if it's a party, ask him why we weren't invited.'' She sat up abruptly. ''You do think that's all it is, don't you?''

He glanced back out the window. ''I don't know. Clothahump's almost three hundred years old. You can make a lot of enemies in three hundred years. I've never known him to be up this late.'' More breaking sounds drifted across the space between the trees. What if Sorbl's life wasn't the one in danger?

Leaving the window he walked to the rear of the bedroom and opened the large carved armoire that stood there. In addition to clothes, boots and other personal effects it contained a small, seamless ramwood chest. He opened it and removed a curious, double-stringed instrument from the padded interior.

''If you think there's trouble,'' said Talea, watching him, ''why don't you take your fighting staff instead?''

Jon-Tom cradled the duar against his chest, fiddled with the tuning fweeps. ''If it's a party I'd look a pretty fool barging in with weapons. If Clothahump's just chasing Sorbl maybe I can calm him down. And if it's something else, I'll be better armed with this than the staff.''

''Not with *your* voice.'' She slid down beneath the covers until only her eyes were visible. Her voice was muffled by the blankets. ''Hurry back. If you can get them to shut up over there maybe we can make a little noise of our own over here.''

''Just stay like that.'' He was backing toward the doorway. ''Don't move a muscle, not an eyebrow. I'll be back before you can blink.''

She blinked, murmured teasingly. ''What, back already?''

He turned and walked fast for the parlor, wondering if he ought to take a lantern and as quickly deciding against it. He hadn't mastered any fire songs yet and his precious supply of matches was down to four. Besides, he didn't need any more light, not with the moon half full on a clear night.

As he shut the tree door behind him the chill night air scratched his throat. He bundled the robe's heavy collar up tight. Based on where the moon was pinned to the sky he thought it was between three and four A.M. An uncivilized time to be awake, much less to be tramping through hibernating flowers clad only in furry slippers and a downy robe. He knew he cut an absurd figure in the moonlight, even though there were only small nocturnal flying lizards and phosphorescent branch crawlers present to observe his passage.

As he neared the wizard's tree he slowed to peer in the front window. The parlor was dark, which strongly suggested that Clothahump was not in a partying mood. The skylight which looked down into the laboratory was equally blank.

Probably nothing more than the usual wizard-apprentice infighting, he groused silently. Here he'd roused himself out of a warm bed and away from a warm woman to find out that the combatants had retired for the evening immediately prior to his arrival.

Might as well make a thorough job of it, he told himself, to placate Talea's suspicions if nothing else. He made his way around to the back of the tree. A huge root half the height of man emerged from the flank of the great oak to plunge at a gentle angle down into the earth. Set into the side of the root was a door which led not to a root cellar, but into the rear of the wizard's kitchen. The door was secured with a massive padlock.

A few appropriate notes from his duar sufficed to spring the seal. The magic words the wizard employed would have taken less time, but Jon-Tom always had a hard time remembering them. Pulling the door aside, he peered inward. No light, but this time he thought he could make out the muffled mutter of distant conversation. There was more than one voice and the whole conversation sounded agitated. He thought he recognized Clothahump's solemn tone and Sorbl's high-pitched whine.

But other voices were present.

It was not unknown for wizards to entertain visitors at odd hours, but such meetings were always held in the front parlor, not in the kitchen. He hesitated as he thought about returning home to get his ramwood fighting staff. But having already refused to bring it, such a return would only make him look foolish in Talea's eyes. Anyway, he didn't need the ramwood. He had his duar.

He felt his way down the steps that led into the tree. They led him into the back of the pantry, which was filled with preserved crawfish, river greens, bottles and jars of spices and flavorings and dressings and every other sort of victual that might appeal to the palate of a discriminating two-hundred-and-fifty-year-old turtle.

Carefully he opened the pantry door. A dim glow bulb cast faint light through the kitchen. The voices, much louder now, came from beyond. The lab was to his right down a narrow corridor. The dining room lay straight ahead. Closing the door quietly behind him, he tiptoed past the stove where Sorbl the owl toiled daily and leaned against the kitchen-dining area divider.

It was easy to make out what was being said. The voice that was currently speaking did not sound like that of an invited guest.

"Where is it? I'm getting tired of asking the same question, wizard!"

Jon-Tom clutched the duar close to his chest and slowly nudged the door outward. The glow bulbs in the dining room were running at maximum intensity and he could see clearly. Wings fastened to his side, his clawed feet tied together and his beak taped shut, Sorbl sat bound to a chair. Clothahump had been secured to another chair in the center of the room. The dining table had been shoved to one side.

Three figures confronted the stubborn wizard. None looked to be the sort one would invite to elevate the general level of conversation at a casual soiree. A tall, muscular wolf leaned on the shaft of his battle-axe and picked his teeth. Jon-Tom saw that he had only one eye. The other socket had been filled with a large cabachon citrine which sparkled piss-yellow in the glow-bulb light.

A civet cat lounged against a chair next to him. The cat's

sword rested in its sheath and he held a bucket from which rose thick steam. To his right stood the portly individual who had been doing most of the talking Jon-Tom had overheard. The guinea pig was not cute. At four feet he had to stretch to lean over the back of the chair to which Clothahump was tied. He wore a suit of thin chain mail which jangled as he hopped up and down in anger and frustration.

Clothahump had retreated completely into his shell. The wizard's hands, feet and head were not visible. The guinea pig was leaning over the opening in the top of the shell and screaming inside. Ugly scars showed on his neck where the hair had never grown back.

"Come out of there, damn you! I'm tired of talking to a carapace." He started to reach inside with a paw, thought better of it and did not. Then he stepped back and nodded to the civet cat. To Jon-Tom's horror he saw that the bucket held boiling hot mud, which the cat was preparing to dump down Clothahump's shell.

The threat was sufficient to induce Clothahump to slowly stick out his head. He squinted in the light, his hexagonal glasses unsteady on his beak. Obviously he and Sorbl had been surprised while sleeping, before either could take any defensive action.

"For the last time, I am telling you to get out while you still have a chance." Clothahump sniffed disdainfully. "I am the world's greatest wizard. Tying me to a chair will not prevent me from turning all of you into walking flagons of pain. I will strip the flesh from your bones, slowly and agonizingly. It is only out of the goodness of my heart and out of sympathy for such blatantly ignorant morons as yourselves that I have not done so already!"

The wolf cast a hesitant glance in the direction of his leader, but the boss of the bandits wasn't fazed in the slightest by the wizard's threat.

"Typical turtle drivel. If you could do anything to us you would have done so already. Without ready access to your potions and powders you're helpless. Empty threats irritate patience already grown thin. For the last time, I say, tell us where your gold is hidden!"

"For the last time," Clothahump replied in an irritated mutter, "I tell you that I have no gold. I have better things to do with my time than spend it amassing a useless fortune. My house is rich in knowledge only, a treasure beyond compare which lies forever beyond the grasp of your soiled fingers. As my servant can attest, I keep on hand only enough money to pay my household expenses, which are not exorbitant." At this blatant attempt to deflect the thieves' attention to him, Sorbl squirmed nervously in his chair, his vast yellow eyes wider even than usual.

The guinea pig spat on the clean floor. "Everyone knows that wizards like to keep treasure close about 'em." He cast sharp glances in all directions. "There are riches in this tree. I can smell them." His whiskers quivered as he looked back into Clothahump's eyes.

"The sun will be up soon and I'm tired of talking. I've no time for visiting noseybodies." He nodded to the civet cat. "Let's see how the old fakir likes having something a little warmer than his shell next to his skin."

The cat grinned and raised the steaming bucket. Clothahump eyed it until the first drop of hot mud began to slide over the rim. "No, wait. I'll tell you."

Holding the bucket in position, the cat glanced to his leader for instructions.

"All right, that's better. What's a little lost gold to the 'greatest wizard in the world'?" The guinea pig shoved his bristly face right up against Clothahump's. "Tell us your secret place, then, and be quick about it."

"A moment, if you please, to catch my breath." The bandit gestured curtly for the civet cat to back off. "I must think—I am very old and have not had the need to check on the condition of my hoard for some time. As your small minds have no doubt already noticed, this tree contains many more rooms than one would think to look upon it from outside."

"I've seen dimension-expanding spells at work before."

The guinea pig was tapping his sword sheath impatiently. "Don't try to impress me with such as that, and don't think to stall me, either."

"Please be quiet." Clothahump closed his eyes, bowed his head forward. "I have to concentrate."

Heretofore, Clothahump's reputation had been enough to keep would-be thieves away from his sanctuary. These three were much bolder than the rest—or much stupider. They didn't know enough to be frightened. That did not lessen the threat they posed to the old sorceror.

Three common thugs. Well, he could deal with them easily enough.

He took a step back and kicked open the door. It slammed against the dining room wall with a sound like a cannon going off. The civet cat nearly dropped the bucket of hot mud he was threatening Clothahump with while the guinea pig did a complete turn in midair. Raising his battle-axe, the wolf bared his fangs and assumed a defensive pose.

Jon-Tom glared down at the trio of intruders, well aware that he towered over the tallest of them. "It's too early in the morning for fun and games." He ignored wolf and civet cat and spoke directly to the guinea pig. "That means it's time for sensible beings who want to live to see another morning to be in bed. That includes bewhiskered butterballs with bad table manners. The lot of you have five seconds to clear out before I reduce you all to gibbering mush."

So saying and having already chosen a suitable tune, he plucked out a few chords on the duar. The civet cat jumped away from the noise and tossed the mud bucket aside, splattering the floor. The wolf winced visibly. So did Sorbl for that matter, but not Clothahump.

"My boy, I cannot recall a previous occasion when I had reason to compliment you on your usually atrocious timing, but this makes up for it. Thank you for saving me from an indecorous situation."

Wary but far from trembling in his sandals, the guinea pig glanced back at the bound wizard. "Who is this singing fool who carries no weapon and challenges us clad in his nightclothes?''

"This is Jon-Tom," said Clothahump. "Just as I am the greatest of all wizards, so is he the greatest of all Spellsingers. And while I do not have access to my magic potions and powders, as you have so carefully noted, you will also note that he carries his instrument of power with him. With a few fragments of song he can spin the world like a top. Or strip the fur from incautious intruders." He looked past the guinea pig. "Have mercy on them, Jon-Tom. I know your temper, but none have suffered yet." Now he turned to fix a warning stare on the civet cat.

"You still have a chance, albeit a fast vanishing one, to leave here with your heads still attached to your disreputable necks. Avail yourselves of it or I will not be responsible. I cannot restrain the spellsinger forever."

The wolf was starting to retreat toward the far door. "Mebbee we better do as he says, Squig."

"Sure is a strange looking one," agreed the civet cat in a rasping tone.

Having chanced so much and nearly accomplished all, the guinea pig was not quite ready to concede defeat.

"So you're a spellsinger, eh?" As he spoke he was drawing a short, thick-bladed knife from his belt. Jon-Tom did his best to ignore this as he glared down at his adversary.

"That's right, fatso. I've defeated demons with powers beyond your comprehension, have freed wandering perambulators to cavort openly between the stars, have battled otherworldly sorcerors and whole armies of plated folk. Now take your weakling minions and begone, lest I loose my wrath on you all!"

As a threat it was magnificently purple, but ineffective. The guinea pig gestured with the knife, twisting the blade through the air.

"How about if I loose the blood in your veins? Since your throat is out of reach, I think I'll start on your legs."

"A short serenade is in order then." Jon-Tom launched into song. Months of practice in the tree while the world around him lay blanketed in cold and snow had made him proficient. As the first notes emerged from the duar there was the taste of magic in the air.

He'd chosen the song carefully. It was designed to turn the intruders' own weapons against them. This it did. Unfortunately, it did so with the unpredictable selectivity that Jon-Tom had come to know at his peril. There were several weapons for the magic to fasten upon: the battle-axe of the wolf, the knife of the guinea pig, the sword of the civet cat. In addition to his sword, the civet cat also possessed a natural weapon which was much superior to all the other weapons in the room combined. This consisted of the skunk-like glands that flanked its anus. It was this weapon which the spellsong loosed against thieves and innocents alike as the dining room was flooded with the most awful stink imaginable.

Flinging aside his formidable axe, the wolf put both hands over his mouth and raced for the far doorway. Knife raised, the guinea pig halted as though he'd run flat out into a brick wall, bent over and began heaving his dinner all over the floor. Also his lunch, breakfast and the undigested remnants of a previous day's salad. As the only one in the room capable of standing his own effluvia, the civet cat grabbed his leader by the collar and began dragging him in the wolf's wake.

Meanwhile Clothahump had retreated back into his shell to take advantage of what little protection it afforded him from this pernicious assault while Sorbl was retching uncontrollably in his bonds. Jon-Tom struggled to segue into a song that sang of sweetness and sugar. He'd defeated the intruders without having to shed a drop of blood, but the victory had proved messy nonetheless.

Civet cat, wolf and guinea pig had fled and he did not think they would soon return. As he sang away the stink his own stomach quieted.

Eventually Clothahump's head popped out of his shell. Eyes watering, he gingerly extended hands and feet. His words were woozy but complimentary.

"That was very nicely done, my boy. There are no rules in war, but next time it would be better if you could settle on some alternate method of sending our assailants fleeing in panic." Indecipherable sounds of internal unpleasantness issued from Sorbl's vicinity. The owl's feathers were sodden with vomit. The dining room stank of something long dead and only recently exhumed.

Jon-Tom staggered to his mentor on shaky legs. "Sorry, sir. It wasn't quite what I had in mind, but with that knife waving at me I didn't have time to be particular."

The wizard nodded sagely. "What you have in mind never does seem to be quite what happens. Come, help me with these bindings." He was struggling to loosen the ropes that bound his shell to the back of the chair, nodded toward a cabinet. "Carving knives in the lower drawer. They will make quicker work of these restraints than my thick fingers." He glanced back toward the door that led to the hallway and grinned slightly.

"It seems we have seen the last of our robbers. I am sure they will not try to come back."

"I don't blame them." Jon-Tom worked with one hand while holding his nostrils pinched with the fingers of the other. "I'm ready to leave myself."

Locating the drawer Clothahump had indicated, he chose the largest of the butchering knives within and turned to cut the wizard loose. As he turned around a terrific pain went through his right foot. Neglecting to look where he was stepping, he'd spun right into the upturned blade of the battle-axe the wolf had abandoned in his precipitous flight, with the result that the naked steel had laid open his right slipper from his little toe to his heel. The wound was not deep but was exceedingly painful.

Stumbling, he grabbed for the nearest chair for support. The chair overbalanced and he went down on top of it. As he fell he tried to stabilize himself, but the pain in his foot prevented him from doing so.

He did not worry about striking the floor, did not concern himself with damaging the chair. What troubled him beyond measure was what found itself caught up between his body, the chair and the unyielding floor. A sickening crunch filled the room as he landed. Even Sorbl, until now preoccupied with his own predicament, let out a cry of shock.

Jon-Tom rolled fast to his right, knowing as he did so that it was a futile gesture. It was already too late. Short of reversing time, the damage could not be undone. Nor could it be wished away. He sat up slowly, ignoring his bleeding foot, and stared.

Then he bent to pick up the shattered splinters of his irreplaceable, priceless, silenced duar.

II

The wooden necks had been broken in several places. The resonating chamber resembled a squashed brown melon. Tiny wires and internal pieces of intricate boxwork had been reduced to toothpicks. It was just short of a total loss, a ludicrous parody of the instrument it had been a moment earlier.

Having finally freed himself, Clothahump climbed down off his chair and waddled over to inspect the ruins.

"You wish the benefit of my wizardly mien and my store of experience in such matters?"

Jon-Tom could only nod, speechless. Clothahump fondled several pieces, twirled loose wires around one finger, then looked up at his tall friend. "You sure broke the shit out of it."

"I don't need three hundred years of accumulated wisdom to tell me that," the spellsinger replied sourly.

"Just underscoring the seriousness of what you've done. I never saw a human who could fall gracefully."

"As opposed to a turtle?"

"No need to discuss unrelated matters now. I do not believe it was your fault."

Jon-Tom was too furious at himself to cry. "You were right the first time. I'm a clumsy slob and I deserve this for not watching where I put my big feet."

"When you two finish exchanging compliments and commiserations, would one of you mind untying me?" Sorbl struggled in his bonds. "I need about half a dozen baths."

"A truth from the beak of the unwashed, so to speak. Life never ceases to amaze me." But despite his sarcasm, Clothahump untied the apprentice himself instead of asking Jon-Tom to do it. "Seven baths, I should say. One would think someone accustomed to exotic smells could control his stomach a bit better."

"I'm sorry I do not have your control, master." Sorbl slid out of the chair and tried to shake out his wings. "I think I received the full blast of that cat's rear end."

"No excuses. Go and get yourself cleaned up. Your odor is exceeded in unpleasantness only by your appearance. Hurry your cleansing. We now face a much more serious problem than the mere intrusion of some simple robbers. We have a broken duar to deal with."

As Sorbl departed, walking stiffly, the wizard turned to rejoin Jon-Tom as the tall young man lovingly laid the remnants of his instrument on the dining table.

"I almost wish you'd given them the gold, sir," he murmured disconsolately.

"I could not do that, Jon-Tom. As I told them, I hoard no gold." He nudged bits and pieces of the duar with a finger, peering at the debris through his thick glasses.

"What now?" Jon-Tom asked him. "Without the duar I can't make music, and without music I can't make magic. Can you fix it, sir?"

"I am a wizard, my boy, not a maker of tootles and tweets. I can shatter mountains. Reassembling them or anything else again is a matter for a different sort of expertise. A simple drum or flute I might repair, but this," and he gestured at the table, "is beyond my skills. I am not ashamed to admit this. Such a task is beyond the ability of but a very few unique craftsmen. To make a duar whole again requires the talent of one who understands how the stars sing to each other. I always did have a tin ear, insofar as I have ears at all."

Jon-Tom could sense what the wizard was leading up to. "It would be too much to hope that someone like that resides in Lynchbany or points nearby, I suppose."

"Too much by many leagues, I fear. Broken instruments are simple to fix. Broken magic is much more difficult. Something like your duar which combines both is almost impossible to make well again. I know by reputation of only one craftsman who might, I say might, have the mastery to make your instrument whole once more. His name is Couvier Coulb. It is rumored he resides in the town of Strelakat Mews, which lies in the jungle south of far Chejiji."

"I don't know where that is."

"Because you have never traveled that far south, my boy. For that matter, neither have I. It is a long journey."

Jon-Tom sighed. They'd been through this before. "How did I know you were going to say that?"

"Because you have a good memory, not because you are prescient. Chejiji is a seaport on the upper southern shore of the Glittergeist Sea. If you wish your instrument repaired, that is where you will have to go."

"I don't know, sir. I just don't know." He sat down in an intact, unvomited-upon chair. "I've never gone on a long trip without my duar. How am I going to protect myself?"

"Disconcerting as it seems, it appears you will have to rely upon your fighting skills and your wits." Jon-Tom couldn't be sure if the wizard was disparaging one talent or both. "If I have done nothing to sharpen the latter this past year then I have failed as a teacher. Be you magician or spellsinger, sorceror or cardsharp, necromancer or solicitor, in the final analysis one lives or perishes by one's wits."

Jon-Tom summoned a weak smile. "You've been a good instructor, sir, and I *have* learned a lot. It's just that knowing I'm going to have to find this Couvier Coulb without being able to rely on my spellsinging to help me along the way is pretty scary."

"It will not be the first time you have faced adversity only to emerge triumphant, my boy. I have confidence in you. Bear in mind that this is not the usual dangerous quest you are about to embark upon but merely a long excursion, as it were. You are simply going to find a repairman to have something fixed. I foresee no dangers lying in wait for you."

Clothahump's words cheered him a little. What was he so despondent, so concerned about? He'd undertaken long journeys before, often opposed by supernatural forces. There would be none to harass him this time. He was overreacting.

Still, there was one danger he could not avoid, one that would have to be dealt with immediately.

"How the hell am I going to tell Talea that I have to go away again?"

The wizard smiled ruefully. "That is something, my boy, that you will have to do without any magic to back you up."

"You're going *where*? No, never mind, I heard you. I don't understand, but I heard."

"I have no choice, Talea. Logic says so, Clothahump says so. I don't want to go, but of what use is a spellsinger without his instrument?"

Watching her stride angrily back and forth in the dimly lit bedroom he found it increasingly difficult to stand up to her. She was wearing the diaphanous gown which had been given to her by the grateful citizens of Ospenspri. It shone like mauve smoke and revealed more of her than it hid. Motile points of crimson light lived in the material and drifted about from place to place like diatoms on the crest of a wave. They tended, for whatever reason, to gravitate to the high points of her body.

She halted in front of the single window. The moonlight

enhanced the nearly overpowering effect of the gown and served to unsettle him further.

"Why doesn't Clothahump go?" she finally whispered.

"Clothahump is the greatest wizard in the world. He doesn't run errands for students. People run errands for him."

"Convenient. Sometimes I think all his moaning about his advanced age is so much rot." As abruptly as it had bubbled forth her anger vanished and she ran to him, holding him close. "I don't want you to go, Jonny-Tom! You've been through so much since you came here. We've hardly had any time together at all and now you want to go running off halfway across the world again."

"Talea . . . ." He put his hands on her cheeks and turned her face up so that he could look into her eyes. "I don't want to any more than you want me to, but I have to do this. Spellsinging can't be faked. I have to have that duar repaired."

"Can't you try spellsinging with another instrument?"

He shook his head. "I've tried. The duar is as much responsible for my success at magic as is my singing. The two are inseparable."

"Can't you buy another one, then?"

"There isn't another one, light of my life. I wish it was that easy. This particular duar has special qualities that, when combined with my singing, allow me to make magic happen. The way the strings weave in and out of reality, the intricate interior of the resonating chamber—it can't be replaced. Only fixed, and Clothahump can't fix it. Nor can anyone else in the Bellwoods, or even Polastrindu. I have to find this Couvier Coulb."

She pressed herself tight against him and the temperature inside the tree rose noticeably. "I don't want to lose you, Jon-Tom. You stayed inside my mind for almost a year until I found you waiting for me there, and I don't want to lose you. You've gone off on so many of these dangerous journeys that I'm afraid your luck may have run out. Even a retired thief can read the odds, and it's time for them to turn against you. I *can't* let you go. I won't let you go!'' She was sobbing uncontrollably now. He didn't know whether to push her away, try to comfort her with words of reassurance, or simply let her cry out her sorrow on his shoulder.

What should have been an obvious thought finally occurred to him. ''Why not come with me, then? You've never seen the Glittergeist. We can relax on our ship, make a real vacation out of it no matter haw long it takes us to get to Strelakat Mews.''

The tears dried with astonishing speed and she took a step backward, her sorrow changing abruptly to outrage.

''You want me to *what*? Leave here, now, to run off with you on some endless ocean voyage?'' She made a sweeping gesture at the bedroom. ''This tree isn't half decorated yet. In two days the curtain maker will be here from Lynchbany, and then there are the carpets to be seen to and do you think that can be done in a day?''

''Well I. . . .''

''Not a chance! Have you ever tried to order carpeting for a tree? Everything's round and curved. There's not a decent square corner in the place. If you think I'm going to spend the rest of my life walking on wood shavings like your precious senile old wizard you've got another thing coming, Jon-Tom!'' She was circling the room now, rather like an eagle homing in on its chosen prey. Jon-Tom harbored no illusions as to which role he occupied in this little domestic play. She was alive with the irrepressible energy which had first attracted him to her. Trouble was, it was now directed at him and not some nameless enemy.

''I've got painters coming in a week. We're going to have to dye some of this wood. I refuse to spend the rest of my life in a house where all the walls are the same color, even if it is an oak tree. And you want me to drop all that so I can run off and carouse with you? You've got your nerve, Jon-Tom!''

Was this the same Talea he'd first encountered so many months ago who'd come to him for help in loading one of her mugging victims into the back of a wagon? The same fiery haired, short-tempered little terror who was as quick with her sword as her tongue? His mini-Brunhilde had metamorphosed into a hausfrau.

"Cripes, Talea, you've become domesticated."

She shook an angry finger at him. "Don't you swear at me, Jon-Tom. You're going to run off and leave all the decision making to me." She had him backed against a wall now. "You'll do no such thing. You're going to stay here and help me with the decorating, help me choose colors and patterns and weaves and landscaping."

"Talea, if I don't get the duar repaired I can't spellsing. If I can't spellsing I can't earn a living. And if I don't earn a living you won't have any money to pay painters and carpet makers and landscapers."

Her finger froze in mid-wag, drifted to her lower lip as she considered this new bit of reasoning thoughtfully. "Yes. That's true. Though I could always go back to work to support us. I'm a little out of practice but. . . ."

Now it was his turn to anger. "You'll do no such thing. You're a respectable woman now."

"I thought I warned you to stop calling me names."

"I'm not going to have you go running off knocking people in the head in dark alleys. How can you think of going back to thievery and robbery?"

"Easy. I did it for years. I'm a thieves' guild member in good standing, I've kept up my dues, and if I get caught you can always come visit me in jail. At least that way you'll be close to me."

"No way." He tried to say it with an air of finality. "You're going to stay here and do all those things you were just talking about. You're going to furnish and decorate this tree exactly the way you want."

"I could just work weekends," she argued in a small voice. "A good thief can make a lot of money on the weekends."

"No, dammit!"

Her voice fell even further. "Just one teensy little mugging a week?"

He sighed in exasperation. "I don't know quite how to explain this, Talea, but I'll try it one more time. Where I come from that kind of business is frowned upon morally as well as legally. It just doesn't sit well with me."

"Nobody has any fun where you come from." She crossed her arms and pouted.

"I admit ethics are a little more, well, liberal in this world, but that's how I feel about it. Besides, I couldn't just sit around and live off my wife's earnings."

"Why not?" She was genuinely surprised. "Most men I know would be glad to."

"I'm not most men. About the best I could do would be to give up spellsinging and magic and try to make a normal living as a musician."

"Not with your voice you couldn't." Seeing the look that came over his face she hastened to comfort him, her anger vanishing as rapidly as it had materialized. "I guess you're right, you and that hard-shelled, hardheaded old fraud. You'll have to go. I'll stay here and keep tree until you return."

He could see she was trying to bolster her own spirits more than she was trying to reassure him. "After all," she continued, "it's not like you're going off to try and save the world this time. You're just running a long errand. Like a vacation, right?"

"Right." He smiled lovingly down at her. "You're sure you won't come? It'll be an adventure."

She grinned up at him. "After my encounter with that wolverine and his perambulator I'm kind of adventured out. I like little, safe adventures, Jon-Tom, not the awesome world-shaking ones you seem to go in for. I think I'll just stay here and enjoy the feeling of being married until you come back. It's still a new sensation for me. That's enough of an adventure for me for now." Suddenly she looked worried. "Or do you think I'm getting old? After all, I'll be twenty-three in three months."

He gave her a light kiss. "I don't think you'll ever get

old, Talea. I think you'll still be looking to crack skulls and pick pockets when you turn ninety."

"That's one reason why I love you so much, Jonny-Tom. You know how to say the sweetest things to a girl. Go on, get your duar repaired. Take your time and stay clear of trouble."

"I'll be back in no time, you'll see. I'm just taking a long cruise, that's all. What could happen?" He pulled her to him, lowering his lips toward hers as . . . .

A loud *crash* sounded from overhead. She pulled away from him, her mood twitching from affectionate and conciliatory to angry once again.

"And while you're at it, as long as you're going *far* away, take that unspeakable vile water rat with you and see if you can't lose him somewhere in the middle of the ocean!" A second thump followed the first, not quite as loud as its predecessor but still aggravating.

The notion of having an attic in a tree was a radical one. But, he'd argued with Clothahump, if one can have a cellar, why not an attic? The wizard had shrugged and complied. After all, it was a wedding present and one could expand dimensionally upwards as easily as down. It proved a convenient place to store unpacked wedding gifts, extra furniture, household supplies, and those items which one has no use for but which are obviously so useful they cannot be thrown away. Counted among the latter was a grotesque stone sculpture which had been a present from one of Clothahump's friends, a whole collection of arms and armor which Talea cooed over and refused to part with despite Jon-Tom's insistence that they were going to live a normal, peaceful life, and one five-foot-tall, bedraggled, foulmouthed, perpetually hungry otter.

Jon-Tom blinked as wood dust drifted down from the ceiling. "I don't think Mudge is ready to leave."

"You don't make it a question," she snapped. "You make it an order."

"But Mudge is my friend. We've been through a lot, the

two of us, and because he helped me out this last trip I feel like I owe him something."

"Any old debts between you have long since been squared. Don't you remember what he said after our wedding? That he'd only stay on here for a few days. That he just wanted a place to kick up his heels and relax for a week. That was months ago, Jon-Tom. He's been freeloading ever since, putting his feet up on my best furniture, tracking mud in every time he goes swimming in the river—and to top it off he stinks and he has rotten table manners."

"All otters have rotten table manners," Jon-Tom mumbled, aware it was a feeble defense. "They're not what you'd call a disciplined bunch."

"Disciplined my ass! The lot of them are crazier than a coterie of cuckoos. I thought maybe Mudge would quiet down after you and I got married, but he's worse than ever. I don't know how many times I've caught him trying to peek at me while I'm taking my bath."

"You ought to feel flattered. Usually Mudge won't waste a glance on anything without fur."

"You think so, do you? He's got you flummoxed too, then, because I happen to know that among the many diseases he's infected with is terminal satyriasis. That otter will screw anything that moves and probably a few things that don't. Sometimes I think he prefers the latter because whatever he's glommed onto can't run away."

"Come on, Talea. Mudge wouldn't lay a paw on you."

"He doesn't have to. All he has to do is look at a female, but I don't expect you to understand that. Anyway," she said, raising her voice and not caring if the rest of the Bellwoods overheard, much less the sole occupant of the attic above, "I want him out of my house; fur, claws, filthy teeth and all. You've the perfect excuse for it now. Tell him you're off on another journey and you need him to serve as guide and companion. Isn't that what you always told him?" She wore a deliciously predatory smile now. "A perfect reason to drag him off with you—and dump him somewhere."

"Talea, I just can't. . . ."

She spun on her heel and marched over to the other armoire, began rummaging through the contents. Underwear and clothing went flying as she dug. "Where the hell did I put that sword?"

"Talea, we don't want to do anything foolish."

"Foolish?" She spoke without looking back at him. "You get that rat out of here in one piece or I'll have him out in sections. Ah." She removed her old sword from the bottom drawer, managing to look thoroughly incongruous standing there in the phosphorescent nightgown hefting a shaft of unyielding steel in her right hand. She was as adept with it, he knew, as any soldier.

He leaned back against the wall as he watched her head for the door. "Don't you think," he said softly, "that if you're going to fight that a little more substantial armor would be in order?"

She glanced down at her nearly naked self, suddenly conscious that she was not exactly dressed for traditional battle.

"Don't worry." He walked over to where she stood fuming silently and gently removed the sword from her hand, laid it aside. "I promise I'll take Mudge along, if that's what you want. He could use the exercise anyway. His current condition is partly your fault. None of us suspected that in addition to knowing how to use a sword and bow and arrows and pike and knives and fighting staff and battle-axe and mace that you could handle a cook pot and stove equally well. He's gotten fat on your cooking, as have I. As soon as I assure him there's no danger involved this time and that I'll be paying all expenses he'll be eager to come along. That's Mudge, always raring to visit new places and explore new lands and cities."

"Sure he is. He might find a whorehouse he hasn't visited before. You promise you'll take him with you?"

"I promise."

She put her arms around his neck and stood on tiptoes

against him. There was nothing between his body and hers save a nightgown and bathrobe, and those hardly counted.

"In that case, why are we standing here wasting the rest of the night talking when we could be over there not talking?" She nodded toward the disheveled bed.

He swallowed. "Don't you think maybe I ought to start packing as long as we're already awake?"

She tugged him gently in the direction of the sheets. "You need some rest before starting on such a long journey. I'll help you pack. The first thing we need to find is your staff, and I know right where it is."

III

He had in mind to make an early start, but it was mid-morning before Talea finally let him crawl out of the bed. The pale brown sheets were all twisted around her as she lay sprawled in the middle of the mattress, watching him as he dressed. She looked like a vanilla swirl in the middle of a chocolate sundae.

"Maybe I could put off leaving for another week or two."

She laughed at that as she sat up, shaking out covers and her shoulder length red hair. "I don't think so. Another night's 'rest' and neither one of us will be able to walk."

He slipped on his boots, shaky as he balanced first on one leg, then the other. "You know where my old backpack is?" She nodded. "Give me one change of clothing, plenty of dried jerky for noshing on between towns, and anything else you think I'll find useful. That and my staff, and I'll have Mudge ready to go by the time you have everything packed."

"Pity you can't leave your staff here."

"Sorry. I might need it on the trip." He ducked the pillow she threw at him. "What's left of the duar's already packaged for the trek. You can tie it to the top of my pack." He tested one boot, then the other. "I feel naked going off like this, without that instrument resting against my ribs."

She put her head down on the remaining pillow. "I wish you weren't going, Jonny-Tom. But since you are, I'm going to think every day what a safe, relaxing time you'll be having. You'll make the best possible ship connections and you'll be back here weeks early." She rolled her eyes ceilingward. "Just don't forget to put out the garbage when you leave."

He made a face as he left the room.

The spiral staircase was located just off the parlor. As he climbed toward the attic he went over what he was going to say to Mudge. Getting the otter out of the house was going to be harder than pulling a tooth.

"Mudge?" He raised the trap door and peered into the room. "Mudge, you awake yet?" No reply. The sharply slanted roof forced him to stay in the center of the chamber. It was filled with piles of gifts, many of which had been forced on him by the grateful citizens of Ospenspri, the city he and Clothahump had recently rescued from the deleterious effects of the wandering perambulator. Most remained unopened. A single porthole allowed sunlight to enter from outside.

Beneath the glass stood a beautiful brass and turquoise bed which had been a wedding gift from one of Lynchbany's most prominent citizens, an old friend of Clothahump's. The reason it reposed in the attic instead of downstairs in the master bedroom was that despite its exquisite workmanship it was impractical, having been built for the shorter humans inhabiting this world. It fit Talea perfectly, but his longer legs hung over the end. They decided to keep it anyway. Some day there might be one or two little spellsingers who'd need a place to sleep. So they'd reassembled it in the attic.

Presently it was occupied by a single furry shape not unlike a large rug in need of washing. Mudge's head lay beneath the covers facing the foot of the bed. His flexible rear end protruded from the sheets and stuck up in the air, the tail twitching spasmodically like an undersized brown flag in response to the otter's depraved dreams. Mudge didn't live quietly and he didn't sleep quietly, something else Talea held against him. He tended to bounce around in the bed despite the muffling effects of Clothahump's best silencing spells. Worse, he tended to walk in his sleep. He also talked in his sleep, which led to the discovery that he spouted more obscenities when unconscious than he did when he was awake.

Jon-Tom bent over to regard his somnolent houseguest. "Mudge? Mudgey-Wudgey? Time to get up." He yelled at the buried head. "Wake up, dammit!"

The otter's rear end subsided slowly like a leaky balloon. A head emerged from the bunched sheets near the foot of the bed. Brown eyes blinked sleepily up at him.

"Cor', wot a bloody racket. Wot's up, mate?"

"Me, and now you, and soon business."

The otter frowned, smacking his lips. "Now wot sort o' business might any civilized person be 'avin' so early in the mornin'?

"Mudge, it's almost lunchtime."

"Lunch?" The otter's eyes snapped all the way open. He was instantly and fully awake, exploding from the bed to slide supplely and with extraordinary speed into his clothes. "Why din' you say so? Missed breakfast already, 'ave I? Well, we'll make up for it some'ow. Tell me then, lad, wot succulent viands 'as the beauteous Talea prepared for us this charmin' midday?"

"Nothing to swallow this morning but a bitter pill, Mudge. A bunch of thugs broke into the wizard's tree earlier and tried to rob him. I woke up, snuck over there, and routed them."

" 'Tis a true selfless 'ero you are, mate. 'Aven't I always said so?"

"No, you've always said that I was a prime idiot for sticking my nose into other people's troubles, but that's beside the point. I fell on my duar and broke it."

That gave the otter pause. "Broke the duar, you say? Bad?"

"Reduced it to fragments. Clothahump says it can only be fixed, if it can be fixed at all, by a master craftsman named Couvier Coulb who lives in a town called Strelakat Mews."

The otter sniffed, his whiskers twitching. "Never 'eard of it." He bent over to gaze into a small mirror, preening himself. "Well, we all 'ave our little unexpected errands to run from time to time."

"We sure do. You're coming with me."

"Wot?" Mudge looked up from the mirror, placed his feathered green felt cap on his head between his ears. "Before lunch?"

"No," Jon-Tom replied in exasperation, "we can eat first."

"Well that's all right then." Fully clad, the otter sauntered toward the staircase. "Where is this Strelakat place? Up near Malderpot? Or east over by Polastrindu?"

"Neither. It lies inland from the southern shore of the Glittergeist."

"Wot, down near Yarrowl?" Mudge hesitated, then shrugged. "Well, that's not but a few days journey by public conveyance. I could use a bit of a change o' scenery. Join me in a quick swim?"

"Mudge, Strelakat Mews lies somewhere in the jungle south of the city of Chejiji, which is clear across the ocean. When I said the southern shore, I meant the *southern* shore."

Mudge cocked a suspicious eye on his friend. "Do you know 'ow far that is, mate?"

"I have an idea."

"Then here's another idea for you to 'ave: count me out. I've 'ad me fill o' travelin' to far distant lands, I 'ave, especially in your company. Nasty things tend to 'appen to folks taggin' along with you, Jon-Tom."

"There'll be no trouble this time. We're just taking a trip to get a duar repaired. We're not marching off to save the world this time."

"Get this straight, mate: *we* ain't marchin' anywhere. Besides, I ain't got the stomach for another ocean voyage. One with you were enough to last me a lifetime. I'll just stay right 'ere."

"I didn't want to bring this up, Mudge, but you've been staying 'right here' ever since Talea and I got married."

"Right, and don't think I 'aven't appreciated the 'ospitality. I've enjoyed every day and every meal, just as I've enjoyed the company."

"Talea seems to feel otherwise," he said quietly.

"Ah, that sweet bare skinned redhead." Mudge spoke wistfully. "Always was like that, 'idin' 'er true feelings behind a fake wall o' temper. That's just to show the world 'ow tough she is. When she says yes she means no, and when she says no she means yes."

"She had her sword out a few hours ago. I think that means 'no.' "

"Wot a sense o' humor. You're a lucky male, Jon-Tom." The otter chuckled.

"I believe," he continued dryly, "she intended to come up here and cut your heart out."

The otter shook his head. "Wot a laugh, your Talea!"

Jon-Tom glanced toward the stairway. "In fact, I think I hear her coming up now."

The otter's smile vanished instantly and he bounded back behind the bed, the amused expression on his furry face now replaced by one of stark terror.

"Don't let 'er get me, mate. I've seen 'er like this before. She goes crazy. You can't talk to 'er, no one can, not even you."

Jon-Tom suppressed a smile. "I think she's gone back down—for the moment. No promises, but if you agree to accompany me I think I can calm her down long enough for us to slip out of the house without bloodshed."

Mudge looked uncertain. "Got to cross the 'ole Glittergeist, you say?"

Jon-Tom nodded slowly. "And then an unknown stretch of jungle after we leave the boat."

The otter considered silently before replying. "I ain't so sure I wouldn't be better off just takin' me chances with Talea's sword."

"Don't tell me you're afraid of a little bitty gal like Talea?"

"You 'aven't seen that 'little bitty' one fight the way I 'ave. She's ruthless as a magistrate on 'angin' day."

Jon-Tom turned and started down the stairs. "You coming with me or not?"

"Give me another minute to think it over, mate," the otter pleaded.

"I can hear her banging around down there with that sword. Sounds like she's getting herself good and worked up."

"Okay, okay." The otter rushed out from behind the bed. "Just keep 'er off me, will you?"

"Let's go," Jon-Tom suggested. "It won't seem so bad on a full stomach, although," and he glanced down at the bulge that was straining the limits of the otter's waistband, "you don't look like you've been empty for some time."

"Right. Always a good idea to eat and then talk. Besides, if she's wieldin' a servin' spoon she can't handle a sword." He was careful to follow his host down the stairs.

"A wonderful meal, luv." Mudge leaned back in his chair as if to accentuate the compliment, wiping grease and fragments of food from his lips. "All those years you and I were pickin' pockets and relievin' undeservin' citizens o' their oversized wallets and you never dropped a 'int that you could cook as well as you could cut."

"We all have hidden talents, Mudge." Talea was cleaning off the stove as she spoke. Clothahump's tree-expanding spell hadn't provided for a separate dining area so the rough-hewn table was located in the middle of the kitchen.

"That we do," the otter agreed contentedly. "Wot might you suppose mine would be?"

"I think you'd make a fine salesman," she replied, wiping her hands with a damp rag. "You've always been as fast with your tongue as with your feet."

"Crikey, that's wot all the ladies tell me. But, says I, why haul a lot o' goods around the country to sell when 'tis easier and cleaner to relieve folks o' their coin without burdenin' them with shoddy goods in return?"

"Something called morals." Jon-Tom was finishing the last of his lunch.

The otter's brows drew together. "Morals, morals—let me see now. I'm sure I've 'eard that word somewhere before, lad, but at the moment its meanin' escapes me. Some sort o' fruit or somethin', ain't it? Grows up north somewheres?" Jon-Tom could only shake his head ruefully.

Mudge slipped out of his chair and stretched. " 'Tis been a wonderfully relaxing few days, it has, but I know when I've overstayed me welcome. No, you needn't try to talk me out o' leavin'." He put up a restraining paw despite the fact that his hosts were not exactly imploring him to change his mind. "Far be it from me to strain a friend's largess. I can see that 'tis time for old Mudge to be movin' on. They say the opportunities for ungainful employment in Malderpot are 'ot just now. I think I'll mosey on up that way and check out the scenery, so to speak."

Jon-Tom put his fork aside. "Just a minute. Aren't you forgetting something?"

"Forgettin' somethin'?" The otter mumbled to himself for a moment, then he said brightly, "O' course. Don't worry, mate, I'll see to me kit and me weapons before I takes me leave. Wouldn't do for old Mudge to go traipsin' off without 'is weapons, now would it?"

"Certainly not, considering the length of the journey that lies ahead of us."

"Us? Long journey? Oh, you mean that brief ocean

voyage you were tellin' me about. I'm sure it'll do you well, mate. The sea seems to agree with you. When you get back you 'ave to look me up so you can tell me all about it."

Jon-Tom's sense of humor was ebbing rapidly. "You're forgetting something else. You're coming with me, remember? You agreed."

"Piffle. Surely you didn't take that serious, lad? Now, if your life were in danger or it were a truly serious situation, why, I wouldn't 'esitate to tag along to back you up."

"You don't think the fact that my duar is shattered is serious?"

Mudge shrugged. "Serious for you maybe; not serious for anybody else. Not my responsibility, it ain't. As I said, if you were off to save the world . . . ."

"You'd be so eager to come along you'd be tripping over your own feet, I know," Jon-Tom said evenly. "Now you listen to me, Mudge. You go upstairs and pack your things, but not for Malderpot. We're leaving for Yarrowl in half an hour."

"Yarrowl? I ain't got no business in Yarrowl, mate." The otter stared back at him out of steely dark eyes. "I might accompany you for a day or so just so's to make sure you start off on the right road, but then I promise you mate, I'd just kind o' slip away quiet-like some night in the woods."

"You never did anything like that before."

"Me conscience were never clear about it before. Knowin' this time that I weren't abandonin' you to some 'orrible danger, I wouldn't have a second thought about it."

"You're going to do exactly as Jon-Tom says." Both of them turned to look at Talea.

"Don't you o' all folks go appealin' to me ethics, redfur."

"Why would I appeal to the nonexistent?" She walked from the sink to a nearby cabinet that held her household papers, searched through the second drawer until she found several sheets clipped together. As she spoke her eyes traveled down the pages.

"Mudge the otter: Expenses Incurred." The otter gaped at her, then at Jon-Tom, who wore an equally blank expression. "Room and board; three meals a day, sometimes four; evening snacks, transportation to and from Lynchbany; laundry—want me to read you the totals, or should I just go on with the list?"

"Now wait a bloody minute, luv! I'm your bloomin' friend from years back, I am. Did I charge you for the times I bailed you out o' damp jails, or protected your arse against a concealed blade? Wot's all this rot about expenses, then?"

She handed him the papers. "Keep that for your records, if you want. I have a copy."

Mudge's eyes ran rapidly down the list. "This is bleedin' outrageous, is wot it is! 'Tis not only illegal and immoral, 'tis outright insultin'. Wot kind o' friend o' me youth are you, anyways?"

"A cautious one. That's one thing *you* taught me. Of course," and she smiled sweetly at the furious otter, "we can forget the whole bill."

"You're bloody right we can." He ripped the sheets to shreds and with great dignity deposited them in the middle of the table. "That don't mean snake-pucky. 'Tis fit for nothin' but wipin' one's arse."

"I'm sure you noted that toilet paper was included on the list," she replied calmly. "On the contrary, that is a perfectly valid contract. Reception of services is sufficient proof of agreement to pay for services received. That's one thing *Jon-Tom* taught me."

"Bloody solicitor," the otter grumbled, glaring up at Jon-Tom. "I made no such arrangements to pay for anythin' when I came to stay 'ere as your guest."

"The judge won't know that. Who do you think he'll believe, Mudge?" She walked over and stroked the fur on the back of his neck. He jerked away, but not very violently. "The honest, respectable wife of a noted local citizen, or a thoroughly disreputable peculator like yourself?"

"Peculator?" The otter turned on Jon-Tom. "Will you listen to this female, mate? You're ruinin' 'er, you are."

"Oh, I don't know." He leaned back in his chair. "She doesn't look particularly ruined to me."

"Which'll it be, Mudge?" She looked at her husband. "You were right. This *is* almost as much fun as carving someone up with a knife."

"It's pretty much the same thing where I come from, light of my life."

Mudge sat down heavily. Talea didn't let up on him. "Answer me, water rat. Do you ship out or pay up?"

Displaying his unparalleled mastery of the blue funk, the otter stared at the floor for several moments. Finally he squinted up at Jon-Tom. "You promise me this ain't no ruse? You ain't tryin' to trick poor Mudge into takin' off on another o' your wild, life threatenin' trips to the backside o' hell?"

Jon-Tom solemnly raised his right hand. "I swear we're only taking a little ocean voyage to get my duar repaired. I don't anticipate any trouble and I'm not going to go looking for any."

"Huh," the otter grunted. He swiveled his head to look at Talea. "Wot 'appens when we gets back?"

"I tear up all copies of your bill."

"Bill, that's a laugh." He licked his lips and whiskers. "Do I get me room back?"

"Over my dead body."

"Wot if this don't turn out to be the picnic Jon-Tom claims it to be?"

"I'll bury you in the backyard. That far I'll go. I've no objection to having you around so long as I don't have to feed you, listen to you, or smell you."

"You always was generous to a fault, luv. Was one o' the things I liked about you. Almost otterish." He smiled in spite of himself. It was impossible for Mudge to stay gloomy for long. "Ah well. If one's to be outfoxed 'ow better than by the sauciest vixen in the 'ole Bellwoods." He rose to confront Jon-Tom. "I'll be comin' along then, mate, but I warn you: If you're tryin' to pull a fast one I'll be away from your side faster than a celibate at a doxy's convention.''

''No tricks, Mudge. I promise. You and I are going to relax and enjoy a pleasant sea voyage, at the conclusion of which we'll do a little business with a master craftsman. Then we'll come home. That's all. I've never been that far south or on an ocean voyage that long. It ought to be educational.''

''Aye, that's wot worries me. Every trip I've accompanied you on 'as been too bloody educational.'' Spying an unconsumed slice of Talea's delicious tokla bread, he lunged toward the table and plucked it off its plate. He did not offer to share it with his traveling companion.

IV

Their backpacks filled to bursting with the savory produce of Talea's kitchen, anxious spellsinger and reluctant companion paused to pay their respects to Clothahump before striking off on the southern road. They found the wizard berating Sorbl for some unspecified offense which the owl insisted loudly was more imagined than real. Upon concluding his lengthy admonition, the wizard turned to the matter of his friend's imminent departure.

"Though she needs none, I will look after Talea in your absence, Jon-Tom. I pity anyone who troubles her while you are away."

"So do I. Talea can take care of herself, but I appreciate the concern. What about you, sir? Are you doing all right?"

"Actually, my boy, I am feeling fitter than I have in some time." He glanced back over his shell. "Things would be better still if I could beat some sense into that useless famulus of mine. Time will tell if Sorbl is to become something more than an alcoholic sponge. I have only just completed an extensive insurance spell for the city of Folklare and I may have to go up there in person in order to check the installation.'' He lowered his head and peered over his glasses to where a bored Mudge was leaning impatiently against the tree.

''Your education is proceeding apace, I see, for it must have taken magic indeed to convince that one to accompany you.''

''Not my magic. Talea's.''

Clothahump nodded knowingly. ''I always thought that young woman had hidden talents, in addition to the visible ones.''

''Pity I never 'ad the opportunity to plumb 'em,'' commented Mudge. The otter's hearing was acute.

''Lay off, Mudge. We're married now.'' This warning only served to increase the width of the otter's smirk. Jon-Tom gave up and looked back down at his mentor. ''I have this,'' and he gestured with his ramwood staff, ''but I feel naked without the duar.''

''Try not to dwell on what you do not have, my boy. Soon Couvier Coulb will make it whole again. Perhaps you can convince him to fashion you a new set of interdimensional strings. Though made of metal, those you have salvaged will not last forever. Now then, when you reach Yarrowl and after booking your passage to Chejiji, I suggest you stop at a certain shop in the commercial district. It is known only by the name of its owner, which is Izfan ab-Akmajiandor, but who is called locally Dizzy Izzy. He is something of an eccentric, something of a local legend, and very much a dealer in precious and unique articles. He trades in clocks, toys—and musical instruments.''

Jon-Tom felt a rush of excitement. ''You think maybe he . . . ?''

''No, my boy. No one but Coulb himself might repair your duar. Still, there is no telling what Dizzy Izzy conceals beneath his shop counter. It is said he deals in devices as eccentric as himself. You might find something to your liking in his inventory."

"Another duar?"

"Too much to hope for, but who can say? Certainly it is worth a visit to find out."

"You hear that, Mudge? If this merchant has another duar in stock we may not have to go all the way to Strelakat Mews."

"Much as that's a development devoutly to be desired, mate, I ain't 'oldin' me breath." The otter was cleaning beneath his claws with a pocket knife. " 'Tis occurred to me that if duars o' such power as yours were that common, the roads would be overflowin' with would-be spellsingers."

"If Clothahump thinks this shop is worth checking out we'll certainly pay it a visit."

Mudge shrugged. "Makes no matter to me. I'm just an indentured servant on this excursion, I am."

"Don't belittle yourself. I've always valued your advice and I don't value it any less now."

"Is that so?" The otter stopped picking his nails and jabbed the knife in Jon-Tom's direction. " 'Ere's a bit o' advice, then. Before you destroy yourself and any unfortunates who 'appen to be unlucky enough to be in the immediate vicinity, give up this spellsingin' business and take up some practical profession."

"Mudge, spellsinging is all I'm trained to do. That and the law."

"Never thought I'd live to 'ear meself say it, but better a live solicitor than a dead spellsinger."

"Thanks for the advice, but you're not getting out of this that easily."

"Easily? Hell, you watch me, mate. I'm just warmin' up, I am."

They bought seats on the southbound coach, changed at the small town of Wourmet, and rattled into Yarrowl several days later. Located where the Tailaroam River emptied into the Glittergeist Sea, the port was abustle with traffic as cargo was transferred from barges and keelboats to ocean-going freighters or animal-drawn wagons destined for the numerous towns and cities sprinkled through the vast forest known as the Bellwoods. In such a crossroads of commerce anything might be purchased. Perhaps, Jon-Tom thought to himself, even something as exotic as a duar.

They found the shop of Dizzy Izzy without much difficulty, only to find themselves confronted by drawn shades and a sign in the window that read:

Open from 8 to 8

Jon-Tom tried to see through the beveled glass and around one of the shades. "Nothing moving."

"There wouldn't be. 'Tis too early, or 'ave you forgotten wot 'is wizardship told us? This 'ere storekeeper's a member o' the lemur persuasion. 'E's open from eight at night 'til eight in the mornin', not the other way 'round."

"I remember now. So we're too early, not too late." He checked the nearby public clock. "We have enough time to eat first."

Mudge licked his chops. " Supper it 'tis , then! Washed down with a pint or two, wot?"

"No booze, Mudge. Not here, not yet. First we have to get on the boat, then you can drink yourself silly if you've a mind to, but if you get yourself good and plastered in a strange city I might not be able to find you again. You tend to wander aimlessly when you're liquored up."

"I do not," replied the otter with some dignity, "ever get 'liquored up.' Drunk occasionally, inebriated once in a while, but never liquored up. Sounds like someone fillin' a bloomin' 'orse trough."

"Yes, that's not a bad metaphor." The otter made a rude noise as they started up the street.

Lights showed behind the shades when they returned from eating. It was not quite eight and they had to wait outside for another few minutes until the proprietor opened his doors. The indri wore canvas pants and vest over his black and white fur, and his bright yellow eyes stared at them from behind round rose-colored glasses with thin lenses.

"Come in, come in. You're early, friends, or late, depending on your time of day preferences."

Izzy's shop was a delight, the shelves crammed full of intricately fashioned clocks of all kinds, small mechanical toys, music boxes and animated banks. But Jon-Tom's attention was drawn instantly to the right-hand wall, on which hung a collection of musical instruments. Many of them were new to him, and several were so alien in design and construction he could not tell by looking at them whether they were intended to be strummed, tootled, or beaten.

A series of small drums wound round a central post like fruit on a branch. Grotesque horns hung next to attenuated woodwinds. On the floor was a pipe carved from the trunk of a single tree. It must have weighed a hundred pounds or more and had fingering holes the size of Jon-Tom's fist.

"Bear pipe," Izzy explained. His voice was high and reedy, not unlike that of some of his stock. "I sold the former owner a duplicate of much lighter wood and accepted this in part payment. It's been here a long time."

"I can see why," Jon-Tom said. "No one but another bear could lift it."

"So true, but I enjoy watching customers try. Sometimes a big cat will get it off the ground. Then they find they don't have the lung power to operate it. What maybe perhaps possibly can I do for you, sir? By your stance and attire I divine you are a person of means, for all that you appear to enjoy associating with lesser lifes. I will be most very muchly pleased to help you, just as soon as your friend returns the small gold music box to the cabinet from which he has removed it."

Jon-Tom whirled to glare back at Mudge. The otter sheepishly removed an exquisitely made music box in the shape of a clavier from his inside vest pocket and put it back into the open display cabinet in front of him.

"I were just 'avin' a close look at it, mate. 'Tis a pretty thing and I thought of buyin' it, I did."

"I know, and you had to see whether or not it would ride comfortably in your breast pocket."

"Very comfortably I'm sure," said Izzy agreeably. "My name, you should know, friends, comes from my dancing talent and not any inability to take care of business."

"Pfagh." Mudge made a show of sauntering over to inspect a clock that was at least as tall as he was. " 'Tis all right for me to look at this one or do you think I'll try an' walk off with it when you ain't lookin'?"

"I'd put nothing not at all never past an otter." The indri smiled back at Jon-Tom. "What appeals to you, friend? What can I sell you? A timepiece?"

"I have plenty of time. I need something else. I am a spellsinger."

The indri peered intently at his customer over the rims of his glasses. "Truly absolutely for sure so? A spellsinger? I've never met one myself though I once had an encounter with a substantial rumor."

Jon-Tom indicated the sack secured to his backpack. "Got a busted duar with me. I don't suppose you could fix it?"

"A true duar? Far beyond my meager skills, friend magic music maker. I'm no dabbler in the arcane arts."

"Then I don't guess you'd have one for sale, either."

"Ah ah, because I do not myself personally me deal with magic does not mean I am unwilling or unable to trade in it. Sadly unfortunately discouragingly I have no duar to sell you. In fact, in all the years I have been in this business I have never so much as seen set eyes upon viewed a duar. I however have an item or two that might do for you."

The first instrument he produced from below his counter resembled a piccolo with Pinocchio syndrome. Tiny secondary pipes emerged from the central tube like the branches of a tree. It was fashioned of holly wood and inlaid with mother of pearl.

"Difficult hard troublesome to play, but it is said that in the right hands it can make rain and snow."

"I'm not a weatherman. I need something more versatile."

"I understand comprehend got you." Izzy put the flute aside and placed a pocket accordion on the counter. There were only four keys on each side of the little squeezebox. Jon-Tom gave it a try out of curiosity. It made a sound like a overweight hog trying to sing Wagner. Mudge looked pained.

"What does it do?"

"A proper musician can bring food and drink into being and the quality of the food varies according to the sweetness of the song."

"Forget that then," said Mudge. "If we 'ad to depend on the smoothness of 'is voice to get us out o' trouble we'd 'ave been dead a 'undred times over by now." He nodded curtly at the squeezebox. "Tryin' to make food with that we'd bloody well starve to death."

Jon-Tom made a face at the otter but pushed the instrument back across the counter. "I don't know how to play the thing anyway."

Izzy looked discouraged. "Then I suppose assume guess I must let you have the one item which might really be of use to you."

Jon-Tom's face lit up when he first saw the instrument the indri removed from a locked box behind the counter, but his initial excitement faded as he inspected the workmanship more closely. There were similarities to his own instrument, but a duar it was not. There was a resonating chamber, smaller and simpler than his own, different controls, and only one set of metal strings. They did fade into insubstantiality where they crossed the resonating chamber, but they did not vanish entirely into another dimension.

"A suar." Izzy plucked idly at the strings. "This little beauty was owned by a pinheaded prestidigitator who used it only on holidays."

Mudge had sauntered over to inspect the instrument closely. "Stuff the sales pitch, bug eyes. Do it work?"

"So I am told, though the owner was hardly what one

would call a master of magic. Perhaps in more skilled hands . . . ." He left the thought unfinished.

"Looks a lot like an ordinary mandolin." Jon-Tom accepted it from the indri. "If it wasn't for this," and he indicated the place where the strings faded from view, "I'd say you were trying to sell me an ordinary musical instrument."

"Not for three hundred gold pieces I'm not."

"Three hun . . ." Mudge choked on the figure, then put a hand on Jon-Tom's arm. "Come on, mate. I never thought I'd meet a bigger thief than meself, but 'tis finally 'appened."

"Too expensive," said Jon-Tom.

The indri tried to appear indifferent. "As you wish. Another willing to pay will come along. Music is cheap. Magic is expensive."

Jon-Tom hesitated, ran his fingers experimentally over the strings. Strange to be strumming one set instead of two, but it reminded him of his electric guitar back home in a way the duar never could. "Can I try it out?"

"Certainly of course naturally." The indri bestowed a frosty stare on Mudge. "I wouldn't want you to think I was trying to cheat you."

Jon-Tom tried a few impassioned stanzas of Pink Floyd's "Money." The result was not what might have been hoped, but neither did it prove the storekeeper a liar. A tiny white cloud materialized in the air of the shop, drifted about uncertainly for a minute, then excreted a miniature lightning bolt. Instead of thunder the cloud made a noise like a cash register and a shower of coins began to rain on the indri's counter. The cloud eventually gave out and dissipated, but not before exactly three hundred large coins lay in a gleaming pile on the hardwood. The only problem was they were silver rather than gold.

"Best I can do," Jon-Tom said apologetically.

"Ah well." Izzy surveyed the pile. "It is a suar and not a duar."

"But the magic works. I can spellsing with this." Jon-Tom held the instrument out at arm's length. "The power is there, but not the strength. I'll just have to scale down my expectations. Will you take the silver and,'' he considered carefully, ''five pieces of gold? We still have an ocean voyage to pay for.''

''Done! Finished, completed, agreed upon.''

Mudge sidled up close to his friend. ''You could've bargained 'im down and got it for a lot less, mate.''

''A lot less than what, Mudge? We got it for a song.''

The otter was eying the pile of silver hungrily. ''Then 'ow about givin' us another demonstration, mate? Just for entertainment value, wot?''

''Mudge, you ought to know by now I can't get results by singing the same song more than once. Not with this. It just doesn't have the power.''

''Pity. Well, at least you're a spellsinger once more, 'eaven 'elp us.''

Jon-Tom nodded. ''It's not a duar, but it seems to be the next best thing. Properly utilized it ought to get us there and back in two pieces.'' He turned to the delighted shopkeeper. ''Thanks, Izzy. See you again sometime, maybe.''

''I most sincerely surely hope so, friend.''

Mudge trotted alongside his taller friend as they started down the street. ''I thought you had just enough lucre to get us to this Scream Cat place and back. You just 'anded that big-eyed thief five gold pieces.''

''No matter, Mudge. We have this now.'' He tapped the suar.

''I was afraid that was wot you were goin' to say,'' the otter sighed.

''Come on, Mudge. Have you forgotten already? I sang us up a boat once before. Given all the practice and study I've had these past months I see no reason why I can't sing up another. That way we can save our money and enjoy a few luxuries along the way.''

''Yeah, like stayin' alive,'' the otter grumbled.

''Have a little confidence. You've seen what I can do.''

''That's wot worries me.''

''Don't. Let's find ourselves a fine inn and have a good

night's sleep. In the morning we'll find an empty dock and I'll sing us up some automatic piloting yacht or something."

"Or something," Mudge mumbled, but under his breath.

Despite Jon-Tom's insistence he'd prefer to work without an audience, Mudge managed to hustle up a bevy of spectators to watch the spellsinger at work.

"Step right up, folks! Feast your eyes on the wonder o' the day, a real live spellsinger about to perform 'is bafflin' an' mystifyin' trade." He stepped in the path of a strolling merchant. "'Ere now mister moneybags, 'ave you ever seen real magic before? I mean *real* magic, in the light o' day, without any tricks or gimmicks?"

"No, but I. . . ."

"See the spellsinger conjure up a 'ole ship out o' thin air! Bet you ain't never seen nothin' like that in your simple, dull-as-daffodils life, 'ave you?"

"No, but I. . . ."

"Much less a ship crewed by as sexy a lot o' naked lovelies as ever twisted their legs 'round a mizzenmast?"

The merchant suddenly halted and strained to see through the rest of the assembling crowd. "How much?" he said enthusiastically.

Jon-Tom did his best to ignore the jostling, eager crowd as he strummed the suar and considered what song to sing. The harbor of Yarrowl lay spread out before him, full of tall sailing ships and smaller craft. The thick aroma of salt mixed with that of cargoes from distant lands and the raw sewage which the ships discharged into the bay.

Surely he was accomplished enough to execute a simple transportation song before a crowd of rubbernecking onlookers? Wasn't that what being a professional was all about? Mudge stepped smartly past, jingling his purse full of coins and grinning behind his whiskers. The otter looked exceedingly pleased with himself.

"Not bad, mate. Maybe there's somethin' to this spellsingin' business after all. With your talents and mine we could do ourselves proud."

"Don't forget, Mudge, that I have to make a boat appear

or else you'll have to give all these people their money back."

"Yeah, let's see some magic," shouted one of the spectators, a small black bear clad in a silvery toga and leather cap. The cry was echoed by several others in the crowd. They had business to attend to and were starting to get edgy.

Jon-Tom leaned over to whisper to his companion. "Maybe you should have waited until I had a chance to try a simpler spell first. This isn't a duar, remember."

Mudge put a reassuring paw on his friend's shoulder. "I 'ave confidence in you, mate. I know you won't let me down, or your public either. Didn't you always tell me you wanted to perform for an audience?"

"Yes, but that just involved singing, not magic." He eyed some of the heavily armed spectators uneasily. "And this isn't quite the type of audience I always dreamed about."

"Now listen, mate, 'ere I've gone to the trouble o' linin' up enough money to pay for our 'ole journey and then some and you're 'avin' second thoughts. 'Tis unbecomin' for a spellsinger. Wot would 'is sorcerorship say about this distressin' lack o' self-assurance?"

"I just wish you hadn't promised them so much, that's all. Naked crew members! I've no intention of conjuring up any such thing."

Mudge winked. "Right, but they don't know that. Ah, a couple more potential customers. I'll just slip over quiet-like and ease them into the audience while you're gettin' started." He melted into the semicircle of onlookers. A couple of margays regarded Jon-Tom out of wide eyes.

How had he let the otter talk him into something like this? Nothing for it now but to try. If he failed they could always return the money Mudge had collected. He strummed the suar again, having already settled on a song. With its single set of strings, the suar was much easier to play. No reason not to proceed with confidence.

Half closing his eyes and trying to concentrate on the water next to the dock, he began to sing. The crowd quieted immediately, hushed and expectant.

Despite Jon-Tom's best effort the first song produced nothing save some mutterings of discontent from his audience. He tried again, his fingers a blur against the suar strings. He felt confident and in control of himself and his music. If anything he was in better voice than usual.

Not so much as a single gneechee appeared.

The water lapped against the shore, driftwood bumped against the dock pilings, and the crowd stared at him unpleasantly. Wrong song, he told himself. Wrong instrument, too, but he had no choice there. Try another tune, and fast.

This time it went much better. Perhaps he simply needed the warm-up. The air above the water began to fluoresce. A few oohs and aahs rose from the crowd. Crabs clinging to the base of the pilings scattered. But while some of the onlookers claimed to be able to see outlines forming in the mist above the water, nothing solid materialized.

"Where's the damn boat?" an elegantly attired wallaby demanded to know.

"Yes, where are the females?" asked the tall hare standing next to him.

"This we can see for free in any tavern," growled a large spectator near the rear of the crowd.

"I'm still warming up." It sounded lame even to his own ears, Jon-Tom knew.

"You said that after the first song," hissed a lynx. Scarred and missing one ear, this tough looking customer was fingering something short, sharp and curved. "Let's see something—or let's have our money back."

"Magic isn't science," Jon-Tom pleaded. "Sometimes it works and sometimes it doesn't."

"We were guaranteed magic."

"I want my gold back!" shouted a tall simian from the crowd.

"What do you mean 'guaranteed'?" Jon-Tom asked the lynx. "Nobody can guarantee magic."

"Your friend the water rat did." Light flashed off the curved knife the lynx was manipulating.

"He did? Mudge?" Jon-Tom strained to see into the crowd. There were representatives of many species facing him, but not one otter. Especially not one particular otter. "Mudge!"

The otter had disappeared along with his sackful of money. It appeared that Talea's threat to sic the Lynchbany law on him had finally lost its hold. Having taken the opportunity to acquire some traveling cash of his own, he'd departed for distant parts unknown, leaving Jon-Tom to deal with an increasingly sullen, angry crowd which had been "guaranteed" a demonstration of real magic making. That was something Jon-Tom couldn't promise Clothahump, much less a mob of newly fleeced citizens.

"Look, you have to understand that *I* didn't promise you any magic. I can only try. That's all any spellsinger can do. It was the otter who made all the promises."

"We don't argue that." The voice was that of a squat long whiskered mole who eyed Jon-Tom from behind thick, extremely dark glasses. He was brandishing a four-inch-long bone blade. "But he ain't here no more, minstrel, and you are."

"I'm not a minstrel." Jon-Tom overtopped most of the crowd. Now he tried to take advantage of his height to make himself as imposing as possible. "I am a *spellsinger*."

"Then prove it," snapped the mole, "and I don't mean by making pretty colors in the air."

"You're damn right I'll prove it!" He was shaking, partly from anger and partly from fright. "I said I'd conjure up a boat and conjure up a boat I will."

While he'd been arguing with the crowd a far more appropriate song had come to him. Confident now, he turned back to face the waters of Yarr Bay. Once more he began to sing, once again his fingers danced over the suar's strings, and this time something far more cohesive than colored lights began to take shape atop the water. No gneechees swirled curiously around it, but he wasn't singing for the gneechees this time. He was concentrating on his song.

Part of the problem stemmed from the fact that not many rock songs dealt with boats or ships. He didn't dare use the

Beach Boys' " Sloop John B." again. That had been a near disaster. So the song he sang now was one of his own devising, improvised words set to the official theme music by Walter Sharf for the old Cousteau television specials. Add a little reggae and what more suitable combination of themes for calling up a proper boat? Perhaps he might even create a copy of the famed *Calypso* itself. Let the natives sneer until he confronted them with the reality of a modern, diesel-powered craft.

Several members of the crowd broke and ran. Most remained to stare in awe. Yes, conjure up the *Calypso* with its radar and complex electronics! Doubt his ability, would they? Double-stringed or single-stringed instrument in hand, he'd show them what a spellsinger was all about.

Twisting and flickering, the intense lights pirouetted above the disturbed surface of the bay. As he brought his vibrant, improvised tune to a rousing conclusion the lights softened and ran together, began to condense and solidify to form a cloud of pink incandescence which finally blew apart to reveal floating lightly on the water—a boat.

On its bow it bore the outline of a golden merman and the legend CALYPSO. Unfortunately, it wasn't the famed *Calypso* itself that bobbed gently in the backwater eddy. It wasn't even a reasonable facsimile.

It was a zodiac, one of the inflatable rubber craft that the crew of the *Calypso* utilized for short excursions away from the main ship. It was not very impressive.

"What the hell's that?" The lynx leaned forward and squinted at the black skinned apparition.

"Floats it does, but t'aint no boat for sure," commented someone else near the back of the crowd of onlookers.

"Of course it's a boat." Now Jon-Tom was angry as well as frustrated. "Any idiot can see it's a boat. What else *could* it be but a boat?"

"It's no boat." A rat clad in shorts and a shirt with puffed sleeves waded into the murky water to poke at the zodiac's flanks. "It's just a big balloon." He tapped the big black outboard motor that hung from the zodiac's stern. "What's this funny-looking hunk of metal for?"

The crowd's initial astonishment was rapidly giving way to a general feeling that they'd been had. To them a boat was a creature the length of a dock and tall as a three-story building, with billowing sails, intricate rigging and a wooden hull. What a boat was not was a flattened bunch of black balloons. Knives began to appear in profusion, brandished in company with numerous homicidal expressions. They'd wanted a boat, they'd paid for a boat, and by the ancestor of every creature present they were damn well going to have a proper boat or else they were going to take it out of this so-called spellsinger's hide.

And where was the crew of lithesome lovelies?

"All right," Jon-Tom told them, "I'll prove to you that this is a boat."

"Pillows," growled the lynx, taking a step forward. He grinned, showing dirty fangs. "You know what I think? I think I've been cheated, that's what I think."

"It's a goddamn boat!" Trying not to show the anxiety he was feeling, he walked into the water, pushed the rat aside, and sat down in the back of the zodiac. The bow rose slightly.

"See? A bunch of pillows wouldn't support my weight like this." The mob was crowding toward the water's edge, muttering loudly. "And this is a magic oar." He primed the engine, praying it would start when he hit the ignition.

The mole peered through his black glasses at the outboard. "Looks like a bunch of junk to me."

"No, I'll prove it, see? All you have to do is press this button." He did so. The engine rumbled, making the crowd retreat slightly. It coughed, spat and died.

"Hornets," shouted the lynx, "he's got hornets in there!"

"I don't see any," said the rat. "It's a trick. He's trying to scare us with tricks!"

The mob surged forward. Praying as hard as he ever had in his brief life, Jon-Tom stabbed the ignition button again and held it down. Come on baby, he said silently, turn over, turn over!

The engine threw black smoke in the face of the advancing lynx, kicked in, and sent the zodiac shooting out across the calm water of the bay, snarling like a lost motocross bike. It was followed by a number of sharp-edged pointed objects which fell far short of their goal. A few choice, equally pointed insults did reach him but did no damage.

But what now? His outraged audience did not appear pacified by this incontrovertible proof that the object he had conjured up was indeed a boat. Probably still looking for the promised crew, he mused. They continued to jump up and down on the shore, screaming unheard imprecations and gesticulating obscenely in his direction. He would have to wait and circle back up the river after nightfall, find some secluded anchorage, and try to make his inglorious way back to Lynchbany under cover of darkness.

First he had to wend his way through the harbor traffic. Bearing down on him already was a huge ocean-going catamaran. The double hull contained the lower class passenger compartments, the upper deck the rooms for those traveling first class, while the cargo was slung in nets between the hulls. This enabled the catamaran to run smartly up over a low dock without having to remove cargo from inside the ship.

He turned to port and the catamaran appeared to swerve to bear down on him. Each hull boasted a pair of masts, one square-rigged for speed, the other fore-rigged for maneuverability. It wasn't maneuvering to his liking now. Had someone on shore somehow communicated with a relative or friend in charge of the ship? The zodiac could run circles around anything in Yarrowl harbor, but it was distressing to think the entire city might be roused against him so quickly.

As the starboard hull of the big ship slid past him something tumbled over the side. Instinctively he winced, but it was only a rope. He recognized the face leaning over the railing.

"Don't just squat there like a bug on a rock, mate," Mudge shouted. "Grab hold and tie on!"

In disbelief Jon-Tom gaped at the otter. Then he swung the zodiac around and accelerated to catch up with the catamaran. Catching hold of the trailing line, he secured it to the hole in the zodiac's bow and shut off the engine as sailors pulled him close to the hull. A sea ladder was extended to him. Making his way carefully hand over hand, he soon found himself standing on the deck looking back at curious sailors and well-dressed passengers. A grinning Mudge saluted briskly and then stepped clear. Jon-Tom brushed his hair out of his eyes and started for the otter.

"Hold off a minim, mate. I know wot you're thinkin'."

"No you don't. If you did, you'd already have jumped overboard."

Mudge continued to retreat, well aware he could dodge Jon-Tom's lunges with ease. "Think it through, lad. You really didn't think you were goin' to conjure up a proper craft with that shadow o' a duar, did you?"

"Why not?"

"Because you couldn't do it when you *'ad* your duar, that's why."

Jon-Tom halted. Three times he'd sung his song, and the best he'd been able to do was the little zodiac. A fine craft for exploring a lake or cruising up a river, but not the sort of thing one would choose to cross an ocean in, especially after the couple of gallons of fuel the engine contained ran out.

"Soon as I saw 'ow things weren't goin' with your spellsingin'," the otter went on, "I sort of took the first opportunity to make a discreet exit and locate emergency transportation. A fine ship an' a cooperative captain 'ave agreed to carry us as far as the island kingdom o' Orangel. That's where this vessel's bound. Orangel's more than 'alf the way to Chejiji. From there we won't 'ave no trouble 'irin' transportation to the southern shores, or so says our Captain. A substantial payment insured a slight change o' course to pluck you from the water. Money we now 'ave in plenty, thanks to your performance."

"Mudge, you guaranteed those spectators magic. You of all people should know that spellsinging isn't an infallible discipline, much less when I'm trying to make it work with a back-up instrument. Suppose I hadn't been able to conjure up my small inflatable craft and get away? What then?"

"Now don't let's go gettin' ourselves all upset over might-'ave-beens. The facts o' the matter are that you did produce this charmin' little boat an' that it did spirit you safely away from that pustulant seep o' ignorant gawkers. O' course, 'ad it not done so and 'ad you not been able to outswim your critics then I expect I would've returned 'ome sadder an' richer to convey me regrets to your beloved, thence to continue on life's merry way after sheddin' a sorry tear or two for me lost friend. All o' which is so much snakesnot, since you're standin' 'ere safe, sound and much better off than when you started singin'."

"That's a pretty cold assessment of what could have happened, Mudge."

"'Tis a cold world, mate, as I've 'ad occasion to mention before. T'wasn't so bad, now were it? I took the time to make sure there were none among your avid audience likely to outswim you. No otters."

As the novelty of the fleeing human and his inflatable boat began to pale, the sailors and well-dressed promenaders on the upper deck started to disperse.

"Let's 'ave no more talk o' despair an' disasters that weren't." Mudge encompassed sea and sky with a sweeping gesture. "See wot a luvely day it is. We're off to this Stubborn Kit Mail place an' we're goin' in style. Wait 'til you sees the cabin I've reserved for you. Ain't this wot you wanted?"

Jon-Tom's voice had fallen to whisper as he made the grudging confession. "I guess so."

"Right! said the otter cheerfully. "An' when we get to Orangel we can sell that inflatable doohickey you conjured up for a pretty piece, wot?"

Jon-Tom leaned close. "It would take several dozen individuals with steel lungs to inflate it properly."

"Or one wizard," the otter countered. "But why trouble yourself with details like that? Such things are for the buyer to contemplate. If your conscience is beginnin' to bother you already, just let ol' Mudge 'andle the sellin'."

"What, and have us run out of another town?"

The otter was shaking his head sadly. "You may make a great spellsinger some day, mate, but you'll never know 'ow to sing the proper tune to carry a business. Come on, the Captain wants to meet you. 'E's never met a real life spellsinger before and I told 'im you were the best who ever picked up a duar. 'E's invited us to dine at his table tonight." Mudge winked lecherously. "I've taken the liberty o' invitin' a couple o' ladies o' compatible species to join us."

"Those days are past, Mudge. I'm a married man now."

The otter spat disgustedly over the railing. "A fine trip this is goin' to turn out to be."

V

Contrary to this prediction Mudge did not perish of terminal boredom as the voyage proceeded. After trying and failing repeatedly to interest his tall companion in a little shipboard rousting and jousting with members of the opposite sex, Mudge finally took to spending much of his time below decks among the second-class passengers. There he could gamble and drink unhindered by Jon-Tom's admonitions to keep it clean because there was no place out in the middle of the ocean to run if he was caught cheating at cards or dice.

Actually Jon-Tom was enjoying himself. The sea was calm, the winds gentle but steady, the sun warm and relaxing as the graceful ship sailed steadily southward. The cuisine was new and intriguing, much spicier than he was used to. Every few days professional dancers and musicians entertained on the vast rear deck of the catamaran.

Jon-Tom guessed the number of paying passengers at

forty, so there was plenty of room to move about on what was essentially a cargo vessel. The crew was helpful and unobtrusive. Only Talea's absence prevented him from relaxing completely. As he was the only human on the ship, he missed her more than ever.

They were three-quarters of the way to Orangel when Mudge came trudging up to him. Jon-Tom was sprawled across two deck chairs, soaking up the sun, but he sat up fast when he got a look at his friend.

"Something wrong, Mudge?"

The otter responded with a gargling noise that sounded vaguely like "Yeh."

"You don't look so good." He sat up and put a hand on the otter's shoulder, gripping it hard. Mudge blinked, seeming to see him for the first time.

"Oh, 'tis you, mate. That's good. Wot did you say? Oh, I'm fine, I am. That is, I think I am. Come to think of it, I guess I ain't sure."

"Something you ate?"

This set off a fit of coughing, followed by a smile, then a look of dazed amusement. "Come with me, lad. I've somethin' to show you."

Jon-Tom allowed himself to be led to the inner railing of the portside hull on which they were standing. Safety nets had been strung between the twin hulls and a number of passengers were cavorting in the shark-free pool thus created. As the catamaran skimmed the waves the current would push the swimmers into the back net, whereupon they would clamber out of the water and walk along a narrow catwalk until they could dive back into the upper end of the net pool, thus repeating the process.

"Don't you see her?"

"Where?" Jon-Tom leaned over the rail. There were a dozen passengers in the nets. Then he saw one who was a blur in the water. As he watched she concluded her swim and climbed the stairs leading to the main deck. There she shook herself out, dried herself further with a towel, and snuggled down into an empty deck chair to allow the sun to finish the job. She wore some flimsy swimming costume which was more decoration than concealment.

Mudge had his elbows propped on the rail and his muzzle cupped in his paws. "Now I ask you straight, mate," he said with a sigh, "did you ever see anything o' flesh an' blood on this world or in any other that were 'alf so beautiful as that?" As he spoke the object of his desire twisted in her chair, plucked a lace handkerchief from a small bag and used it to dry her whiskers one at a time.

Jon-Tom regarded the lady otter a moment longer before his attention was caught by Mudge's expression. The bemusement he had noted before remained, now buffered by a peculiar intensity. It was not the standard gaze of unalloyed lechery he was familiar with. This was something different.

"'Er name's Weegee." Mudge's voice was distant, unfocused. "She's a typical forest products buyer on 'er way 'ome from a shoppin' trip up the Tailaroam. I believe the Earth rotates around 'er."

The otter's tone, his choice of words and his posture combined to make a statement Jon-Tom was not long in assessing. Only a natural disbelief caused him to hesitate before noting the obvious. It was as if a basic law of nature had been contravened, as though one of the great pyramids at Giza had crumbled to dust in a single day.

"Mudge, you're in love."

"So good o' you to notice." Not once did he take his eyes from the vision of sleek brown-furred loveliness sprawled on the deck chair not far away.

"No, I mean *really* in love, Mudge. As opposed to in lust. I can hear it in your voice and see it in your face."

"Then I expect 'tis so, spellsinger. I've never felt like this before, I 'aven't. Why, me insides 'ave turned all to crikleberry jelly."

"You know her name, so obviously you've met. Why don't you introduce me?"

"Wot, now?"

"Why not now?"

"Well, I don't know—yes I do. Come on, mate."

Jon-Tom allowed the otter to lead him onto the central deck. The lady was lying half asleep and Jon-Tom had to prod his companion to say something, as it seemed Mudge would have been quite content simply to stand there and stare until they docked in Orangel.

"Amber face, are you awake, luv?"

She opened her eyes and quickly took in the both of them. "Hello, Mudge."

A sweet, seductive voice, Jon-Tom thought, one that curled around each vowel as slickly as an otter would curl around a fish; toying with it, playing with it before finally devouring it. He was conscious of bottomless black eyes studying him intently. "This must be the friend you spoke of." She half twisted, half jumped out of the deck chair, gave one leg a final shake. Water droplets sparkled in the air.

"Come now, tall man, bend down and give us a kiss." Jon-Tom glanced uncertainly at his companion, only to find Mudge grinning back at him. So he bent over and tried to bestow a quick peck on one furry cheek. Much too fast for him, she turned and treated him to a full otterish buss on the lips, which consisted of a rapid-fire series of wet bewhiskered smacks smelling vaguely of mackerel. Contact with a cold black nose completed the extraordinary sensation, not unlike having one's mouth attacked by a fishy jackhammer.

She pulled back and cocked her head sideways at him. "He's shy. You didn't say he was shy."

"'E's married an' a spellsinger an' 'e's from another world. Wot did you expect, luv? Normalcy?"

"Not from a spellsinger."

Straightforward as an arrow, Jon-Tom thought, shifting uncomfortably under that uncompromising stare. Otters were not a subtle race. He watched as she reached over to muss the fur on Mudge's forehead just below the brim of his green cap. Diaphanous material swirled around her lithesome form and her fur gleamed like brass in the midday sun.

"So you're his best friend?" Jon-Tom glanced at Mudge in surprise. The otter shrugged.

"Well, for want o' a better choice. Anyway, you're 'ere."

"That sounds more like it," he said.

"What am I to make of your companion, Jon-Tom? He's been trying to get me into bed with him from the moment we met. Do you think I should?"

"Ah, hey now, friends, I—that is . . ." He stopped stammering when he saw they were both grinning at him. Mudge put an arm around her and she didn't resist or pull away.

"She's just teasin' you, mate. You ought to know otters that well by now. We took care o' that little detail right away."

"Yes, and we have a lot of work to do to get it right," she added pleasantly.

"Uh *huh*. Swell meeting you, Weegee. Now if the two of you will excuse me, I have an appointment to make a fool of myself somewhere else."

"Don't do it here," she chided him. "I'm sorry if I embarrassed you. Mudge said you were easily embarrassed and I wanted to find out for myself. Now come and sit down." She grabbed his arm and practically yanked him into the empty deck chair next to hers, sat down and crossed her short legs over her lower torso, the latter a spine-destroying trick that only someone with the backbone of an otter could manage.

"Now then: tell me all about yourself."

Jon-Tom flicked his gaze sideways. "Hasn't Mudge done that already."

"Yes, but I've known Fastfingers long enough to realize that in addition to his many talents he is also an incorrigible liar. So tell me about yourself, and about him, and about anything else you think I might be interested in. I'm all ears." She wiggled the short brown ones atop her head. "Mudge says that you're as trustworthy, honest and open as you are naive and ignorant."

"I see." He looked up at his companion, who had

suddenly found something of interest to study in the water below. "I'd be glad to. When I first found Mudge and dragged him from the gutter in Lynchbany where he was lying in a drunken stupor . . . ."

The otter's outraged bark echoed throughout the ship.

As the days passed Jon-Tom rarely saw Mudge far from Weegee's side. The more they talked, the better he liked her. She was one of those rare otters whose sense of playfulness and joie de vivre did not prevent her from functioning effectively in an urban context. Most otters didn't have the patience to make a go of it in the world of commerce.

She found the stories of their travels and adventures fascinating. Who wouldn't, considering what he and Mudge had been through this past year? And when the otter's embroidery grew too elaborate, Jon-Tom was always there to inject a dose of reality into his companion's narcissistic fantasies.

He was delighted to see that Mudge's feelings for her were being reciprocated and that what he initially viewed as a typical shipboard romance was ripening into something deeper and more substantial. He was quite prepared to lose a traveling companion to true love. Mudge had never been thrilled about galavanting around with the spellsinger anyway.

For his part, in spite of all the trouble Mudge had caused him in the past, Jon-Tom was quite fond of the irrepressible otter. Weegee might be strong enough and stable enough to settle him. Mudge needed that kind of influence if he was to see middle age. Nor did Jon-Tom have to build the otter up in Weegee's eyes. Mudge did quite a good job of that all by himself, and Weegee was sensible and perceptive enough to discard ninety-five percent of everything her paramour said. The remaining five percent was remarkable enough, if only Mudge would realize it.

It was a pleasure to watch their relationship grow, to witness the change in Mudge from indifferent seducer to protective companion. To see him finally mature a little from drunken carouser into a thoughtful, attentive being.

Until one day hopes new and old were shattered at a single stroke.

The alarm rang at night when all of the passengers and most of the crew were asleep. It was only through the courage and alertness of one of the night watch, a brave little aye-aye with an outsize voice, that the warning was given at all and utter disaster thereby averted.

At the first clang of the alarm bell Mudge was out of bed and donning clothes and weapons. Jon-Tom was still struggling with his pants when a couple of heavily armed pangolins came stumbling into their cabin. Each was barely four feet tall and carried a short hooked sword. One wore a bloodstained bandana around his head. Neither was dressed to waltz.

After breaking in the door the first intruder ran straight into Mudge's short sword, which pierced the throat just beneath the chin and above the animal's armor. Blood gushed in all directions as the second pangolin swung at Mudge, who somehow managed to dodge aside while the first fell on top of him. So involved was the intruder with the otter that he neglected to spot Jon-Tom on the other side of the room. The club end of Jon-Tom's ramwood staff rectified this oversight while simultaneously putting out the invader's lights.

"Thanks, mate!" The otter shoved the body of his assailant aside and bounded to his feet. Shouts mixed with an occasional scream filtered down from above. "Let's up an' at 'em."

After a discreet survey proved the hallway to be deserted, the otter led Jon-Tom toward the stairs at the far end.

"Hurry it up, mate."

Jon-Tom was trying to run and step into his pants at the same time. "I'm coming as fast as I can, or do you expect me to fight without any pants?"

"Why not? Would you rather be embarrassed or dead?"

Wearing only his pants, a bare-chested, barefooted Jon-

Tom followed his friend up the stairway. They emerged on deck in the midst of darkness, confusion and carnage.

Another ship had fastened itself to the portside hull. The ketch was old and beat-up but evidently seaworthy enough to tackle the much larger caramaran. It was also home to an astonishing variety of cutthroats and thugs, who continued to swarm over the gunwales onto the freighter.

Their plan was as simple as their intentions were obvious: wait until dark, then slip quietly aboard and exterminate the officers and crew in their bunks. Then they could sample cargo and passengers at their leisure. Unfortunately for them the alert aye-aye had died a hero's death while sacrificing his life to raise the alarm. This had roused not only the crew but the passengers as well, most of whom knew their way around a weapon or two. As this was not Bel-Air or Brentwood, most of the citizens carried some form of personal defense. As a consequence the pirates found themselves badly outnumbered and being forced steadily back toward their ship.

A few had managed to secure some booty in those first frantic minutes before the ship's complement had been aroused. They hurried back toward the ketch with their arms full of stolen goods. The deck was slippery with blood. The dangerous, uncertain footing was more to the pirates' disadvantage than that of the defenders.

Jon-Tom watched the energetic Captain Magriff lead the counterattack, his crew silently and determinedly following the badger as they plunged into the pirates' midst. With the aid of the passengers they were slowly overwhelming the attackers.

A few unlucky brigands were cut down as they tried to make it back to their ship. The survivors tossed what they'd been able to steal over the side, followed it down the lines and cut themselves free. Those on board the catamaran sent a stream of curses and insults in their wake.

Jon-Tom and Mudge listened as the ship's officers argued with the captain. Several were for putting on additional sail and turning to pursue their fleeing assailants. Magriff would have none of that.

"Stow that spray, gentlebeings. We nay go chasin' after phantoms this night. Listen to your heads for a minute instead o' yer hearts. With a strong wind at our backs we might overtake 'em, but the breeze tonight is light and out o' the east instead o' the north. Not only would we have to work a change in course, but in such a light wind a smaller boat could easily outmaneuver us. And they might have friends a-waitin' for 'em somewhere out on the dark sea. It would not make good sense to go a-chasin' in pursuit o' some wounded blackguards only to find ourselves confronted by two or three vessels o' the criminal class. Our first responsibility be to our passengers and cargo. Remember that and belay any talk o' wild pursuits." He stepped up onto a capstan.

"Mister Foison, check the stores and see what we have lost. See to the below decks cargo as well. I'll want a list of damages for insurance purposes. Mister Opoltin!" A tall, sinewy marten with blood on his muzzle snapped to attention. "You and Doctor Kesswith see to any injured. Passengers first, crew second, officers last."

"Yes sir!" The marten vanished.

Two crew men arrived with the body of the dead aye-aye. The primate who had saved the ship was barely three and a half feet tall. His long tail lay curled stiffly over his back.

"Saved the ship and surely saved us," murmured the captain. "A hero's burial at sea as befits a good sailor, and company damages to his survivors. I'll see to it." The badger turned to his third mate. "Check with the doctor and let me know who else be hurt. You," he snapped at another officer, "get a squad up here armed with mops and brooms. Buckets and scrubs, mister Seevar. Let's get this mess cleaned up and this deck looking shipshape. Double the watch until further notice. We nay want to chance bein' surprised again."

Mudge was staring out across the ocean. His face was alive, his eyes shining. "That weren't such a bad evenin's entertainment, now were it?'' The otter loved a good fight, provided the numbers were on his side. He looked back at his taller companion and frowned.

''Hey now, mate, you've been cut.''

Jon-Tom touched his left side. The small trickle of red was already drying up. ''Just a scratch.''

The otter nevertheless inspected the shallow gash closely. ''So it 'tis.'' He grinned up at the tall human. ''Remember when our good friend Clothahump first brought you into this world and dumped you on top o' me?''

''Sure, I remember. You tried to run me through, but you were too scared to strike a hard blow.''

''Wot, me scared o' a bald scarecrow like you? I just saw no reason to kill when I could strike a warnin' blow first.'' The otter peered past him at the crowd still milling about on deck. Everyone was too excited to go back to sleep. ''Wonder where Weegee is? Surely she wouldn't 'ave missed a good knockabout like this.''

''Maybe she slept through it.'' He leaned on his staff, suddenly exhausted. The sleep he hadn't enjoyed was starting to catch up with him. From the position of the moon it had to be around three or four in the morning. Nocturnal fights weren't to his liking.

''She'll be damned upset if she did.'' Mudge darted down the nearest gangway, leaving Jon-Tom alone on deck as the passengers began to return to their cabins and the crew to bed or duty stations.

Except for the unlucky aye-aye who'd sounded the alarm, there were no fatalities among the ship's complement. There were wounded, however, and dead pirates to be unceremoniously dumped overboard.

He started back toward his own bed only to find an anxious Mudge confronting him at the top of the stairs. ''She ain't in 'er cabin, mate. I don't suppose . . . ?''

Jon-Tom shook his head. ''I haven't seen her. She probably came up through the other hull. Don't worry, Mudge. She's on board. She has to be. Maybe she's down in the galley having something to eat, or maybe she's helping with the wounded.''

''That'd be like 'er.'' The otter pleaded gently. ''Could you 'elp me 'ave a look-see, mate? I'd be obliged. Wouldn't be able to sleep until we found 'er.''

''Of course.''

But Weegee wasn't in the dining area, or was she helping to bind up the injuries the crew had suffered. Word was passed to the captain, who ordered an immediate search to ascertain passenger Weegee's location. As time passed and one crew member after another reported negatively to the bridge, Mudge grew progressively more frantic.

Enlightenment came not from one of the searching sailors but from a passenger who happened to overhear their concern. She was immediately escorted to the bridge to tell her tale to Jon-Tom, Mudge, the captain and his first officers. The jerboa belle was still clad in a lacy pink nightdress which had been torn in several places. As she spoke she nervously preened the black tuft at the tip of her tail. Her eyelashes were nearly as big as her feet, Jon-Tom noted.

''The otter you speak of was near me. We shared cabins by the place where the pirates first came on board. She went out on deck with her knife.''

Mudge nudged his friend in the ribs. ''Told you Weegee weren't the one to pass up a good fight.'' He raised his voice slightly. ''Bet she's restin' in somebody else's cabin right now, wot?''

''I'm afraid she may not be,'' said the jerboa sadly. ''I am sure now that I saw her go over the side in the arms of an agouti.''

Jon-Tom swallowed. ''You mean you think she's on the pirate ship?''

The jerboa nodded, her whiskers trembling. Obviously a high-strung type. ''If she is still alive, the poor brave thing. I told her not to join the fight until the rest of the crew appeared, but she would not listen to me.''

''That's Weegee for sure,'' Mudge muttered. ''You're

sure now, lass, that this agouti took her onto the boat and that they didn't just land in the water?

"As sure as I can be, for I listened and there was no splash." She put her narrow bewhiskered face in her hands and began to sob. "It would have been so much better had she died on board here. A nasty business, nasty."

"You didn't see them kill her?" Jon-Tom asked the question because he knew Mudge couldn't.

"Why should they kill her?" The jerboa looked up at them, wiping at her tears. "A live prisoner is worth infinitely more than a dead one, especially a brave attractive one. I think I saw the pirate captain order the poor thing taken below decks to keep her from escaping." She shuddered. "He was a frightening looking fellow. I think he must have been the captain because he was standing atop the center cabin giving orders. A leopard, big, nearly as big as you." She nodded toward Jon-Tom. "Almost handsome he was, but there was nothing attractive in his demeanor." A finger went to her lips as she continued playing with her tail.

"You know something—I didn't think of it at the time, but his tail didn't look quite right."

"A strange thing to say," commented Magriff. "How do you mean, madame?"

"Well, it looked as if the last half of it was stiff and frozen. It didn't twitch once, didn't move at all. Almost as though it was artificial, yes, that was it. Artificial." She looked pleased at finally puzzling it out. "I am sure that at some time that leopard's tail had been cut off and that a false end has been substituted for the missing piece."

Jon-Tom listened in disbelief. He and Mudge had once made the acquaintance of a leopard with half a tail. It was not an acquaintance either of them wished to renew.

"Mudge?"

"Anythin's possible in the world, mate," said the otter grimly. "Old Corroboc's dead, but we watched 'is bastard crew go sailin' off in another direction on this very same ocean not that many months ago."

Jon-Tom remembered their narrow escape from the bloodthirsty pirate parrot Corroboc. His first mate had been a muscular, sadistic leapord named Sasheem. Sasheem of the prosthetic tail. There could not be two of them, not even on an ocean as big as the Glittergeist.

"I wonder how many others of the original crew are with him?"

"Don't matter, mate. Sasheem's who matters. That cat would remember us for sure. Get 'is claws into us and 'e'd disembowel us as slowly as possible, lookin' into our eyes all the while. Not out o' any misplaced sense o' loss over 'is late unlamented captain but to satisfy 'is own sense o' revenge. Made a fool of 'im, we did, and a cat like that don't forget."

"We'll just have to deal with him as best we can. If our fuel holds out I think we can catch them in the zodiac."

"Now wait a minim, mate. Wot about wot I just said about Sasheem, and that murderin' lot? You know wot'll 'appen to us if they get their paws on us?"

Jon-Tom hesitated. "All right. This is your decision to make, Mudge." He nodded toward the dark water. "That's your lady out there, not mine."

The otter stared blankly back at him, then turned and stumbled over to the railing. "Weegee!" he shouted at the top of his lungs. "You 'ear me, Weegee? Damn you for gettin' me into this. Damn you from your whiskers to your bloody beautiful tail, an' double-damn you for makin' me fall in love with you!"

Jon-Tom put a comforting hand gently on the otter's shoulder. "You really mean that, Mudge? Or is it just another term of convenience for you?"

" 'Ow the 'ell should I know, mate? I ain't never felt like this before. 'Ow the 'ell do you *tell*?"

Jon-Tom stared down into the otter's eyes. "There's one simple way. Is she worth dying for?"

"Dyin' for." The otter looked past him. The captain and officers remained discreetly behind on the bridge. It was lonely on deck now, lonely and quiet enough to hear the sound of the waves slapping against the catamaran's hulls.

"I never thought a lady were worth gettin' excited over, much less dyin' for—but this one, Weegee. I dunno."

"How do you feel, inside?"

"Angry. 'Urt, upset. 'Urt outside too, far as that goes. Shit. This is a ridiculous position to be in."

"Another fine mess you've gotten yourself into, Stanley?"

"Wot? Wot's that ?"

"Forget it." He waited another minute, then turned toward the nearest gangway. "I'm going back to sleep. It's still a ways to Orangel and I'm flat worn out."

A furry paw grabbed him by the belt. "Now 'old on a minim there, mate. You ain't goin' nowheres."

"Oh?" Jon-Tom was glad he was facing the other way so that Mudge couldn't see the grin spreading across his face. "We going someplace else then?"

"You bet your bald arse we are. We're goin' after me true luv, that's where we're goin'."

Jon-Tom looked back and down. " 'True love'? Am I hearing these words from that mouth or am I imagining them?"

"We're wastin' time. With just the pair of us in a small open boat you'll 'ave all the opportunities you want to snigger at me an' make jokes."

"What do you mean 'the pair of us'?"

"You're comin' with me. Remember? Friends to the end, you watch my backside, I watch yours?"

"Let me see now." Jon-Tom struck an exaggerated pose. "Am I listening to the same otter who's always having a fit because he's stuck tramping all over the place with me? Who can't stop cursing his ill luck at being my companion on similar journeys? Who is constantly bemoaning the fact that fate has made me his friend?"

"There's only one Mudge 'ereabouts, an' it 'appens to be the selfsame one you're foamin' at the mouth about, only maybe just a titch changed. Even an otter can change, you know. Let's not babble on about past disagreements. You owe me, this time. I've pulled your arse out o' the fire often enough, an' I've the singe marks to prove it. You really think this boat o' yours will run out of fuel somewheres in the middle o' the sea?"

All business now, Jon-Tom considered. "I don't know. I wish I'd paid more attention to Clothahump's hydrocarbon spells. I'd take a shot at it with the duar, but with this suar I'd probably just gum up the engine."

"Then we'll need us a sail. As for dealin' with me luv's abductors, I don't need no magic. I'll rely on me other old friend." Fingers flipped the short sword into the air. It did a triple twist and he caught it neatly in one paw. "Sword and longbow and don't sing me no lullabies, pater, because it ain't firewood I'm off to cut." He glanced back at Jon-Tom. "Sasheem'll be onto us the moment we put in our appearance."

"I know that," Jon-Tom replied solemnly.

"Wish we 'ad your striped sassyface Roseroar with us. She'd like to meet up with Sasheem 'erself."

"And I'd like for her to also, but she'd sink the boat." He looked over the side. The zodiac trailed alongside the catamaran like a puppy on a tether. "I'm sure we can rig a brace for a small mast. With luck we won't need it. How are you at tracking on water?"

"I'm an otter, mate. Not a fish."

"Then we'll have to try and raise some porpoises because we've no idea which way the pirates went." He waved vaguely at the night. "East isn't much of a heading to go on. We need something more specific."

Mudge came up close and put both paws on the human's waist. "I'll never forget this, mate."

"Damn right you won't."

Even as they were helping to outfit the zodiac with a flexible mast and sail, the ships' crew tried to discourage them from setting out on what they perceived to be a futile and possibly fatal excursion. The first mate stared out into the night.

"You'll never find them. Too much ocean out there."

"We're not going completely blind. They won't be expecting any pursuit, so they're likely to head for the nearest landfall. Captain Magriff's already told us there are no islands between here and the coast, so we'll be able to track them after they make land if not before."

"Aye," said another sailor, "but which landfall are you talking about? That's a lot of coastline to be searching."

"I think they'll head due east, give or take a few degrees. They'll need a place where their wounded can recover. The sooner they're put on land, the better they'll do."

"Perhaps your magical oar will let you overtake them and allow you to sneak up on their stern at night." The sailor sounded dubious. "You're both crazier than a couple of loons."

"That's wot luv does to you," Mudge told him.

"Not to me." The nimble-fingered vervet secured a package of supplies to the inside of the boat.

In an hour they were done. In addition to receiving the mast, the zodiac had been stocked to overflowing with provisions. Jon-Tom brought out his purse and turned to pay the first mate. The sloth raised both massive paws.

"The captain says that the company will absorb the difference." He nodded toward the zodiac, winked through sleepy-lidded eyes that were nevertheless quite alert. "He's putting it in the manifest as part of the cargo that was taken by the brigands. If you should find them and rescue the otter's lady and by chance manage to cut a few throats in the process, he says to tell you that will be repayment enough."

Still he hesitated until Mudge tugged insistently at his arm. "Wot are you waitin' for, mate? Didn't you 'ear the bleedin' sailor? Don't look a gift badger in the mouth."

The money might come in handy elsewhere, Jon-Tom told himself. "Give Captain Magriff our thanks and tell him we'll thank him in person when we get to Orangel."

"*If* you ever get to Orangel, which all of us doubt most sincerely. We wish you all our luck." He hesitated, then said in a slightly different tone, "The otter keeps saying to everyone that you're a true spellsinger." Jon-Tom nodded. "Good. Magic's the only thing that might get you away from where you're heading alive. Don't see how it can help you track those ruffians, though."

"But it can." He had one leg over the railing preparatory to climbing down the sea ladder into the bobbing zodiac. "We'll just ask the locals which way they went."

"The locals?" Another sailor indicated the open ocean. "What locals?"

"The local yokels, o' course," shouted Mudge as he helped cast off.

Crew members crowded the railing as the zodiac fell behind the catamaran. A few waved farewell. The expressions they wore were not reassuring. It took three tries before the engine caught. Then Jon-Tom swung it sharply to the right and the zodiac leaped into the night like a flying fish breaking foam.

The catamaran's running lights were swallowed up all too rapidly by the open sea. It was very empty out on the ocean. Fortunately the sea was calm, though they felt the swells more strongly in the much smaller boat. Jon-Tom hadn't really considered how they might cope with a real storm. He prayed they wouldn't have to.

Mudge was relaxing in the bow. "Which way, master mariner?"

"East, I guess. Until we can find some help."

"No time like the present," the otter said pointedly.

Jon-Tom sighed resignedly. "Here." As they switched places he showed Mudge how to keep the zodiac on course. Then he settled himself in the bow and slid the suar into playing position.

The zodiac boasted a built-in compass. All they needed now was a proper heading. But which way in the darkness besides east? Once while sailing to distant Snarken they had encountered the only intelligent inhabitants of the open sea. Now he would have to try again, knowing that even a successful effort might be doomed to failure. Porpoises were notoriously uncooperative. They tended to spend all their time telling anyone they could get to listen to them the most excruciatingly bad jokes.

He had to try, because they could help. If they could identify the pirate ship and provide directions, he and Mudge might actually have a chance to save Weegee. But what to sing? He leaned back against the inflated wall, reflecting that if nothing else the zodiac was a comfortable boat to ride, and began to murmur a gentle seasong. His voice would not carry far, but porpoises had exquisitely sharp hearing. Perhaps they'd be lucky.

It seemed it was not to be. The sun was rising and he was nearly sung out when a surge almost lifted them out of the water. Jon-Tom's expectations were dashed when he saw that they had been dumped not by porpoises but by a vast school of far smaller swimmers.

Doffing his clothes, Mudge went over the side, as at home in the water as he was on land. Jon-Tom was beginning to get anxious when the otter finally reappeared, licking his whiskers and holding up two small fish from which the heads had been neatly removed.

''Sardines. Tasty, but they ain't much for givin' directions.'' Climbing back aboard, he set the rest of his snack aside as he shook himself off and picked up a towel.

''Sing like that, mate, an' we'll never starve, but we won't find wot we're looking for either.''

The surface of the sea was silver with schools of the tiny fish. ''Suar works all right,'' Mudge continued, '' but don't seem to 'ave the power of a regular duar. You sing for a big boat, you get this floatin' mattress. You sing for porpoises, you get sardines. Proportional magic, I expect.''

''What's proportional magic?'' a new voice squawked quite unexpectedly, nearly causing Jon-Tom to jump out of the zodiac. The slick grinning head had emerged right behind him. It was joined by a second, then a third, like so many toofs lining up at the feeding trough.

''It did work,'' Jon-Tom said triumphantly to Mudge, who nodded grudging assent.

''What worked?'' one of the porpoises inquired.

''My spellsinging. My music. I used it to call you up, and here you are.''

"Call us up?" They looked at one another, then back at Jon-Tom. "You didn't call us up, man. We came for the fish. Never have seen so many in this part of the world." Two of them dropped back beneath the surface.

"Well, it worked, anyway," Jon-Tom mumbled. "I called up sardines instead of porpoises, but the porpoises came after the fish."

"You don't need to draw pictures for me, lad." The otter was slipping back into his shorts. "Main thing is they're 'ere an' we've made contact of a sorts."

"Contact," squeaked the remaining porpoise. "Speaking of contact, have you heard the one about . . . ?"

Jon-Tom put an arm around their visitor and patted it affectionately on top of its head. It was rather like slapping a bulging hot water bottle. The sound was sharp and hollow, the porpoise's skin smooth and solid as an off-road tire.

Thus greeted, the porpoise glanced over at Mudge. "Tell me, citizen of both worlds, is the man always like this?"

"'E's just a friendly soul, 'e is."

"My turn first," Jon-Tom said, having decided on his line of attack earlier. "This story concerns the shipmaster and the eel."

"Wait, whoa!" The porpoise let out several short high-pitched squeals that sounded like miniature train whistles. In seconds the zodiac was surrounded by bobbing heads wearing attentive expressions.

"Better make it funny, mate," Mudge whispered warningly.

"Don't worry."

He spent the next half hour repeating every old Richard Pryor and Woody Allen joke he could remember, adding cetaceanic gags whenever possible. His audience roared at every one.

There was only one drawback. Every time he told a joke he was compelled to listen to one from his audience. These were invariably as bad as they were filthy and risque. Whether they understood them or not, Jon-Tom and Mudge laughed uproariously at all of them.

The steady supply of fresh food and jokes combined to

put the notoriously mercurial porpoises in a convivial mood. Finally convinced he'd gained their confidence sufficiently to talk as well as joke with them, Jon-Tom made the request. It was batted around from one cetacean to the next and a reply was not long in forthcoming.

"Yeah, I've seen the landwiller craft you describe." The speaker was a small bottlenose leaning over the starboard side of the boat. "What about it?"

"Could you tell us which way they went?"

"Easy. Follow me and I'll see you set on the right track." He then proceeded to taildance a compass heading, repeating it several times until Jon-Tom was positive he had it down pat.

"You're not leaving?" asked another, a big yellowside. "You haven't heard all our new jokes yet."

"We're in a desperate rush. Besides, we don't want to hear them all at once. Let's save some for next time."

"Why the hurry?" It was the bottlenose who'd provided the heading. "Ordinarily none of us would give a damn, but for a landwiller you've been awfully accommodating." A chorus of agreement came from his companions.

While Mudge railed silently at the loss of precious time, Jon-Tom told their seagong friends the story of the pirate attack and kidnapping. This last produced a chorus of outrage among the members of the school, for porpoises are quite family oriented.

"Nothing for us to do, though," said the bottlenose, sounding regretful. "We never involve ourselves in the affairs of landwillers or the details of their shallow, meaningless lives. But we will convoy you for a while to make sure you keep to the proper course."

"We appreciate it."

"You're welcome," sounded the high-pitched, squeaky choir.

Jon-Tom pointed at the engine. "Don't let this frighten you. It's only a bit of otherworldly magic. It's going to make a lot of noise. There are blades attached to the bottom that will cut if you get too close, so I suggest you back off a ways." The porpoises complied.

A couple of stabs on the ignition brought the engine to vibrant life. It coughed several times—and died. Jon-Tom's fears were confirmed by the position of the needle in the little gauge atop the engine.

"Magic's gone out of it, eh, mate?"

"The gasoline has. Same thing."

"Then we'll just have to raise sail and hope we don't fall too far behind 'em."

As they struggled to set the jury-rigged mast in place, the bottlenose swam over and plopped his head on the side of the zodiac. "It didn't frighten us, man. When does it get loud?"

"I'm afraid it's dead," Jon-Tom told the porpoise. The spell's run out."

"Too bad." He hesitated, bobbing lightly in the water, and then dropped clear. Jon-Tom could hear him whistling to his companions. The call was taken up by others. Soon squeaks and querulous squirps and squeals filled the air around the boat. The bottlenose reappeared.

"Landwillers often carry interesting toys they call 'rope' with them. Do you have any ropes?"

Jon-Tom looked puzzled, then began hunting through their overstock of supplies. There were several strong coils of hemp in addition to the rigging Mudge was unpacking. As it turned out, they found a much better use for the rigging. The sail became superfluous.

The bottlenose shouted to the two landwillers when all preparations had been completed. "Ready?"

"Ready," said Jon-Tom, bracing himself.

"Then hold on, man!"

They began to move through the water. Slowly at first, then more rapidly as the porpoises gained confidence in the makeshift harness. In a couple of minutes the zodiac was rocketing across the swells twenty miles an hour faster than the engine could have driven it. In fact, the empty engine was acting as a drag. With the wind blowing his long hair back into his face, Jon-Tom unbolted the outboard and dumped it over the stern. Then he leaned back against the padded hull of the zodiac and watched the four dozen porpoises rising and falling in unison as they pulled the little craft through the water. Other members of the school paralleled those pulling, shouting encouragement while awaiting their turns.

Not only would they not fall behind the pirate ketch, they might overtake it by morning. Sometimes a good joke was the best magic.

VI

As morning dawned the fleeing ketch still had not put in an appearance. The porpoises pulled tirelessly, laughing and giggling among themselves, competing to see who could pull the hardest or make the grossest joke. Once Jon-Tom was nearly thrown overboard as the porpoises on the right gave an especially hard surge. Mudge caught him just in time, and a good thing, too. So self-centered were their voluntary steeds they might have continued swimming eastward, arguing about punch lines and forgetting their lost passenger until it was too late.

Morning gave way to midday and still no sign of their quarry. The shore of the eastern continent dominated the horizon, a fringe of bright sand backed by tall greenery. The zodiac slowed to a stop and the porpoises began slipping out of their harness. A familiar bottlenosed face peered apologetically over the gunwale.

"We have to leave you here. The water is growing

shallow and there is a lot of fresh mixing with the salt. Fresh water makes us itch. If not for that we would take you onto the beach."

"That's all right." Jon-Tom was helping Mudge raise the sail. "You've done more than enough already. I just wish we could've located the ketch."

"We followed its course true. It must be somewhere close. Perhaps those you track made a last minute change of course to enter a hidden anchorage. Seek carefully and we're sure you'll find what you're looking for."

We'd better, Jon-Tom reflected as he surveyed the inhospitable shoreline. The last thing he wanted was to spend endless days cruising aimlessly up and down the coast. By that time the pirates might be long gone via some overland route, and Weegee with them.

A few last excruciatingly bad quips were exchanged. The school turned and raced back toward the open ocean. They were something to see, Jon-Tom reflected, leaping clear of the water and swapping jokes and laughter like a chorus of kids who'd been inhaling helium.

It grew downright steamy as he and Mudge sailed the zodiac along the beach, searching for possible landfalls.

"Doesn't look very promising," he murmured. The swampy, humid terrain was a nightmarish tangle of cypress and morgel roots. Giant fither vines let down long air roots. They could maneuver beneath much of this cellulose mesh but couldn't penetrate far into it.

"There has to be a channel or an inlet somewhere."

"That's for damn sure, lad. No way could the best sailor in the world slip a big boat like that ketch into this mess. Which way, then?"

"South, I guess."

"Any special reason?"

"Just a hunch. Besides, home lies northward and sailing in that direction feels too much like retreating."

The otter nodded and swung the sail around to catch as much of the hot breeze as possible. Obediently the zodiac turned southward.

"We can't be too far off." Jon-Tom made this appraisal as evening neared. "The porpoises were sure they followed the right course."

"I wouldn't bet a tin coin on anything that lot o' seagoin' sardine strainers said." The otter was lying on his back on the starboard hull, legs crossed and staring lazily at the sky. "Pleasant enough country, though a smidgen on the damp side."

"We'll find a place to anchor tonight," Jon-Tom said grimly, "and continue on south tomorrow. If we don't find them by then we'll turn about and try farther north. I can't believe the porpoises were deliberately leading us on."

"Why not? 'Ow can you take seriously anyone wot don't 'ave no 'ands?"

Jon-Tom followed the coast as it curved slightly to the east. They were preparing to tie up to the buttress roots of a huge morgel when Mudge suddenly dropped the line he was holding.

"You 'ear that, mate?"

Jon-Tom straightened, stared into the swamp. Small insects were beginning to emerge from the trees. The hisses and hoots of flying lizards reverberated in the evening air.

"I don't hear a thing, Mudge."

"Well I sure as 'ell do!" The otter dumped the rope back into the zodiac and pointed. "That way." Reaching up, he began pulling them into the trees.

"Mudge," Jon-Tom said warily, "if we go in there at night we're liable to find ourselves good and lost by morning."

"Don't worry, mate. It ain't far."

"What ain't—what isn't far?"

"Why, the music, o' course. Sounds like celebratin'. Mebbe 'tis our friends, 'avin' themselves a high drunken old time. Mebbee drunk enough so's they won't know we're about and we can sneak right up on 'em before they know where their bleedin' pants are an' steal sweet Weege away."

"I still don't hear any music."

"Trust me, mate. Well, trust me ears, anyways."

Jon-Tom sighed, adjusted the sail. "All right, but just the ears."

As the vines and tangled branches closed in over them he grew steadily more apprehensive. Bogart had a hell of a time getting the African Queen out of country like this and he wasn't Bogart. At last he was able to draw some relief from the knowledge that Mudge hadn't been affected by the heat. The otter was no crazier than usual.

There was definitely music coming from up ahead.

Mudge stood in the bow, sniffing nervously at the air, his small round ears cocked sharply forward. The tangle of roots and branches began to thin until they found themselves sailing up a slow-moving river whose banks were festooned with low-hanging vegetation. It was almost night now, but the otter's eyes saw clearly in the dark.

"Over there." Squinting, Jon-Tom was just able to make out not one but several small boats of unfamiliar design. The big pirate ketch was not in sight. "Anchored somewhere else," the otter muttered. "Mebbee still out at sea. They 'ave to use them smaller craft to make it through the swamp."

A large bonfire lit the woods behind the beached boats, which were drawn up on the first bit of solid land they'd encountered since leaving Yarrowl. Something small and leathery landed on Jon-Tom's forearm. He let out a muffled yelp of pain and slapped at it, watched as it fell, twitching and stunned, into the bottom of the zodiac. The half-inch long reptile had thin, membranous wings, a narrow, pointed muzzle. His forearm was starting to redden and swell where the invader had bitten him.

Mudge turned from his lookout position near the bow and picked it up. After a cursory inspection, he tossed it over the side. "Bloodsucker. Bet there are plenty in this country. Foulness with wings, wot?"

"I don't see anyone guarding the boats."

"Who'd they 'ave to guard 'em from? Anyways, sounds like they're 'avin' too much fun. Crikey, that looks like a row o' bloomin' 'ouses. Mighty domestic, this lot."

The line of shacks, lean-tos and cabins hardly qualified as houses. Shelters would've been a more accurate description. Some appeared to stand erect in defiance of gravity.

Jon-Tom was nonplussed by the sight. "This doesn't look right, Mudge. The houses don't fit, there's no sign of the ketch, and that singing doesn't sound like the chorus of a bunch of drunken brigands to me. I'd swear some of the voices are female."

"One way to find out."

They tied the zodiac to a downstream cypress and cautiously headed toward the makeshift village, Jon-Tom cursing the low-hanging branches and thick roots as he fought to follow the agile otter. There was a small gap between a couple of the cabins and they slowly followed it toward the light and singing. All of the cabins were built on stilts, a necessity in a swampland that doubtless flooded every wet season.

Beyond the semicircle of structures was the bonfire whose glow they'd spotted from the river. A covey of musicians were playing a rollicking tune to which numerous members of the little community were dancing and jumping. None of them were dressed like pirates. Mudge's black nose was working overtime.

"They don't cook like pirates, neither. Wonderful smells! You know wot?" He glanced up at his friend. "I bloody well think we've come to the wrong place. These folks ain't buccaneers."

"Of course we no buccaneers. What you two?"

Jon-Tom spun, to see a young lady muskrat leaning out of a cabin window looking down at him. She had a corncob pipe stuck in one corner of her mouth and a bright yellow polka-dot bandana wrapped around her head.

"Yeah, ever'body!" she yelled.

The dancing slowed and the music stopped as the villagers turned in the direction of the shout.

"Right, let's not overstay the welcome we ain't been given." Mudge started to back up the way they'd come, but Jon-Tom put out a hand to hold him. The otter shook it off.

"Wot's the 'old-up, mate? Wot are you waitin' for? Let's make a run for the boat while we still 'ave the time."

"So we can do what? Continue sailing blindly along the coast until we hit a submerged root or something? Maybe these people can help us."

Reluctantly Mudge held his ground, muttering. "Aye, 'elp us into the cookpot."

A fox, several squirrels, and a sleepy-eyed porcupine approached to confront the strangers. "Now what we got here, you think?" The fox's clothes were of simple materials and design, frayed at the edges but clean. Nor did Jon-Tom fail to note the long sharp skinning knife sheathed at his waist. One of the lady squirrels walked right up to Mudge and put her nose against his, sniffing interestedly. He drew back.

"'Ave a care for the familiarities, luv. We ain't been properly introduced."

"Doen flatter youself, water rat. I already married." She looked up at the fox. "Smell clean, no blood on 'em. Not recently, anyways."

"You're not pirates," said Jon-Tom.

The fox and the squirrel looked at each other and then burst out laughing. The porcupine let out a gruff guffaw.

"Us, pirates?" said the fox. "We fisherman, crabbers, swampfolk. What you?" He had to lean back to look up at Jon-Tom, since he was no taller than Mudge. "Big man; never seen one big like you. Pirates. You hungry?"

The thought of a hot meal overcame Mudge's initial hesitations. Also his second and third ones. "Now that you mention it, mate, I could do with a spot o' tea an' fish."

"Good!" The fox turned to yell over his shoulder. "Play-on music! Get the food ready." He grinned up at Jon-Tom, showing sharp teeth. "Time to eat anyway, an' now we got company time." Putting a paw on the tall human's arm, he gently led Jon-Tom toward the roaring, crackling blaze.

"Hey, Porge, what you stop playin' for? The field mouse who sat in the front of the band was staring at Jon-Tom.

"Hey, I doen know." He put his lips to his double

harmonica. The other musicians resumed their serenade and a few of the villagers struck up a brisk dance, but most were moving toward a line of roughhewn tables laden with food. There was a lot of red and yellow in the food, though whether from spices or natural coloring Jon-Tom couldn't tell. He didn't care. Not after a day eating cold rations in an open boat.

One thing they didn't have to worry about was poison. All the food came out of common pots and portable ovens and casseroles. Jon-Tom and Mudge joined the other villagers in heaping it on individual plates.

"So where you two funny fellas come from?" the fox asked him.

"Up north." Someone shoved a ladle full of vegetables and two or three different kinds of meat onto his plate. He hunted around until he located a cut-off stump that would do service as a chair. "North by a roundabout route." Since no one profferred a fork or any other silverware, he dug in with his fingers.

The first bite nearly blew his palate off. There was a big pitcher of cool water nearby and he gulped a third of it without wasting time hunting for a glass.

"Take small bites," the lady squirrel advised him. Jon-Tom nodded, picked carefully at his plate as he enviously watched Mudge downing huge mouthfuls of the fiery concoction. The otter saw him staring, sidled over to sit on the ground next to the stump. He gestured at the village, the fire, the inhabitants.

"Wonder who these people are and where they came from? Whichever, they sure as 'ell can cook."

"So you think we pirates?" The fox sat on Jon-Tom's other side. "That pretty funny, man. What you want to find pirates for? Most folk want to avoid them."

It was hard to talk, what with his mouth having been thoroughly numbed by the steady barrage of peppers and other spices. Everything between his lips and upper alimentary tract had been blitzed by a combination of food and liquid that most closely resembled carbonated turpentine. He made an effort to communicate.

"Last night some of them attacked the ship my friend and I were on and made off with his intended."

The fox looked solemn. "I see now. Nasty goingson. Take a little money and goods, that business, but people-stealin' we doen agree wid."

"You wouldn't happen to have any idea where this particular bunch of cutthroats might have their landing, would you? We were assured it was right around here someplace."

For an instant Jon-Tom thought he saw a spark of recognition in the fox's eyes. Then his host was leaning backward and staring at Jon-Tom's pack. "Hey I never see instrument like that before. Funny-lookin' thing. You musician? Maybe you give folks a little music, who know, maybe you jog somebody's memory." He winked.

Jon-Tom smiled back. "Sure, I'd be happy to."

"Careful now." Mudge put his plate aside. "We don't wish to scare the lot o' them into the woods."

Jon-Tom gave his companion a sour look as he strode past the fire to join the village band. They welcomed him curiously, checking out his suar. Rather than launching into some alien tune, he chose to listen until he could pick up on their own music. It wasn't difficult. The rhythms were simple and the melodies straightforward. He jumped in at an opportune moment and let the beat take him, his fingers moving faster and faster over the suar's strings. He found he was enjoying himself immensely, almost wished for a real guitar instead of the suar he was forced to make do with.

If his duar had been intact he could have given them some magic to go along with his music, but the latter seemed more than enough. Villagers set their food aside to join in the dancing; swirling and flying around the fire. One egret executed a move that had Jon-Tom laughing off and on for half an hour.

Still, despite his best efforts to blend in and make himself a part of the band the suar didn't sound right. If only he could play it differently, the way he'd seen similar instruments in identical circumstances played. Then there it was, just as he wished for it, near at it. From a terrapin tapping his feet nearby Jon-Tom plucked a device that looked like a cross between a saw and a cheese slicer but was less biting than either. Bowed across the suar's strings it made the instrument sound very much like a country fiddle.

The dancing and singing didn't slow down even when a muskrat and a drunken mongoose fell to fighting. The battle only inspired Jon-Tom's fellow musicians to play faster.

Eventually the celebration petered out as couples wandered off into the woods or back to their cabins. Soon Jon-Tom and the terrapin were the only ones still playing. By mutual agreement they halted together. It was time to call it a night. Jon-Tom was plumb tuckered, but also elated. Making music was as good as making magic, especially when one had an appreciative audience.

The grateful fox escorted the visitors to an empty cabin.

"About these pirates now, friend." The fox ignored the otter's query.

"You had enough to eat?"

"Yeh, plenty, but. . . ."

"Good. You be hungry all over by morning, you see. Maybe you get rid of supper quick-like unexpected in middle of night. Light up swamp." He chuckled. "Just watch out for gator an' snake or maybe you lose more than your food." Laughing to himself, he sauntered back out toward the clearing. Jon-Tom noticed that he was slightly bowlegged. A couple of lady mice were raking out the coals from the fire.

He leaned back on the bed which was soft and almost long enough to accommodate his gangling frame. Mudge sat on the edge of a nearby cot.

"What do you make of that?"

"I dunno, mate," said the otter thoughtfully. "Friendly enough. Never met a chummier bunch. Never saw so many people ready to drop everythin' an' 'ave a good time with strangers."

"Never saw any folks it was so hard to get a straight answer out of, either."

"Too many good spirits maybe, lad."

"Possible. Or maybe they don't like talking about pirates because it's unhealthy. That would make sense if the schmucks we're after hang around this part of the country a lot. We'll find out in the morning if we have to corner one of these happy chappies and tie him to the breakfast table."

"Until then, let's try and get some sleep."

A paw on his shoulder woke Jon-Tom. He couldn't hear anything over the din of night critters from within the swamp, but he could see a furry shape standing in the darkness staring down at him.

"Mudge?" His eyes were reluctant to open.

"No. You be quiet, man."

The silhouette turned and approached the otter's bed.

"Don't worry about me, stranger," Jon-Tom heard his friend whisper. "I've been awake ever since you set foot to board."

"So I see." No doubt their visitor also saw the glint of moonlight on Mudge's knife.

" 'Tis a bit early for breakfast and a shade too late for sweet goodnights. Wot is it you want?"

"To help you. I listen during dancing and talking and bullshitting, hear whole story. Got one for you."

Jon-Tom was sitting up on his cot now. As his eyes grew used to the light he saw that their nocturnal visitor was about Mudge's size and shape. At first glance he thought the stranger wore a mask to disguise his identity, then he realized the mask was part of the face.

"Name is Cautious." The raccoon was looking out the cabin's front window as he spoke. "I hear much of what you talk with fox and others. You looking for your beloved."

"My loved, anyway."

"Love what matters." He was wearing vest and short pants with a hole cut in the latter to allow the bushy gray tail egress.

"The fox told us he'd discuss Mudge's problem in the morning."

Dark eyes winked at him. "Fox say anything to change the subject."

"So you *do* know something about the pirates."

"Sure we know 'bout 'em. We sell them food and other supplies and sometime two or three of us go help work fix up their boat. Their ship-place not too far south of here."

"We just didn't sail far enough," Jon-Tom muttered half to himself..

"You sell them supplies; wot do they pay you with?"

The raccoon shrugged. "Money, goods, none of it earned honest, you bet. We're isolated village here. Do pretty good business with them and don't ask too hard where payment come from." He spat disgustedly to one side.

"Only you're different." Jon-Tom was wide awake now.

"Pretty sick of whole stinkin' business, but nobody listen to Cautious. Ever'body listen to fox who he say if we doen sell them food then next village inland or one beyond that will get the gold. He say we not cutting anybody's throat. Me, I think you take the money, you take the blood that come with it, you bet. Once in while you get paid with silk dress or boots that got funny stain on 'em you know don't come from maker's mistake, you know what I mean."

"We know wot you mean, mate." Mudge put his knife up.

"Now maybe they take your lady someplace and trade her for gold. Not around here. Swamp folk doen traffic in live people. Others do."

"Why are you telling us all this?" Jon-Tom was slipping into his clothes.

"I ask myself: Cautious, you mean anything of what you say or you just full of swamp gas? So I decide to come help you fellows because what you lost lot more precious than gold. I doen know, maybe we get killed this night, but I can take you to where pirates sleep. Help you much as I can."

"Damn decent of you. Just show us where they are and

Mudge and I will try and do the rest. This isn't your fight. There's no reason for you to risk your life."

"Me, I ain't got much life." His face was sad. "Two year ago big storm hit swamp. Big wave come all the way in from sea, right through village. Most of us know it coming so go up in trees until wave go by, then climb down and fix up house." His voice grew raspy. "My mate and two cubs way out picking oysters. They doen get back in time and I doen get out in time to warn them. Oysters get washed away, wife and babies get washed away." He swallowed hard, his voice breaking. It was dead silent inside the cabin.

"So that's why you want to 'elp us?" Mudge finally murmured.

"That why I know what you feeling. Storm take my loved ones from me. Pirates take yours. Can't do nothin' about storm, maybe can do something about pirates. So you doen worry about ol' Cautious, you hear?"

"We hear." Jon-Tom considered. Could they believe the raccoon, put their trust in him completely? Was the story about losing his family just that, a clever story they were about to buy unknowingly?

The same thought had occurred to Mudge. "No offense, mate, but 'ow do we know you ain't making this tragedy up as you go along? 'Ow can we be sure you ain't plannin' to sell somethin' besides shellfish and shellac to these pirates?"

"Maybe I leave you find them on your own." Cautious took a step toward the doorway. Mudge restrained him.

"Easy, guv'nor. Consider our position 'ere."

The coon hesitated, glanced from otterish visage to human. "Hokay. This time I forget you say something like what you said. You say it again and I disappear into trees."

He led them out the back of the cabin. The village was silent, sleeping off the previous evening's binge.

"Come on now, quick. I hear about your boat."

"What's the rush? Just because everyone else was intentionally evasive doesn't mean they'd try and stop us."

"No telling what they might do. Swamp folk like that.

Party with you one night, put you in the gumbo next. Fox and others make good living off pirates. You sneak up on their camp and steal one of their prizes, maybe you jeopardize that living. Better go quiet."

"Me feelin' precisely."Mudge pushed aside a branch. It snapped back to smack Jon-Tom in the gut. Murmured curses rose above the drone of the crickets.

"Funny boat," Cautious commented when they reached the place where the zodiac was tied. "Sure like to see animal builder took skin from."

"It's an artificial fabric, not a skin." Jon-Tom was looking anxiously in the direction of the village. There was no sign of pursuit. "It came from a polyethelene plant."

"Must be some damn fine big leaves." The raccoon gestured downstream. "We go that ways toward ocean some then cut back in through hidden channel. Try to sneak up on them from other direction or they see us for sure."

Mudge nodded. "You can bet your arse on that. The one runnin' that crew's the suspicious type."

"What you say? You know this bunch of picaroons?"

"We've 'ad occasion to chat with 'em before." Mudge paddled steadily down river. "Their Captain's got a score to settle with us, so we'd just as soon snatch back me lady quiet-like and slip away same."

"Oh ho. Gets to be interesting, this business."

"Take Mudge's word for it; you don't want to make this bastard's acquaintance."

"Hokay. Had few dealings with them myself. Mostly fox, he go and do business with them. How you come to know them, eh?"

Jon-Tom and Mudge took turns relating to their guide the tale of their earlier encounter with Sasheem and the rest of Corroboc's crew. By the time they had finished the story the sun had put in an appearance, peeping uncertainly over the tallest trees. Shafts of light sliced down through the vines and moss. They were paddling through a deep water inlet over a sandy bottom.

"Good place for big boat, but we coming up on them

from behind. We find a good spot to leave this funny-skinned craft and go through trees, get your lady, then run like crazy back same way. If lucky, I doen think they see us."

Jon-Tom frowned at the sky. "We'll have to wait a whole day until it's dark again."

"No problem." He settled down in the bottom of the boat. "This good place for sleeping."

"So close to their camp?"

"Doen worry. They never come in swamp. Stick to open water and their boat. Why you think they buy food from us instead of looking for it themselves?"

"What if they take Weegee and sail off?"

"You worry too much, man. You say they just got beaten off your big ship. Now they got to rest up and lick their wounds."

"'Ow about you, mate? Won't they miss you back 'ome?"

"Nobody is missed until they been gone two weeks maybe. Ever'body go hunting and fishing back in swamp for long time, nobody miss them. Miss you maybe, but not me. I bet they figure you get tired and leave early. Maybe fox and others suspicious, maybe they want to talk more, but I think they all just relieved you gone. Now you not their problem anymore. They know you don't know where to find pirates, so they forget you real soon."

To Jon-Tom's considerable surprise he found he had no trouble sleeping away most of the day. His body was more than willing to make up for all the sleep he hadn't enjoyed out on the open ocean. When he woke again it was to see the sun setting behind the swamp and the nearby sea. He felt fully rested and ready to begin the tricky business of effecting Weegee's rescue.

They secured the zodiac to a large hollow fastump and concealed it with palm fronds and moss. Then they started into the woods. Jon-Tom had the usual hard time ducking branches and stepping over protruding roots and was glad it wasn't far to the pirate encampment. They heard it before they could see it.

Drunken laughter, shouts, blithe obscenities filled the air. Cautious gestured for them to slow down as they neared a place where much of the underbrush had been cleared away.

It was an ideal anchorage. Morgels and cypress gave way to a wide sandy beach. The action of the current had cut a small inlet into the shore and a crude dock had been built out into the water. The ketch was moored to this ramshackle jetty. On the beach a single large one-story structure had been erected. It had the look of an old warehouse. Perhaps at one time some hopeful entrepreneur had tried to start a plantation in this part of the world, only to eventually abandon it and several smaller outbuildings to the unyielding swamp from whence it had subsequently been reclaimed by the pirates.

A few of the brigands were much closer than the beach. All were in an advanced state of intoxication. They were lying or standing around an isolated wepper tree, playing paddle ball with something hanging from one branch. Jon-Tom had to physically restrain Mudge from rushing forward.

Weegee's wrists and ankles were bound together by a single rope. Her head hung toward the ground. She had not been gagged. As far as her tormentors were concerned this only added spice to the game. As they swung her dizzily back and forth she tried to take a mouthful of flesh out of each of her persecutors, who would dance aside as her teeth neared them, laughing and taunting one another. Two of them were utilizing long paddles both to protect their fingers and enhance the sport. The solid bang of wood on fur and flesh echoed across the clearing.

"Rotten bloody bastards."

Jon-Tom kept his hand on his friend's trembling shoulder. "Easy, Mudge. We've rested all day. They haven't. At the rate they're collapsing they'll all be asleep soon enough. Then we'll get 'em. Don't look."

"I 'ave to look, mate. I 'ave some faces to memorize."

Jon-Tom's appraisal of the pirates' condition proved correct. Half an hour later the last one erect took a wild swipe at the swinging body of Weegee before crumpling to the ground. The onlookers waited another ten minutes to be sure the corsair's stupor was all-encompassing before Cautious gave the word.

"We go get her away fast, you bet."

"Right." Jon-Tom rose and broke through the remaining brush. "And remember, Mudge; no unnecessary killing."

The raccoon frowned at the man, then looked to the otter. "He always talk like that?"

"Don't pay 'im no mind. 'E can't 'elp it. The poor sod's the victim o' a deformed set o' ethics."

Staying close together they emerged into the clearing. There was no sign of Sasheem or the rest of the crew. Probably sleeping on board the ketch or inside the main building, Jon-Tom reflected.

Weegee was unconscious, exhausted and dazed from hanging upside down for too many hours. Mudge greeted her with that delicate rapid-fire succession of kisses otters employ as he put a paw over her mouth to keep her from shouting out in surprise. She bit him gently.

"About time you got here."

Mudge worked on the knots securing her wrists and ankles. "Wot made you so sure I was comin'?"

"Because I'm your only true love. You told me so, at least four dozen times on the ship."

"Right, but I've an ignoble memory."

"It's good enough for me." Mudge reached for his knife to cut the main rope and she hurried to protest. "Better not, unless you're prepared to catch me. If I fall on my fundament it's liable to shatter, considering the pounding it's taken the past couple of days."

"Creeps." He used the point of the blade to work the knots free. Jon-Tom finished the job as the otter set her gently on her feet. Her muscles were so cramped she could hardly stand, let alone walk. As she fought for balance an old seadog came limping out of the main building. He was missing one leg and walked with a crutch. Jon-Tom recognized him as an original member of the pirate crew from their earlier sojourn on Corroboc's ship; this was the one who had tried to warn the unfortunate captain of the danger Jon-Tom and his companions presented.

There was no time to retreat. The veteran saw them and began yelling at the top of his aged lungs. "Up, everybody up! By my tail, the water rat and the magician have come back for us!"

Mudge let Weegee balance against the raccoon, slipped his longbow off his back, and put a feathered shaft into the alarmist's neck. Too late. The cry did none of Weegee's recent tormentors any good because Cautious, utilizing a wicked little curved knife, rapidly made the rounds of the inebriated and cut their throats where they lay.

The only survivor was a lynx who had passed out unnoticed beneath a bush. He reached out to trip the retreating Jon-Tom and send him sprawling.

"Clumsy man," Weegee chided him, "get on your feet!"

Not enough time, as pirates erupted from the warehouse.

"This way quick or we are lost." Cautious beckoned frantically from the undergrowth.

Jon-Tom rolled to his knees and stood, holding his ramwood staff out in front of him. Weegee and Cautious had already vanished into the vegetation and Mudge wasn't far behind. He was alone in the middle of the clearing.

A great calm settled over him. Perhaps it was better that it end this way. Mudge had helped him so many times it seemed only fitting that Jon-Tom should perform a final service for the otter. After all, this was their world, not his. Better Mudge and Weegee should live out their lives where they belonged than sacrifice themselves in aid of an alien. He flicked the concealed switch in the staff's shaft and six inches of steel snapped out of the base.

"Come on then. What are you waiting for?"

The onrushing brigands slowed to a halt, eyeing him warily. "I know 'im." The speaker was a muscular beaver with a patch over his left eye. "That's the spellsinger, it is." Murmurs of recognition came from those around him.

None wanted to be the first to challenge the tall human. Those who had sailed with Corroboc remembered the havoc Jon-Tom and his companions had wrought. They rapidly enlightened those newer recruits who hadn't been on that earlier expedition.

The stand-off was purely mental. The instant Jon-Tom turned and tried to run they would realize he was afraid of them and cut him down in a minute. If he charged they might scatter in panic—but if just one stood his ground and fought back, the others would realize they had nothing to fear from their taller opponent. Nor could he allow the stalemate to continue indefinitely. Time favored numbers.

Carefully he set the ramwood aside and swung the suar around in front of him. He was relying on the hope that enough time had passed for the pirates who remembered him to have forgotten the details of what his duar looked like. If he could conjure something, anything at all, even a small cloud of harmless gneechees, it might be enough to frighten his opponents away.

But before he could commence playing a new figure, taller and more massive than any of the other brigands, forced his way through the line. He halted a safe distance from the spellsinger. Half a dozen stilettoes were sheathed in the bandolier that crossed his broad chest. His tail twitched back and forth, back and forth, and only the first half was flesh, fur and blood.

"Greetings, man. I never expected to see you again."

"Hello, Sasheem. Roseroar sends her regrets."

"Regrets? What regrets would the tigress leave with me?"

"That she wasn't able to bid you farewell in person."

The leopard chuckled, quite able to appreciate the bloodthirsty humor inherent in Jon-Tom's remark. "I'm sure the big lady would have made a coat out of me if she'd had half the chance." He examined the clearing, the rope dangling empty from the tree, the several sailors lying sprawled on the ground with their lives leaking from their slit throats. "You'd risk your life for a single female?"

"I see no reason to trouble you with my motives, which I doubt you'd understand. You remember me. You remember Roseroar. You should remember the others as well."

"Ah, the otter with the touchy manner and toilet mouth. One arrives, two depart. A relationship?"

"Weegee was his," Jon-Tom struggled for the right word, "fiancee."

Sasheem nodded. "Some sense at last. Not a bad swap; a spiteful and sharp-toothed female for a spellsinger."

"Who said anything about a swap? I'll be leaving now." He took a step backward.

Sasheem kept the distance between them unchanged. "No, I don't think you will, spellsinger, or you would have gone already." Sure enough, the sharp-eyed leopard had spotted that which had escaped the notice of his colleagues. "That's not the same instrument you carried before. I know that a spellsinger must have a certain special instrument else he will be unable to perform his magic. Can it be that you have misplaced both?"

Jon-Tom strummed the suar, smiled thinly at the big cat. "Take another step closer and find out."

"Careful, mate," said the lynx on Sasheem's flank. "Remember how he betwitched us the last time. Maybe he's just taunting us. Mayhap this stringed snake he holds is as dangerous as the other."

"If it is, then why is he standing there wasting his time talking to us while his friends put space between them?"

Jon-Tom was staring at him. "'Mate.' He called you mate. Aren't you the captain now?"

Sasheem seemed surprised. "Captain, me? Of course I'm not the captain here. I've never aspired to captaincy."

There was a commotion among the brigands in back. Jon-Tom watched as the pirates parted to let someone through.

"No. It *can't* be. I saw Roseroar take you apart."

Recent memory notwithstanding, it *was* a three-and-a-half-foot tall parrot that hopped out in front of the semicircle of respectful, edgy buccaneers to glare sourly at the dumbfounded spellsinger.

VII

Jon-Tom realized he was not going mad. The parrot was not Corroboc, though the relationship was unmistakeable. Though no expert in the distinguishing characteristics of fowl, there were too many similarities of aspect and posture between this bird and the late pirate commander for coincidence. At the same time the differences were as blatant as the similarities. Corroboc had boasted one false leg and an absent eye while this new arrival was missing neither. He was quite intact save for his left wing, which was splinted and bandaged.

"Captain Kamaulk." Sasheem favored Jon-Tom with a toothy smile. "Brother to our lamented missing captain and inheritor of his titles and property."

"Better he should've left you alone," said the parrot, "and I could have stayed with my ledgers. Or did you maybe think my featherbrained fool of a brother ran this business by himself? Because pirating is a business, make no mistake of that. Corroboc was clever with a ship and a sword but not with figures. That end I handled. Now I am forced to manage both. So a mutual acquaintance of yours took him apart, har? We wondered what had happened to him. What a nice surprise that the guilty parties should choose to drop in. It seems we will have vengeance out of this last raid if not much profit. Your death will salve my poor brother's heart.''

''He didn't have a heart. Corroboc was the most vicious, evil, sadistic, venal low life it was ever my displeasure to encounter.''

Kamaulk looked pleased. ''I'm sure that wherever he is now he's delighting in your flattery, but it will do you no good. He's dead and it's up to me to decide your fate.'' He rubbed his beak with his unsplinted wingtip. ''What do you suggest, Sasheem?''

''Sell him in Snarken. Money's better than vengeance. A spellsinger will bring much more on the open market than an ill-tempered lady. A fair trade, I calls it.''

''*If* he can be induced to cooperate.''

Jon-Tom listened dazedly to the conversation. He felt like a participant in a bad dream. There couldn't be two Corrobocs. Nature wouldn't permit such a dual abomination. Of course, Kamaulk wasn't the same bird as his brother. Already it was clear that this more bookish of the unholy pair was less impulsive and more stable than his deceased sibling. That didn't mean he'd hesitate to have him drawn and quartered if he decided it was in the best interest of the ''business.''

''You claim he is a spellsinger. I don't doubt your story, but if that is the case then why hasn't he turned us all into toads or himself into an eagle?''

''I believe he has lost his instrument of power, sir.'' Sasheem nodded toward the silent Jon-Tom. ''The device he carries is not the one he used on us when he was a prisoner on your brother's ship.''

''I don't like these uncertainties. Figures are always certain. I cannot believe he is confronting us in this fashion without purpose.''

"I see what he up to!" A lanky dingo pointed frantically toward the inlet.

Everyone turned. Kamaulk flapped his wings, settled down on Sasheem's shoulder. From this high perch he was able to gaze out across the river.

"I've never seen a small craft like that," the leopard commented. "It must belong to the magician."

"Broken loose from its moorin's," suggested one of the other pirates.

"No," insisted the one who'd raised the alarm, "see, 'tis all camouflaged like, filled with moss and twigs and such."

"A diversion, designed to distract us?" The parrot cocked a querulous eye at Jon-Tom who, knowing nothing, said nothing.

"The others are hiding under there," said the dingo. "The female prisoner and the others who helped her. It has to be."

"Trying to slip past right under our noses. Be damned. An extra ration of grog for you, Gorswont." Kamaulk snapped orders. "Oreyt, Tomooto: take down the ship's boats and we'll cut them off. They've no sail."

The pirates rushed toward their ship, but not before the parrot instructed a lynx and three others to stay behind to watch Jon-Tom.

"Ware close the spellsinger. If he attacks, defend yourselves and call for aid. If he tries to flee, hamstring him." Sasheem's eyes narrowed. "How much power you have left I do not know, man, but we'll most surely find out when we return with your companions. A little cooperation on your part may be all that keeps me from having your lady friend disemboweled before her lover's eyes. Remember that."

Jon-Tom watched as the leopard raced to join the rest of his mates with his captain riding his shoulder. Then his eyes fell as he examined his guards. They held their spears and swords uneasily.

Could he bluff them? Clearly they were discomfited at

having been left behind to guard this master of unknown abilities. All four would have been much happier chasing after the drifting zodiac.

"Beware!" This admonition, delivered in his best courtroom tone, caused two of the guards to retreat a couple of steps. "My patience is at an end. Run while empathy lives in me or I will truly turn you all into toads as the first mate suggested."

The lynx looked to his companions for support and held his ground. "Better a dead lynx than a dead toad. Sasheem and the Cap'n will kill us sure if we let you go."

Jon-Tom studied the quartet. In addition to the lynx there was a broad-shouldered wolf carrying a razor spear that was half blade, a squirrel with a scimitar, and a spectacled bear who wielded a massive club. Spikes projected from its business end.

He could outrun the bear but not the wolf or the lynx. On the other hand, he could probably overpower the squirrel and maybe the other two, but the bear could fell him with one swipe. Kamaulk had chosen the group of guards with care.

A bold try on Mudge's part to disguise the zodiac and try drifting past the pirate's camp, but it hadn't worked. Kamaulk and his crew would run them down before they could reach the sea and raise sail. A gallant effort. Feeling slightly giddy, he raised the edge of his right hand to his brow.

"I salute thee, Mudge, but even the master of tricks and ruses can't win 'em all."

As the side of his hand touched his forehead a small tree fell square on the bear's head. Bruin eyes rolled up like small window shades and he toppled over in a heap.

"Magic!" The squirrel let out a squeal and turned to run—right into a knife thrown from the bushes. Never one to squander a heady opportunity, Jon-Tom slammed the butt end of his ramwood staff into the side of the wolf's skull. Mudge brought the lynx down with an arrow before he could get ten yards toward the jetty.

Cautious and Weegee emerged to greet him. Hardly a

minute had passed since his unexpectedly efficacious salute. Meanwhile the rest of the pirates were paddling furiously down river in their exuberence to overtake the drifting zodiac and its cargo of leaves and moss.

"Thanks," he told Cautious. "Hi, Weegee. Short time no see."

She smiled up at him. "I'd like to put this habit of getting separated behind us, tall man."

He looked over his friends' heads. "Pretty damn smart. I thought you were out there trying to sneak past, too."

Her eyes dropped. "Actually, we had kind of a noisy argument about it. I'm a little ashamed to admit I tried to talk Mudge out of trying to rescue you."

"Don't give it another thought. I know how otter minds work. I once had to journey across half a world with a dozen of your kind. I figure if I survived that, I'm the next best thing to invulnerable.

"You're a dear thing, for a human."

Mudge rejoined them, having lingered over the dispatching of the unfortunate lynx. He was panting hard. "Aye, tried to talk old Mudge out o' savin' 'is mate, she did, but I wouldn't think o' leavin' you to the tender mercies o' Sasheem and 'is bird-boss. 'Avin' blown a dozen opportunities to abandon you to a well-deserved fate before today, I figured I might as well keep me record consistent."

"You all crazy, you people. Ever'body know otters crazy, but not humans." Cautious was shaking his head dolefully.

"I've been breathing otter fur too long." Jon-Tom patted Mudge on the shoulder, then nodded at the river. "What now? They're almost to the boat."

"Going be plenty mad when they find crocodile dung in the bottom instead of us."

"We thought that after expendin' all that effort they deserved to find somethin'," Mudge explained blithely.

"They're going to be a lot madder when they get back here and find these four." Jon-Tom gestured at the bodies of the four guards. "We'd better not hang around to watch."

"Agreed." The raccoon pointed into the swamp. "Not

enough time to steal big boat. Take too long to get sails up and maybe they got somebody left on board to watch. They think we try and run toward nearest town. That be my village. So we go other way, south, and pretty soon by and by they give up and forget about us."

"South. What's south of here?"

"Nearby, nothing. Farther away, who know? Maybe another village. Maybe we find somebody to sell us a boat. Maybe we borrow one. But can't go back to my home. That be first place they check, you bet. Kamaulk a smart bird. Also I think maybe fox plenty mad at me by now. So if it okay, I tag along." He jerked a thumb in Mudge's direction. "Otter here, he say you trying to get to Chejiji. I've heard about that place from other travelers, you bet. Always wanted to go there but never had reason. Got one now, by golly. Need to keep head out of stewpot."

"You really think they'll give up the chase after a while? I don't know this Kamaulk, though he seems to be a lot like his unmentionable brother, but this is twice we've left Sasheem looking foolish. He won't like it."

"Likes got nothing to do with it. He not in charge. Pirates know ocean pretty well. Me," and he tapped his gray-furred chest with a thumb, "I know swamps pretty well. Ground this way," and he started toward the trees, "is higher and dryer. We make pretty damn good time, you bet, and soil still damp enough to soak up our footprints. They have to be better trackers than I think they are if they try to follow Cautious in swamp."

Mudge jogged along behind the raccoon. "Right. Suppose we give 'em the slip? Then what? We can't walk all the way to bloomin' Chejiji."

"I tell you we find boat. If not, I make one maybe."

"We could borrow one, like you said." He was speaking to Cautious but looking at Mudge as he spoke. The otter's reply astonished him.

"Nope. No more o' that for me, mate. I'm givin' up thievin', I am."

"What's that? You sure you didn't catch the butt end of that lynx's sword on your skull?"

The otter looked slightly embarrassed. "Tweren't entirely my doin', mate." Jon-Tom looked sharply at Weegee, who continued to stare resolutely and noncommitally straight ahead. "An' it ain't final. But I'm givin' it serious consideration."

Cautious interrupted to suggest they save their breath for running, as it was important they put as much distance between themselves and their soon to be furious pursuers as possible before daybreak. In the dim moonlight the raccoon quickly and unhesitatingly chose the firmest, most direct path through the dense forest. Nor was Cautious's wetland expertise the only thing they had going for them. Having slept away the day, Jon-Tom and his companions were fully rested, whereas the pirates had spent the entire day awake and the evening drinking. They would give out a hundred yards into the trees.

Weegee did not enjoy the advantage of a full day's rest. When even her boundless otterine energy threatened to run dry they paused long enough to rig a stretcher of saplings and reeds. Jon-Tom and Mudge carried her through the dense vegetation as Cautious continued to lead the way.

Kamaulk was sure to cut the chase short, Jon-Tom reflected. The parrot was a practical sort. Corroboc, had he been alive and present, would have driven his men to the point of collapse in pursuit of the escapees.

But they couldn't take the chance that the pirate captain would act sensibly. They pressed on until a few hours before daylight. By then he and Mudge were too tired from carrying Weegee's stretcher to run any longer. Cautious agreed to a stop and all were asleep within minutes of each other.

They'd pulled it off, Jon-Tom mused tiredly as he drifted into unconsciousness. As he fell asleep a pair of parrots kept winking in and out of his mind's eye; one less a leg and eye, the other intact save for a splinted wing.

He rolled over and exhaled, trying to get comfortable on

the damp ground. "Good thing Kamaulk's wing was hurt or he could have flown over the zodiac close enough to see there wasn't anyone under the camouflage. Lucky break."

"Lucky my derriere." Weegee let out a snort. "Right after they tied me to that frigging tree he waddled over to check me out. Sort of inspecting the merchandise, you might say, with an eye toward future sales. He got a little intimate and I bit the shit out of his wing."

A steady high-pitched whistle emanated from the dark shape lying next to her. Mudge was already sound asleep.

"I understand. You bit him because he was fondling you?"

"Hell no. I bit him because he was insulting me. Sonofasnake underestimated my value by at least fifty gold pieces, the green-feathered little turd."

"Oh." He closed his eyes again, feeling himself fading rapidly. A leaf or something settled on his chest. Or something.

He sat up fast. Bright yellow eyes with black slitted pupils mooned back at him. He let out a yelp as the fat little lizard-like creature stuck out its tongue at him in a natural expression of curiosity and not derision. It was barely six inches long and Jon-Tom immediately perceived his howl of surprise as a loud overreaction.

The thing rose straight into the air. It was able to do so because in place of arms and legs its body rested on four miniature rotors. Six feet off his chest it stopped, hovering like a cross between a hummingbird and a toy helicopter. A look around revealed dozens of the intensely colored insectivores flitting among the trees.

His shout had roused the rest of his exhausted companions. Red-eyed, they studied the flock of helipoppering lizards as they dove and darted through the swamp. Each displayed several tiny patches of luminescence along its flanks. Running lights, Jon-Tom mused.

They were unfamiliar to Mudge and Weegee, but Cautious expressed surprise at the ignorance of his traveling companions.

"Squirks. Harmless little things, and tasty."

Mudge swatted at one that dove at his face, mistaking his whiskers for worms. They could motor forward or backward with equal agility, Jon-Tom observed with delight. They darted back just out of reach whenever he took a gentle swipe at one. Their flattened tails served as rotors.

He went to sleep with one buzzing curiously above his ear.

Cautious awoke first, well after the sun had put in its daily appearance. There was no sign of the pirates, so they lingered long enough to make a quick meal of backpacked supplies before resuming their trek southward. Morgels and cypress began to give way to drier land dominated by rail-thin evergreens and blue magnolias. One tree put forth silvery blossoms that vibrated when they were touched. Mudge pronounced it distant kin to the familiar belltrees of home, though this variety hummed instead of tinkling.

"Like I thought. Our friends they doen know this country. They stick to water robbing. I think we pretty okay now. Soon maybe we find a new town and rent ourselves a boat."

"You could probably go back now," Jon-Tom told the raccoon.

"I'd rather go with you, if you doen mind. Most of my people they happy in swamp, doen care about rest of the world. I always want to see other places."

"You stick with bald-bottom 'ere, then." Mudge nodded toward his tall friend. "You'll see more of it than you ever wanted to. I know that for a fact, I do, because I've traveled farther than 'ere an' there with 'im, an' me without ever 'avin' a choice in the itinerary."

They marched all that day and into the morning of the next without encountering so much as a sign that another village might be near. Jon-Tom didn't mind the hike, so long as they didn't have to slop through mud and ooze and tangled vines. On dry land his long legs enabled him to keep pace with his more energetic companions.

Once Mudge draped a long thin section of vine across Jon-Tom's back, sending the youth into a panic believing a snake had fallen on him. Weegee leaped instantly to Jon-

Tom's defense, insisting that such juvenile gags were beneath Mudge's station. All otter Weegee was, but far more mature than most. No wonder Mudge had been attracted to her.

By mid-afternoon they were wading a shallow inlet less than a foot deep when Cautious suddenly raised a paw to call for a halt. He was staring into the trees opposite, his nose working the air.

"Relatives, enemies, or wot?" Mudge inquired.

"Fire. Something's burning. Something big."

Jon-Tom turned a fast circle. The broad stream they were crossing was devoid of trees. "No reason to get excited. If it is a fire and it's coming this way, we're in the best place to cope with it. There's nothing out here to burn."

"Maybe so, man," said Cautious, "but where I come from we've heard rumors of funny things people down here do with fires."

Weegee was eyeing the forest dubiously. "Strange we don't see any smoke."

A distant rumble became audible. Cautious's eyes grew wide. "Run!" He turned to his right and started splashing wildly downstream. "This way quick, you bet!"

Jon-Tom followed without knowing why he was doing so. "I don't understand. We're in the middle of a stream. This is as safe a place to be as any. Why are we running?"

"The slinkers are burning the water!"

Jon-Tom almost stumbled as he put his foot in a hole, managed to regain his balance. "That's insane. Why would anyone want to burn the water, even if they could?"

"Doen you hear, man?" Indeed, the rumble was growing steadily louder. The raccoon turned and headed toward the nearest bank. It was still a good distance away.

At last they could see the smoke. A peculiar pale blue smoke preceded by a tremendous commotion in the water. The approaching blur began to separate into individual shapes and the hair on the back of Jon-Tom's neck stiffened.

The water was indeed on fire, though whether the liquid itself burned or the smoke rose from some volatile substance that had been dumped on top of it he couldn't say. As to the disturbance preceding it, this was a stampede of epic proportions. Driven before the advancing flames was a huge herd of alligators and crocodiles, gavials and other toothed denizens of the shallow stream. Hundreds of them half swimming, half running, pounding their frantic way toward the smokeless sea. A few managed to escape onto the banks, but most continued to flee downstream.

"They catch them this way, the slinkers do, and cut them up for the meat and hides. This must be how they drive them, you bet." Cautious had more to say but not the chance to say it as all four of them found themselves wrenched upside down and lifted skyward. Hanging in the big net they were able to watch the reptilian stampede thunder by beneath them. Nearby, other nets held batches of furiously spasmodic crocodilians.

"Get off me 'ead, luv," Mudge was shouting.

"I'm not on your head, dammit."

"I'm tryin' to get at me knife. If we can cut ourselves out o' this before the bleedin' owners show up. . . ."

"Too late. Too late for sure," said Cautious, interrupting him.

A dozen locals had materialized out of the fading flames. Slinkers, the raccoon called them. Mostly rats and mongooses averaging four feet tall. Jon-Tom picked out a few minks among the group. They wore neither civilized clothing like Mudge and Weegee nor the relaxed attire of Cautious's people. Their fur was streaked with long splashes of blue and ochre paint. Head bands were decorated with fragments of crocodile hide and trade feathers. Other feathers were tied to short tails. Most carried spears except for a few who gripped stunted machetes. Their speech was unintelligible.

Except to Cautious. "Degenerate talk. Very primitive, these people."

"Nothin' primitive about their net work," Mudge grumbled.

"They trying decide what to do with us."

The tallest of the mongooses ordered the captives released

from their prison. Someone tugged on a concealed rope and the four travelers landed in a messy heap in the shallow water. Jon-Tom tried to position his ramwood staff, but the slinkers were too fast. He found himself nose to point with an ugly looking spear. Hands were tied and weapons appropriated. Weegee vied with Mudge to see which of them could fashion the most egregious insults to heap upon their captors as they were led into the woods.

The natives were impressed by Jon-Tom's unusual size, but hardly overawed. Around them dozens of slinkers were slaughtering imprisoned crocodilians. They worked fast; killing, bleeding, and skinning. Jon-Tom was glad his own skin was too flimsy to be of any profit.

"What will they do with us?" Weegee sounded concerned. It was too soon to panic.

"I doen know. We try stay away from this part of the swamp, my buddies and me. They talking now about food."

"That ain't promisin'," Mudge muttered to the raccoon.

"We might make a break for it when they're not watching," Jon-Tom suggested.

"With our hands tied?" Weegee favored him with the kind of smile one reserves for an idiot child. "Look how good they are with those skinning knives. I'm sure they're just as quick with these spears. We wouldn't get twenty paces."

The river was far behind them now as their captors marched them through the undergrowth. This didn't trouble Jon-Tom's companions, but the needles and occasional thorns scratched and bit him.

By evening they'd reached a village. The individual huts were not as architecturally advanced as those of Cautious's town, but they were cleaner.

The elderly mongoose who emerged from the largest hut to greet the returning hunters wore a particularly elaborate headdress. If not for the fact that this individual looked like he would gladly issue the order to have the captives cut up starting with the soles of the feet and working slowly upward, Jon-Tom would have laughed at the sight he and his attendant minks presented in their primitive garb. He kept his expression neutral. This wasn't a play and none of the participants were acting.

The mongoose in charge of the hunting party approached this chief, or headman, local premier or boss or whatever he was, and started talking. Cautious listened closely, struggling with the awkward speech.

"They're trying to decide whether or not we're gods and how best to venerate us, right?" said Weegee sarcastically.

"I'm afraid not. I think maybe they talk about which one of us taste better." He glanced up at Jon-Tom. "Trend seems to favor you, Jon-Tom, since you got most meat on you bones."

"They can't eat me. I refuse to be eaten. I haven't spent a year battling perambulators and wizards and demons and pirates to end up in somebody's cook pot."

The raccoon shrugged. "You can tell them that but I doen think they going to be impressed."

Jon-Tom was acutely conscious of the sharp spear points pressing close around him. "Talk to them, dammit. Tell them I'm a powerful magician, a spellsinger. Make sure they know what a spellsinger is."

Cautious took a step forward. "I try, but doen hold your breath."

The head hunter and the chief turned to the raccoon, who began speaking in a halting but passably forceful manner. Their expressions indicated Cautious was making himself understood.

The raccoon finished his speech. There was a pause, then the chief stepped forward, shoving Cautious aside, and examined Jon-Tom with new interest. Though he was among the tallest of the villagers, he barely came up to Jon-Tom's waist. A finger poked him in the belly. Jon-Tom tried not to flinch.

Turning his head, the chief spoke to Cautious, who swallowed and translated.

"Chief he say he think maybe you taste pretty sweet, but

he doen want to eat a magician. He want to know what kind of magic you can make."

"Tell him I can give everyone in his village their heart's desire, the thing they each want most in the whole world."

Mudge's jaw dropped. "'Ave you taken leave o' your senses, mate? That's too bloomin' big an order even for a duar, much less that piddlin' substitute lyre you're pluckin' these days."

"Don't worry, Mudge. I know what I'm doing. Tell him, Cautious."

The raccoon took a deep breath and relayed the reply. The mongoose's eyes grew wide. He took a couple of steps back from the tall human as he spoke.

"He say he pretty impressed, you bet, if you can do this thing. For whole tribe?"

"For the whole tribe," Jon-Tom reiterated, staring at the chief as he spoke.

This time it wasn't necessary for Cautious to translate, the chief getting the gist of it from Jon-Tom's expression and attitude. Again the head slinker chattered away and Cautious strained to make sense of his words.

"Chief say you try this thing and if you tell the truth there be no reason to keep you here. He say he want to know how you can tell what everyone want most in the world."

"Tell him all they have to do is think of it, and I will know."

This produced quite a commotion among the assembled hunters and every other villager within earshot. The entire population had clustered around the hunting party and its captives. They babbled among themselves until the chief raised both paws for silence. Then he sat himself down in front of Jon-Tom, crossed his short legs, and spoke briefly to Cautious.

"Chief say you go ahead."

"I'll need my instrument, my suar, to work the magic."

As soon as this was translated one of the hunters quickly handed it over, after first checking the resonating box to make sure it held no concealed knives or other weapons.

As he tuned up, Mudge sidled up next to him. "I don't know wot you 'ave in mind, mate, but it can't work. You ain't got the wherewithal without your duar to grant even one o' these charmin' fellas the thing 'e most wants in the 'ole world, let alone the 'ole bleedin' bunch of 'em."

"Of course I can't. What kind of fool do you think I am?"

"I expect I'm fixin' to find out."

"I just want to get them thinking hard about something, anything. With everyone concentrating on his heart's desire, I'm going to try and put the village into a trance. Remember how we put Corroboc's whole crew to sleep? I don't think I can do that here, especially without the duar. They're too sharp-eyed and alert. But I do think I can put them into a hypnotic trance because they're doing half the work for me by concentrating hard on a single thought. Then while they stand around swaying with stupid contented smiles on their happy faces, we can get the hell out of here."

"I don't 'ave any better ideas. But if this don't work they ain't goin' to be real pleased with us. Not that they've exactly invited us to join 'em in song an' dance as it is." He stepped back.

"What's he going to try?" Weegee asked him.

"Paralyze 'em with the sheer beauty o' 'is voice, m'luv."

"Tell them to start concentrating on what they want," Jon-Tom told Cautious. "In order for the magic to work they have to think of that and nothing else. They must shut out all other thoughts. I want them thinking as hard as they can."

The raccoon nodded, translating for the chief and everyone else nearby. The word was passed through the assembled villagers. Many of them closed their eyes to enhance their concentration while those who kept them open stared expectantly in Jon-Tom's direction. If only they were as friendly an audience as they were attentive, he thought.

Having already settled on his song, he began to strum the suar's strings. Almost immediately a faintly phosphorescent green cloud formed over the villagers' heads. Whispers of astonishment and awe greeted this rapid manifestation of true magic.

Unfortunately, while visually impressive, it distracted them from concentrating. He had to tell Cautious to remind them to ignore things like the green cloud or none of them would get their wishes. The cloud did have the effect of convincing the doubters among the hunters, however. Everyone was concentrating intently now.

As he sang on, a few gneechees put in an appearance. Not many, certainly far fewer than would have been drawn to the music of his duar, but enough to show that the spellsinging was working. There seemed to be something wrong with them, though. Instead of swooping and darting in familiar patterns, they shot through the air in short, jerky bursts. A couple even smashed into the ground and bounced dazedly away.

What this erratic behavior portended he couldn't imagine and didn't have time to consider. What mattered was that the tribe continue to concentrate. He could see them beginning to drift, to lose consciousness where they stood. A foul odor abruptly assailed his nostrils. Odd, but then his spellsinging often produced unexpected side effects. He could see that his companions smelled it, too.

"Wot the bloody 'ell's that aroma?"

Next to him, Weegee put both paws over her nose. "Jon-Tom, it's awful."

Indeed it was, but he was afraid to stop singing or playing. The horrible miasma spread and intensified.

Cautious tried to retreat a few steps, nodding toward the villagers closest to him. "I think it coming from *them*."

Indeed, every one of the villagers, from the chief down through the hunters to the lowliest infant seemed to have suddenly acquired the most abominable body odor. Nor did they appear in the least hypnotized by the spellsinging. One by one they opened their eyes and began to discuss the atrocious effluvia that now permeated their fur. Mutterings of disgust and anger filled the air as neighbor shied away from neighbor.

"That settles it." Mudge could barely keep his breakfast down. "Not that there seemed much doubt wot fate they 'ad in mind for us before, but 'tis confirmed now."

Jon-Tom continued to play until it was clear his song wasn't producing the desired effect. "I don't understand. I played that perfectly. The words were so apt."

"Must've been somethin' in your pronunciation, mate, or maybe it 'as to do with your usin' this 'ere suar instead o' your duar. You tried to get 'em thinkin' all the time. Wot you got 'em was *stinkin'* all the time."

"We'll have to try again." As he said this a pair of the senior hunters were heading toward him, gesturing angrily with their truncated machetes. "Cautious, tell them it'll be all right, tell them I made a mistake but I'm going to fix everything. Tell them *fast*."

The raccoon translated. The hunters hesitated, glared threateningly at the man in their midst but held their ground. He began to sing again. It wasn't easy because of the odor, but he had no choice. Once again the green cloud intensified. No onlooker could doubt the human was a magician. The trouble was that his variety of magic wasn't very agreeable.

He sang hard, trying to concentrate particularly on his enunciation, phrasing each lyric precisely. Once more the spellsinging took effect. Once more the result was not quite what he'd been striving for.

"Terrific, mate." Mudge gazed at the villagers surrounding them. "You've made 'em our friends forever."

The odor had not gone away. Not only was the tribe still stinking worse than an antiquated sewage plant, the second spellsong had induced a second additional change in their demeanor. Every one of them, irrespective of species, had turned a shocking shade of pink.

"You couldn't make them think," said Weegee, "so you made them stink and pink."

"I just don't understand," Jon-Tom muttered to himself. "The songs both sounded so *right*."

"I wouldn't try tellin' 'em that, mate. Not that you could

make 'em any madder. Wotever you do don't say you can't change 'em back or they'll 'ave us on the spit on the spot."

"Got it." He turned to Cautious. "Tell the chief that the magic doesn't always work right the first time. I'm sorry for the unpleasant results, but after I rest I can make everything right again. When this kind of magic occurs you have to wait a while between spelling or you just make things worse."

Clearly the chief and his advisors didn't care one whit for this explanation, but they didn't have much choice. Jon-Tom knew it and they knew it. The mongoose snapped an order. A platoon of furious, brightly hued and extremely smelly hunters promptly herded Jon-Tom and his friends to one end of the village and into a large, sturdy wooden cage. This was suspended from a thick rope fashioned of interwoven vines which ran through a wooden pulley hung from a high overhead branch. The captives bounced helplessly as they were hauled up until the cage dangled twenty feet off the ground. Looking down between the bottom poles they could watch the villagers jabbing weapons and fingers in their direction.

"I don't mind that," Mudge commented, "but I wish they'd do it from a distance. They stink somethin' terrible, an' they look worse."

Weegee slapped a paw over his mouth. "Whatever you do, luv, don't laugh. Keep in mind 'tis Jon-Tom they need to fix things. The rest of us are expendable. That apparently hasn't occurred to them yet. Let's not give them a reason to think of it." He nodded and she removed her paw.

"I ought to 'ave bit your fingers, luv, but you're right." He sat on one of the poles that formed the bottom of the cage. "So 'ow do we get out o' this one, spellsinger?"

Jon-Tom leaned against a corner of the prison and brooded. "I thought I was getting us out of it." He was staring at the suar, trying to wish an additional set of strings and better controls into existence. "I wish Clothahump was here."

"Wot's this? Losin' a bit o' our confidence, are we?"

"Hey, gimme a break. At least they're not getting ready

to barbecue us. Maybe the magic was unconventional, but it did buy us a breathing spell."

Weegee had a delicate lace handkerchief wrapped around her muzzle. "Poor choice of words, Jon-Tom."

"I don't know wot you're all cryin' about. I've smelled worse in me time."

"I've no doubt of that," she told him, "judging from the descriptions of some of the dens of iniquity Jon-Tom's told me he's dragged you out of."

"Wot's that?" The otter shot a look in his tall friends's direction. "Wot false'oods 'ave you been feeding 'er when me back were turned?"

"Only the truth."

The otter threw up his hands., "The truth? Ain't you got no more brains than to tell a lady the truth, mate?"

"What do you mean by that?" Weegee snapped, and the two of them launched into a violent argument that if nothing else took their minds off their present precarious situation. Cautious sat down and cleaned beneath his claws. Jon-Tom envied them all their ability to relax.

Worst of all was, he found himself wondering what he would taste like.

VIII

They were provided with food and water the following morning. By late afternoon their captors had evidently decided how to handle their unwelcome guests. A creaking announced the lowering of the cage as a half dozen warriors slowly let the rope slide through its pulley. Jon-Tom clutched the bars and peered downward.

"Better think fast, mate. Looks like they think your magic's 'ad about enough rest."

"I'll tell them they'll just have to wait. I need more time to recharge my batteries."

"I wouldn't count on it. Take a look at their eyes. If your batteries ain't recharged by now, I expect they're goin' to 'ave a go at removin' 'em."

"Maybe they're bluffing," said Weegee. "If they kill you they won't have anyone to restore their normal color and smell."

"So if 'tis a standoff, then why are they lowerin' us

down? Can't be for casual conversation an' I ain't anxious to be invited to dinner."

"Be ready." Cautious was checking out the forest as they descended. "We may have to make a run for it, you bet."

A run for it. That was something movie cowboys did, Jon-Tom mused. Like heading people off at passes and saving the ranch. He was a spellsinger. Spellsingers didn't run. They didn't get eaten, either. He thought furiously. Maybe they could head these primitives off at the impasse.

As it turned out they were not to be marched to the kitchen, though when they saw what was waiting for them Jon-Tom wondered if that fate might not be preferable.

"Well now," said Kamaulk, "it's a genuine pleasure to see you again. The way you departed one might think you didn't care for our hospitality."

Jon-Tom's heart sank as he saw the pirate captain, Sasheem and other members of that bloodthirsty crew standing among the natives. They'd have a much more difficult time escaping from the parrot than they would from these superstitious primitives.

"How'd you find us?"

"When you abandoned our company we were quick to send word all up and down the coast. Money talks, tall man. A runner from this tribe heard about our open offer of payment. We hastened here as fast as the word reached us. I've already settled a price with this chief. Seems he's anxious to be rid of you. I don't think he trusts your spellsinging anymore. Sasheem, relieve our friend of his burden, won't you?"

"With pleasure, sir." The first mate and a couple of assistants proceeded to strip Jon-Tom and his friends of weapons, packs, suar and everything else useful.

"What do you intend to do with us?" Weegee stood straight as she asked the question though in her case she thought she already knew the answer.

"Ain't decided yet. Now me dear departed nest-brother, he wouldn't be hesitating. He'd have the lot of you gutted on the spot. Myself being of a less wasteful nature I can't decide whether to try and sell you somewhere for a profit or keep you to satisfy my less businesslike cravings. But I promise you'll be the first to know when I've made my choice."

"If you take me away from here I won't be able to return these people to normal."

Kamaulk chuckled. "You haven't been paying attention, spellsinger. The chief and I have already discussed the little problem you created here. Their color is already beginning to come back. So is their smell. Have a look and a sniff."

The pirate was correct. Pink was shading back to brown and black and the rich aroma of raw sewage was less offensive than it had been the day before. Jon-Tom was downcast.

"The spell fades. It never did that when I worked with the duar."

"You should be thankful." Sasheem smiled hugely at him. "We arrived to rescue you just in time." The other pirates found this sally vastly amusing.

"Not sure I wouldn't 'ave preferred the cookpot," mumbled Mudge.

"Come now, I'm not so uncivilized as that." Kamaulk rubbed at an eye. "I doubtless will end up selling you, though perhaps not quite all of you. You see, Sasheem here has grown fond of you and wishes to keep some small remembrance of your numerous meetings. I have not yet decided which part of each of you I am going to allow him to retain. That will depend on the behavior you exhibit between now and the time I have you sold. Keep that in mind lest any new thoughts of escape enter your heads."

Sasheem fingered his knife. "Eunuchs are in high demand on the western shore of the Glittergeist."

"Definitely ought to 'ave opted for the cookpot," said Mudge miserably.

They were marched in single file out of the village between lines of snarling, gesticulating hunters. Then the pirates turned west instead of north.

"Heading for the sea. Got a boat on the beach somewhere, you bet." Cautious sniffed at the air. "Told you pirate folk stick to ocean. Pretty long walk from here, I think. Be night soon." He threw Jon-Tom a significant glance.

His meaning was clear enough. Despite Kamaulk's warning they had to try to get away before the pirates got them back aboard a boat. Once safely at sea Sasheem would muster all his arguments, insisting it was dangerous to let them live, probably regaling Kamaulk with an exaggerated list of Jon-Tom's abilities and in general doing everything in his power to convince the new captain that it was safer to have the human and his companions dead than to try and wring a few gold pieces out of them. Excepting Weegee, of course.

They didn't stop for dark until a scrawny, swarthy coyote tripped over a root in the darkness and got up cursing. "We need to halt 'ere, Cap'n" He carried a long pike and was gaudily clad in reds and greens. "The boys don't relish tryin' to find the beach in the dark." Murmurs of agreement rose from the other crew members.

"Aye, sir, we're about done in."

" 'Tis been a long enough day and enough marchin'. I'm for makin' camp here."

Sasheem glared at them. "Nonsense." He jabbed a thumb skyward. "The moon gives plenty of light."

"We'll do better to rest tonight and make better time in the morning," the coyote argued stubbornly. "One never knows what one might meet in a strange wood at night, especially in this unknown country."

The leopard let out a low snarl. "Surely you don't fear the simpletons we just left?"

The coyote spat at the ground. "First mate, I ain't afraid of anything natural. We're just plain tuckered, we are. I'm second to none in me desire to be back aboard a seaworthy vessel, but even a fanatic needs his sleep. Now that we got what we come for I don't see the need to rush. They ain't goin' anywhere."

Kamaulk put a restraining wing on his second-in-command's

arm. "I'm tired myself. The past few days have been a strain, har. This is a good place to nap, dry and cool. Even if we were to reach the beach we'd have to spend the night on the sand before sailing home. The currents along these shores are tricky and I don't care to try the breakers at night. Let the crew have their sleep."

A smart captain, Jon-Tom reflected, and therefore more dangerous than the impetuous, hotheaded Corroboc. He knows how to listen to his men and play them off against each other.

Sasheem set an ample guard over the prisoners and around the temporary encampment just in case the hunters they had bargained with were tempted to try and repossess their former property. The fat, badly scarred beaver who had been assigned to watch glared down at Jon-Tom, angry at having been singled out while his comrades fell to sleeping.

Jon-Tom and Mudge put their heads together and whispered, but in the end it was Weegee who determined their next course of action. She sat up straight and spat on both of them. Man and otter separated in surprise.

"I'm fed up with the lot of you!"

"Luv, wot are you on about? We risked our necks to rescue you from these bastards. Just because things didn't work out the way we planned. . . ."

"Planned my arse. You don't plan, you stumble, you ignorant twits. You don't consider the unforeseen possibilities. My luck that my 'rescuers' turn out to be the biggest trio of dummies this side of Snarken."

Mudge rose. "Now you listen to me, you bristle-nosed bitch!"

"Don't call *me* names, fuzznuts. I've about had it up to here with you and your pimple-brained man-boy. You're no good as rescuers and you're no good as anything else. At least this bunch," and she jerked her head in the direction of the sleeping pirates, "has some guts. Take him, for instance." She indicated their guard. "You can tell just by looking at him that he's too smart to get himself in a fix like this. Males like that, they've been around. They know the score, how to take care of themselves." The beaver made a show of ignoring this verbal by-play, but he consciously tried to suck in his gut and stand a little taller.

"A real male would know how to take advantage of every situation, no matter how delicate, without getting himself in a bucket of trouble. Wouldn't he?" She batted her lashes at the beaver, who pretended not to notice. She began to twist about on the ground in a seductive manner. "It's been so long since I've had a good lover I've damn well forgotten what it's like."

The beaver swallowed, watching her movements out of one eye.

"Don't you think," Weegee cooed to him, "you and I could slip away for a few minutes and show these bottle-brains what a real male and female can do?" She cut her eyes right. "There's a couple of nice, thick bushes over there."

"I—I can't." The guard's lips were twitching. "Sasheem would have my tongue out if I left my post."

"But you're not leaving your post. Your job is to keep an eye on us, isn't it? Those useless neuters are securely tied. So am I for that matter. Why, I wouldn't be able to keep you from doing just any old thing you might want to do. And you will be keeping an eye on me, won't you? Along with other things?"

The guard turned, studied Jon-Tom, Mudge and Cautious. "One of them might get loose."

"Why don't you tie their necks together?" Weegee suggested brightly. "That way if they try to run off they'll just choke each other. If they trip and fall two of them will break the third one's neck—not that that'd be any loss. Besides, we'll just be a few feet over there."

"How do I know I can trust you?"

"What could a little weak thing like me do, all tied up like this?"

The temptation was too much for the guard. Drawing a length of heavy rope from his belt he quickly secured the three males neck to neck, so tightly the hemp burned into

Jon-Tom's skin. Then he lifted Weegee under her arms and dragged her off into the bushes. Mudge rolled over to face Jon-Tom.

"Let's 'ave a chat, mate."

"About what?" Jon-Tom was looking past him into the underbrush where the guard had taken Weegee.

"Anything you want," the otter said tightly, "but let's talk."

So they talked, trying not to listen to the sounds coming from the bushes until Weegee reappeared. She ran bent over and low and though her wrists were still bound behind her, she made short work of their bonds with her sharp teeth. Her clothing was more disheveled than ever.

"How'd you get away from him?" Jon-Tom asked the question because Mudge couldn't.

"I waited and let him do as he pleased, whispering sweet sillinesses into his ears and moaning and whistling, and when he was about done I kissed him as hard as I could and kicked his nuts up into his throat, that's how. Then I picked up a rock I'd selected earlier with my feet—he forgot that we otters are very agile with our feet—and I hit him in the head. Many times. Until he stopped moving. I don't think he'll move again."

Cautious was the last to be untied. As Mudge and Jon-Tom were helping him slip free of his bonds, Weegee vanished back among the bushes only to return a moment later with the guard's knife and spear.

"We've got to get our backpacks and stuff." Jon-Tom rubbed his wrists where the rope had cut into them. "We've at least got to get the sack my duar's in."

"How much is me life worth to you, mate?"

"Mudge, you know I can't leave that behind."

"Some'ow I knew you'd say somethin' like that." The otter sighed. "Wait over there." He pointed toward a clump of small trees. Not the bushes where Weegee had been dragged.

They did as he bid, waiting for what seemed like an hour but was only a few minutes. Jon-Tom was about to suggest going after him when he reappeared, moving silently through the darkness, his own pack on his back and Jon-Tom's trailing along behind him. Jon-Tom winced every time the sack containing the pieces of duar bounced off the ground.

"Couldn't you have been a little more careful with that?" He grabbed the backpack's straps and swung it onto his shoulders.

"Do tell? You ought to be grateful I risked me life to sneak back for that lousy sack o' kindlin'."

"I am, because you're the only one I know who could have done it."

"Oh, well, since you put it that way. I expect I am. Anyone else would 'ave woken the lot of them."

At about that time a shout rose from the pirate encampment, followed by a couple of sleepy queries.

"Would have, eh?" Weegee smacked him across the snout. Mudge slapped her back and Jon-Tom and Cautious had to forcibly separate the two lovers.

"Ain't got time for this, you bet," Cautious chided them. Jon-Tom was trying to peer into the woods as the alarm spread slowly through the brigands' camp.

"Which way? Toward the beach?"

"I doen know the beach. I know the woods." The raccoon pointed southward. "We go that way."

At first the cries and shouts of the pirates faded behind them, but soon they gained in strength.

"Following for sure." Mudge scampered alongside Jon-Tom. "I 'ave this uncomfortable feelin' they won't be so quick to give up on us this time. We've embarrassed 'em once too often."

"I agree." Jon-Tom ducked a low-hanging branch, felt the wood scrape the top of his scalp. "I'm afraid Sasheem will prevail."

"They won't take us alive." Weegee kicked a bush aside. "Think we can outrun 'em?"

"I don't know." He glanced skyward worriedly. "I wonder if Kamaulk's wing is healed enough for him to fly. I didn't notice any other avians in the crew."

"Lucky break." Mudge leaped a rivulet. "Be 'ard put to spot us at night through these trees anyway."

At times the pirate's cries would drift away, only to return stronger than ever as one of their number picked up the tracks of the escapees. Once they splashed down a shallow stream and temporarily lost their pursuers completely, only to have them eventually pick up the trail yet again. Cautious tried every trick he knew, but the pirates persisted. This time they wouldn't tuck their tails between their legs and give up. And if they couldn't shake them at night, Jon-Tom knew, they'd have twice the trouble losing them in the daytime.

He was tired already. His heart pounded against his ribs and his legs felt like silly putty. Even Mudge and Weegee were showing signs of exhaustion. Not even an otter can run forever.

Suddenly Jon-Tom stopped, nearly stumbling. Mudge crashed into him from behind and wheezed angrily up at his friend.

"Wot's the matter with you, mate? Come on, we've got to keep movin'."

"Hold on a minute."

"We ain't got many minutes."

Jon-Tom ignored this as he moved curiously to his left. Mudge looked back into the woods, then at his companion.

"Are you daft, lad? Wot is it you're 'untin' for?"

"Don't you feel it?"

"Feel wot?"

"Something our friends are likely to overlook." He was pushing leaves and branches aside now, let out an exclamation of satisfaction when he found what he was looking for.

A cool, slightly damp breeze emerged from beneath a rocky ledge.

"There's got to be a cave down there. Pretty big one, too, judging from the strength of the wind coming out. Maybe we can't lose them up here, but I think they'll be less likely to come looking for us below, even if they're lucky enough to find this opening." He started scanning the forest floor. "Find something we can make torches out of."

There was plenty of dried moss. Wrapped around branches, these made serviceable faggots.

"How do we light them?" Weegee had already searched her clothing. "I don't have any flints with me. Can you sing a fire spell?"

"No, but I've got these." He fumbled in his pack. Sure enough, he had four matches left of the box he'd been carrying when Clothahump had first yanked him into this world. Saying a silent prayer, he struck the first alight. He was greatly relieved when the moss on the first torch caught instantly.

Weegee was wide-eyed. "If not magic, what do you call that?"

"Matches. I'll explain later." He touched the lit torch to the others. "Come on. If I fit, everyone'll fit."

Cautious stepped in front of him. "My eyes are better in the dark than anyone else's here, you bet. I go first. You follow, Jon-Tom, stay close to my tail. Maybe if I fall in big hole, you got something to grab. If not, I warn you before I bounce." He grinned, clapped the man on the shoulder, then turned and ducked lithely beneath the ledge. Jon-Tom followed as Mudge and Weegee brought up the rear.

The cave sloped steadily downward, a claustrophobic tube. Jon-Tom began to wonder if this had been such a bright idea. His palms were rubbing raw on the slick, unyielding limestone.

Without warning the ceiling rose and everyone was able to stand. Torches revealed a graveled path leading steadily onward.

Weegee surveyed the dark tunnel ahead. "Isn't this far enough? I'm not very fond of deep places."

"Are you fond o' bein' slowly skinned alive?" Mudge nodded back the way they'd come. "If they do find the openin' they're liable to hear our voices or see the light from these torches. The farther we go the safer we'll be."

Cautious had advanced several yards in front of his companions. "Opens up more, I think."

"Let's go on." Jon-Tom followed the raccoon. He'd always liked caves.

Roughly a hundred feet beneath the forested surface the floor of the tunnel leveled out and their torches illuminated a subterranean world of baroque loveliness. Except for rock that had fallen from the ceiling the surface they were walking on was smooth and firm, having been scoured clean ages ago by a now vanished underground river. Water dripped from stalactites into shallow rimstone pools.

"A live cave." Jon-Tom held his torch close to one pristine limestone soda straw. "Still growing."

"Strange places, caves. 'Tis better to stay out of 'em." Mudge was studying the floor, looking for tracks. "One never knows wot sort o' evil spirits lurk in their depths. O' course in this case, we already know the nature o' the evil spirits lurkin' about above."

The torches were holding out well, burning slowly and steadily, and the extensive winding chamber showed no sign of diminishing in size. Jon-Tom allowed Cautious to lead on. The farther they got from Sasheem and Kamaulk and the rest of their murderous ilk the safer he'd feel. Eventually they'd find a convenient stopping place, extinguish all of their torches, and rest.

Unless they discovered the entrance to the cavern the pirates would have to give up. Not even Sasheem and Kamaulk's exhortations could keep the crew roaming a trackless forest for days on end. Even if they did discover the cavity beneath the ledge they probably wouldn't enter, since the brigands tended to be more superstitious even than Mudge. Eventually the practical Kamaulk would have to admit he'd been outwitted again. His crew would mollify him by assuring him it was no crime to be fooled by a magician.

The beauty surrounding them tended to take their minds off their distant pursuers. A cluster of stalagmites rose fifteen feet from the floor, gleaming beneath their coats of pure white calcite. Frozen flowstone waves clung like draperies from the walls and gave off charming musical tones when

Mudge tapped them with his claws. Iron oxide stained several draperies, giving them the appearance of huge slabs of bacon. Miniature travertine dams held back the drip water.

Long thin stalactites called soda straws hung from the ceiling, each with its bead of lime-saturated water dangling from the tip. One chamber was filled with helictites, twisted stalagtites that grew every which way in defiance of gravity. There were cave pearls and fried eggs and a whole phantasmagoria of wondrous speleotherms to admire. Jon-Tom identified stalactites and stalagmites that had grown together over the eons to form columns, tiny pale troglodytes that had to be cave crickets, long snaky wires. . . .

Long snaky wires?

Hands shaking, he bent over and held his torch close to the motionless cable. The insulation was frayed and disintegrating but there was no mistaking what it was.

Weegee leaned over his shoulder, her musk strong in the still air of the cavern. "What the devil is it?" Ignoring her, he began tracing the cable along the ground. She looked over at Mudge. "What's wrong? Why doesn't he answer?"

Mudge bent low over the frayed cable, plucked a bit of torn insulation and smelled of it. His eyes were on his tall friend's back. "I've an idea. 'Tis insane, but no more insane than many things 'e an' I 'ave encountered in our travels together. Whether it bodes good or ill only the fates can say, those interferin' blabbermouths."

Jon-Tom was examining the narrow cleft in the wall from which the cable emerged. By turning sideways he could just squeeze through. Several minutes passed before his companions were drawn by a shout from beyond. Clothahump couldn't have followed, but Cautious and the two otters slipped easily through the gap.

They came out in another decorated chamber seemingly no different from the one they had left. The cable continued to snake along the floor until it terminated in a square metal box. Another cable in somewhat better condition emerged from the other side of the container. Jon-Tom was studying it closely as his three companions gathered around.

"What is it?" Cautious inquired.

By way of reply Jon-Tom flipped open the box's lid. A large plastic switch stared back at him. Hardly daring to hope, he turned it to the right. The primitive wiring not only still worked, it was connected to an as yet undiscovered power source. Mudge and Weegee jumped involuntarily as powerful argon lamps came to life and illuminated much of the chamber in which they stood. Cautious made protective signs in front of his body.

"No jokes this time, mate. Where 'ave you brought us?"

"I don't know. I sure as hell don't know, Mudge."

Quickly overcoming his initial surprise, Cautious had wandered over to stare at one of the high intensity lamps. "Strongest glow-bulb spell I ever see."

"Don't touch it," Jon-Tom warned him. "They look old and I bet they get real hot real quick. This whole setup's at least forty or fifty years old."

"So where do we go from 'ere, mate?"

"One of two ways, Mudge. Either we go back the way we came or we follow the cable and lights the other way and see if they lead to a dream come true."

"I'd rather they led to a decent eatin' place, but I think I'd settle for a dream come true. I sure as 'ell ain't going back up yet. Weegee?"

"If you trust Jon-Tom that much, how can I do less?"

"Doen make no much difference to me," added Cautious. "You lead now, tall man."

The cables led to another switch box, and another, and a fourth. Since the limits of the power supply had to be finite, Jon-Tom turned off the lights behind them each time he turned on the next set ahead. As old as the system was he didn't think it would take much to overload it.

Once the roof dropped, and they all had to bend to clear the ceiling. When it lifted so they could stand again the cavern had become another tunnel similar to the one they had descended but with one important addition.

Concrete steps spiraled upward directly ahead of them.

"Wot's up there, mate? Or rather, wot do you *think* is up there?"

"Not our piratical friends. As to anything else, I'm afraid to guess."

"If we're not to come out in the forest we left," said Weegee, "where are we to come out, Jon-Tom?"

"The mind boggles." He started climbing.

The steps wound their way up a narrow chute which had been artificially enlarged. As they neared the top they could smell warm air. A roof had been built over the hole. Several of the crossbeams had long since fallen in. The entrance to the cave below was either infrequently used or infrequently maintained.

When they got to the top of the stairs they found themselves surrounded by stone walls. A double door of heavy planks sealed the exit and was secured by a fat padlock. Jon-Tom bent to examine it but was gently nudged aside.

"Are you forgettin' in whose company you're travelin'?"

Using a knife and another small tool from his pack, it took Mudge about two minutes to pick the lock. The doors were shoved aside.

They found themselves standing atop a grassy knoll surrounded by trees very different from those they had left behind. There was no sign of the sandy-soiled cypress, pine and hardwood forest. The earth underfoot was thick with crumbled limestone, shale and clay. As for the trees, Jon-Tom recognized live oak right away. It took him longer to figure out that their neighbors were mesquite.

Off to their right stood a single building devoid of life. Climbing a few dozen yards the other way put them atop the highest part of the hill. From this vantage point they should have been able to see over the forest to the distant shore of the Glittergeist. There was no sea to be seen; only mile upon square mile of dense forest broken by a single wide, paved trail.

As they stood and stared, a bulky monster came chugging down the trail. It roared twice.

"Wot the bloody 'ell is that?" Mudge stammered.

" 'Tis horrible to look upon." Weegee turned her face to Jon-Tom. "Where have you brought us, spellsinger?"

The monster was the size of several elephants. It had eighteen legs, all of them round, and as it thundered southward Jon-Tom could just make out the legend inscribed on its flank.

PIGGLY WIGGLY

Dumbfounded, he watched the eighteen-wheeler until it vanished into the woods. Fingers tugged insistently on his sleeve.

"Out with it, mate. You know where we are, don't you?"

Jon-Tom didn't reply, continued to gaze dazedly at the highway. Mudge turned away from him.

"E's bloody well out of it for now, 'e is."

"There's a sign of some sort." Weegee waddled over to the wooden square that topped a post marking the end of a dirt road. She couldn't make out the alien hieroglyphics on the other side but Jon-Tom could. Mudge dragged his friend over. The sight of the familiar lettering shocked him back to reality.

"It says, 'Welcome to the Cave-With-No-Name' " and underneath, in smaller letters, " 'San Antonio – 64 Miles'."

" 'San At-nonio'?" Mudge's brows drew together and his whiskers twitched. The sun was beginning to set over the eastern horizon. At least that were unchanged from the real world, he reflected. "I know Jarrow and I know Lynchbany an' Polastrindu an' half a 'undred other cities, but I ain't never 'eard o' no San At-nonio."

"I didn't think Hell would have quite so many trees." Weegee was examining a pair of acorns.

"We're not in Hell," Jon-Tom assured her. "Just Texas."

"I don't know where that is either."

"My world." A slow grin spread across Jon-Tom's face. "We've crossed through to my world." He walked back to the cave entrance. " 'Cave-With-No-Name'. That's appropriate. There must be a permanent passage down there between your world and mine. Whoever developed this cave started to run a new cable through to the chamber on your side and gave it up. Maybe ran out of money. This setup hasn't been worked on in years, maybe decades. Clothahump often postulated that such permanent gateways might exist."

"Wot makes you think 'tis permanent?"

"Want to go back and see if Kamaulk and Sasheem and the others are waiting for us by the ledge opening?"

"Not just right away, mate. I expect we could 'ang around 'ere for a day or two and then go back. Don't know as 'ow I could stand it much longer than that." He sniffed ostentatiously. "Air 'ere smells peculiar but not as you always told me."

"That's because we didn't come out in the middle of a big city. Just as well. Would've caused quite a stir." Bending, he picked up an empty metal container. It was brown, red, battered, and said DR. PEPPER on the side. It was the most beautiful thing he'd seen in over a year. He might've been fondling the Hope diamond. Tears started from the corners of his eyes. "Home. Damn, I finally made it."

Cautious was turning a slow circle. "So this your world, eh? Doen look so impressive to me."

Jon-Tom couldn't bring himself to cast the empty can aside. "We didn't emerge in the most impressive neighborhood, for which we can all be grateful. The culture shock on both sides would've been too much to handle." He took a deep breath, gestured toward the entrance to the cavern. "I think the rest of you'd better keep out of sight over there until I see if anybody's home."

Mudge frowned. "Why? We got bad breath or somethin'?"

"You don't understand. In my world, people like you and Weegee and Cautious don't talk."

"Oh, right you are, mate. You told me that before."

"What's he talking about?" Weegee asked.

Mudge put his arm around her and directed her toward the

cave. "I'll explain it all to you, luv. It beggars understandin', it does."

As soon as his friends had concealed themselves Jon-Tom stepped up on the porch of the building which was at least as old as the wiring he'd encountered below. Clearly this was not one of the tourist highspots of the Lone Star state. He rapped twice on the screen door before noticing the small sign set inside.

GONE BOWLING – BACK IN A WEEK

Someone who knew how to relax, he reflected. On a hunch he opened the unsecured screen door and tried the door knob. Locked. He hunted around the opening. Displaying either country trustworthiness or bucolic naivete, the owner had left a key on top of the nearby light. He had to jiggle it in the lock but soon had the door open.

The sight froze him. So long, it had been so unbelievably long. So many extraordinary things had happened to him that he found himself paralyzed by the sight of the ordinary.

It was all real, from the souvenir postcards in the wire rack atop the candy counter to the telephone and cash register and rack of antlers. With difficulty he restrained himself from tearing into the neat rows of Milky Ways and Baby Ruths and Hershey's with Almonds.

The den of the old house had been converted into a greeting room for tourists. Snug and lined with pine, it fronted a single bedroom and a small unimpressive kitchen which nonetheless held out the promise of the first familiar food he'd seen in a year. He forced himself to stay clear of the refrigerator and pantry until he'd thoroughly checked the rest of the premises. There was a bathroom and a garage out back. The garage was empty.

A shout brought him back to the front porch. Mudge was peering around the edge of one of the doors that led to the cave. "Is it safe or ain't it, mate? Do we come on in or run back down?"

"It's okay, there's nobody here now. Come on in."

The otters and Cautious were fascinated by the plethora of unfamiliar objects that filled the old house. The kitchen in particular was a treasure house of alien delights, not the least of which took the form of half a dozen cans of Chicken of the Sea tuna. After Jon-Tom instructed him in the use of a can opener Mudge went a little berserk.

An hour later he was patting his bulging belly. "One thing about your world, mate: 'tis fillin'." He held up a small oblong can. Wot's in 'ere?"

Jon-Tom had the lights on in the kitchen. It was getting pitch dark outside. "Sardines. Slow down. We don't want to eat everything at once and I don't know how I'm going to pay the owner for what we've eaten."

"We'll leave 'im an IOU."

"You leave an IOU? That'd be a first." He sipped slowly from a cold bottle of RC. Pure luxury sloshed down his throat. "It's funny. All the spells Clothahump and I have tried over the past year, all the arcane tomes we've consulted, and here we stumble across a permanent link between our worlds because we're running for our lives from a bunch of two-bit pirates."

"If it is permanent and doesn't close down on us while we're sitting here stuffing our faces," Weegee said darkly.

Jon-Tom lowered the bottle from his lips. "I think that gate's been there as long as the cave itself. The terminated cable running through the passage shows that it's been open between worlds for a number of years, anyway. Think of it! We can travel back and forth between my world and yours at will. Columbus was a piker compared to us." He chuckled at the thought. "I can't wait to see the reaction when you and Mudge and Cautious appear on the Six O'Clock News."

"Now wot might that be?"

Jon-Tom was explaining network news to the otter as he fried himself some bacon and eggs. The explanation was inelegantly interrupted by a voice from the kitchen doorway.

"Nobody runs out on Kamaulk twice in a row and lives to brag about it, not even if they run all the way to another world."

IX

Jon-Tom dropped the skillet. Sizzling bacon and runny eggs splashed over his boots. Kamaulk stood framed in the lower half of the doorway, holding a small crossbow in his wings. Behind him Sasheem held a throwing knife in each paw.

"Crap!" Mudge glanced at his friend. "Guess you're right, mate. I expect the passage between our worlds is permanent enough. Would 'ave to be. Proof of it is that sewage flows both ways."

Kamaulk hopped into the kitchen, his eyes flicking over the strange sights and familiar former acquaintances with equal alacrity. "Demonic contrivances. There's money in demonic contrivances. There's much here that can be turned to profit."

Jon-Tom forbore from pointing out that the household goods the parrot was eyeing enviously didn't belong to him. Somehow he didn't think appealing to the pirate's sense of fair play would garner them much credit. Mudge was trying to sneak his paw down to the longbow lying near his feet when a stiletto slammed into the table two inches from his belly.

"Don't try that again." Sasheem stepped into the room. "I've no patience left where any of you are concerned. Try me one more time and no matter what the captain says I'll put the next one between your eyes. Or hers." He favored Weegee with a cursory nod.

"Nice to see you again, lass." The voice was colder than the ice cubes in the refrigerator's freezer compartment. It came from the beaver who slipped into the room beneath Sasheem's arm. A thick bandage was wrapped around his head. It was the guard who'd been assigned to watch them last night. His expression was not pleasant. "I've pleaded with the Cap'n to let me take charge of you special. I've a few kicks you lent me I'd like to return."

"Belay that for now, Woshim. You haven't earned anything here."

"But Cap'n, you said . . . ."

"Not now," Kamaulk snapped. "A fascinating place you've led us to. We will need a suitable guide to show us the best way to profit."

"I'll guide you to the garbage dump."

"You'll do better than that, spellsinger. By my tail feathers you will. Or your friends will die one by one, as slowly and painfully as Sasheem can make it. You will stay here to explain this world to me. We will take the others back with us as hostage to your good intentions. We marked the path with care. Tracking you through that cave was not easy."

"How did you track us?"

Mudge snorted. "Ain't you lived long enough in our world to figure that by now, mate?" He tapped his glistening black nose.

Jon-Tom had forgotten. In the pristine atmosphere of the cave their scents must have lingered in the air like road markers. Even so it had taken guts for Kamaulk and his crew to follow them through that black underworld, up the obviously alien concrete stairway. How many of them had that kind of courage? He tried to see past Sasheem into the den. How badly were they outnumbered? Surely the whole crew hadn't agreed to follow their captain into darkness.

Of one thing he was certain: If Kamaulk was able to march Mudge, Weegee and Cautious back to their world he'd have a permanent hold on Jon-Tom. He'd have to do exactly as the pirate directed in order to keep his friends alive. Eventually Kamaulk would grow sated with the products of Jon-Tom's world, or else he'd figure out some way to derive what he wanted from it without any help. Then Jon-Tom and the others would become expendable. He had to do something *now.*

As bemused and amazed as they were by this new world they'd stumbled into, Jon-Tom didn't think Kamaulk was dazed enough to allow him to try a song on the suar. For that matter he had no idea if his spellsinging would work in his own world. As he thought furiously, time and opportunity were slipping away. The pirates were divesting their captives of their rewon weapons. With sorrow Mudge watched his longbow and short sword taken by other hands. Jon-Tom was relieved of his ramwood staff and suar. Their backpacks were not touched. Apparently Kamaulk was convinced they contained nothing likely to present a significant danger to him or his crew.

The parrot was inspecting the gas range, determined not to show hesitation or fear in front of his troops. He sniffed at the stove, picked up the skillet Jon-Tom had dropped and placed it back on the open burner.

"Cooking device. Very interesting." He peered beneath the skillet. "Where does the fire come from?"

"Gas."

This brought forth laughter from several of the pirates. Kamaulk made a face and whipped out a long stiletto with a hollowed handle. "Do you take me for a fool?" He ran the tip of the blade up one leg of Jon-Tom's pants, not cutting the material but letting him feel the edge. "I said I didn't want to kill you. That does not mean I am adverse to marking you a little."

Jon-Tom found he was starting to sweat. "Dammit, it's a gas stove!"

"Even Kizewiz doesn't make that much gas." A bulky anteater guffawed from his place in the doorway.

"It's not that kind of gas. See?" He reached for one of the stove controls and almost lost a finger as Kamaulk brought the blade down against the plastic.

"Be careful what you do, man. I am sure you can guide me in the use of these devices with nine fingers as well as with ten."

Very slowly Jon-Tom adjusted the flame. "See how it works? A special kind of gas enters the house through pipes and runs into this stove. You use a small fire to light the gas."

"How do you stop it?" Jon-Tom demonstrated. Kamaulk nodded, satisfied.

"And this?" He tapped the refrigerator handle with his knife.

"It keeps food from spoiling." Maybe Kamaulk wouldn't get bored with his survey of modern inventions. The longer he could stall the captain the more time there was to think of something. Not that there seemed much anyone could do with a bunch of heavily armed pirates milling around in the other room.

"Pull the handle."

Kamaulk did so and jumped back as a puff of chilled air struck him. He blinked, then waddled forward to study the porcelain-on-steel interior.

"Wonderful." He looked back at Sasheem. "We're going to take some of these marvels back with us. Trade will make us the wealthiest company of buccaneers the world has ever seen." He glanced curiously at the portable TV that sat atop one of the kitchen cabinets. "And what is that thing?"

"Television. Magic picture box." He tried not to reveal the sudden surge of excitement that raced through him as he winked at Mudge. The otter's expression did not change, but Jon-Tom saw him stiffen slightly.

Kamaulk squinted at the blank screen. "What does it do?"

"Turn the knob on the bottom right all the way to the left, then pull it out 'til it clicks." He gathered himself. Maybe they would get lucky. If a sufficiently loud, violent show flared to life it might startle or frighten the pirates enough to enable Mudge and himself to get their hands on some weapons. Starsky and Hutch, a war movie, the evening news, anything really repellent and noisy.

What they got instead was a tape of the Royal Ballet doing the pas de deux from the Nutcracker Suite. He cursed helplessly.

"Lovely." Kamaulk turned the volume down to an acceptable level and grinned at Jon-Tom. "You see how quickly I adapt to new things. But why are there only humans in the picture?"

"That brings up something about my world you aren't going to like." As he began to explain, the lights went out.

"Freeze! Everybody!"

There was barely enough time for Jon-Tom to identify the accent as Spanish before a number of things happened all at once. Kamaulk yelled an oath, Jon-Tom leaped toward his friends and shouted for them to drop to the floor, Sasheem roared and charged and thunder and lightning echoed through the little house.

"Great rubbing post of God, what was that?" Weegee whimpered.

Jon-Tom shushed her. "Quiet. Whatever you do, don't breathe another word when the lights come back on. Understand? Say nothing unless I give you a sign, no matter what happens. Mudge, Cautious, that goes for you, too."

Mass confusion reigned in the den as the remaining pirates practically broke down the screen door in their anxiety to flee. Jon-Tom could visualize them scrambling in panic to reach the tunnel that led back to their own world. The air in the kitchen stank of gunpowder and blood. Then the lights came back on.

Standing by the back door was a swarthy man in his late

thirties. He had curly black hair, a thin mustache, and one finger on the light switch. Jon-Tom thought he was a dead ringer for one of the extras who composed the background of *Miami Vice*. The sawed-off twelve gauge he cupped against his forearm was no prop.

Directly across the floor Sasheem lay sprawled on his back with a gaping hole in his chest. Kamaulk had flown up onto a cabinet and perched there, staring wide-eyed at the body of his first mate and wondering whence his brave crew had fled.

"Madre de dios." The intruder took his hand off the light switch and stared down at the dead leopard. Another Latino paused in the den door, a large pistol dangling from his fist. His eyes flicked over the spotted corpse before coming to rest on Jon-Tom and his friends.

"What thee hell ees going on here?" He looked to his buddy. "I was comeeng een thee front door an' theese damn zoo nearly run over me."

"Big cat jumped me." The other man's accent was not as thick as that of the pistolero. "What's with all these animals in clothes?"

Mudge made as if to reply, clammed up as Jon-Tom frantically put finger to his lips. The otter nodded imperceptibly and both movements went unnoticed by the armed intruders. They were too busy examining Sasheem's body.

The pistolero muttered the name "Cruz" and that worthy turned to point the sawed-off in Jon-Tom's general direction. "You. You tell me what's going on here. Where the hell did all these animals come from?" He leaned to his left and saw Cautious squatting under the kitchen table. "That's the biggest damn raccoon I've ever seen."

"They're mine." Mudge nipped him on the leg but he winced and ignored it. "They belong to me. I'm an animal trainer. These are all specially trained performers." He nodded at Sasheem. "When you turned on the lights you panicked the leopard. He's really quite harmless. A great loss."

"Hey mon, he panicked me pretty good. I was just

defending myself. You part of a circus or something? We didn't see no tents outside."

"More of a private traveling show. I'm kinda down on my luck. Got kicked out of the company. At least they let me take my animals with me. Maybe you could give me a hand? I understand about the leopard. Just tough luck."

"Give you a hand?" Cruz grinned in a way Jon-Tom didn't like. "What's with the getup?" He indicated Sasheem's vest and short pants, the sword lying next to the leopard's body, and the bandolier of stilettoes that crossed his broad chest.

"I told you, they're all trained. It's all part of the act."

"I never saw an act like that."

"Hey, I deed once." The pistolero's eyes lit with recognition. "In Vegas. You know, mon, them Siegfreed and Roy guys? They dress some of their animals up."

"Is this your place?" Jon-Tom asked innocently.

Cruz found this very amusing. "Let's just say we use it as a stopover on our way north. You might say we're traveling salesmen, Manco and I. A raccoon that big. What kind of tricks can your animals do?"

Jon-Tom stared hard at Mudge and Weegee. "They can't do anything unless I tell them to. But I've trained them to walk on their hind legs all the time."

"That's about enough of this bilge-pus." Everyone's eyes went to the top of the high cabinet. Cruz gave Kamaulk the approving eye.

"Biggest parrot I ever saw, too. That's a sharp outfit you've got on him."

"What the blazes are you two morons blabbering about?"

Jon-Tom tensed, but Cruz and his partner found Kamaulk's comments entertaining rather than insulting. "Hey, that's pretty good! You teach him all that?"

"Not exactly." Jon-Tom's throat was dry. "He kind of picked up a lot of it himself. He's very clever. I don't know myself what he's going to say next."

"Bugger the lot o' you!" The pirate folded his wings

over his chest. "Do what you will with me. I'm not frightened of you."

"Cute." Cruz forgot about the parrot and turned his attention back to Jon-Tom. "You, I'm not so sure you're cute. More like a problem."

"Look, let's just forget about the trained leopard and I'll let bygones be bygones, okay? I didn't know this was your house and I'll be glad to pay for the food. I had to do something. My animals were starving. And I've got to try to catch the others before they've gone too far." He took a hopeful step toward the far door, grunted as Cruz shoved the business end of the sawed-off into his belly.

"Your pets'll just have to wait, compadre. You don't need so many animals anyway. Why don't you hitch a ride with us? We'll drop you at a phone and you can call the local animal shelter."

"Oh, that's not necessary. I don't want to cause you guys any trouble."

"No trouble at all." Cruz gestured with the shotgun. "We're ready to leave right now. See, we just stopped for a few minutes to pick up some luggage we have to deliver up north. Chicago. We don't mind company." His expression darkened. "Out back now. Bring your animals with you if you want."

"What about my stuff?" He gestured toward the backpacks and weapons.

Cruz walked over, picked up the ramwood staff, then Mudge's longbow. "Check 'em out, Manco." The other man obediently went through both packs.

"Cleen."

"Okay, you can have these." He tossed both packs to Jon-Tom, who caught them gratefully. "These other toys," and he admired Mudge's short sword as he held it up to the light, "I think maybe we keep with us. I know a good pawn shop in Chicago." He grinned. "Payment for your ride, no?"

Under watchful eyes Jon-Tom, his friends and Kamaulk were herded out back of the empty garage and into a waiting truck. With all the noise and confusion attendant upon the pirates' earlier arrival he hadn't heard it drive up. It was a U-Haul with a fourteen foot bed. The back end they scrambled into was filled with cheap household furniture. He frowned. Furniture movers didn't usually travel with heavy artillery. Cruz secured their weapons in a steel footlocker.

"Go on, all the way back." They obliged. The metal door was rolled down and locked. Jon-Tom heard the click as it was latched from outside.

There were no windows, but the truck had been heavily used and there were a couple of spots where roof and walls didn't quite meet. Starlight was visible through the cracks. At least they wouldn't suffocate. The truck lurched backward, then started forward, picking up speed. Heading down the dirt road that led away from the house, no doubt.

He smelled Weegee close by. "Is it all right to talk now, Jon-Tom?"

"What do you mean, is it all right to talk now?" Kamaulk sounded at once puzzled and bitter at the hand fate had dealt him. "What are the two strange humans going to do with us?"

Jon-Tom ignored him. "It's okay to talk, Weegee."

Cautious made a disgusted noise. "Your world not very hospitable, man. Doen think I like it much. Is always this violent, people throwing thunder and lightning at each other?"

"No. We just got lucky."

"That's right, mate, Lady Luck loves travelin' in your company, she does." Mudge was working his way back to the rolling door. "If they take us too far from that place we'll never find our way back."

Mudge, you don't know the half of it, Jon-Tom thought worriedly. The one named Cruz had mentioned Chicago. They couldn't go to Chicago. No way could they go to Chicago. They had to get back to the Cave-With-No-Name.

"You're all frightened." Kamaulk's tone dripped contempt. "Even you, man, in your own world."

"You bet your green feathered ass I'm frightened."

"Pagh! You should prepare to meet your fate with dignity."

"You meet your fate with dignity, buttbeak. Me, I'm goin' down kickin' an' screamin'. Hey, wot 'ave we 'ere?"

"Where?" Jon-Tom could barely make out the silhouette of the otter. Mudge was fumbling with a large oak trunk.

"Somethin' in 'ere smells peculiar. Luv, 'and me my pack, would you? That's a good lass." Weegee passed his backpack over. Mudge fumbled inside, removed a couple of small bits of metal and went to work on the trunk's lock. Jon-Tom didn't see the point of it, but at least it kept his companions' minds off their incipient demise.

The trunk produced a pair of Samsonite suitcases, also locked.

"Can you make a little light, mate? These locks are new to me."

Three matches remained in Jon-Tom's back pocket. He struck one alight, held it close to the latch of the first suitcase. Mudge leaned close, squinting.

"Bloody tricky clever, this design."

"Can you spring it?"

The otter grinned at him in the matchlight. "Mate, there ain't a lock in *any* world that your bosom buddy can't figure. Just give me a minim to think 'er through."

The match burned Jon-Tom's fingers and he flung the stub aside, lit a second. "Only one match left, Mudge."

"Don't matter none, mate. I can work it by feel."

"You always could," said Weegee, and the otters shared a not so private giggle.

Two minutes of quiet, intense work remained before Mudge had all four suitcase latches sprung. He opened the first. Jon-Tom leaned forward.

"I can't see a damn thing. What's inside?"

"Nothin' much, mate. Just some plastic bags full of funny smellin' stuff. Maybe a better whiff . . ." and he used a claw to slit one of the plasticine sacks. As he did so he leaned forward and sniffed deeply.

Someone must have lit a fire under all his toes because he

suddenly leaped off the floor of the truck and fell backward over a crushed velvet sofa.

"Mudge—Mudge, you okay?"

"Okay? *Okay*? Okay ain't the *word,* mate. Weegee m'luv, have yourself a sniff, but just a bitty one."

Curious, she did exactly that and let out a whoop as she jumped halfway to the roof.

"Hey, what is that stuff? Take it easy, you two. We don't want to let our friends up front know what we're doing back here." He had to forcibly keep Mudge away from the open suitcase.

"What is it? I'll tell you wot it is, mate. That there is pure stinger sweat, that's wot it be. More than I've ever seen in one place. More than ever were in one place. It explains a lot to me. I expect 'tis worth as much in your world as in mine."

"Stinger sweat?" Jon-Tom frowned, thought hard. He didn't have to think too hard.

Shotguns. Business in Chicago. Stop to pick up some luggage. Clear bags of funny smelling stuff.

"What color's the powder, Mudge?"

"Why, 'tis white, mate. Wot other color would it be?"

"Christ." Jon-Tom sat down in a conveniently close-by chair. It bounced and rocked as the truck fought its way down the dirt road but his mind was on something other than the smoothness of the ride. "It sure does explain things. This whole deal: the van, the furniture, it's just cover. Those two guys are coke runners. Two suitcases full of cocaine. Jesus." He got out of the chair and against Mudge's protests shut the suitcase. They they checked its mate. It was just as full. He lifted first one, then the other.

Allowing for the weight of the suitcases, he estimated that between them they contained between eighty and a hundred pounds of pure uncut "stinger sweat."

"I need you thinking straight, Mudge. That stuff will mess up your head."

"I know, mate, but wot a delightful mess."

"Jon-Tom's right," Weegee admonished him. "Besides,

you told me you were going to stay away from thosesuch temptations."

"Aye, luv, but blimey, a whole *case* full!"

"Keep an eye on him," Jon-Tom instructed her. "Mudge has a good heart, but where temptations are concerned he's weak."

"Weak? Like 'ell I'm weak. I can resist anythin' if I put me mind to it."

"It's your nose I'm worried about you putting to it." He tapped the suitcase. "If I left you alone with this for five minutes you'd snort your brains out. Everyone needs to be sharp if we're going to get out of this."

"And 'ow might we be goin' to get out o' this, your magicship?"

"I want to go home," said Cautious suddenly. "Back to sane world."

"So do I. I mean, I want to help the rest of you get home." What did he want, he asked himself abruptly? Did he even know?

"Hey, I can hear what they two fellas saying up front." Cautious was leaning against the front wall of the truck.

"Impossible," Jon-Tom said. Then it occurred to him he was arguing with a raccoon, a creature who could hear a beetle crossing a dead leaf thirty feet away in the middle of a forest. Trying not to make any noise, he and the two otters clambered forward to stand close to their masked companion. They waited silently, hardly daring to breathe while he listened.

Finally Jon-Tom couldn't stand it anymore. "What are they saying?"

"They laughing a lot. Talking about what they going to do when they get to a place called Vegas."

"Vegas? Las Vegas? I thought they said they were going to Chicago."

"Won't you ever learn anythin' about life, mate?" Mudge shook his head in the dim light. "Why should they tell us where they're 'eadin'?"

It made sense, Jon-Tom mused. Logical destination, empty interstates, plenty of loose cash for making big deals, and people visiting from all over.

"Quiet," said Cautious. After a minute, "They talking 'bout us now."

"Us? You mean, the rest of you?"

"Yeah. they going to sell us. To zoo or something like whatever that be. Sure they can get lot of money for us."

A pair of five foot tall otters, an equally big raccoon and a parrot that could swear a blue streak certainly would tempt any zoo or circus director, Jon-Tom thought.

"What about me? Are they saying what they're going to do with me?" He could see Cautious's eyes glint in the darkness.

"They ain't going to sell you. Ain't going to let you go, neither."

"I thought as much." That's why they hadn't worried about the possibility of him finding their cocaine shipment. If by some miracle or an otter he stumbled across it, he wouldn't live long enough to tell anyone about it. They'd dump him along some lonely stretch of desert road, between Flagstaff and Las Vegas would be a likely place, and the buzzards would do their autopsy long before the Highway Patrol.

"We've got to break out of here. Even if they decide to let me go I'm damned if I'll see my friends sold to some rotten sideshow."

He could visualize Mudge and Weegee stripped of their clothing, put on display in a glass cage in a Vegas casino, poked and probed by double-domed researchers and callous zoologists. See the amazing talking otters! See the giant talking raccoon!

On the other hand, if he didn't get lonely for their own kind, Mudge might do rather well living in the lap of luxury surrounded by gambling and liquor. Best not to mention such a possibility to his impressionable and occasionally mentally erratic friend. Certainly Weegee wouldn't opt for such a life.

Would she?

An answer to his unasked question took the form of soft sniffling from nearby. "Mudge, I don't like this world. I want to go home."

"So do I, luv, so do I. Mate, you've got to do somethin'."

With these confessions in hand he felt better about his chosen course of action.

"Mudge, they think they've locked our weapons away from us. Have they?"

The otter bent over the steel footlocker. "Give me three minutes, mate."

Actually Mudge was wrong. He needed four. Once they were rearmed Jon-Tom ordered everyone to move to the back of the truck.

"That way those guys up front won't hear me spellsinging."

"Spellsinging, fagh!" Kamaulk rocked back and forth atop a dresser. "Don't expect us to believe in that, har. That's a feeble joke you've been fooling people with all along."

"Believe in what you want to believe in, Kamaulk. The rest of us are getting out of here."

"Think you that? Well, on the off chance you may be right . . ." he turned and started hollering toward the driver's compartment. "Hey you humans up front! Your captives are preparing to—mmmpff!"

Using a couch for a trampoline Cautious had landed on the parrot in a single bound. Mudge gave the raccoon a hand subduing the spitting, snapping parrot. Kamaulk's intent was clear enough: he'd hoped to secure his own freedom by spoiling their attempt to escape. Jon-Tom almost felt sorry for the bird. He had no idea what kind of world he'd stumbled into. Much of the furniture was secured with rope and they soon had the pirate bound and gagged to a chair.

"That takes care o' 'im." Mudge turned to look grimly up at Jon-Tom. "Now let's take care o' us, mate. If you can."

"Everybody keep close together. I'm not sure what's going to happen if this works." As they crowded tight against his legs he let his fingers fall across the suar's strings, wishing desperately it was his trusty duar instead. One good solid spellsong. That's all he needed from his store-bought instrument. Just one hefty spellsong.

Nothing for it but to begin.

"Hang on, everybody. I'm going to try and sing us home."

"That means you'll go back with us, mate." Mudge looked up at him. "Wot about you? You wanted to come back to your own world more than anythin'. Now you're 'ere."

"Shut up, Mudge, before you talk me out of it. I'm not going to stand for having you and Weegee and Cautious doped up and treated like a bunch of freaks."

"Well, if 'tis good dope. . . ."

"Mudge!" Weegee looked up at Jon-Tom. "Why would anyone want to do that to us, Jon-Tom?"

"To find out why you're intelligent. To find out why you can talk."

She shuddered. "This world of yours is a horrible place."

"Not horrible, really. There are some good people in it, just as there are bad. It's not all that different from your world."

"Hush now," Mudge told her, drawing her close. "Let the man concentrate on 'is spellsingin'."

Jon-Tom sang beautifully, softly. His voice and the dulcet tones of the suar rang through the truck. He sang until his throat was raw and his fingers were numb as they rumbled over rough roads and smooth. And nothing happened.

They were on a highway now. The truck hardly vibrated and their speed had increased. He finally gave it up.

"I'm sorry. Not surprised, but sorry. Clothahump told me time and again it wasn't easy to bounce people from one world to another. But I had to try."

"Don't take it too 'ard, mate. Maybe if you 'ad your duar. . . ."

"I'm not sure it would make any difference. I'm not sure magic works in my world."

"Dull place then. Don't worry about Weegee and me. We'll make out all right. Won't we, luv?"

"Sure. We'll manage."

They wouldn't, he knew. If they kept silent whenever anyone else was around they might be able to slip away to freedom one day. But what kind of freedom would that be? The freedom to roam an alien world, cut off from others of their kind, unable to go home? Fugitives in a strange land.

"I hear a new sound." Cautious pressed his ear to the rolling door that sealed the back end of the truck. "Some animal is chasing us."

Jon-Tom frowned. "Dogs maybe." On the highway? They were doing at least fifty. "Is it still there?"

"Coming closer. Screaming steady-like."

Screaming? Then his eyes got very wide. "Police siren."

"Local cops? Crikey, that's bloody wonderful."

"Not if they see us." He was thinking rapidly. "If they do they'll want to haul us all in as material witnesses, and that only if they've a lead on these guys as dealers. If not, they'll probably just let 'em go. Maybe the truck has a taillight out or something. We're sure not speeding. No, we've got to get out of here *fast*."

The siren was clearly audible now. The truck slowed, pulled over onto the shoulder. "Be quiet. I want to listen." He climbed onto a desk and leaned close to one of the cracks in the roof. He could just hear one of the patrolmen ask Cruz for his license. Then the words, "Open it up" and Cruz replying politely but tensely, which was to be expected.

"Hey, what's wrong, officer? We haven't done anything. You said we weren't speeding, and there's nothing the matter with our truck."

"It's not that, buddy," Jon-Tom heard the cop reply. "Routine inspection. We're looking for undocumented aliens."

Jon-Tom hadn't thought of that possibility. He wondered how someone checking on the presence of undocumented aliens would react to the sight of two giant otters and a five-foot-tall raccoon. Probably not what the patrolman had in mind. No immigration law would allow for Mudge and Weegee.

And just like that the old Genesis song popped into his head. He immediately launched into the first stanza, not caring if Cruz or the cops or anyone else overheard. Mudge and the others packed themselves tightly around him as he sang, wishing Phil Collins was there to back him up with voice and drums.

"Hey, eets no fun, bein' an illegal ayleeun . . . ."

"Come on, pancho, open it up." The patrolman stood impatiently next to the back of the truck. Cruz was fiddling with the lock, taking his time and wondering how he was going to explain the presence of a kidnap victim. They could always insist he was just some crazy hitchhiker they'd picked up. Maybe he'd just take his animals and split, glad to get away.

"Really, officer, I don't know what kind of shape our stuff is in back here. My poor Consuela and I packed for days and days. If everything has shifted it's all going to fall out."

"We'll help you pick it back up." The patrolman sounded tired. He also had the build of an ex-linebacker and was in no mood to coddle suspicious characters at two in the morning. Cruz knew he'd stalled about as long as he could. "Open it, or we can open it at the station."

"Oh no, no need of that, officer. It's just that this lock here, it's kind of rusty." He took a deep breath and rolled up the door. "See, nothing but furniture and one . . ." he broke off. There was nothing in the back of the truck *but* furniture. There were no giant otters, no oversized raccoon, and no lanky, bigmouthed young Anglo. They had *gone*.

The cop turned his flashlight on the furniture. Something *was* moving in the middle of the household goods. The light picked out the shape of a large colorful parrot with bound wings and beak. It struggled mightily to squawk a protest but was too tightly tied.

"That's no way to move a household pet," the patrolman declared disapprovingly.

Cruz stammered a reply. "I know, man, but Consuela wouldn't listen to me and. . . ."

"Never mind. I'm not looking for birds. If you guys were smuggling endangered species you'd sure as hell have a load of more than one." He leaned back and yelled toward the cruiser parked in front of the truck. "Skip that call in, Jay. These guys are clean." By way of apology he offered Cruz a reluctant, professional smile. "Sorry to hold you up, buddy."

"Hey, no sweat, mon. We all got to do our jobs." Cruz waited until the big patrolman had climbed back into his cruiser and driven off into the warm Texas night. Then he shouted for his partner.

"Manco, get back here, mon!" When his companion arrived he saw on his boss's face a mixture of confusion and glee. "The kid and most of his animals got away, but the cops didn't find the coke."

Manco peered into the truck. "You sure? Somebody's been into that trunk."

"Whaaat?" Cruz jumped into the back of the truck. He ignored the struggling, sputtering parrot. "Oh, *mierda*." The two of them started pawing through the furniture, tossing pieces out the back of the truck, not caring if they broke on the unyielding pavement.

Two hours later they sat staring out the back of the truck, forced to admit defeat.

"I don't understand," Cruz was muttering disconsolately. "How the hell did they get out of the truck? It was still locked when that cop and I opened it up. How did that skinny bastard get *out*?"

"Maybe the animals chewed their way out?"

"I didn't see no hole in the roof."

Cruz dropped his head into his hands. "What are we going to tell them in Vegas?" He was running his long fingers through his straight black hair. "That a college kid and some trained animals made off with forty kilos of coke from the back of a locked truck?"

Manco looked wistful. "I got relateeves een Cheeleh I ain't seen seence I was a keed."

"Terrific. Except we ain't got no money for airline tickets and I forgot to renew my Visa. How about you?"

"Just a few bucks for expeenses. But thee man doesn't know when we're supposed to show. We've got a chance to get away."

"Without money?"

Manco gestured into the truck. "We steel got that beeg talking parrot. We can sleep eento Vegas and sell eet for plenty, then go straight to the airport."

Cruz perked up slightly, turned to gaze at the bird in question. It stared back at him with an alarmingly intelligent eye. "What if we can't get it to talk? We aren't animal trainers like that kid."

"Hell, it'll talk. I know a leetle about birds like that. Give them some food, you can't shut them up. Thees one ought to be worth a fortune."

"It sure as hell can say more than polly wanna cracker. Maybe we get out of this yet." He slapped his compadre on the back. "All right, Manco. We go to Vegas, dump the furniture at some pawn shop and sell the bird. Then we take the first Aeromexico south. I've always wanted to see South America."

"That's thee spireet, mon." They rolled down the back door and ran back to the front of the truck, ignoring the spitting and struggling of the big green parrot who represented their ticket to safety.

X

It was a beautiful beach, the kind of pure white sand beach that exists only in travel posters and, oddly enough, in the middle of New Mexico. Gypsum sand, powdery and canescent as sugar. It climbed unmatted ten feet from the water's edge before the first palm trees appeared. Beyond the beach the water was as transparent as the lens of an eagle's eye. It lay like glass over submerged beach until finally giving way to deeper water and the distant spray of surf on a barrier reef.

Jon-Tom looked down at himself. He was intact and unharmed. Mudge and Weegee embraced nearby while Cautious had squatted to inspect an empty shell. Eventually the two otters separated.

"Where the 'ell are we, mate?"

He was staring up the beach. "Far south of where we escaped from the pirates, I'm guessing. Of course, we could be on the other side of the world, but I'd say we've moved about as far as we moved in the back of that truck. Time of day's different, too. Tonight we can check the stars."

"I wouldn't worry about no remaining pirates." Cautious tossed the shell aside. "They won't stop running 'til they get back to their boat, you bet. I don't think it much matter anymore. Kamaulk was brains and Sasheem the muscle. Others pretty well lost without those two."

"Then 'tis about time we 'ad a rest." Mudge was stripping off his shorts and vest. Weegee matched him item for item, throwing her shoes at him and beating him into the water. Jon-Tom watched as they swam and dove with the agility of a pair of furry porpoises. Mudge rolled over onto his back with a sinuous motion no human could hope to match and shouted back toward shore.

"Come on in, mate. The water's swell. Fresh is better, but this ain't bad."

Jon-Tom hesitated. He'd been skinny dipping with Mudge before, but Weegee acted almost human. Cautious was already trotting down to the water. Now the raccoon looked back.

"I understand. You humans, you shy because you ain't got no fur hardly." Then he plunged into the shallow lagoon.

Hell, Jon-Tom thought. It took him a few minutes to strip. The water was warm and refreshing, wiping away the sweat and dirt of the past several days, washing away the memory of the pirates and the tribefolk who'd captured them, relieving some of the stress that had built up during their trek south.

"Odds are that he sinks," said Weegee, watching the human's clumsy attempts to emulate the otters' agility in the water.

"Not 'im, luv." Mudge lay on his back, floating, letting the sun warm him. " 'E does all right for a 'uman, the way 'is arms an' legs are arranged notwithstandin'."

They spent the whole day cavorting in the lagoon. The palm forest was full of tropical fruits and when they desired something more substantial, it took the otters only minutes to produce armfuls of edible shellfish. One particularly tasty mollusc was available in such quantities it threatened to permanently expand Jon-Tom's waistline. Mudge called it a seckle. It was flat on the bottom and full of blue spines on top and when toasted tasted just like abalone. Cut and polished, the shell would make beautiful jewelry. That led him to thoughts of Talea, and home, and induced a melancholy the otters understood and did not comment upon.

It was evening and they were sitting around a fire Cautious had built on the sand. Recognizable constellations shone overhead, indicating they had indeed returned to the world of the otters a number of miles south of where they'd entered the cavern. Jon-Tom had tried resinging the alien song, to no effect. Clothahump had warned him that such special spells often worked only once. He wasn't going to get back home that way.

Their clothes had been washed and now hung on a palm branch nearby.

Finally Mudge could stand the silence no longer. "Wot's ailin' you, mate? Thinkin' about your ladyluv?" He pulled Weegee closer to him. Together the otters regarded their human companion.

"I wish she were here."

"'Ell, she's better off back in the good old Bellwoods. Clothyrump will watch over 'er. I wish *we* were back *there*. Ain't no 'arm goin' to befall 'er."

"I'm not worrying about harm befalling her. I'm wondering if we could find that cave again."

"I don't see why not. Might take a bit 'o 'untin', but I'm sure we could find the inlet where our playful seagoin' friends anchored their craft and then work our way south from there. Why?"

"If it's the permanent gate between our worlds that I think it is, it means I can go home anytime I want."

The otter stirred the fire with a stick. Something that looked like breadfruit but tasted like sugared tangerine was roasting on the coals. "If that's the case, why go all the way to this Screaming Kitty Muse place?"

He shrugged. "We might run into trouble trying to find the cave again. If so, I'd like to have an operational duar with me. Also, I'm kind of interested to see if I can make magic with it in my own world. Or just great music. But Talea's my main concern. I love Talea and I. . . ."

Mudge raised a restraining paw. "Spare me the sappy 'omilies."

Weegee whacked him in the ribs. "Like hell." She smiled at Jon-Tom. "Go ahead. I love sappy homilies."

"It's just that I can't imagine life without her."

"That's good. Go on," she urged him, a contented expression on her face.

"I don't know what to do."

"No problem, I'm thinking." Cautious poked at the fire. "You go get your instrument fixed, then we go back and get your lady, and lastly you both walk back through passage to your world."

"It's not that easy, Cautious. That's what's tearing me up. Talea's never known any world but this one. Remember how you three reacted to mine? And we were in one of the simpler, easier to adapt to parts. In someplace like downtown Los Angeles you might've gone crazy. I don't know if Talea could handle it."

"Don't underrate 'er, mate. She's pretty tough, that redhead. I think she'd manage it."

"I'm glad you think so, Mudge, because I'm not going back without her."

"Right." He hopped to his feet, pulled Weegee up after him. "Now that that's settled, I've something to show you, luv."

"Mudge, I've already seen that."

"Not like this you ain't." Together they strolled off into the bushes.

Jon-Tom stared out over the silent lagoon. A cry of pain and surprise shattered the mood. Wordlessly, he and Cautious ran for their weapons, then turned and raced after the otters.

"What happened?" he asked breathlessly as they practically ran into Weegee. It was Mudge who answered. He was leaning againt a bush, holding his right foot.

"Tripped over this bleedin' thing I did, but it don't 'urt no more. No it don't."

Jon-Tom's gaze dropped to the ground. What Mudge had stumbled over in the poor light was a medium-size cerulean blue Samsonite suitcase. A second case lay nearby, half buried in the sand.

"We didn't see them earlier because they came through here in the weeds," Weegee commented. "They must have been close enough to have traveled through on the same spellsong, Jon-Tom."

"One of them was right next to my foot when I started singing in the truck." He started to pick one up but Mudge beat him to it, began working on the locks.

The hundred pounds of cocaine was still inside, snug in its plasticine sacks.

Mudge danced gleefully around the suitcases.

"Mudge, we can't keep this junk."

The saraband ceased in mid-leap and the otter gaped at him in the moonlight. "Can't keep it? Wot the 'ell are you sayin', we can't keep it? You want to haul it back through the cave so you can give it back to those two delightful blokes who were ready to sell us into slavery and kill you?"

"Of course not, but we can't keep it. It's too damn dangerous."

"Oh matey-mine," the otter moaned, "don't you go all ethical on poor Mudge now. Not now o' all times." He picked up a bagful of white powder. "Do you know wot this 'ere stuff is worth? There's them in places like Snarken an' Polastrindu that would pay through the nose for a pinch of it, so to speak. Weegee and me, we wouldn't 'ave to work another day in our lives."

Jon-Tom was adamant. "I haven't fought my way across this whole world and learned how to be a spellsinger so I could stoop to dealing drugs."

"Fine! Let me stoop. I'm a 'ell of a stooper. I'm the best damn stooper you ever saw. It ain't entirely your decision to make anyways. This ain't no kingdom an' you ain't no bleedin' emperor."

"I know that."

"The rest of us 'ave as much right to this booty as you do. We sure as 'ell 'ave gone through enough to earn it."

"It's not a question of who has the right, Mudge. It's a question of what is right. The people of your world aren't used to drugs of such potency."

"'Ow the 'ell would you know? I could tell you stories."

Jon-Tom tried a different tack. "Well, they're not used to this type of drug."

The otter let out a snort. "Stinger sweat is stinger sweat no matter wot world it comes from."

"Mudge, it's dangerous stuff. I don't want any part of dealing it."

"No problem, mate. I'll take care o' all of it."

"Jon-Tom's right, Mudge."

The otter spun, stared at Weegee. "Wot do you mean 'e's right, luv? 'E ain't been right since 'e slid out o' 'is mother's womb, an' I think 'e's gettin' less right every day."

She gestured at the suitcases. "If he says it's dangerous, I'm inclined to agree with him. After all, this comes from his world, not ours."

"But luv," Mudge pleaded, "don't you see wot this could mean to us?"

"I think I do, yes. Mudge, I haven't led the kind of life you have." She looked apologetically at Jon-Tom. "Not every otter is an incurable hedonist like my sweet Mudge. Some of us do have higher aspirations and a semblance of morality." She stared hard at her lover. "Do you know what we are going to do with this otherworldly poison, sweetness?"

Mudge turned away from her, in obvious pain. "Don't say it, luv. Please don't say it. Can't we keep one packet?" She shook her head. "'Alf o' one?"

"I'm sorry, Mudge. I want to start off our life together on a higher plane."

"Fine. Let's just 'ave a few snorts of this an' . . . ."

She grabbed a suitcase in each paw and while she wasn't strong enough to lift them, she was able to drag them through the sand. An admiring Jon-Tom followed her as she trudged toward the lagoon.

Mudge parallelled her, sometimes arguing with his paws, sometimes pleading on his hands and knees. "Don't do this, Weegee. If you love me, don't do this."

"I do love you, Mudge. And if you want to prove your love for me you'll help me with this thing."

"Don't ask me that. I won't stop you. By all the powers that live in the ground and make tunnels I should stop you but I won't. But don't ask me to 'elp."

"Piffle. Don't make such a fuss. Here." She dropped one of the suitcases. "I know you can do it. I know what you have inside you."

"Right now 'tis mostly pain."

"I'll dump this one and you do that one."

Jon-Tom and Cautious stood side by side higher up the beach and watched as the otters waded into the shallow lagoon. A horrible keening sound drifted over the water.

"Never heard an otter make noise like that," Cautious commented.

"Me neither." Jon-Tom watched small puffs of white rise into the air as sack after sack of pure cocaine was ripped open and scattered upon the tide. When the last had been emptied the suitcases themselves were left to sink peacefully into the pale sand.

Weegee came trotting back to rejoin them. Splashing sounds rose from the water behind her. Jon-Tom peered over her.

"What's he doing back there?"

She shook her head, sounding disgusted. "He's out there in the water trying to snort half the lagoon, the stupid fuzzball. But all he inhales is water. Then he sits up spitting and choking for three minutes before he tries again. Let's go back to the fire. He'll either give up or drown pretty soon now. I'm not going to baby him. He's no cub. Just slightly retarded."

So they sat and waited and nibbled on the roasted seckles until Mudge, looking more pitiful and bedraggled than Jon-Tom had ever seen him, came trudging back to flop wetly down in his spot. He said nothing at all the rest of that evening. The depth of his depression was demonstrated by his refusal to join Weegee in the bushes for some post-dumping discussion.

Morning returned him to something like his usual effervescent self. He was simply too full of life to remain morose for long.

"Easy come, easy go, they say." He was rearranging the supplies in his backpack. "Time to move on an' no use to lookin' back."

"You got over that fast enough," said Jon-Tom.

"Wot's the point in stayin' down?" He rubbed noses with Weegee. "Besides, when you make a commitment you either stick to it right down the line or you don't."

"Pretty impressive coming from someone who's never made a commitment to anything in his life."

"There's a first time for everythin', mate. I never met anyone like the Weeg 'ere before, either. Life's chock full o' endless surprises, wot?"

"What indeed. What do you think about the beach ahead, Cautious?"

The raccoon was staring southward. "Might as well go this way if it's the way you need to go, man. Maybe this time we find some friendly folk to sell us boat."

Off they went, Mudge and Jon-Tom shouldering their packs, Weegee skipping along the shore and occasionally bending to inspect the small treasures the sea had washed up, and Cautious leading the way, his alert eyes constantly scanning the tree line for signs of movement.

"I wonder wot old Kamaulk's up to an' 'ow 'e's makin' out in your world." Mudge glanced up at his tall friend. "You don't suppose Corroboc 'ad a third brother lyin' about somewheres?"

"Let's hope not. Two of that ilk are all I ever want to encounter."

"I were thinkin', there's a chance, just a chance mind now, that someone as clever an' resourceful as that parrot might be able to talk 'is way out o' trouble. Those two 'umans who were goin' to sell us to some sideshow weren't exactly wot you'd call any world's brightest. If Kamaulk could convince 'em 'e were more than a trained pet 'e might be able to get them workin' for 'im. If they came marchin' back through that cave passage with a few o' those lightnin' throwers like the kind they used to kill Sasheem with they could make a lot o' trouble."

Jon-Tom looked uneasy. "I hadn't thought of that." The idea of an enraged Kamaulk returning with armed humans from his own world was more than disconcerting. "We'll just have to hope that nobody believes him."

But as they marched along the beach he found himself brooding over the image Mudge had called forth. As if they didn't have enough to worry about with just trying to reach Chejiji.

"I'm telling you, Lenny, you ain't never seen nothing like this."

The neatly dressed man leaned back in his leather chair and fiddled with his glasses. "Boys, I've booked acts at the Palace for fifteen years. There *aren't* any acts I haven't seen."

Cruz stepped back from the desk. "And I'm saying you haven't seen anything like this because there ain't never been anything like this. This damn bird is unique. Almost weird how it talks."

"Yeah," chipped in Manco. "I mean, you don't have to prompt heem to talk or nothing. You just loosen hees beek an' hee starts talkeeng nonstop. Hee's smarter than a cheempanzee."

"And big." Cruz held his palm a meter off the floor to show just how big. "I've never seen a parrot this big."

"A macaw." The booking agent steepled his fingers. "Macaws get pretty big."

"Not like this. And broad in proportion. Almost heavyset."

"Well." The agent glanced pointedly at the clock on the far wall. In fifteen minutes he was due to watch a quartet of former showgirls who'd developed a specialty juggling act which included watermelons, chain saws, flaming torches and, most important for Vegas, strategic articles of their clothing. Sort of a nudey version of the Flying Karamazov Brothers. He was looking forward to interviewing them a lot more than he was these two street clowns, the good dope they'd slipped him in the past notwithstanding.

But they'd been convincing enough to get past his secretary and there was in their spiel an almost childlike certitude that gave him pause. It was one thing to waste your time on every fruitcake that wandered in off the street convinced he owned a million-dollar act, quite another to dismiss them out of hand only to see them turn up headlining the lounge over at the MGM Grand or Circus Circus the following night. Fifteen years' time with the company or no, that was a good way to find yourself out on the street shilling for the cheap joints downtown. He studied the two expectant visitors. Had they actually managed to latch onto something special? Or had they stolen it from another performer? There was such a thing as a one-in-a-lifetime novelty act.

Wild thought, of course. Talking parrots were a dime a dozen. Cockatoos were always in demand because of that old TV show that was still big in syndication, that, what was it—Berreta, or something. No, that was a gun. And every animal act he'd ever seen required the presence of a trainer to cue the critter. There was no such thing as a spontaneous animal performer. All required direction. Yet these two insisted theirs could perform alone. Dare he risk passing on the five minutes needed to check it out?

Cruz watched him waver. "Listen, the bird's outside in the back of our truck. All you gotta do is come look at him." He was begging and trying not to. "I promise you, Lenny, once you've seen and heard him I won't say another word. I won't have to."

"Is that a promise?"

"Promise. I swear."

The agent sighed, rose from behind his desk. ''You boys better not be wasting my time. And don't try fooling me with a hidden mike or something. I've seen every scam in the book.''

''No tricks, Lenny.''

He followed them toward the door. ''I can't figure your angle. You two don't look like animal trainers.''

''We ain't,'' said Cruz agreeably. ''We just sort of acquired the bird. As payment for a debt.'' What the hell, he thought. ''We gave a guy a ride and he paid us with the parrot.''

''Just sort of acquired it, huh?'' Well, that wouldn't matter. All that mattered was whether or not the act would astonish the blue-hairs from Topeka.

They entered his outer office and he told his secretary he'd return in a few minutes and to make sure the juggling chorines didn't leave until he had a chance to check out their act. Flanked by Cruz and Manco he strolled across the main floor of the casino, past ranks of jangling slots and the intense preoccupied stares of the quarter-feeders. They exited through the marbled front lobby.

Out on the edge of the vast parking lot he halted suspiciously. ''Where is your truck, anyway?'' Not that he was carrying a lot of cash, but it still paid to be prudent. These weren't two kids from Boise, after all.

''Take it easy, mon.'' Cruz pointed to the far corner of the parking lot. ''It's right over there.''

The truck was parked off by itself next to several large commercial buildings which stood on the lot next to the casino. There was a bank and a big discount drugstore complex, then another casino. The lot was brightly illuminated.

''Why didn't you just bring the bird to my office?'' the agent grumbled as he stepped over a large puddle.

''I said he was *big*.'' Cruz jumped the same puddle. ''The other thing is, well, when he does talk he's pretty blue.''

The agent considered. A few four-letter words wouldn't

hurt a talking bird act. Not in Vegas. "What else can he say?"

"I told you, mon. Pretty damn near anything you can think of. Whoever trained him really knew what the hell he was doing. He sounds just like a person." They reached the truck. As they turned the rear corner Cruz acquired the look of a man who'd just said hello to a two-by-four with his forehead.

The back of the truck had been rolled up.

Cursing, he climbed inside. The agent could hear furniture being thrown around. "Something wrong?" he said mildly to the other member of the pair.

"We didn't leave thee door up. Hey, Cruz, I thought you lock eet."

"Lock it?" The other man's voiced echoed from inside the truck. "Why lock it? To keep somebody from stealing this junk? I don't see no ropes, so he didn't get loose in here. Maybe somebody got curious and lifted the door and he hopped out." He jumped down out of the truck, his eyes scanning the parking lot, the agent forgotten. "He's got to be around here someplace. His wings were tied. He couldn't fly away."

"Are you sure?" The agent's voice was tinged with sarcasm. "I've seen plenty of acts where the birds did that." The two men ignored him. Manco ran down the alley between the drugstore and the bank.

"Sorry, boys, but I've got another act to review."

Cruz put a hand on his arm. "Just give us a minute, please, just a minute. He's got to be close by somewhere. We ain't been gone that long."

"Hey, down heere!"

Cruz let out a sigh of relief. "See? I told you it was a smart bird." Reluctantly the agent allowed himself to be led into the alley. The casino doorman had seen him leave and would be after him in two minutes if he didn't return.

It was more service road than alley and plenty wide. He didn't think the two men had robbery on their mind. If so, they would have jumped him already, behind the truck.

Halfway down the road was an elderly gentleman who was not a casino patron. The agent knew this immediately because the man was wearing a long overcoat. You don't wear overcoats in Vegas in the springtime. The smell of liquor was stronger here than at the gaudy bar in the casino. The man was swaying unsteadily, obviously uncomfortable at being the object of so much unexpected late-night attention.

"Hey, lay off. I didn't do nuttin'."

"We know, mon." Manco was standing close to the rummy, licking his lips and look farther down the alley. "We're just lookeeng for sometheeng."

"Ain't we all. Me, I'm lookin' for the ten grand I dropped in this burg six years ago. Lost it in there." He nodded toward the nearby mirage that was the casino. "No offense. They were honest cards." The agent aknowledged this with a slight nod.

"It was a big bird." Cruz traced shapes in the air with his hands. "About this size."

The rummy's eyes narrowed as he fought to concentrate. "Big bird. All tied up?"

"Yeah! That's him. You seen him?"

"Yeah, I seen him. Me an' my buddies." He turned and sort of gestured with his whole body. Cruz and Manco sprinted down the alley. The curious agent followed at a more leisurely pace.

A small fire crackled behind a pair of massive dumpsters. The group of bums clustered around it tensed, then relaxed when they saw that their visitors weren't uniforms. A few lay against the rear wall of the bank. Others rested on their backs, staring up at the stars and remembering better nights.

Cruz arrived out of breath. "We're looking for a bird. Big green parrot."

"Parrot?" One of the old men sat up and frowned. "We ain't seen any parrot."

"Hey." A younger down-on-his-luck gestured with a half empty bottle. "He must be talking about the chicken. That belonged to you, huh?"

"Chicken?" Cruz talked like a man who'd just had Novocain. "What chicken?"

"The big green chicken. Hey, look man, we didn't know he belonged to anybody. He just sorta came hoppin' down here and, well, some of us ain't had a square meal in three days. He was big enough to feed the bunch of us and what with him all trussed and ready for the fire, well—hey, don't cry, man. What was it, somebody's pet?"

Cruz couldn't answer. He just put his face in his hands and sobbed. His partner stared past the fire at the small pile of bones on the far side. "That weren't no cheeken, mon. It were a parrot. A talking parrot. A special talking parrot."

The younger bum leaned back, shrugged, and picked at his upper left bicuspid. "I don't know about special, but he sure was delicious."

The agent sighed. "Sorry, boys. I've got another act to review."

"That's all you got to say, mon?" Cruz stared blankly at the ground. "You're sorry? Somebody ate the most unique act in the history of this town and you're sorry?"

"Hey—that's show business."

With the pure white sand beach gleaming beneath their feet, the pale blue sea on their right and the warm sun shining down through a perfect cloudless sky it was impossible to believe anything was wrong with the world, Jon-Tom reflected.

"Wonder 'ow far from 'ere it 'tis to this Chejiji." Mudge kicked a shell aside. "Not that I'm complain' about the walk. This is charmin' country. Plenty to eat an' easy to catch, but even paradise can get borin' after a bit."

"I've no idea, Mudge. All I remember is that it lies southwest of here and we haven't begun to turn west yet. It might take weeks to hike there."

"Months," put in Cautious.

Weegee was cleaning her lashes. "I, for one, have no intention of hiking hundreds of leagues. If we don't find a village where we can buy or rent a boat pretty soon, I think we should seriously consider stopping and trying to make one.''

''A raft's not out of the question. There are plenty of straight palms we could use.''

''Sure thing, mate,'' said Mudge. ''An' while you're at it, 'ow about singin' up some saws an' 'ammers an' nails. Come to think o' it, why not sing up a couple o' ships' carpenters as well. Because speakin' for meself, I don't know a damn thing about shipbuilding.''

''Come on, Mudge, we built ourselves a raft once before.''

''When we were travelin' to fair Quasequa? You're forgettin' one thing, mate. You spellsang that one up.''

''Oh, that's right. Well, we'll do something soon. I promise you won't have to walk all the way to Chejiji, Weegee.''

Mudge leaned over and whispered to her. '' 'E's always makin' promises like that, 'tis Jon-Tom. Sometimes, through no fault o' 'is own, 'e actually keeps one or two.'' He raised his voice. ''Anybody 'ungry besides me?''

''You're always eating. I don't think it has anything to do with hunger.''

'' 'Tain't much to life if you don't indulge, mate.'' The otter scampered into the palms, returned a few minutes later with several large chunks of real breadfruit. It peeled apart in flat, faintly green sections.

''Now for somethin' to put on it.'' His eyes fastened on the water's edge. ''Ah, the very thing.''

Jon-Tom observed the otter working with his knife and flinched. Mudge was dicing several large, pale-hued jellyfish which had washed up on shore.

''You can't eat those, Mudge. They're poisonous.''

''Now mate, when 'ave you ever known me to eat anythin' that weren't 'ealthy, much less bloomin' delicious?'' So saying, the otter slipped several quivering slabs of coelenterate between two pieces of breadfruit and commenced chewing noisily. Despite Jon-Tom's fears, he didn't fall over kicking and twitching. Instead, he handed a sandwich to Weegee, who bit into it with obvious gusto.

She looked up, dripping jelly from her whiskers, her muzzle smeared. "Mudge is right, Jon-Tom. It's lovely. Have some."

"I don't know." He warily approached the sandwich the otter proferred. "Where I come from jellyfish are anything but tasty."

"We've already 'ad a taste o' 'ow perverse your world is, mate. Now 'ave a taste o' ours."

Feeling queasy, Jon-Tom took the sandwich. Droplets of jelly oozed from the edges. His stomach jumped.

"Go on, mate," Mudge urged him. "If I wanted to poison you I've 'ad a dozen better opportunities than this."

Jon-Tom closed his eyes and took a deep bite out of the sandwich. His mouth froze and his taste buds exploded. Raspberry. He chewed, swallowed the wondrous concoction, and took another bite. Grape. To his utter astonishment each bite had a different flavor. Huckleberry, cherry, lingonberry, pear and so on.

"Mudge this is marvelous!"

"O' course it is. Didn't I recommend it? Would I suggest indulgin' in anythin' that weren't absolutely amazin'?"

"Given your degenerate and occasionally despicable life, yes you would. But I've forgiven you such history." Weegee tapped his nose with the sandwich.

Mudge put his arm around his ladylove as they strolled down the beach. "That's a dear."

"I just don't understand." Jon-Tom was on his second sandwich.

"Wot don't you understand, mate? Why the 'ell do you suppose they're called jellyfish?"

"That's just not the way it is in my world."

The otter made an obscene noise. "Your world don't work proper. 'Tis smelly an' impolite an' brutal. One day I expect you'll be goin' back through your tunnel or cave or wotever that passageway we found is, but you'll 'ave to make the trip without me."

"Or me." Weegee shuddered slightly. "I don't think I could take that again."

"I understand. I don't expect you to go with me."

Cautious had moved out ahead, scouting for the shellfish which constituted his favorite food. Now he beckoned for them to join him, having found something less tasty but far more significant. Jon-Tom saw the prints right away. There were quite a few. They were similar but subtly different.

"All related." Cautious traced several with a finger. "Foxes, wolves, dingoes, like that. Doen often see species exclusivity so much."

"Maybe they're just part of a larger community," Mudge suggested.

"Could be." The raccoon nodded down the beach. "Goes that way. Fresh, or they would've been washed away by now. I think we better go careful from here, you bet, until we find out whose back yard we playing in."

They abandoned the exposed beach in favor of moving through the trees. The village was not far. It was located on the far side of a clear stream. A number of double outriggered canoes lay drawn up on the sand. They looked solid and seaworthy, especially the larger ones.

"Transportation!" Jon-Tom was already selecting a favorite from the line of boats. "I told you we wouldn't have to walk all the way to Chejiji."

"'Old on a minim, mate. We don't know as 'ow these 'ere chaps are in the boat rentin' business, much less 'ow they'll react if we go stompin' into their town uninvited. Let's just 'ave ourselves a bit o' a sit-down 'ere and study our prospective suppliers, wot?"

"I thought you were sick of walking."

"Sick in the feet, but not sick in the 'ead. 'Aven't you learned anythin' about me world yet? Fools rush in where sneaky types fear to tread. I ain't no fool."

"Remember the attitude of the last villagers we encountered." Weegee was peering around a large fern.

"All right, but this looks like a completely different kind of village."

He was right about that. The owners of the outriggers were in no wise similar to the primitives who'd sold them back to the pirates. On the other hand, Mudge's caution proved well-founded as observation revealed they were not the type of folks to spend their time helping old ladies across the creek, either.

Most revealing was the high-walled wooden corral that dominated the center of the village. It did not look especially sturdy, but the tops of the walls curved inwards and were lined with sharp thorns. The intent was clear: to prevent anyone inside from climbing out. Presently the corral had a single occupant.

Each villager wore a single massive necklace from which hung long, brightly colored interlocking leather strips. Hammered breastplates of thin metal were secured to the leather. The individual in the corral was attired in a similar garment, but Jon-Tom didn't think he wore it voluntarily. For one thing the leather was dyed dead black. There were no bright colors, no additional adornments of beads or quills. For another, he was pacing restlessly back and forth as he tried various sections of the wall. Nor was he related to canus or lupus.

Jon-Tom recognized the pattern. Appaloosa, and a handsome member of the breed he was. This world's breed, for only in fantasy did any stallion of his own world sport broad wings like those attached to the shoulders and ribs of the corral's inhabitant.

"Look there." Cautious was pointing toward a big fire pit. Two spits were suspended over the shallow excavation. Villagers were filling it brimful with wood and coconut husks to make a hot blaze.

It looked as though the community was preparing for a large luau. But was the flying stallion secured in the corral to be an honored guest or the main course?

"What do you make of it?" Jon-Tom asked his companions.

"From the way that 'orse is runnin' back and forth and nudgin' at those posts I'd say e'd rather pass on tonight's supper," said Mudge. "But there's one thing that don't make no sense."

Jon-Tom found himself nodding in agreement. Indeed,

you'd have to be blind not to have noticed it already. For while the walls of the corral curved inward and were topped with sharp things, the enclosure remained open to the sky. The nervous fluttering of the stallion's wings showed they were not broken or otherwise visibly damaged. Therefore the inexplicable question remained.

If he was in the kind of danger he appeared to be in, why didn't he simply spread those powerful appendages and fly away?

XI

"That black collar they've got on him must be some kind of ceremonial harness." Weegee was as puzzled by the apparent dichotomy of the stallion's imprisonment as the rest of them. "Even if it was solid lead I don't see it weighing him down enough to prevent him from taking off. He's a big, strong animal."

"Make no sense for sure," Cautious agreed.

"'Tis all to our advantage." Mudge pointed to a long outrigger with a sturdy mast set in the center. "Look at that beauty. If we can make off with 'er we'll 'ave ourselves a leisurely cruise to Chejiji in no time. This is goin' to be a cakewalk. While they're 'avin' themselves their barbecue me an Weegee will swim across an' slip that pretty from its moorin's. We can do this stream underwater easy."

Jon-Tom made no effort to hide his shock. "Mudge, we can't just run off and let them cannibalize a beautiful animal like that."

"Who says?" He nodded toward Weegee. "That's *my* idea o' a beautiful animal, not somethin' with hooves instead o' toes."

"But what about the commonality of intelligence among the warm blooded? Have you forgotten that one of our best friends on our previous journey was a quadruped?"

"I ain't forgot old Dormas. Who could? But she ain't set for the banquet tonight and I don't know that winged stallion from nothin'. Just because 'e's got wings don't make 'im anythin' special."

Cautious looked upset. "It ain't right. Ain't right that those who can speak an' think should try eat each other."

" 'Ow do you know that 'orse can speak an' think? Maybe 'e's a dumb throwback. Sure as 'ell's somethin' wrong with 'im. Otherwise why don't 'e up and fly away? Maybe 'e's livin' out a deathwish."

Jon-Tom watched the stallion as he endlessly paced the interior of his prison. "We could fly to Chejiji a lot faster than we could sail there. You're right, Weegee, about his size. A flying percheron. He's big enough to carry all of us."

"I don't like bein' off the ground, mate. I get airsick, I do, if I 'ave to climb to the top o' a small tree. You're pissin' into the wind anyways. 'E's in there and we ain't. Tonight we 'elp ourselves to a boat and slip out o' 'ere an' tomorrow mornin' we'll be out on the open sea. Worst you'll 'ave out o' this is a bad dream or two."

"Logically you're right, Mudge. Emotionally you're all wrong."

The otter found this amusing. "Now there's a switch, wot?"

"How about this, then? Suppose we cross the stream and free him while the villagers are busy preparing for their feast."

" 'Ow about we tie an' gag you an' dump you in the boat, and untie you when you've come back to your senses."

"I'm going in after him. Are either of you with me?"

The otters exchanged a glance. Weegee dropped her eyes and said nothing. Disappointed, Jon-Tom looked to the last member of their little party.

"What about you, Cautious?"

"Just my name, that. I go with you, man." He looked back toward the village and the corral. "This not right for sure."

"You're both out o' your bleedin' minds. Jon-Tom, you ask too much this time, you do."

Jon-Tom pleaded with his friend. "It won't be dangerous. Cautious and I will sneak up there when no one's watching and cut the ropes securing several of those corral posts. Then we'll run him out of there. Meanwhile you and Weegee can be stealing a boat. We'll meet you where the stream flows into the lagoon. Cautious and I and maybe the stallion will swim back to join you. We'll all be out to sea before anyone in there realizes that their main course has departed for parts unknown."

"That's fine, mate. You write it down. We'll make copies to pass out to them cannibals in there just so's they know for sure 'ow they're supposed to play their bloomin' parts."

They waited until the sun fell behind the palms. Mudge watched as Jon-Tom and Cautious started across the stream.

"You better make it downstream on time, mate. I ain't 'angin' around waitin' on you. Not this time. You 'ear me?" But Jon-Tom's ears were full of water and he didn't hear. Or maybe he did hear but chose not to reply.

"Bloody idiots. I tried to warn 'em."

Weegee put a paw on his shoulder. "They'll make it. Don't worry."

"Worry? Why the 'ell should I worry about them? They've got plenty o' time. We've got plenty o' time." He turned to embrace her but she pushed him away.

"Not to be distracted we don't. Let's go get that boat." She trotted toward the water. Grumbling, Mudge followed.

A single drum kept up an unvarying, monotonous rhythm that imbedded itself in Jon-Tom's consciousness. He would hear it in his dreams for days thereafter, he knew—assuming this improvised rescue attempt came off successfully. With Cautious leading they picked their way through the reeds, dripping wet from having swum the stream. It was a warm evening and Jon-Tom felt refreshed instead of chilled. More than ever he knew they were doing the right thing.

They stopped behind a hut, crouching low. "See anything?"

"Most people over making preparations for big fire," the raccoon whispered. "Here I don't see anything and nobody. We go quick now."

They raced across a small open area and found themselves standing next to the corral. The stallion saw them, glanced anxiously back over a shoulder, and trotted toward them. His voice was deep and resonant.

"Who are you, where'd you come from?"

"Friends." Jon-Tom tried to see past the horse. "How'd you come to be in this fix?" Cautious was already using a knife on the thick ropes which held the corral posts together.

"I was traveling to visit friends. A terrible storm struck one night and the small craft I was traveling on foundered. I fear many of my shipboard companions were not strong swimmers. There were high waves and then rocks. I washed ashore alone and came this way looking for help. Instead I found these terrible people."

Cautious had freed one of the posts. Jon-Tom helped the raccoon tie it down quietly.

"You'd better hurry." The stallion was looking toward the fire pit. "My name is Teyva, by the way. Hurry or they will eat you as well. This is a terrible land."

"Depend which part you live in." Cautious strained against the knife.

"Why don't you just fly out of here?" Jon-Tom indicated the black leather collar. "Surely that doesn't weigh that much."

The stallion glanced down at the ring around his neck. "No, it's not heavy. I think the meaning is more ceremonial than anything else. This is what they place on the people they plan to eat. The fence is too high for me to jump."

"I didn't say jump, I said fly. Why don't you fly away?"

Teyva looked at the ground and his voice fell. "I can't."

"Have this in a minute." Cautious grunted as he pulled on the post. "Why not."

"I just *can't*."

Something struck Jon-Tom in the small of the back, propelling him into the corral through the gap he and Cautious had opened. The raccoon sailed in alongside him. Man and coon rolled to their feet in time to see a dozen grinning, well armed villagers starting to put the posts back in place. Cautious's knife lay next to the feet of a muscular wolf. He picked it up and stuck it into his belt. They'd approached so quietly neither Jon-Tom or Cautious had heard them until heavy feet landed in their backs.

Now they resecured the posts. Their tongues hung out as they regarded their new prisoners. Not a word was spoken.

"Plenty quiet people for sure." Cautious started forward. "I can climb this fence, I think." He started forward until an arrow landed in the ground a foot in front of his big toe. Jon-Tom looked up into the trees. There wasn't much visible among the branches. Intimations of bows and flashing eyes.

"That's where they came from. That's why we didn't hear them sneaking up behind us. They've probably been watching us ever since we came out of the river, trying hard not to laugh."

"Plenty dangerous people all right. Think nobody watching, they watching all the time."

"Not wasteful, though." Jon-Tom nodded at the arrow. "That could have gone through your foot." He turned away from the corral wall. "Pretend we're stuck, that we've given up."

"We are and maybe I have." The raccoon sat down heavily.

"Not necessarily."

"What are you talking about? You're just as helpless as I am," said Teyva.

"There's a six-inch blade concealed in the bottom of my

staff." Jon-Tom gestured with his ramwood stick. "And I have an instrument in my pack."

"I don't think music will help."

"You don't understand. I'm a spellsinger."

"You'll never be able to spellsing yourself out of here, man. You won't have time."

Jon-Tom turned, studied the dark silhouettes of the trees. "Maybe, maybe not. Is that why you haven't flown off? Because you're afraid they'll put an arrow through you before you can get above the treetops?"

The stallion turned away. "Oh no, that doesn't worry me. I could be up and gone before the quickest among them could take aim. They don't worry about that, though, because they know I can't fly out of here. Because they know what's wrong with me."

Jon-Tom rested a hand on the enormous wing which lay folded back against the stallion's right flank. He could feel the muscles beneath, the play of tendons the size of his thigh. The horse looked strong enough to fly off with a grand piano strapped to his back.

"You look all right to me. If you're not worried about being shot down and there's nothing wrong with you then why the hell don't you fly out of this lizard coop?" He tugged appraisingly on one of the leather straps that hung down the stallion's sides, the black leather that was the mark of a chosen victim. "If as you say there's something wrong with you, I sure as hell can't see it."

"That's not surprising. It's not something that shows." Teyva swallowed in embarrassment. "You see, I am afraid of heights."

Jon-Tom stared open-mouthed at the stallion. Sometimes he wondered if he wasn't fated to personally make the acquaintance of every psychologically damaged individual in Mudge's world.

As for the villagers, they were delighted to welcome two new additions to the night's feasting. To make them feel at home they busied themselves adding two new small spits to the pair of larger ones. The fire pit was widened. The main course would now be preceded by two appetizers. Surely a benign providence had smiled on them, blessing them with fresh food which walked right up and practically begged to be consumed.

Why, one of them wouldn't even have to be skinned.

Jon-Tom studied the posts from the inside. The blade hidden in the base of his ramwood staff would make short work of the ropes holding them together, but it would also expose him to the attentions of the bow-wielders in the trees overhead. He doubted they'd allow him enough time to cut his way through.

"We in stew for sure."

"Maybe not. Mudge and Weegee are still out there."

The coon blew his nose. "Nothing plus nothing gives nothing. I think we better try and figure way out of here ourselves. Don't think you ought to count on your otter."

"He's come back for me before."

"Did he have new lady with him at that time?"

"Well, no."

"Then you ain't talking 'bout same otter no more. Which you think he choose between? New life with her or old friendship with you?"

Instead of making that choice Jon-Tom wandered over to Teyva. The stallion paid him no mind as he inspected the arrangement of leather straps that dangled from neck and back, and wondered if their captors would try dressing him in similar garb. In his heart Mudge was coming to save him, but his mind agreed with Cautious. They'd better try and figure a way out by themselves—and fast. Teyva represented the best chance of making an escape. Work on him instead of the fence.

"A flying horse that's afraid of heights. Doesn't make any sense."

The stallion glanced back at him. "Neither does a spellsinger from another world, but you're here."

Jon-Tom adopted his best professorial tone, the kind he used when tutoring befuddled first-year law students. "Why don't you stop staring at that fire pit and relax? I've had some experience in matters like this. Maybe if we work on it we can find a cure for what's ailing your mind."

"I am relaxed. Just as relaxed as anyone can be when they're preparing to be the main course at a cannibal feast. As for your curing me, man, you are welcome to try, but I must warn you that as things stand now I begin to get nervous rearing on my hind legs because it puts my head so far from the ground. On the ship I spent all my time in my room because I couldn't bear to look over the railing. The surface of the ocean was too far below."

Not good, Jon-Tom told himself. "Have you always been this way?"

"As far back as I can remember. When I was a colt I used to run and hide from my playmates because I couldn't bear to watch them soaring freely through the air, playing tag with storm clouds, while my own inner fears bound me to the earth. Oh, I tried to fly, man. Believe me I tried!" He unfurled his magnificent mottled wings and flapped them vigorously, but as soon as two hoofs rose more than an inch off the ground he immediately tucked his feathers against his body. He had a wild look in his eye and was shivering visibly. Clearly the mere thought of flying was anathema to him.

Cautious was shaking his head, watching. "Damndest thing I ever see."

"Don't help," Jon-Tom said sharply to the raccoon. He turned back to Teyva, smiling comfortingly. "When did you first realize you were afraid of flying, as opposed to actually being physically incapable of flight?"

The stallion spoke shyly. "Oh, I knew that from way back. If you're searching for some pivotal event, some deep dark secret of my past, you don't have to look far. When I was *very* young I was told, though I can scarce remember, that I had begun to fly on a training tether, as is the custom with young colts. Apparently, and I can hardly credit this though I am assured it is so, I was braver than most. I tried to fly right out of the stable that was my home. Right over the stable door I went like a shot, a door about your height, man.''

"What happened?"

"I tripped." He shuddered visibly. "My legs hit the top of the low door. One hoof caught on the latch and the rest of me tumbled over the other side."

"Bruised yourself pretty good?"

"Not at all. You see, the tether was around my neck and the door was taller than I was. So I was trapped against it, hanging from my neck. I tried to right myself by flapping my wings but they were pinned between my back and the door. I hung there against it slowly strangling until a mare who was a friend of my dame happened to come strolling by. She bit the tether in half, but by that time I had blacked out. That memory has remained with me always. Now if I try to fly all the fear and pain comes rushing back in on me and I feel as though I am strangling. You see, there is no great mystery about it. Just as there is nothing I can do about it."

Jon-Tom nodded. "Perfectly understandable."

Teyva eyed him in surprise. "It is?"

"Certainly. You can't fly if you're grounded by a childhood terror. Many people know the cause of their irrational fears. They simply have no idea how to overcome them. The first thing you have to realize is that your fear *is* irrational. That all took place a long time ago, when you were barely an infant. You have to convince yourself there's nothing wrong with your mind, just as you know there's nothing wrong with your wings, your legs or any other part of your body." He took a couple of steps forward until he was practically eyeball to eyeball with the stallion.

"You can overcome your fear, Teyva. All you have to do is talk yourself out of it. There's no tether around your neck except the one in your memory. You can't choke on a memory. Doesn't the fact that you're about to be gutted and spitted and served up as someone's dinner make you want to get out of here?"

"I have no more interest in becoming a premature meal

than you do, but there's nothing I can do about it." Again he flapped his great wings. The backblast of air from those powerful limbs blew dust in Jon-Tom's fact. Teyva rose off the ground an inch, two inches, three, half a foot this time before dropping back to earth. He was sweating and beginning to froth at the mouth.

"I just can't do it," he said tightly. "I can feel the tether around my neck. I can feel it tightening and constricting, cutting off my breath. If I got ten feet up I'd black out from lack of air and come crashing down. I *know* it." He glared at Jon-Tom. "You don't know what it's like, that feeling. You can't imagine it. So don't try to tell me that you do."

"I won't." Jon-Tom wanted to be patient, to be gentle. Unfortunately, the light from the fire pit was beginning to glow brightly. There was no time for patience or gentleness. He had to push.

"Let's try something."

"They've gone an' got themselves caught, the stupid twits." Mudge was squatting in the middle of the big outrigger he and Weegee had spirited away from the boat landing, looking back toward the village. Two wolves had been guarding the trim little vessels, but some commotion among the huts had providentially drawn their attention. Now Mudge knew what the cause of the commotion had been, and providence hadn't been involved.

"They ought to 'ave been 'ere by now."

"Give them another few minutes."

He turned to stare at her in the darkness. "No. I know that Jon-Tom, I do. The poor bald-bodied ape don't 'ave the brains of a worm. Got 'imself caught 'e did. Well, we did our best. I tried to warn 'im, but no, 'e 'ad to go an' play the noble man, 'e did. It were 'is choice, it were, an' it don't 'ave nothin' to do with us. We've a life of our own to live. 'Tis time to go." He hopped out of the boat and leaned his shoulder against the side preparatory to pushing it off the low sandbar where they'd beached the hull.

Weegee leaned out and rubbed her nose against his to get his attention. "We can't just let them die like that, Mudge."

"We didn't make the choice on 'ow they're goin' to die, luv. They did that themselves. Wot about me and you then, eh?" He stood straight and kissed her, leaning over the gunwale to do so. Then he ran a finger over her whiskers. "I never met no one like you, lass. Never expected to. Never planned on settlin' down because I never thought I'd 'ave a reason to. Now I've got me a reason an' I ain't blowin' it because some nitwit of a 'uman from another world 'asn't got the sense to know when to mind 'is own business. Jon-Tom's been pullin' idiotic stunts like this ever since I've known 'im, which is as long as 'e's been in our world. I knew 'e'd pull one too many one day and that would be the end o' an interestin' friendship. Today's that day. 'E's made the choice. There's no one else at risk in this. This time the fate o' the world don't 'ang in the balance. 'Tis just Jon-Tom, an' fate's decided 'is end 'as come."

"Someone once told me that fate never decided anything."

"Wot fool told you that?"

She leaned close. "You did, Mudge."

He pulled away from her but he couldn't get away from her eyes. "Damn all females to 'ell anyway. You 'ear me, Weegee? I say damn you!"

"I heard you." She slipped over the side into the water. "We'll have a nice long mutual cursing session later. Right now we're wasting time."

Together they swam for the village, easily outracing the startled fish that crossed their path.

Jon-Tom's halting attempts at equine psychoanalysis were going nowhere fast when he was interrupted by the sound of a gate opening at the far end of the corral. At first he thought the cooks had come for them, but the opening was only to permit the injection of some new ingredients to the stew. These ingredients were unceremoniously tossed inside. The gate was slammed behind them.

He didn't wave. "Hello, Mudge. Hi, Weegee."

Teyva pawed the earth. "More of your friends? You certainly do have a number of foolish acquaintances, man."

Mudge was brushing himself off. The expression on his face ought to have been sharp enough to cut through the pen all by itself. "You don't know the 'alf o' it, four-legs. I should've brought me longbow but the water would've ruined it. Should've brought it anyway an' taken the chance. Too bleedin' late now." He ran back to the gate and bestowed some choice epithets on his captors.

"Very smart this bunch." Cautious was cleaning his tail. "You got to be real quick or they drop down on you from trees."

"I'll keep that useful advice right where it'll do the most good," the otter growled. "Only trouble is 'tis about three minutes shy o' bein' of any use. I didn't think to keep an eye on the trees. Didn't see no monkeys livin' 'ere." He stared straight at Jon-Tom. " 'Course they got one now."

Weegee walked slowly up to Jon-Tom. "This is my fault. Mudge didn't want to come. He was probably right, but I insisted."

"Wot do you mean I didn't want to come? Are you sayin' I 'ad thoughts o' abandonin' me good mate 'ere to the cookpot without at least tryin' to save 'im?"

Weegee turned on her paramour, stared at him for a moment, then looked quietly back up at Jon-Tom. "Everything you told me about him is true." She strolled over to whisper something to Cautious. Meanwhile Jon-Tom, vaguely aware that he might be missing something, walked over to rejoin his brave friend.

"I appreciate the effort, Mudge. I'm just sorry you didn't succeed." He nodded toward the gate. "You bought us some time, anyway. They're going to have to enlarge the firepit again." Through the fence posts they could observe the delighted villagers doing just that.

"Why don't they just cook us one at a time?" the otter muttered.

"That's what I do not understand," said Teyva.

"Maybe it's some spiritual thing. The bigger the banquet

and the more prey they cook at once the better it bodes for future hunting, or something."

Mudge cocked an eye at him. His tone was bitter, resigned. "I knew if I just stuck with you long enough, mate, I'd wind up dead before me time. You know, at the end o' every one o' our previous little jaunts you've always clapped me on the shoulder an' said 'Well done, Mudge. Well done.'" He jerked a thumb toward the gate and the firepit beyond. "I'll be well done for sure this time." He turned his gaze on the flying horse.

"Wot 'ave you found out about the cause o' all this distress? You were right about 'im bein' big enough to carry all o' us. So why don't we just climb aboard and 'ave 'im fly us away?"

"He's afraid of heights," said Cautious.

Mudge's eyes narrowed as he stared at the raccoon. "Wot's that? I didn't 'ear that."

The disgruntled Cautious raised his voice. "I said he afraid of heights."

Mudge was silent for a long moment as he digested this. Then he walked slowly up to the huge stallion until his black nose was barely inches from Teyva's muzzle.

"Mudge, don't..." Jon-Tom began, but he could no more keep the otter quiet than he could have halted a flood of biblical proportions.

"So you're afraid o' heights? With wings that'd shame a 'undred eagles an' muscles like that?" He tried to kick the stallion in the chest but his short legs wouldn't reach high enough. "You four-legged coward. You winged sissy. You namby-pampy cud-chewin' pitiful excuse for a member o' the equine persuasion! Wot use are you?" The otter continued to heap insults on the flying horse until Teyva buried his head beneath one of his wings. Only then did the thoroughly disgusted Mudge turn away.

"Thanks, Mudge." Jon-Tom was shaking his head. "You really helped the situation, you know that? Here I'm trying to convince Teyva he *can* fly by building up his self-esteem a little and you—"

"Do wot, mate? Tell the truth? 'Tis a tough life and I ain't one to coddle another bloke, especially when 'tis my life that's at stake." He sat down and rested his head in his paws. "I only 'ope that when they cook me they use plenty o' sage. I always liked sage."

Jon-Tom turned his attention back to the stallion and tried to peer beneath the concealing wing. "Come out of there, Teyva. That's not helping anything."

"Yes it is. I feel bad enough already and I'm going to die and you're all going to die because you tried to help me. I don't need any more shame."

Weegee was standing next to the gate. "Time for last minute expressions of regret or whatever. They're coming for us."

Moving in solemn double file, a long line of villagers was approaching the corral. A dull chant rose from the rest, who were assembled around the firepit.

"Please come out of there," Jon-Tom pleaded with the multicolored wing. A reluctant Teyva peeped out from behind the feathers.

"It is no use, man. I appreciate your efforts on my behalf, but you're wasting your time. It has been tried before."

"Maybe we can fake them. Pretend like you're going to fly away. Shock them into hesitating for a while at least." He put one hand on the black leather strap that ran down the stallion's spine. "Do you mind?"

"Better you should be composing yourself for the last moment, but if it makes you feel better, go ahead."

Jon-Tom put a foot into the lower leather straps and swung himself up on the broad, muscular back. From his new height he had a different perspective on Teyva's size and power. The stallion would have the wingspan of a small airplane.

"Mudge, Weegee, Cautious: get up here behind me."

"Wot for, mate? If that useless lump o' 'orseflesh could fly 'e'd be long gone from 'ere before now an' we wouldn't be in this fix."

Weegee spoke as Jon-Tom gave her a hand up. "Do as he says, Mudge."

"Do as Jon-Tom says, do as Jon-Tom says. I've been doin' that for over a year and look where 'tis got me."

"All right, then do what I say. Get up here!"

"An' now I'm takin' orders from a dumb female." Grumbling under his breath, he rose and walked to the stallion's side.

With Jon-Tom in front and the two otters and Cautious behind, there wasn't much room left on Teyva's back. Mudge was sitting more on the stallion's rump than his back, which suited the otter just fine. According to him, that was the part of life he'd been getting ever since he'd met up with Jon-Tom.

"Turn and face them."

"Why?" Teyva asked Jon-Tom. "I would rather not see the fatal blow coming."

"Turn an' face 'em like the man says," Mudge bawled. "Maybe it don't make no difference to you, but I'm damned if I'm goin' to die with a spear up my arse."

Silently the stallion pivoted.

"Now spread your wings like you're preparing to take off," Jon-Tom told him. With a sacrificial sigh the stallion complied.

The gate opened. The villagers parted to form two lines leading from the corral to the firepit. Two wolves, a couple of dingoes and a bat-eared fox came marching ceremoniously down the aisle. Each carried a knife the size of a machete.

"'Ere comes the anointed butchers," Mudge muttered. "'Old 'em off as long as you can with your staff, mate."

Jon-Tom ignored the otter as he studied the bloodletters. They wore black straps similar to those that had been placed on Teyva. The last wolf in line held an armful of smaller leathers. Obviously it would not do for the three smaller captives to go to their deaths improperly attired.

Leaning close to the stallion's ear, he whispered. "Now make like you're getting ready to fly."

Obediently Teyva began to flap his great wings. They

reached from one side of the corral to the other. He rose off the ground almost a foot this time before settling back to earth and nearly collapsing to his knees.

"I can't," he said hoarsely. Jon-Tom thought he could see tears beginning to spill from his eyes. "I just can't do it."

"Goodbye, Weegee." Mudge leaned forward to clasp her tightly to him. "I'm sorry about all the times we didn't 'ave to spend in bed so that I could show you wot a great lover I am."

"And I'm sorry," she murmured back, "about all the times we didn't have to spend out of bed so that I could learn what a truly fine person you are beneath all the affected crudity and false bravado."

"Me, I'm just plain sorry," said Cautious. The raccoon shut his eyes and waited for the first kiss of the knife.

"Fly," Jon-Tom urged the stallion. "I know you can do it. *You* know you can do it." Remembering an old Indian trick he'd once read about he leaned over and bit the stallion's ear. Teyva started but didn't rise.

"It's no use, my final friends."

The butchers were mumbling some ceremonial nonsense next to the gate. Blessing the sacred slaughtering knives or something, Jon-Tom thought. They had less than minutes left.

"Fly, dammit!"

"Uh, mate."

"Don't bother me now, Mudge."

The otter was fumbling with the left inside pocket of his battered old vest. Curious in spite of himself Jon-Tom looked back. No doubt Mudge wanted to present him with some final offering, some last token of his esteem to cement the bond that had sprung up between them during the past months. Something meaningful. Something that looked just like a four-inch square packet of white powder.

Weegee's outrage was palpable. "Mudge!"

"Sorry, luv. I'm weak, I guess. Never made a promise that weren't some'ow qualified." He handed the packet to

Jon-Tom. "As the time for spellsingin' seems past, maybe 'tis time to try a little spellsniffin'. Give 'im a whiff o' this—just a tiny one, mind now."

"Right, yeah, sure." Jon-Tom snatched the packet. In his frantic efforts to break it open he almost dropped it. When he ripped it down the middle Mudge winced as though the tear had gone through his back fur. Clinging to the stallion's neck with his left arm he profferred the gaping bag with his right. "Open your eyes, damn it."

Teyva blinked, saw the bag. "What is that? I have already made my peace with the universe. There is nothing more to do."

"I agree, right. This will help relax you. Take a sniff."

The stallion frowned. "It looks like sugar. Why sniff instead of taste?" The chanting rose in pitch and the official butchers were spreading out in a semicircle to make sure no panicky captive could dash past them.

"Please, just inhale a little. My last request."

"A foolish one, but if I can make up a little at the last for all the damage I've done I will do so." Bending forward, the stallion dipped his nostrils to the packet and inhaled deeply. Teyva was quite a large animal. Most of the contents of the packet vanished.

A couple of minutes slid by. Then the lead wolf raised the ceremonial blade and struck. It cleft only empty air.

Teyva hadn't so much taken off as exploded two hundred feet straight up.

The shockingly abrupt ascension caused Jon-Tom to drop the packet and the remainder of its euphoric contents. Cautious and Weegee had to grab Mudge to keep him from diving after it. With his tremendous wings beating the air to a blur, the stallion hovered like a hummingbird above the corral and its stunned occupants. Teyva not only had the wingspan of a small plane; the extraordinary rapidity of his wing beats made him sound like one.

"Well what do you know." He studied the ground far below. "You were right, man. That *is* the ground down there, isn't it?"

Jon-Tom's heart was pounding against his chest as he clung to the black leather straps with a death grip. "Yes. Quite a ways down, in fact."

Teyva spun in midair. "My but this is interesting up here." He glanced down again. "Look at them all jumping up and down there. They seem quite exercised about something."

"I imagine it's our escape."

"Oh yes, our escape. We have escaped, haven't we? They were going to kill us." His gaze narrowed. "Cook us and eat us. Nasty mean old people. We should teach them a lesson."

"No no! I mean, we don't have time to teach them a—nooooo!"

Folding his wings against his flanks, the stallion dropped like a stone toward the corral. What the startled villagers below took to be war cries were actually screams of utter terror. Wolves, foxes and others scattered in all directions. Some didn't flee fast enough and the stallion's front hooves cracked a few skulls. Teyva repeated his stuka-like dive several times. Then he hovered over the center of the village and emptied his bowels and bladder. Having lastly knocked over a brace of torches, thereby setting half the village on fire, he fluttered overhead and surveyed the havoc he'd wrought with an air of equine equanimity.

"That ought to teach them to think twice about trying to eat any helpless strangers." He glanced back at Jon-Tom. "I owe you everything, man. What can I do for you?"

Aware that his skin must by now have acquired something of a greenish cast, Jon-Tom fought to form a coherent sentence. "Could you take us to a town called Strelakat Mews?"

"I don't know where that is, I'm afraid."

"How about Chejiji, then?"

Teyva's expression brightened. "Ah, Chejiji! Of course I know Chejiji."

"And quickly."

"Why quickly, mate?" a woozy but exultant Mudge inquired.

"Because I'm getting dizzy and I don't know how long I can keep this up. I guess I neglected to mention it while I was trying to cure Teyva of his fear of heights, but *I'm* afraid of heights. Always have been."

"Oh, this is going to be fun!" And to demonstrate how much fun it was going to be the stallion executed a perfect loop-the-loop, thereby allowing Jon-Tom to add the contents of his stomach to the gifts Teyva had already bestowed on the devastated populace below.

"Afraid of heights, man?" The stallion let out a whinny that could be heard across half the continent. "What a foolish notion! It seems to me that I was once afraid of heights. I can't imagine why. You must let me talk to you about it sometime."

"You betcha." Jon-Tom wiped his lips. "Could we go now—please?"

"To Chejiji it is." He leaned forward, a determined look on his face, and in a minute they were out over the silvery expanse of the ocean.

"Wait, wait a minute!"

"I thought you said quickly."

He pointed downward. "We have to get our things. That is, if you think you can handle a little additional weight."

"Weight? What is weight?"

Mudge searched until he located the outrigger where he and Weegee had stowed their backpacks. Teyva executed another heart-rending dive, waited impatiently while they gathered up their supplies.

"I could carry the boat as well, if you like."

"That won't be necessary." Jon-Tom resumed his seat on the stallion's broad back. With weapons, food, and the splinters of his precious duar once more in hand they rose again over the water.

Anyone on shore who chose that moment to look skyward would have seen a most unusual silhouette crossing the face of the full moon, and might also have heard the whinny of pure delight the stallion Teyva emitted. Might have also heard the sharp smack of paw on furry face accompanied by a feminine voice saying, "Mudge, don't try that again."

"But luv," another voice then plaintively replied, "I never did it on the back o' a flyin' 'orse before."

Arguments, whinnies and wings shrank toward the starlit horizon.

XII

Teyva was all for striking out straight across the open sea, but Jon-Tom didn't trust the stallion's navigational skills enough to abandon the coastline entirely. So they stuck to the shore, following it steadily southward until it began a long westward curve that would carry them to the vicinity of Chejiji. The farther they flew the more they saw that this part of the world was virtually unpopulated. Not even an isolated fishing village appeared beneath them.

''Not bad country.'' Cautious gazed down from his perch at the terrain slipping past below. ''Wonder why so empty?''

''Tropics, swampland,'' Jon-Tom commented. ''Hard to fashion a city in dense jungle.''

Mudge pointed suddenly. ''Somebody did. 'Ave a look at that, would you.''

''Bank left,'' Jon-Tom directed their mount. Teyva dropped his left wing slightly and they began to turn.

Below them, hidden by vines and creepers and parasitic

trees, lay the ruins of a great city. The massive stone bulk of huge pyramids and decorated walls poked through the choking vegetation. Shattered towers thrust skyward like broken teeth.

"Wot do you make o' that, mate?"

"I don't know." Jon-Tom drank in the sight of the ruined metropolis. "Plague, tidal wave this close to the ocean. Who can say?"

"Let's 'ave ourselves a closer look, wot?"

Jon-Tom looked back in surprise. "Why Mudge, I thought you were anxious to get back to civilization."

"That I am, but lost cities tend to be chock full o' things forgotten. Maybe bushels o' corn an' dried-up old vegetables, maybe bushels o' somethin' else."

Jon-Tom chuckled. "I don't think we'll find any buried treasure, but you can look if you want to. Set down atop that big temple or whatever it is over there, Teyva."

"As you wish, my friend, though I hate to land. Flying is such pleasure."

The stallion's wing beats slowed. They fell in a descending spiral until he touched down gently on the apex of the ancient pyramid.

From the ground the lost city was more impressive than it had been from above. It extended an unknown distance back into the dense jungle, where the vegetation was so thick it was impossible to tell where city ended and rain forest took over.

A small building sat atop the pyramid. They entered in hopes of finding some clues to the nature of the city's builders and their fate, but there were none to be seen. No bas-reliefs, no sculptures, no chipped friezes. Jon-Tom found the complete absence of any informative or decorative arts disturbing. It was almost as though the former inhabitants had made a conscious effort to maintain their anonymity down through the ages. All they found were some traces of tempera-painted plaster which mold and moisture had obliterated.

Jon-Tom touched a fragment of blue and pink color. It

crumbled to powder at the touch of his finger. "Jungle's destroyed everything that wasn't removed. It would've lasted in a desert climate, but not here."

"Not everythin', mate!" came a shout.

Mudge had crawled beneath a fallen beam. Now his voice echoed from beyond. "Come see wot I've found."

One by one they slithered through the opening. It was a tight squeeze for Jon-Tom. Teyva's passage was out of the question. He remained outside, waiting on them.

The chamber Mudge had discovered was in a much better state of preservation than anything they'd yet encountered. Perhaps it had been sealed for years and only recently exposed to the air. The plaster frescoes were intact. There were finely rendered scenes of ocean and beach, perhaps the very beach visible from the top of the pyramid. Fish cavorted in the shallows. There were scenes depicting cultivated plants, and weather, and mysterious imaginary beings, but no portraits of the city's builders. They were anxious to illustrate the world in which they lived but downright paranoid about exhibiting themselves to posterity. Jon-Tom could think of one or two cultures in his own world that had phobias about rendering exact images of themselves.

Besides the frescoes the chamber held several relics. A beautifully worked dressing table or desk with matching chair stood against the far wall. Both had been cut from some purplish wood that proved to be as hard as steel. In the center of the desk was an age-stained mirror. Shoved into the back of the chair was a sword that might have been forged yesterday. The handle gleamed like chrome. An indecipherable script covered the visible portion of the blade.

On the dressing table to the left of the mirror sat a golden goblet. Closer inspection revealed that it was full of water and that the base was of pure rock crystal. Anyone drinking from it would be able to see through the transparent bottom.

Except for these singular objects and the wall frescoes the room was bare and plain. There were no windows. The ceiling was fashioned of exceptionally thick timbers of the same purple wood from which the dressing table and chair had been carved. Slate and straw littered the floor, having fallen from overhead.

Weegee shivered slightly. "It looks like somebody just stepped out."

Mudge put a comforting arm around her. "Glad they did. This is where fortunes are made, luv."

"I don't see no fortune," said Cautious. "I see a desk and chair, pretty but not special. Maybe the goblet and sword worth some money, maybe the gold fake."

Mudge approached the dressing table and picked up the goblet. Weegee sucked in an anxious breath, but no ghosts appeared to defend their property. The otter inspected it from every angle, holding it up to the light.

"If this ain't real gold I'll eat me tail. Why don't you 'elp yourself to the sword, Jonny-Tom?" He gestured magnanimously at the chair and the weapon half buried within.

"Thanks, but I'll stick with my ramwood staff."

The otter shrugged as he walked over to the chair. "Don't say I didn't offer to share." He spat into one paw, rubbed it against its counterpart, and grabbed the sword handle with both hands. As his skin made contact with the metal it began to speak. Mudge jumped three feet. A faint yellow luminescence appeared, traveling from the handle down through the blade until the entire chair was glowing brightly.

Weegee was backing rapidly toward the crawlway. "Mudge, you put your hands on too many things."

The otter hesitated, then stepped back to the chair and resumed his grip. "So wot? It ain't doin' nothin'."

"It spoke. I heard it."

"I heard it too," Jon-Tom said.

"I ain't afraid o' no sword voice. 'Tis the edge that concerns me."

"Higher," said the sword.

Mudge licked his lips, feeling suddenly less bold, but followed the weapon's instructions by sliding his paws upward a few inches.

"That's better."

Like a recording, Jon-Tom thought, moving closer. Same inflection, tone, and decibel level as the first time. Not a suggestion of intelligence so much as programming. It reacted to the touch of a living creature, no more.

"I sense and I respondeth."

Mudge let go of the shaft, but this time the glow didn't fade.

"Respondeth? Wot the 'ell kind o' talk is that?"

"Hush," said Weegee. The sword continued.

"Knoweth all who stand before me that I am the One and Sole True Sword. This chair is my home and I standeth guard o'er it for ever and ever."

"Wot, not forevereth?" Mudge said sarcastically. The sword ignored him.

"Those who placed me here did so in the full knowledge that only a true hero can remove me from my home and take me out into the world where I may defend and profit such a hero greatly." Now voice and luminescence faded together, but a faint aura clung to the weapon's haft.

"Pagh!" Mudge stepped back. "That's a waste, then. Of no use to anybody."

"How do you know?" Weegee looked at each of them in turn. "We should try to remove it. Maybe there's a true hero among us."

Mudge found this vastly amusing until she batted her lashes at him. "You first, Mudgey. You're my true hero no matter what happens."

Mudge swelled with self-importance. "That puts a different light on it, luv, though I think I'm wastin' me time. Never let it be said I let a request from a lady go unattended."

He walked back and studied the sword from every possible angle while his companions looked on anxiously. At last he hopped up into the chair, reached over and grabbed the handle of the sword with both paws, and heaved mightily. His whiskers quivered and the strain distorted his face.

"Is it coming?" Weegee asked anxiously.

He finally released the sword, let out a gasp and slumped

over. "Is wot comin'? The sword, or me 'ernia?" He climbed down. "I told you I weren't no 'ero, much less a true one. Never 'ave been, never will be, an' furthermore I don't aspire to it. I'll settle for bein' yours, luv." He looked to his right. "Why don't you try it, mask-face?"

"Be some surprise for sure, but why not?" The raccoon hopped up into the empty seat and gave a tug on the sword. He didn't strain himself. "Sorry. Doen have the strength to be hero."

Jon-Tom was studying the chair. "Maybe brute force would work. I wonder if we could knock the chair over and let Teyva have a go at it."

"Not me," said the flying horse from beyond the crawlway. "I don't want to be a hero. I don't want the responsibility. All I want is to fly. Speaking of which, could you hurry things up? I feel like I've been standing here simply for *hours*." It had only been a few minutes, but the stallion was idling in overdrive.

"Won't be much longer." He looked to the only female member of their little band. "Weegee?"

"What, me?"

"Sure, go on, luv." Mudge gave her a nudge forward. "Just because that snippy section o' steel said ''ero' don't mean it couldn't be talkin' about a 'eroine."

"I wouldn't know what to do with a sword like that." She hesitated. "I feel a lot more comfortable with a knife."

"You feel a lot more period," Mudge chortled, "but give 'er a try anyways."

She did so, and was unable to move the sword an inch. Mudge turned to gaze up at his tall friend. "I guess 'tis up to you, mate. If there be any among us likely to qualify as a true 'ero I expect 'tis you. Either that, or for the looney bin."

Jon-Tom had to admit this was true. Had he not been thrust into that role several times during the past year, and hadn't he emerged intact, unscathed and successful? Perhaps the sword was meant for him. Perhaps some unseen, unknown power had placed it here knowing he would require the use of it during the remainder of the journey. It might be a thing destined.

Approaching the chair, he put one hand around the haft of the sword, the other around the hilt just below the guard, and straightened, pulling with his legs as well as with shoulders and arms. He tried several times.

The sword didn't budge.

"Why don't you sing to it, mate." Mudge was leaning against the far wall. He wore an expression Jon-Tom couldn't interpret and didn't like.

Finally he had to call a halt to his efforts, if only to catch his breath. "If I had my duar with me don't think I wouldn't."

The sword spoke up. "Knoweth all that I am the One True Sword."

"Ah, says you." He stepped away from the chair.

"Uppity bit o' brass, wot? Meself, I ain't got much use for a weapon wot talks back." He kicked the chair, not hard enough to hurt his foot or do it any damage but hard enough to receive some satisfaction from the gesture. "I got me longbow an' me short sword. Who needs it?" Jon-Tom was staring longingly at the ensorceled blade. "Don't look so downcast, mate. You don't 'ave to be a true 'ero. 'Tis sufficient to be an ordinary, everyday, run-o-the-mill one."

"I know, Mudge. It's just that I thought . . . ."

"You thought wot, mate?" Mudge eyed him penetratingly. "That you were somethin' special? That you were brought to this world for some deep dark purpose instead o' merely by accident? They say contrition's good for the soul. Not 'avin one, I wouldn't know."

"Not having one what? Soul, or contrition?"

"I wouldn't mind having *this*." Weegee plopped herself down in the chair. Ignoring the sword sticking out of the back, she peered into the beveled mirror atop the dressing table and began to primp fur and whiskers. "It would be lovely in a bedroom and . . . ."

She broke off as a soft pink glow appeared within the glass.

"Oh, shit," said Mudge, "not again."

Sure enough, the mirror began to speak, in a slightly less fruity voice than the one which had inhabited the sword.

"Knoweth all who sitteth before me that I am the One True Mirror. That all who peer into my depths shall seeth themselves as they actually are and not as they may thinketh they be: without prejudice, without flattery, without enhancement." The mirror was silent, but the pink fluorescence remained.

"You want it in your bedroom, luv, then you'd better 'ave a looksee."

"Are you sure it's safe? No," she said, answering her own question, "of course you're not sure it's safe. But the sword didn't do anything. All right, why not? It's only a mirror." She leaned forward.

The face that stared back at her was her own, but instead of the tatters she wore as a result of her encounters these several days past with pirates and cannibals and difficult circumstances, her reflection was clad in an exquisite body-length suit asparkle with gold and jewels. Her expression and pose in the mirror combined with the clothing to give off an air of dignity and power.

"I look beautiful," she whispered in awe. "Truly beautiful."

"A true mirror for sure," said Mudge, smiling at her.

"But I look like a queen. I don't own any clothing like that."

"Not yet," Jon-Tom murmured. It was a regal reflection indeed.

She hopped down off the chair and walked into Mudge's arms. "What does it mean, do you think?"

He whispered in her ear. "That you're gonna 'ave a ton o' money, or else we've got a first-class joker on our 'ands."

"Let me try." Cautious squirmed onto the chair. The otters and Jon-Tom joined him in peering into the mirror. Pink diamonds danced along the beveled rim, but there was no change in the image visible in the glass. None at all.

The raccoon waited a moment longer before abandoning

the chair. "I am not disappointed, you bet. I am what you see. Worse things to be."

"To thine own self be true," murmured Jon-Tom softly.

"You next, Mudge." Weegee pushed him toward the chair.

"Now wait a minim, luv. Let's think this through. I ain't sure I want to see myself as I really am. From wot friends tell me it leaves somethin' to be desired."

"Oh go on, Mudge. It's only a mirror."

"Yeh, sure." He readied himself. "Just be ready to pick me up if I faint."

Carefully he sat in the chair, resting his arms on the wooden ones, and turned to face his reflection. It showed a much older otter in the final stages of dessication. Most of the fur had turned silver and the figure was so thin the bones showed in the shoulders and face. Several whiskers on the left side of the muzzle were missing, spittle dribbled from the same side of the trembling mouth, and the right eye rolled wildly and independent of the left. The clothes were ragged and torn.

It was a reflection of a life taken to extremes, of one stuffed to bursting with too much liquor, too much rich food, drugs, wenching and a general overindulgence in all things. Despite intimations of incipient senility, there was no mistaking that lecherous expression. It was Mudge.

Jon-Tom eyed him worriedly as he slid slowly out of the chair. Weegee said nothing but embraced him tightly. He stroked the fur on the back of her neck.

"There now, luv, no need to get all upset."

"It doesn't bother you to see yourself like that?" Jon-Tom asked him.

"Why should it bother me?" He looked around at the trio of concerned faces. "That's 'ow I've always seen myself. Besides, 'tis a reflection of 'ow I am now, not 'ow I'm goin' to end up. Come on now, cheer up. You're depressin' me wot with all these long faces. 'Tis your turn, Jon-Tom."

"I don't know." The image of the decrepit otter still

lingered on his retinas. What might the mirror tell him about himself?

"Go on," said Cautious, displaying unaccustomed assertiveness. "We all done it, you got to do it too. You not afraid of what maybe you see, are you?"

"Yes I am."

"Take the plunge, mate. Probably you'll just see a straight reflection, like Cautious did."

Now that all three of his companions had chanced the mirror he could hardly back out. So he settled himself in the chair, lifted his eyes and stared nervously into the glass.

His lower jaw dropped and he moved his head from side to side, but it didn't change what he saw in the mirror.

"You okay, Jon-Tom?" Weegee was eyeing him with concern. He didn't reply and she looked to Mudge. "What's the matter? What's gone wrong?"

"Maybe nothin', luv. Maybe 'tis just somethin' we ain't smart enough to understand." He held her tightly. "Not every answer in life's an easy one."

There was no image in the mirror, no image at all. Cautious leaned forward and saw himself, and you could see the otters standing a little further back, but Jon-Tom might as well have been invisible. The raccoon helped him up from the chair. Still stunned, he leaned against the dressing table, consciously avoiding any contact with the beveled glass that dominated the center.

"But what does it mean? Does it mean I'm not really here? That I don't really exist?" He felt of his chest, his legs. "I feel real. I feel like I'm here."

Mudge tried to be helpful. "Maybe it means the real you hasn't made itself known yet. Maybe there's somethin' that 'as to be added to make you complete. Hell, I've always thought you weren't all there."

"Mudge, this is no time to be funny. I'm scared."

"Then that's the best time to be funny. 'Ere, let's think about somethin' else for a while. I don't think you 'ave to worry about fadin' away." He searched the chamber and his gaze fastened on the golden goblet. "Wot you want to bet this 'ere bit o' crenulated crockery talks?" He picked it up, as he had once before, but though he held it tightly no glow issued from its hammered sides and no words from its depths.

"You lose," Weegee told him.

"Can't lose when you bet against yourself, luv." He sniffed the clear contents. "Smells like rainwater. Must've dripped from the ceilin'. Pity it couldn't be somethin' a mite stronger."

"As dry as my throat is all of a sudden I'm not going to be particular." Jon-Tom took it from the otter and after a quick look to ensure himself nothing besides water had fallen into it from the ceiling he downed the contents gratefully.

He was about to put it back on the dressing table when the bowl filled with a pulsating blue smoke.

"Knoweth all that I am the One True Goblet. Knoweth all who standeth before me that I will provide sustenance for the thirsty of mind as well as throat."

"Interesting." Jon-Tom turned the empty goblet around in his fingers. "I wonder what it means, 'sustenance for the mind'?" He looked into its depths anew and they heard the voice a second time.

"Beware the Moqua plants."

The blue smoke dissipated. In its wake it left a fresh drink of water.

"Now ain't that somethin'," said Mudge. " 'Beware o' the Moqua plants.' "

"What's a Moqua?"

The otter formed a circle with thumb and forefinger. "Got little bells on it about like this that fill up with tiny bugs. Got nasty bites, they do." There was contempt in his voice. "I didn't need no talkin' utensil to tell me that. But I do need a drink. Pass 'er over."

Jon-Tom handed the otter the goblet and Mudge drained it in a single long swallow. "Water's good even if the advice leaves somethin' to be desired."

It spoke again. "Avoid the lugubrious lescar."

Mudge made a face. "That one's got me stumped. Any you lot know wot a lugubrious lescar is?" Weegee and Cautious shook their heads.

"Hurry up in there." Teyva sounded genuinely impatient.

"Just another minute." Jon-Tom glanced at his companions. "Nobody knows what a lugubrious lescar is?"

"Never 'eard o' it," confessed Mudge.

"Well we'd better stay out of its way, whatever it is." He studied the vessel, peered over the rim at the lady of the troup. "Weegee?"

"Strange, but I feel a sudden thirst." She smiled at him as she took the goblet.

"At least we come out o' this with somethin' useful." Mudge watched her as she sipped. "Melted down, there must be a quarter pound o' gold in that cousin to a tankard."

Jon-Tom was shocked. "Mudge, how can you think of melting something so unique and magical just for its monetary content?"

"Because I think o' just about everythin' in terms o' its monetary content, that's 'ow."

"You could be dying of thirst in the desert and that bottomless water supply could keep you alive."

"Aye, and I could be fallin' down broke in Polastrindu an' the gold in it would keep me drunk forever."

"Jon-Tom's right," Weegee chided him. "You don't melt magic." She'd finished draining the goblet. As it refilled itself for the third time they heard the voice again.

"Buy IBM at 124."

Jon-Tom blinked. Could it be that the goblet's range extended to his world as well? He took the goblet from Weegee and stowed it carefully in his pack.

"We'll decide what to do with this later, but I think it definitely has its uses. Let's go before Teyva decides to depart without us."

They crawled back beneath the fallen beam. Teyva's nostrils flared. "I smell water. I could use a drink."

Jon-Tom sighed. "Cautious, would you get him the

goblet?'' The raccoon obliged, held it for the stallion while he drank, and then repacked it. As he was putting it away Jon-Tom thought he heard it again.

''The solution to the national debt is to . . .'' but the remainder was smothered by the supplies in his pack.

Easy come, easy go, he thought. Better it should tell them how to get to Strelakat Mews.

By the morning of the next day Teyva's wing beats had slowed considerably and the flying horse was beginning to show the strain of carrying four passengers for hundreds of miles. If the stallion were to give out unexpectedly they would land in the ocean. How much farther was it to Chejiji?

''I'm sorry,'' said Teyva, ''but all of a sudden I don't feel so good. Uh, you wouldn't happen to have any more of that white powder on you, would you?''

''It wouldn't matter. What your system needs now is food. You're coming down, Teyva. At this point another jolt would do real damage. Can you go on?''

''I don't know.'' The stallion was shaking his head repeatedly. ''Real tired all of a sudden. Weak.'' He dipped sharply, fought to regain altitude. ''Going down.'' His voice was slurred.

''Look!'' Cautious was leaning out over nothingness and pointing. ''Is that real or am I blind?''

Just ahead a narrow strip of land protruded into the sea. A wide beach lined the green peninsula like lace on an old lady's collar. The far side of the peninsula was dotted with irregular brown and red forms. Buildings, Jon-Tom thought excitedly. It could only be fabled Chejiji. It *had* to be Chejiji.

''We'll have to swim for it.'' Teyva continued to lose altitude.

''Like hell. We've haven't come all this way and overcome everything we have to arrive soaking wet. Lock your wings, Teyva. Just lock them out straight. You don't have to work to fly. We can glide in.''

''I'll try.'' The vast multicolored wings slowed and extended fully. They descended in a slow curve, soaring on the hot air rising from the warm bay below.

For a few minutes Jon-Tom feared they'd land in the shallow water on the near side of the peninsula. Then Teyva struck a thermal rising from an exposed section of reef and they lifted like a hot-air balloon, barely clearing the tops of the tallest trees. Exhausted, the stallion set down on the edge of the harbor district, causing something of a commotion as the shadow of his great wings passed over startled pedestrians.

Jon-Tom and his companions dismounted quickly. "How do you feel?" he asked Teyva.

"Like my wings are about to fall off. In fact, like everything is about to fall off."

"You don't look too good, either. I think we'd better get you to a doctor."

"Let 'im find 'is own doctor." Mudge was in no mood to coddle. "I'm starvin', I am."

"Mudge," said Weegee warningly. He gave her the sour eye.

"I know you can pronounce me name properly, luv. No need to keep demonstratin' the fact."

She smiled sweetly. "Be nice to Teyva, dear, or I'll give you a kick."

"Well matched, them couple." Cautious turned to gaze at the tall stone and tile buildings that lined the harbor front. "Never seen a city like this. Come to think of it, I never seen a big city ever."

The stucco walls, tiled roofs, turrets and battlements suggested a cross between an old Moorish town on the Costa Brava and a leftover set from the film *South Pacific*. They intercepted a ferret wearing a broadbrimmed straw hat and short pants. He was carrying half a dozen fishing poles and attendant paraphernalia which he kept shifting from shoulder to shoulder as they inquired about a doctor.

"For which among you?" Bright sunlight made him squint as Jon-Tom gestured toward Teyva. "A quadruped specialist, then. I recommend Corliss and Marley." He turned and pointed. "Go along the Terrace to the first brick road and turn left. Their office, as I recall, lies not far up that street."

"Great, thanks." Jon-Tom shook the ferret's paw and they headed south.

They found the brick road easily, but Teyva was now so weak he could barely make it up the steep incline, his wings fluttering spasmodically against his sweaty withers. Corliss and Marley's office was a one-story yellow stucco structure topped by a green tile roof. It had a sweeping view of the bay beyond. A few fishing boats were visible out in the calm waters.

Corliss was a nimble-fingered gibbon with an empathetic bedside manner. His long arms and delicate fingers probed the length and breadth of Teyva's body while his partner Marley stood nearby staring through thick glasses and making notations on a pad. One didn't have to be a member of the profession to figure out that Corliss was the manipulative end of the partnership and Marley the brains. After all, Marley was a goat, and it's rather difficult to perform surgery without any fingers.

When Corliss had concluded his inspection the pair consulted. Then the gibbon stepped aside, Marley put down his mouth-stylus, and they voiced their diagnosis simultaneously.

"Worst case of wing-strain we've ever seen." Marley continued on his own.

"What did you do, make the poor fellow fly halfway across the Glittergeist?"

Jon-Tom coughed into his fist. "Something like that. But we didn't make him do it. He volunteered."

The goat consulted his notes. "And his blood pressure, verra strange." He glanced up at the stallion through those half-inch thick lenses. "Are you on enna kind of medication?"

"Ah, no." Teyva looked away. "That is, nothing of a long-term nature."

"Long-term nature?" The physician looked at the stallion's companions. "What does 'e mean, nothing of a long-term nature?"

Mudge started to reply but Weegee slapped a paw over his mouth. Jon-Tom took a step forward. "Our lives were at stake. Teyva here suffered from a fear of flying ever since colthood. We had to resort to the use of a stimulant to break him of that fear."

"Weel you broke him of it, I'd say, judging from the way those wings look. Severe sprain, both of them." He shook his head at the stallion. "No flying for you for a while, my friend."

"Absolutely verboten." Corliss was examining Teyva's right eye, having added drops to dilate the pupil. "Nor would I take any more of that stimulant if I were you. Not if you want to fly anywhere soon except into a shallow grave."

Jon-Tom felt uncomfortable. "Like I said, we had no choice. Everything happened pretty fast. I had no time to measure out a dose."

This failed to placate the gibbon. "As a doctor I have little sympathy for anyone who employs strong drugs without a prescription."

Mudge couldn't stand it anymore, broke away from Weegee's restraining paw. "Look 'ere, knuckles, we were about to be potted an' we didn't 'ave time for careful consideration o' the possible consequences."

Teyva gazed sorrowfully at Jon-Tom. "I am sorry I will not be able to do as I hoped and fly you all the way to Strelakat Mews, but I think I had best abide by the doctors' decision."

Jon-Tom walked up to pat him on the neck. "That's all right. You've done more than enough by bringing us this far, Teyva. We can walk the rest of the way."

Marley looked up from his papers. "Strelakat Mews? What business could you have in Strelakat Mews?"

Jon-Tom indicated the sack containing the fragments of his duar. "I'm a spellsinger by trade. My instrument is badly broken and my mentor, the wizard Clothahump, insists that the only craftsman in the world capable of repairing it properly is a fellow named Couvier Coulb who lives in the Mews."

"That may be, that may be." Corliss was writing on a pad of his own. "I wouldn't know, not being a musician myself."

"Where might we find someone to guide us to this dump?" Mudge asked.

"You can't," Marley told the otter. "It's said the inhabitants of Strelakat Mews can do wondrous things, but nobody goes there."

"Then how can they know that?"

Corliss shrugged expressively, pursing his thick lips. "Who knows how tourists come up with the things they do? Myself, I am not one for the jungle. I much prefer the coast."

"Lovely," growled the otter. "More creepers an' cannibals."

"No cannibals, I'd say." Marley's goatee twitched as he shook his head. "Not between here and the Mews, I shouldn't think."

"Other things, though," said Corliss.

"What other things?" Jon-Tom inquired.

"Don't know. Tourist talk. Traveler tales. Me, I stick to the coast."

"All right then." Jon-Tom's exasperation was beginning to show. "If we can't find anyone to guide us to this place, can you tell us if there's at least someone who can point us in the right direction?"

The physicians exchanged a look. "Try Trancus the outfitter," Marley suggested. "He's the one who would know."

"He's also," Corliss added sagely, "the only one I would trust."

XIII

Trancus the outfitter was a wombat, overweight as were most of his kind. His features seemed to sit loosely in pockets and folds of firm flesh covered by dense black fur. At first he tried to discourage them but when they continued to insist, he agreed to provide them with directions.

"There's a trail that runs straight to the Mews. Sometimes, not often, folks come from there to here to buy what they can't make or grow. I hear it is the most wonderful sort of place, full of talented, kind people. They like to keep to themselves. Seem to find their way to Chejiji lots easier than people from here can find their way there. It doesn't make me glad telling you this, but I will be glad to sell you supplies." And he did.

When they had been appropriately reoutfitted for the hike ahead he closed his shop and waddled to the edge of the city to make sure they didn't miss the trail head.

"You be careful in there." He waved a stubby paw at the

wall of jungle. "Get a few leagues away from good old Chejiji and you never know what you might run into. That's what Mews means: jungle."

"Then what does Strelakat mean?" Jon-Tom asked him.

"Beats hell out of me. We always wondered about that here in the city. If you find out you can tell me. If you come back."

"Now 'ow did I know you were goin' to say that?" Mudge sighed, started up the narrow, muddy track that wound its way among the trees.

"Good luck, friends." They left the wombat waving to them as they filed into the unknown.

Some of the flora and fauna was known to Mudge and Cautious, much of it was new and strange, but nothing challenged their progress. They carried no waterbags, for as everyone knew, jungle water is pure and palatable. There was an abundance of wild fruit and while the atmosphere was humid it wasn't unbearably so. By the second day they were all enjoying the level, easy walk. All except Mudge, who complained incessantly. This was normal for him, however, and everyone ignored him.

One new variety of lizard in particular interested Jon-Tom. Instead of the familiar webbed or feathered wings, this aerial charmer had thin wafers of skin mounted on small bones that rotated on a gimbel-like mount. Spinning at high speed, these provided sufficient lift to raise the brightly colored reptile straight up. Not only could it hover like Teyva, it could also fly sideways and backward. They seemed to delight in bouncing up and down in the air in front of the marchers' faces like so many snakes on yo-yos.

One exceptionally iridescent six-inch specimen buzzed along in front of Jon-Tom for five minutes before flying off into a nearby calimar tree.

"Amazing how they can stay aloft that long."

"Not really, when you consider that anything makes more sense in this soggy country than walking."

"What was that, Mudge?"

"I didn't say anythin'." And for a change, he hadn't. Neither had Cautious or Weegee.

They were walking parallel to a five-foot-high ridge of smooth stone. As they neared the far end the ridge turned its head to block the path. It was large, reptilian, and full of sharp teeth.

"I said that anything was better than walking." The monster let loose with an uproarious guffaw, convulsed by its own humor. The convulsion rippled down the length of the ridge, which they now saw was not fashioned of stone but of flesh and blood. The tail of the snake vanished somewhere far back in the forest. It made an anaconda look like an earthworm.

"S-s-snakes can't talk." It took Mudge a moment to find his voice, when what he really wanted to do was get lost with it.

"Oh so?" The massive head rose twelve feet off the ground and made a show of looking in all directions. "You think there's a ventriloquist back in the bushes maybe?" It laughed again, its great weight shaking the earth.

Jon-Tom leaned over to whisper to Mudge. "Whatever you do, don't make it angry."

"Angry? Looks to me it's 'avin' one 'ell of a fine time." He shut up as the head dipped down to stare at him.

"Besides, there are no such things as snakes my size. I am a dragon."

Jon-Tom had fond memories of their occasional companion, the giant river dragon Falameezar. "I'm sorry, but you look like a snake to me."

The monster did not take offense. "What do you think a snake is, anyway? I can see that you don't know." It sighed. "I'd hoped you weren't as stupid as you look." Another earthshaking belly laugh.

"It all happened, oh, several millennia before the first age of eons ago when a dragon offended the Ur-wizard Ivevim the Third and he placed a curse upon that dragon and all its descendants. What you call snakes are nothing but quadraplegic lizards. I am to a footed dragon as snakes are to lizards. This is a defect over which I have no control, but I am still sensitive to the misidentification."

"That explains how you can talk." Everybody knew dragons were capable of speech. Look at Falameezar, who talked entirely too much. "But you're still the biggest dragon, with or without legs, I've ever seen."

"It's a pituitary condition. At least, that's what the wizard who identified it called it."

"I know a few wizards. Would I know this one?"

"Not anymore." The legless dragon quivered with amusement. "I ate him. Waste of time, really. As a rule wizards tend to be stringy and sour." It smiled at him. "Whereas you look a particularly flavorful quartet."

Mudge took a step backward. "Not me. I'm all fur an' bone, I am. Eat 'im, if you're 'ungry. 'E's big an' slim an' e'd slip down easy-like. You don't want to eat me. I've got bad breath, strong body odor an' I don't cut me toenails. I'd scratch your throat on the way down."

"Mudge," said a disgusted Weegee, "you do yourself no credit by these expressions of base cowardice."

"I know, luv, but wot am I to do? I am a base coward."

They could see the great muscles beginning to tense beneath the skin. "A few scratches don't bother me. There's nothing better than a nice midday snack—except maybe one thing."

"What that be?" Cautious had already resigned himself to ending up in the dragon's belly.

"Why, a good laugh, of course." The monstrous coils relaxed slightly. "Any fool knows laughter's more nutritious than meat."

"Doen look to me, then. Cleverness not my strong suit. Can't recite my last will and testament and make jokes at same time, you bet."

"Come on then, mate." Mudge hissed at his tall friend. "Sing 'im some funny songs or somethin'. Meself, I think everythin' you sing is silly, but this 'ere tree-sized caterpillar obviously fancies 'imself somethin' o' a connoisseur."

"Mudge, I can sing rock and spells and ballads and blues. Even some classical. But I'm no Smothers Brother."

"You're gonna be a smothered brother if you don't do somethin' fast. Please, mate," he pleaded, "give 'er a try."

"Yes, give it a try, man." The dragon's hearing was evidently as acute as his vision. "Help me try to forget the unhappy circumstances engendered by that cursed distant relation."

"Unhappy circumstances?" Jon-Tom stammered. With that gaping mouth so near it was difficult to concentrate.

"The fact that I don't have any limbs, you limivorous biped!"

Closing his eyes to shut out the sight of that bottomless maw, Jon-Tom strove to recall a humorous tune or two. Try as he might, however, he couldn't remember any of Newhart's sidesplitting ditties or those of any of the other great recording comedians. He knew "Hooray for Captain Spaulding" from Animal Crackers but doubted it would have any effect on the expectant serpent coiled around them.

Part of the problem was that while he was used to dealing with serious life-threatening situations this was the first time he and Mudge had faced a threat which insisted on being amused. It was enough to throw any spellsinger off stride and off key. Difficult enough to play and sing when one's hands were shaking and throat was tight without having to be funny at the same time. He lightly strummed the suar's strings in the hope the music might stimulate some humorous reminiscence, but none was forthcoming.

That's when he noticed Mudge arguing quietly with Weegee. Finally she shoved him from behind until he was standing next to Jon-Tom.

"I—I know a joke, I do." The otter's whiskers were quivering.

The dragon shifted his attention from Jon-Tom. "Do you now? Well let me hear it, let me hear it. If I'm sufficiently amused and not too hungry when you've finished I might let you go so you can tell it to another, though I warn you that

I'm hard to satisfy. It usually takes more than one joke and more than one meal."

"Is that right now, guv'nor? We'll see, because this is the funniest, most rib-ticklin', sidesplittin', uproarious, knee-slappin'—skip that latter—belly-bustin' story anyone ever 'eard."

"Bravo. Do tell me."

Jon-Tom looked sideways at the otter, searching for a sign, a clue that Mudge was up to something. Instead of hinting that he was trying to put something over on the dragon, the otter settled down to recite his tale. Not knowing what else to do, Jon-Tom plucked at the suar. Perhaps the music might serve to soothe their adversary somewhat while enhancing the quality of Mudge's storytelling. Despite this determination he found he couldn't concentrate on his playing. Even as he was still trying to think of an effective spellsong, he found himself caught up in Mudge's tale. When he put his mind to it, the otter could be engaging to a fault, and he was pouring every ounce of personal charm and wit into what was developing into a lengthy, complex story. Cautious was listening also. So was Weegee, even though she'd played a prominent part in convincing him to tell the tale in the first place.

For its part the dragon listened intently, its initial casual indifference changing with the telling to enthralled interest. As Mudge rambled on and on, beginning to use his acrobatic body and malleable face to enhance various aspects of the story, the dragon's smile broadened in proportion. It began to chuckle, then to laugh, and finally to bellow with amusement, its lower body whipping convulsively and barely missing Jon-Tom's head while snapping the crowns off a pair of small trees. It laughed and shook and trembled with hilarity, and the only reason it didn't drown in its own tears was that it had no tear ducts.

Jon-Tom found himself smiling, too. Soon he, Weegee, and Cautious were rolling about on the ground, holding their sides. Mudge was hard pressed to retain his composure long enough to finish the extended joke and barely managed to wind it up with a flurry of distorted expressions and a neatly placed punch line. This grand finale resulted in sufficient hysteria to shake leaves from the nearby trees.

Knowing something of the joke in advance, Weegee was the first to recover her senses. She gestured and winked until her companions got the idea and the four of them began, still laughing uproariously, to slink away through the trees. Possibly the dragon saw them but in any event it was laughing too hard to pursue.

"That," wheezed Jon-Tom when they'd made good their escape and he could finally breathe freely once more, "was the funniest story I've ever heard in my life."

"I know." Weegee was leaning against Mudge and he against her. "Mudge told it to me one night on the ship to Orangel. I'm sure I laughed so long and so hard that the crew thought there was something seriously wrong with me. I urged Mudge to tell it to the dragon. He made it even funnier this time. That part about the Baker's College and the traveling lady's choir always cracks me up." So saying she fell to her knees with renewed laughter, clutching at her sore ribs. They were all aching from laughing too much.

"I don't know." Jon-Tom wiped at the streaks on his face. "I can't get past the part where the elephant shows up."

"And the six chimps," Cautious reminded him. "Don't forget about the six chimps."

This provoked a renewed outburst which resulted in all of them rolling about on the ground. When this latest eruption of hysteria was over they were finished, chuckled out, incapable of laughing anymore. Then they picked up their supplies and shuffled off up the trail, unworried by the dragon's proximity. It wouldn't be tracking any prey for days. Mudge's joke had put it in stitches, and it would be some time unknotting its coils.

That night as they were sitting around the campfire finishing their supper Jon-Tom's eyes locked with Cautious's and he said simply, "The elephant."

Cautious replied by saying, "Six chimps," thus beginning the entire round of laughter one more time. Exhausted not by their tense confrontation with the dragon but by Mudge's joke telling, all fell into a deep and restful sleep.

The next day the trail began to climb, winding its way up one steep hillside only to switchback down the other and then repeat the cycle on the slopes of the mount beyond. By mutual consent there was no mention of elephants, chimps, bakers or any other portion of what had come to be known as The Joke. Jon-Tom didn't want to lose any more time. The woods through which they were tramping still qualified as jungle, though it had lost some of the steamier aspects of rain forest. Brush lizards swarmed in the trees, dropping down fearlessly to inspect the travelers. Their relative tameness was a sure sign that this region was little visited.

Civilization in this part of the world hugged the temperate coast and left the vast jungle lands alone. At times the narrow trail they were following vanished entirely, swallowed by the dense undergrowth. This did not slow down the seekers. Not with two otters and a raccoon as members of the expedition.

Cautious was chewing on a leaf from a variety of tree that was new to him. "Not so much many kinds where I come from."

"Far more than where Mudge and I come from, too." Jon-Tom hesitated. Where he and Mudge came from, he'd said. Was he beginning to think of this world as home, then? The thought should have made him uncomfortable. That it did not was surely significant of something.

"Like that one there." The raccoon pointed to a tree full of what looked like flattened apples. "Look like benina tree but is something else."

"You mean 'banana,' " Jon-Tom corrected him.

"What 'banana'? I mean benina. You never seen benina tree, man? Fruit is bigger and yellow. Peels this way." He demonstrated. "You eat one, you can't stop. Want to eat everything on the tree. That why it called what it called. We see someone come back with bad bellyache, holding stomach and moaning, we know he benina tree too long."

"And I suppose that's not a mango?" Jon-Tom indicated a small sapling on their left that was heavy with purplish fruit.

"Look like it but really a mungo tree. And that one there look like nielce but ain't. One next to it got fans like a palm but no nuts, and one here has fruit like shrooms but got branches that look just like a net."

"Like a what?" Then Jon-Tom felt himself going down under the weight of the falling mesh. Mudge hardly had time to utter an oath while Cautious fought to remove his knife.

"Get ready sell your lives again, friends."

The otter was struggling with his longbow. "Wish I could, but I'm afraid by now me own's been 'eavily discounted for anyone in that market."

The owners of the net surrounded their captives, pinning them to the ground until their wrists were bound securely and their legs shackled together. The scenario was distressingly familiar. The appearance of their captors was not.

"What the devil have we fallen into?" He stared in amazement at the figures surrounding them.

"Devil double." Cautious was working on the ropes securing his wrists. "I think they called ogres. I never see one but I heard them described, and brother, these sure fit description."

"Shit, they don't look like much o' anythin', the sorry slobs." Mudge peered up at his companion. "I'm beginnin' to get pretty sick o' this, mate."

"No more than I am, Mudge."

"I mean," the otter continued as they were marched off into the depths of the jungle, "am I bein' unreasonable? Am I bein' greedy? All I'd like is to be able to spend one day in your bleedin' company without bein' jumped by somethin' that wants to kill us, keelhaul us, or cook us. Used to be all I ever 'ad to worry about was stayin' one step ahead o' the local sheriff or tax collector."

"You're just lucky, I guess," Jon-Tom told him dryly. "It

really isn't part of some sinister plot on my part to run into every tribe of homicidal maniacs between the poles."

"Wish I 'ad a pole right now," the otter grumbled. "I know where I'd put it, I do."

Human ogres Jon-Tom could have handled, but this was Mudge's world and not his own. Therefore most of the ogres flanking them were grotesque variations of many species and not exclusively human.

On his right strode a snaggle-toothed wolf. One ear grew from the side of his head instead of the top. His left eye was larger than the right and he had puffy, unwolflike paws. Behind him marched a pair of margays, but instead of the handsome, symmetrical faces common to their breed they displayed long upward curving fangs, piggish nostrils and greatly elongated ears that flopped over their foreheads like those of a basset hound. Their whiskers were kinked instead of straight.

Weegee found herself prodded along by a four-and-a-half foot-tall monstrosity with not one but five stripes running raggedly down its spine. Two of them trailed off to one side instead of continuing on down the tail. One of the major incisors had twisted up and back until it resembled an ivory mustache growing from the upper lip, and both shrunken eyes had shifted over to the left side of the skull. Chipmunk as ogre, Jon-Tom thought. The sight was enough to shake one's faith in nature. Yet none of their captors limped or looked diseased. All seemed healthy, certainly healthy enough to stomp anyone foolish enough to try and escape.

There was a capybara whose distinguishing characteristic was a complete absence of fur on its back and belly. Overhead flew a pair of ravens with three-foot wingspans and necks like stunted vultures. Several humans brought up the rear. They had megalocephalic skulls, hair growing in long strands from their forearms and calves, and pointed, protruding teeth. There was no sympathy to be had from that quarter, not even for a fellow human in distress.

"Wonder where they're taking us?" he murmured.

"Ain't it obvious, mate?" Mudge laid the sarcasm on

thick and heavy. "We're all off to the local snaffleball game. See, this lot o' fancy dandies were a few lads short so they shanghaied us to fill out their roster."

"I imagine they're taking us to their village," opined Weegee.

"Don't worry. I'll use the suar on this simple-minded bunch and we'll spellsing ourselves free like always."

"Mate, did it ever occur to you that each time we gets away from some 'ostile natives or other danger that the odds rise against us for the next confrontation? That we've been pushin' our luck for more than a year now, we 'ave, and that maybe 'tis time for it to run out?"

"It can't, Mudge. Not this close to Strelakat Mews. Not this near to success."

"Cor, you an' your bloody deathless optimism. Damned if I don't think it'll live on without you."

"Hey you, good-looking." A hunchbacked mink with one good eye stepped close to Mudge, eyeing him up and down. "Can I get you something? You want something maybe?"

"Want something? Why sure, lump-lass. I want to leave. I want a million gold pieces. I want two dozen lovely otterish houris to comb out me fur."

"Watch those wishes." Weegee bumped him from behind. "They may come back to haunt you someday."

"Piffle." Mudge looked at the female ogre. "I wouldn't mind knowin' what you lot intend doin' with me and me friends 'ere."

"That's up to the chief." The mink grunted, spat indelicately into the nearest bush.

"How about a 'int?"

The mink's distorted brow clenched. There was a revelation, because she smiled brightly. "Food." She shifted the spiked club she was carrying from one shoulder to the other.

"Hey, 'ow's that for an optimistic assessment o' our chances, mate? Sound familiar, wot?"

"We'll get out of this." Jon-Tom stumbled, regained his balance. "You'll see. We always do. We got away from the pirates, we got away from Cautious's people, and we got away from the normal cannibals. We can get away from the abnormal ones, too."

"Odds, mate, wot about the odds? They're runnin' against us. You can't throw twelves forever."

"I don't need to throw anything but music. All I need is a few minutes with the suar."

The otter sounded reflective. "You know, I almost welcome gettin' stewed. I'm so sick an' tired o' marchin' around the world with you, goin' from one crisis to the next, that me enthusiasm's just about run out." He glanced back at Weegee and his tone softened. "O' course, somethin' new's been added that I kind o' 'ate to miss out on."

"Relax, Mudge. This doesn't strike me as an especially dangerous bunch. Certainly they have no supernatural powers."

"They don't need none, not with all those teeth."

So primitive were their captors that they hadn't bothered to construct even a rudimentary village. Instead they lived in a line of caves worn in the side of a sandstone cliff. As the hunting party approached, a horde of cubs came shambling out to grunt and chuckle at the captives. Two began throwing pebbles at Mudge, who dodged them as best he could and said sweetly, "Why don't you two infants go make like a bird." He nodded toward a twenty-foot-high overhang. Fortunately for the otter the preadolescent ogres were not possessed of sufficient intellectual capacity to comprehend his suggestion or the implications behind it.

The captives were arraigned before the largest of the caves so that the chief of the ogres might inspect them. As befitted a leader of monsters he was an impressive specimen, this mutated bear, standing some seven feet tall. Add to his natural size an extended lower jaw, additional teeth, rudimentary horns, a sharp-edged protruding backbone and it was self-evident he had reached his position by means of something less refined than sweet reason. Strips of plaited vines swung from his massive shoulders together with strings of decorations fashioned from colored rocks and bones. He wore a matching headdress made from the skulls and feathers of numerous victims.

After a brief examination of the four captives he favored each with an individual sneer before turning to bark a query to the leader of the party which had brought them in.

"City folk."

The bear nodded understandingly. "Damn good. City folk less filling, taste right."

Mudge boldly took a step forward. "Now 'old on a minim 'ere, your inspired ugliness." The otter barely came up to the chief's thigh. "You can't eat us."

"Wanna bet?" growled the chief of the ogres.

Jon-Tom advanced to stand next to Mudge, demonstrating moral solidarity if not physical superiority. At least he didn't get a crick in his neck looking into the giant's eyes.

"Mudge is right, dammit. I've had it up to here with everybody we meet wanting to eat us instead of greet us. What happened to common courtesy? What's happened to traditions of hospitality?"

The ogre chieftan scratched his flat pate. "What's that you talking?"

"Wouldn't you rather make friends with us?"

"Can't eat friendship."

Jon-Tom began walking up and down in front of the chief and his aides. "If half you people would learn to cooperate with one another instead of trying to consume your neighbors you wouldn't have nearly as many problems nor spend half as much time fighting one another as you do now."

"I like fighting." The wolf ogre who'd helped capture them grinned hugely. "Like eating, too."

"Everyone likes to eat. But it's an accepted tenet of civilization that you don't eat people who want to be friends with you. It makes for uneasy relationships."

"Need vitamins and minerals." The chief was clearly confused.

"This is a rich land." Jon-Tom gestured at the wall of greenery surrounding them. "There's plenty to eat here. You don't have to eat casual travelers." He shook a finger at the bear. "This business of attacking and consuming anyone who enters your territory is primitive and childish and immature, and to prove it I'm going to sing you a song about it."

Mudge looked skyward and crossed mental fingers. Perhaps the unexpected verbal assault had stunned their captors, or maybe they were simply curious to hear what the afternoon meal wanted to sing, but none of the ogres moved to interfere with Jon-Tom as he slid his suar into position. Meanwhile the otter stepped back to whisper to his lady.

" 'E's goin' to try an' spellsing this lot. I've seen 'im do it before. Sometimes it works, and sometimes it works worse."

Try Jon-Tom did. It's doubtful he ever sang a sweeter and more beautiful set of tunes since being brought into Mudge's world. And it was affecting the ogres. Anyone could see that. But magic had nothing to do with it. It was just Jon-Tom singing about love, about life and friendship, about common everyday kindness toward one's neighbors and the understanding that ought to prevail among all intelligent species. As he sang he poured out all the contradictory feelings he held toward this world in which he found himself. Feelings about how it could be improved, how violence and anarchy could be restrained and how it could be transformed by cooperation into a paradise for one and all.

Tears began to run down mangled cheeks and bloated nostrils. Even the chief was crying softly until finally Jon-Tom put his suar aside and met his gaze straight on.

"And that's how I think things ought to be. Maybe I'm naive and innocent and overly optimistic . . . ."

" 'E's got that right, 'e does." Weegee jabbed Mudge in the ribs.

". . . but that's how the world should be run. I've felt this way for a long time. Just never had the right opportunity to put it into song."

The chief sniffed, wiped at one eye with a huge paw. "We love music. You sing beautiful, man. Too pretty to lose. So we not going to eat you." Jon-Tom turned to flash a triumphant grin at his friends.

The chief gestured to his left. From the cave flanking his own emerged a female bear ogre almost as big as he was. "This my daughter. She like music too. You hear?"

"I hear," she said, blowing her nose into a strip of burlap the size of a coffee sack.

The chief looked down at Jon-Tom. "Such good thoughts should stay with us allatime. I believe in what you sing. You stay and sing to us on all lonely days and nights."

"Now wait a minute. I don't mind sharing my thoughts and music with you, but I'm afraid I can't do it on a permanent basis. See, my friends and I are on a mission of great importance and. . . ."

"You *stay*." The chief's hammer-like hand cut the air an inch from Jon-Tom's nose, then gestured to the young female standing nearby. She wasn't bad looking, Jon-Tom thought. Rather lithesome—for a professional wrestler.

"You stay and marry my daughter."

Whoa! "I'm afraid I can't do that."

Two tons of ogre bear tilted toward him. "Wassamatter, you don't like my daughter?"

Jon-Tom managed a weak smile. "It's not that. It's just that, well, it would never work. I mean, we're not even distantly related, species-wise."

"What was all that you say about all intelligent species working together?"

"Working together, yes; not living together. I mean, living together domestically, in a state of matrimony, like."

"Wot 'e means, your supreme ghoulishness," said Mudge as Jon-Tom's protests degenerated into babble, "is that 'e don't know wot 'e's talkin' about. I know: I've 'ad to listen to 'im spout drivel like that for more'n a year now."

"Something else," Jon-Tom said quickly. "I'm already married."

"Oh that no problem." The chief raised both paws some ten feet into the air and proceeded to declaim a steady stream of incomprehensible gobbledygook. "There." He lowered his paws, smiled crookedly. "Now you divorced and free to marry again."

"Not by the laws of my land."

"Mebbenot, but you living under law of this land now. Come here." He reached out and grabbed him by the right wrist, nearly lifting him off the ground as he dragged him over until he stood next to the daughter. She stood half a foot taller than he did and weighted eight hundred pounds if she weighed a hundred.

"Darling." She put both arms around him and he was treated to the rare experience of a genuine bear hug. The fortunately brief encounter left him with bruised ribs and no breath, as though he'd just spent a week in a chiropractor's office. Possibly she recognized the fact that blue was not his normal healthy color. As he gasped for air the chief raised his arms and declaimed grandly to the rest of the tribe.

"Big wedding tonight, you all come, plenty dancing and singing, plenty to eat. Though not," he added as an afterthought, "any of our guests." A few groans of disappointment greeted this last, but they were swept aside in the general jubilation. The charmingly bucolic scene reminded Jon-Tom of the cheery Night on Bald Mountain sequence from *Fantasia,* with himself as one of the prime performers.

"So 'is gruesomeness is magnanimously lettin' us off. That's big o' 'im."

"I suspect he realized, in his slow dull witted way, that it would be impolitic to eat the bridegroom's companions," Weegee told him.

"Yeah—until after the weddin'. You wait an' see. Or rather you don't wait an' see because we bloody well ain't 'angin' around to find out. First time they takes their eyes off us, we evaporate."

"What about Jon-Tom?"

"Wot about 'im?" Mudge was less than sympathetic. "'E got 'imself into this lovely fix, wot with 'im 'avin' to go on singin' about luv an' friendship an' intelligent species an' all that rot. Let 'im sing 'imself out o' it. We can't 'ang around after the weddin' to find out wot's goin' to 'appen to 'im. Got our own lives to think about, we does, and we 'ave to make a break for it while our charmin' 'osts are still in a good mood." He whispered to the raccoon standing nearby. "Wot about you, Cautious old chap?"

"Afraid I must agree with you this time time for sure. Poor Jon-Tom got himself in one great galloping mess. I don't see way out of, you bet." He chuckled ruefully. "Better he do something before tonight. Making love to mountain could be dangerous. She get carried away, he find himself in pieces like his duar."

Mudge and Weegee concurred with the raccoon's assessment of their friend's connubial prospects.

They put Jon-Tom and his intended in a cave of their own. The floor was of clean sand. There was a table and chairs and a brace of unexpectedly modern looking chaise longues. Not knowing what else to do he lay down on one. The lady ogre immediately settled into the other. It creaked alarmingly.

The official waiting room, he told himself. Just like waiting for surgery. He wasn't allowed to leave the cave but he could see his companions strolling about outside. Apparently they'd been given the freedom of the encampment. This forced his thoughts to work faster still because he knew Mudge wouldn't hang around waiting for him to extricate himself from this new predicament forever. The otter was a friend but not a fool. Jon-Tom knew if he didn't try something fast he'd find himself completely on his own. Meanwhile the female ogre lay in her longue and stared across at him in what could only be described as an affectionate manner.

Frustrated by the continuing silence as much as his unhelpful thoughts he said, "This isn't going to work, you know. I told your father that."

"How you know? Haven't tried it yet."

"Take a good look at us. I see you, you see me. I see different."

"I see two. What more is needed?"

With that kind of axe logic Jon-Tom saw he was in for a long conversation.

"Ever been married before?"

"Once. Was fun."

"But you aren't married now?"

"Nopes."

"What happened to your first husband?"

"He got broke."

"Oh." Better shorten the conversation somehow, he thought rapidly. But his usually fast if not always accurate wits had deserted him. Since his suar and spellsinging had gotten him into this situation it was unlikely he'd be able to use them to extricate himself from it. If only his duar was intact. If only, if only—he wondered if another ogre would find her attractive. He couldn't imagine what she saw in him. Of course, it wasn't him, it was his haunting sweet songs which had enchanted the entire tribe.

"What's your name?" he asked her, not really caring but unable to stand any more silence between them.

"Essaip."

He almost smiled. Cute moniker for an uncute lady. "What should we do now?"

"Anything you want. You to be husband, me to be wife. If you want anything you must tell me. Is wife's duty to wait on her husband, even on husband-to-be. That is the way of things."

"You don't say?" A hint of an inkling of a thought was beginning to take shape in his brain. "You mean that if I wanted you to do something for me, anything at all, you'd have to do it?"

"Except help you run away."

Dead end. Or—maybe not. "Are all the females of your tribe required by custom to act that way?"

"Certainly. Is way of things. Is what's right."

He sat up and faced her. "What if I were to tell you that it's not only wrong, it's unnatural."

That lengthy jaw line twisted in confusion. "I don't understand what you say."

"Suppose I told you—and you have to believe me, remember, because I'm your husband to be—that males and females are equal, and that it's wrong for one to wait on the other all the time."

"But that not right. Has always been this way."

"I see. I wish I had some Kate Millet or Gloria Steinem to read to you."

"I don't know such names. Are they names of magical deities?"

"Some people think so." He rose and walked over to her. It was an awesome body. Those enormous paws with their long heavy claws could tear out his throat with one swipe. The parody of a bear face was frightening. But behind those large, even attractive eyes he sensed an emptiness waiting to be filled, an eagerness to learn. Would she be receptive to new ideas, especially as propounded by an outsider?

"I think you like me, Essaip, even though we are not the same."

"Like you much."

"That doesn't mean you have to live as a slave. It doesn't mean that any female of your tribe has to live in servitude to any male. This is a fact that holds true whether one is talking about otters or ogres. Times they are a-changing, Essaip, and it's about time you and your sisters changed with them."

"How you mean, change?"

"Well, it's kind of like this. . . ."

Mudge was trying to see into the depths of the wedding cave. "I don't 'ear no suar music but I can see 'is mouth movin'. 'E's talkin' up a storm, old Jon-Tom is. I know 'im. 'E can work a different kind o' magic just with words. 'E's sharp enough to confuse a magistrate. You'll see, luv. In a few 'ours 'e'll 'ave 'er spoutin' sweat reasonableness."

Before long Essaip emerged from the cave spouting, all right, but she didn't sound very reasonable. She sounded steamed. When the two guards refused to let Jon-Tom exit behind her she knocked both of them into the bushes.

Another warrior, a large jaguar ogre, stepped in her path and tried to halt her.

"Is not good for bride to leave wedding cave before feast."

"Ahhhh, shaddup you, you—male!" The jaguar's jaw connected with a paw only slightly smaller than a 725-15 radial ply tire.

Other warriors came running to try and quiet the chief's daughter, who had apparently gone berserk. No one bothered to stop Jon-Tom. He strolled past the battle royal toward the staring otters, grinning like the Cheshire cat.

Mudge turned to his lady. "Get ready to leave."

"What? But just because she's fighting with the guards doesn't mean they're going to let us walk out of camp."

"Just be ready. 'Tis like I told you: Jon-Tom don't always need to sing to work magic."

Behind them the rest of the tribe's females had put aside domestic tasks and emerged from their caves. They listened intently as Essaip recited the feminist litany Jon-Tom had relayed to her while she simultaneously fought off half a dozen hunters. Most of the male ogres were off preparing the wedding ground for the nighttime ceremony. They would have found Essaip's speech most interesting. Growls and grunts began to issue from the tightly packed cluster of females.

Weegee picked up a few sentences. "This is very interesting." Mudge tugged on her arm.

"Come on, luv, we've got to be ready to leave when Jon-Tom reaches us."

She held back. "Extremely interesting. I've never heard the like before." Mudge overheard, too. His tugs began to take on an aura of desperation.

Abruptly the fighting ceased. The chief and the rest of the warriors had returned. "Not nice to begin festivities without us," he said disapprovingly. "Plenty of time to play after wedding ceremony complete."

"No wedding ceremony."

The chief gaped at his daughter. "SAY WHAT?"

"No wedding ceremony." Breathing hard, her fur mussed, Essaip was clearly in no mood to back down. "Who you think you are to give order like that?"

"Who I think I—I am your father! I am chief of this tribe!" The giant's face was flushed, a remarkable sight.

"By what right you make such a demand?"

Speechless, the chief waded through his warriors, scattering them left and right, and tried to cuff her across the muzzle. She blocked the blow and caught him with a return right to the chops. Several warriors stepped up to grab her. As they did so they were set upon by the tribe's females. Shouts and snarls filled the hitherto peaceful evening air, along with bits of fur and flesh.

Abandoning the fight, the chief chose instead to confront Jon-Tom as he was trying to tiptoe inconspicuously around the dust of battle.

"You! You have brought this trouble among us. You have been talking to my daughter and filling her head with superstitious nonsense. What evil magic have you worked? Marriage is off. Dinner is back on." He reached for Jon-Tom, who skipped back out of the way.

"Essaip!" He called to her several times, but she was too busy raising male consciousness by cracking skulls to help.

The chief advanced, grinning nastily. "I going to eat you myself, have you raw for dinner. One piece at a time. I think I start with head first." He reached out again. Jon-Tom saw Mudge running to recover his longbow but he knew the otter would never make it in time. His oh-so-clever scheme had backfired. Mudge was right. The odds had finally run out.

A massive shadow interposed itself between him and the chief and thundered, "You not going to eat anyone without my permission." The ground shook as the new arrival moved forward to engage the chief in combat.

"Come on, mate!" Mudge had his longbow in hand, but there was no reason to use it now. "Let's get out o' 'ere."

A bit stunned by the extent of the reaction he'd provoked among the tribe's ladies, Jon-Tom allowed himself to be led from the scene of battle. No one tried to stop him and his companions as they recovered their supplies and slipped unnoticed into the forest.

"Who was that?" he finally mumbled when they had put the village a safe distance behind them. "Who saved me?"

"I'm not sure," said Weegee, "but I think it must have been Mrs. Chief. I still don't understand quite what happened, Jon-Tom. What on earth did you tell the daughter to make her and the other females react so violently?"

"I had no idea how they'd react, to tell you the truth. All I did was sit her down and tell her about . . . ."

"Right, mate," said Mudge energetically, "we can get to all that later, wot? Right now we need to save our breath for puttin' as many trees between ourselves and that lot as we can."

"Sure, but I . . . ."

"Sure but you can talk about it later, when we 'ave a chance to sit down an' chat without worryin' about no pursuit, right?"

Jon-Tom caught the otter's drift and shut up. There was no harm in acceding to his friend's unspoken request for silence. He doubted Weegee needed any otherworldly philosophical help anyway.

XIV

The ogres did not follow. Jon-Tom suspected they wouldn't. They were too busy sorting out their own lives to worry about their former captives.

Mudge should have been cheered by their easy escape. Instead, the otter tramped along enveloped in melancholy, his expression dour. When he replied to questions it was in monosyllables. Finally Jon-Tom asked him if anything was wrong.

''O' course somethin's wrong, mate. I'm tired. Tired o' stinkin' jungle, tired o' runnin', tired o' followin' you 'alfway around the world every time I think life's settled back to somethin' like normal. An' there's somethin' else, too.'' By way of illustration be began scratching under his left arm, working his way around to his back.

''Ever since we left Chejiji I've been itchin'. Last few days 'tis gotten considerable worse. I must've picked up some kind o' rash. Worst place is in the middle o' me back, but I can't reach back there."

"You should've said something, love." Weegee halted and began peeling off his vest. "Let me have a look."

They took a standing break while she inspected Mudge's back and shoulders.

"Well, wot is it?" he asked when she didn't comment. When she finally did speak it wasn't to him.

"Jon-Tom, I think you'd better come have a look at this."

He did so, and was too shocked by what he saw to say anything.

All the hair on the otter's back had fallen out. A glance beneath the arm where he'd just been scratching showed that the fur there was likewise coming out. Weegee brushed her paw across the back of his leg and came away with a whole handful of fur.

"Wot's the matter with you two? Wot's wrong?"

"I'm afraid it's more than just a rash, Mudge."

"Wot do you mean, more than a rash? 'Ave I got leprosy or somethin'?"

"No—not exactly," Weegee murmured.

That brought Mudge around sharply. "Wot do you mean, 'not exactly'? Will somebody kindly tell me wot's wrong? 'Tis just a damn itch. See?" He rubbed his right forearm. When he brought his paw back he'd left behind a bare strip of skin. "Oh me haunches an' little sisters." Horrified, he stared up at Jon-Tom. "You got to stop it, mate." A patch of fur fell from his forehead. "Do somethin', spellsing it awaaaay." He was hopping about frantically, the fur fairly flying off him.

"I'll try, Mudge." He whipped the suar around and sang the most appropriate songs he could think of, ending with a rousing chorus of the title tune from the musical, *Hair.* All to no avail. Mudge's alopecia continued to worsen. When the exhausted otter finally ran down several minutes later there wasn't a tuft of fur on his denuded form.

Cautious regarded him with his usual phlegmatic state. "Never seen a bald otter before. Ain't pretty."

"Wot am I goin' to doooo!"

"Stop moaning, for one thing," Jon-Tom chided him.

"I might as well be dead."

"And don't talk like that."

Weegee was leaning on Mudge, trying to comfort him. Now she pulled away slightly to peer at his spine. "Wait a minute. I think it's starting to grow back already."

"Don't tease me, luv. I know I'm doomed to wander the world like this, an outcast, furless and naked like some mutated 'uman."

"No, really." There was genuine excitement in her voice. "Look here." She raised his left arm to his face. Jon-Tom looked, too. Sure enough, little nubs of fur were sprouting through the skin. They could see them growing.

Mudge all but leaped into the air with relief. "Comin' back she is! Wot a relief. I thought 'twas all over for poor Mudge. Wouldn't 'ave been able to show me face in any o' me old 'aunts. Come on, mates, let's not 'ang around 'ere. I might get reinfected."

By late that night half-inch long fur, dark brown and glossy, covered the otter's entire body. By morning it had grown back to its normal length. Each bristle was unusually thick, but the color and feel were otherwise correct and Mudge could have cared less about the one unnoticeable variation. He looked like himself again.

Toward the end of the day he no longer did.

"When do you suppose this'll stop growin'?" He was staring down at himself and muttering.

"Don't worry about it." Weegee gave him a reassuring caress. "If it gets any longer we can always give you a trim."

Trouble was, it continued to grow and short of swords they had nothing to trim it with. So it continued to lengthen, growing at the same steady extraordinary speed, until it was a foot long. This slowed their progress since Mudge had a tendency to step on and trip over the fur growing from his feet. He'd long since had to removed his boots. Finally it was decided to resort to the use of a short sword, but trimming it back only accelerated the rate of regrowth.

By the morning of the next day the quartet included three anxious travelers and a shambling ball of fuzz. Mudge was reduced to holding the fur away from his eyes in order to see.

"You look like the sheepdog that ate Seattle."

"This is gettin' bloody absurd, mate. Pretty soon I won't be able to walk."

"Then we roll you into Strelakat Mews." Cautious ducked beneath a branch. "I hope among their master craftsfolk there be a master barber."

"And I've about had it with the clever comments!" the otter bawled angrily. He would have taken a swing at the raccoon except that he could barely move his arms.

By afternoon a light rain was falling and, perhaps by coincidence, so was the fur. It came out in four-foot long strands. When the last hank lay upon the ground there stretched out behind them a trail of fur sufficient to fill a couple of goodsized mattresses. Mudge was bare-ass bald again.

Yet new bristles were already starting to appear on his back. By nightfall his coat had grown back to normal.

"Maybe we'll wake up in the mornin' an' I'll be meself again," he said hopefully as he wrapped himself in a light bedroll.

"I'm sure you will." Weegee patted him soothingly. "It's been a terrible couple of days for you but I bet the infection's run its course. You've lost it all, had it come back in multiples, lost that and regained it again. Surely nothing else can happen." She lay down next to him.

The main problem with jungle trekking, Jon-Tom reflected, was that you sweated all the time. Not that it mattered to anyone but him, since odor was an accepted bodily condition in this world. But he wasn't used to smelling as strongly as Mudge, say, and he was finding it increasingly difficult to ignore his own intensifying aroma.

For a change he was the first one up. The camp was silent. Weegee slept comfortably on her side and Cautious lay on his belly not far away. But where was Mudge? Had the otter wandered off in a fit of depression and perhaps fallen into one? The cycle of too much fur–none at all had stressed his stubby companion considerably. A quick inspection of the camp revealed no sign of the otter.

"Weegee." He shook her firmly. "Wake up, Weegee."

She sat up fast. Otters do not awaken gradually. "What's wrong, Jon-Tom?"

"Mudge has disappeared."

She was on her feet fast and he moved to wake Cautious.

"Ain't here." The raccoon turned a slow circle. "Wonder what happened to him, you bet."

"He's always hungry," said a worried Weegee. "Maybe he's just gone berry hunting or something. Let's shout his name simultaneously and see what happens."

"Right." Jon-Tom cupped his hands to his mouth. "All together now: one, two, three . . . ."

"MUDGE!"

This provoked an immediate response, but not from a distant section of forest. "Will you lot kindly shut up so a body can finish 'is bleedin' sleep?"

The voice seemed to come from close by, but though they searched carefully there was no sign of its source.

"Mudge? Mudge, where are you?" Weegee looked up at Jon-Tom. "Has he gone invisible?"

"No, I ain't gone invisible," the otter groused. "You've all gone blind is wot."

Jon-Tom nodded to his left. "I think he's sleeping under that flower bed over there." Sure enough, when he walked over and parted the blossoms a pair of angry brown eyes glared back at him, blinking sleepily.

"Gone deaf, too. I said I were tryin' to catch up on me sleep, mate. Do I boot you out o' bed when you're sleepin' late?"

Jon-Tom took a deep breath as he stepped back. "I think you'd better take a good look at yourself, Mudge."

"Cor, wot is it this time?" The flower bed sat up slowly. "No fur? Too much fur?" He glanced downward and his voice became an outraged squeak. "Oh me god, now wot's 'appened to me?"

What had happened was as obvious as it was unprecedented. During the night Mudge's fur had returned to its normal length and consistency but with one notable exception. The slight thickening they had noticed at the tip of each bristle had blossomed into—well, into blossoms. Each bristle was tipped with a brightly hued flower. Other than being a bit thicker and tougher than most, the petals appeared perfectly flower-like.

Weegee found more than a dozen different types. "Daisies, bluebells, yellowlips, murcockles, redbells, twoclovers—why Mudge, you're beautiful. And you smell nice, too."

"I don't want to be beautiful! I don't want to smell nice!" The apoplectic otter was dancing in an angry circle and waving his arms at the injustice of it all. Petals flew off him as he flailed at the air. He looked like a piece of a Rose Parade float making a break for freedom. Eventually he ran out of steam and settled down in a disconsolate lump—a very pretty lump, Jon-Tom mused.

"Woe is me. Wot's to become o' poor Mudge?"

"Take it easy." Jon-Tom put an arm around a flowered shoulder. A happy bee buzzed busily atop one ear. "I'm sure this conditon will pass quickly just like all the others. And to think you're always calling me a blooming idiot."

Mudge let out a shriek and charged his friend, but Jon-Tom had anticipated the attack and dodged out of the way. Normally Mudge would have run him down, but he was so encumbered by his floral fur that Jon-Tom was able to elude him.

"Vicious," he mumbled. "Vicious an' evil an' sarcastic, you grinnin' ape." He looked down at himself, spreading his arms. "Positively 'umiliatin'."

"Look at it this way," Jon-Tom told him from a safe distance, "if we have to hide from any pursuers you're already perfectly camouflaged."

"Jokes. 'Ere I'm sufferin' terrible an' me best friend 'as to make jokes."

Jon-Tom put his chin in hand and studied the otter with exaggerated seriousness. "I don't know whether we should have you mowed or fertilized."

Even Weegee was not immune. "Don't worry, dearest. I'll make sure to water you twice a week."

Mudge sat down on flowery hindquarters. "I 'ate the both o' you. Individually an' with malice aforethought. Also afterthought."

"Now Mudgey . . . ." Weegee moved to caress him but he pulled away.

"Don't you touch me." He didn't retreat a second time, however.

She began plucking petals from one of his blooms. "He loves me, he loves me not."

By the time she'd finished plucking him there wasn't a petal left on his back. Nor did the flowers rebloom. The bristles that moments earlier had doubled as stems stayed bare.

"See, Mudge? Under the flowers your fur is normal." Together they began removing the rest of the blossoms.

There was a lot of hair and a lot of petals and plucking kept them busy the rest of the way to Strelakat Mews. By the time they were approaching the outskirts of the town Mudge looked and felt like his old self again. The mysterious (if colorful) disease had run its course. A good thing, too, since Mudge and Weegee were worn out from three days of continuous plucking.

There was no road sign, no warning. They didn't so much march into Strelakat Mews as stumble into it.

Jon-Tom had been too preoccupied with other matters to envision the town in his mind, so he wasn't prepared for the enchanting reality. Neither were his companions. It cast an immediate spell over all of them. All the dangers and travails of the long journey were behind now. They could relax, take it easy, and let themselves succumb to the charm of this unique community carved out of the middle of the Mews.

At the edge of the town the jungle had been pruned rather than merely cleared away. Those trees and bushes which put forth large flowers had been left intact to lend their color and fragrance to the periphery. No one pointed this out to Mudge as he was still somewhat sensitive where the matter of blossoms was concerned. Any mention of flowers tended to tilt him to the homicidal.

A single cobblestone street wound its way through town, its very existence as astonishing as the precision with which the stones had been set. Jon-Tom could only try to imagine where the townsfolk had quarried perfect cobblestones in the middle of the jungle.

The first shop they passed was a bakery, from which such wonderful smells issued that even the grumpy Mudge began to salivate. As was true of every establishment they passed, the exterior reflected the inhabitant's occupation. The roofing shingles resembled slabs of chocolate. Surely the window panes were fashioned of spun sugar, the doors and paneling of gingerbead, and the lintels of strudel. Ropes of red licorice bound candy logs together. Yet all was illusion, as Mudge discovered when he tried to steal a quick lick of spongecake fence only to discover it was made of wood and not flour.

A master sculptor's residence was hewn from white marble which had been buffed to such a high polish not even a solitary raindrop could cling to it. Woodworkers' homes were miracles of elaborate carving, baroque with curlicues and reliefs. Seamless joints were covered with fruitwood veneers. Such work was normally reserved for the fashioning of fine furniture.

A painter's house was a landscape of mountains and clouds set down amidst green jungle. A rainbow seemed to move across the face of the building.

"Magic," said Cautious.

"Not magic. Superior artistry. Superior skill and craftsmanship."

They passed a mason's house, an infinity of tiny colored stones set in an almost invisible matrix. A furniture maker's establishment resembled a giant overstuffed settee surmounted by a dining room table. But nowhere did they see a storefront or home that suggested its owner was a maker of musical instruments.

They finally had to stop outside the house of a master weaver. Jon-Tom rang the bell set in the door of woven reeds, a rectangle of brown against walls of dyed wool, alpaca and qiviot. The weaver was a four-foot-tall paca, built like a pear and clad in a simple tunic. She rested against the door jamb while she pondered the stranger's story.

"I don't know that you should bother Couvier Coulb," she said at last.

Jon-Tom relaxed slightly. At least they'd come to the right place. He said as much to the weaver.

"Oh, this is the right place, yes." She looked into his eyes, studied his face. "You've come a long way. And you say you are a spellsinger?"

Jon-Tom slid the sack containing the remnants of his duar off his shoulder and exhibited the contents. "Yes. My mentor, the wizard Clothahump, said that in all the world only Couvier Coulb might have the skill necessary to repair my duar."

"A magical device." She eyed it curiously. "Not many of us here deal with magic, though visitors think otherwise. Shomat the baker now, he can make decorations dance atop his cakes and spin spun sugar webbing spiders mistake for their own. Couvier Coulb knows also a trick or two." She sighed, apparently arriving at a conclusion to some unspoken internal argument. "I can show you where he lives." She stepped out onto the cotton porch and pointed.

"You go to the end of the main street. A trail turns to the left. Don't take that one. Take the one after it. The house you want lies at its end a short walk from town, back in the trees beside a waterfall. You can't mistake it for anyone else's place.

"Be quiet in your approach. If there is no response when you knock on the door, please leave as silently as you came."

Jon-Tom was carefully repacking the pieces of his duar. "Don't worry. I wouldn't be here unless it was an emergency."

"You do not understand. You see, I fear you may have come too late. Couvier Coulb is dying."

XV

Mudge kicked pebbles from his path as they made their way down the street. "Great, just great. We slog 'alfway across the world to get your bleedin' instrument fixed an' the only bloke wot can maybe do it up an' croaks on us."

"We don't know that. He isn't dead yet." Jon-Tom shifted his pack higher on his back. "The weaver said he was dying, not that he was deceased."

"Dyin', dead, wot's the difference. You think 'e'll be in any kind o' shape to work? The inconsiderate schmucko could've waited a couple of weeks till we'd finished our business before gettin' on with 'is."

"I'm sure if he'd known we were coming he would have postponed his fatal illness just to accommodate us."

"Precisely me point, mate."

Jon-Tom looked away. Just when he thought the otter might be turning into a halfway decent person he'd up and say something like that. Though by the standards of this world his behavior was hardly shocking.

They found the second trail and turned into the trees. It was a short hike to the house of Couvier Coulb. They were able to hear it before they could see it because the house itself reflected the mood of its master. This morning it was playing a funeral dirge, which was hardly encouraging. The melancholy music permeated the air, the earth, their very bones, filling them with sadness.

The walls of the house were composed of pipes: some of bamboo, others of dark grained wood, still others of gleaming metal. The ropes which bound them together vibrated like viola strings. Bright beams thrummed with the sonority of massed muffled trumpets. The waterfall which tumbled over a nearby cliff splashed in percussive counterpoint to the melody the house was playing. Sight and sound affected all of them equally. Even Mudge was subdued.

"This 'ere chap may not know 'ow to cure 'imself, but 'e sure as 'ell knows 'ow to make music. Rather wish 'e weren't dyin'. I'd give a gold piece to see this place when 'e were 'ealthy."

"Maybe we ought to just leave," said Cautious. "Go back to town, try find somebody else."

"There is no one else. That's what Clothahump told us. That's why we've come here. We have to see him."

"Wot if 'e ain't receivin' no visitors, mate? Blimey, wot if 'e ain't even receivin' air no more?"

"We have to try."

As they approached the front door the stones on which they trod rang like the plates of a gamelan. The doorbell was a flurry of flutes with an echo of panpipes. It was opened by a matronly possum. Her wise old eyes flicked over each of them in turn, stopping to rest on Jon-Tom.

"Strangers by the look of you. We don't get many visitors. I don't know from whence you come or why, but this is a house of the dying."

Jon-Tom looked to Mudge for advice, found none available. He had come to this place for reasons of his own. Now he would have to deal with the results of his decisions in the same way.

"It's about an instrument. Just one instrument. I don't know where else to go or what else to do. I've come so far in the hope that Master Coulb might be able to fix it."

"Master Coulb cannot rise from his bed, much less replace a reed in an oboe. I am Amalm, his housekeeper." She started to close the door.

"Please!" Jon-Tom took a step forward, forced himself to be patient. "The wizard who teaches me insisted only Coulb could repair my duar. I must have it fixed or I can't spellsing."

The door opened a crack. "You be a spellsinger, young human?" He nodded. The door opened the rest of the way. "A wizard sent you here?" Another nod. "Then there is magic involved. Truly only Master Coulb could help you. If he were capable of helping anyone." She hesitated, then sighed resignedly. "Because you have traveled far and magic is involved I will see if Master Coulb will speak to you. But be warned: he can do nothing for you. Perhaps he can recommend another."

As they entered Jon-Tom had to bend to clear the opening. Their guide continued to talk. "There are other master instrument makers, but none like Master Coulb. Still, he may know of one I do not. After all, I am only the housekeeper. This way."

She led them into a living room which was dominated by a tall stone fireplace. The wind whistled mournfully down the chimney, perfectly in tune with the melody the house was playing. There were several couches, each fashioned in the shape of some stringed instrument.

"Rest yourselves while I see to the Master."

They sat and listened and stared. Wind whistled through the rafters while loose floor slats chimed against one another. The windowpanes resonated like drumheads.

"Gloomy sort o' place," whispered Mudge. "Too bleedin' dignified for me."

"What did you expect?" Jon-Tom asked him. "Bells and laughter?"

The housekeeper returned. "He is worse today, but then he is worse each day."

"What kind of disease is he suffering from?"

"Maybe 'e's just old," Mudge said.

The possum eyed him sharply. "Aye, old he is, but in the prime of health before this affliction brought him down. It is no normal sickness that afflicts the Master. Potions, lotions, painkillers and pills have no effect on it. He is haunted by demons."

"Right." Mudge sprang from his chair. "Thanks for your 'ospitality, ma'am. Time to be goin'."

Jon-Tom caught him by the collar of his vest. "Don't be so quick to panic, Mudge."

"Who's quick? I've thought it right through, I 'ave. See, all I 'ave to do is 'ear the word 'demon' an' it don't take me but a minim to carefully an' thoughtfully decide I'd be better off elsewhere."

"They're not very big demons." The housekeeper sniffed. "Quite small, actually." She held her thumb and forefinger apart. "Such strange demons as have never been seen before. They wear identical raiment and they all look something like—you." And she shocked Jon-Tom to the bottom of his heart by pointing at him.

"Not you personally," she said hastily, seeing the effect her words had produced. "I mean that they are all humanlike." Her eyes rolled ceilingward. "Why they picked on poor Master Coulb, who never did anyone any harm, none of the experts in town have been able to divine. Perhaps it was just his time. Perhaps it was the special trumpet he sold to another traveler who passed by this way not long ago.

"One thing we know for certain: Something angered these demons enough for their own master to set them upon poor Coulb. Every attempt by our local wizards and sorcerors to exorcise them has failed. We even imported an urban wizard from Chejiji but his efforts were no more helpful than those of our own. The evil of these demons is insidious and slow. They kill gradually by poisoning the mind and the spirit rather than the body. Most demons suck blood, but these are worse, far worse. They suck the will out of a person. I feel the Master has little left with which to resist them. They will claim him soon."

"Life's irony," said Mudge. "'Ere stands me friend, a special spellsinger if ever there was one, but 'e can't 'elp cure your master because 'is instrument is broke. An' if it were 'ole, we wouldn't be 'ere now."

"I still have this." Jon-Tom displayed the suar. "My spellsinging's not as effective with this as it is when I'm playing the duar, but I can still rouse a gneechee or two. Let me try. Please?"

"I don't know." She was shaking her head slowly. "Little enough peace has Master Coulb. I've no wish to make his last days, perhaps even his final hours, uncomfortable ones."

"Let us talk to him," Weegee pleaded. "I've seen Jon-Tom's powers at work."

Jon-Tom started but managed to hide his surprise. Exception to the rule she might be, but Weegee was still all otter. When the need arose she could lie as fluidly as Mudge.

"I suppose it can't hurt letting you see him," Amalm murmured. "Perhaps some company would do him good. I will put it to him—if he's awake and able to respond. We'll see what he says." She turned to leave the room.

"Tell him not only am I a spellsinger, but I'm a spellsinger from another world. My magic, if I can make any, might be effective against these demons where that of local practitioners might not."

She looked back at him. "I will tell him, but I don't think it will matter." She vanished into the next room.

"Wot do you think, mate? Can you really do 'im some good?"

"I don't know, Mudge, but even if he can't help me we have to try."

"You mean you can try." Weegee was studying the weakly pulsating windows. "The rest of us can only watch.

I want nothing to do with any demons, no matter how small they may be." She shuddered. "Suppose they take offense at our intrusion and decide to strike us as well?"

"That's a chance we'll have to take."

"Don't you love the way 'e uses the word 'we'?" Mudge walked over to stand close to Weegee. He felt as if the house was beginning to close in around him. Or maybe it was just the tightness in his throat. "Whenever 'e runs into trouble or danger, suddenly 'tis 'we' this an' 'we' that."

"You can leave if you want to, Mudge." Jon-Tom gestured back toward the front hall. "You know where the door is. I won't stop you. All you have to do is walk out."

"Don't tempt me, mate. One o' these days you're gonna tempt me one time too many. So you think I'm going to walk out, wot? Why, I wouldn't give you the satisfaction, you skinny-legged, flat-nosed pale excuse for a feeble fart."

The otter would have continued but the housekeeper had returned. "He is very weak, but your story intrigues him." She smiled warmly. "He loves music, you see, and the idea of meeting a spellsinger, much less one from another world, was enough to rouse him from his lethargy." She shook a motherly finger at Jon-Tom. "You weren't lying about that just to get in to see him, were you?"

"No, ma'am. I am a spellsinger and I am from another world." *I'm just not a spellsinger* in *the other world,* he murmured silently.

"Come then." She turned and led them into the next room.

At the far end of the sitting chamber a stairway led to a second floor. Much more than a revitalized attic, this spacious area had been turned into a comfortable bedroom complete with dresser, chairs, a washtub in the shape of a squashed tuba, and an exquisitely carved bed. The headboard was composed of wood and metal pipes while the foot of the bed comprised ranked wooden keys.

Presently the bed was humming a sad lullaby. Every so often it would strike an odd atonal note, pause as if confused, back up and recommence playing like an elderly musician suffering from Alzheimer's.

Lying in the middle of the bed was a single figure no taller than Mudge and considerably slimmer. In fact, the elderly kinkajou was more closely related to Cautious than to the otters. Couvier Coulb wore a plain white nightdress and white tasseled sleeping cap. His nose was much too dry and his big eyes appeared more deeply sunk into his head than was normal. But they were open. He squinted at them, as was only to be expected of a nocturnal creature awakened during the day. The absence of upstairs windows kept the bedroom comfortably dark during the daytime.

Amalm stood on tiptoes to whisper to Jon-Tom. "Try not to tire him; he's very feeble." He nodded and approached the bed while his companions held back. At the bedside he dropped to his knees to bring his face closer to the kinkajou's level.

"I've crossed part of an ocean and many strange lands to see you, Couvier Coulb."

"So Amalm tells me." The small mouth curled upward in a semblance of a smile. Jon-Tom felt dampness at the corners of his eyes. He had expected to encounter an aged and kindly individual, but hardly one with the mien of a favorite uncle—if one could imagine having a kinkajou for an uncle.

A hand emerged from beneath the sheets. The fingers were narrow and delicate, the grip unexpectedly strong. "I have met many musicians, but never one from another world. How strange I should have the opportunity to do so on my deathbed."

"Don't talk like that." It sounded silly but he didn't know what else to say. "I really am a spellsinger, you know. Maybe I can do something to help you. I've helped people before, but almost always with the aid of this."

Carefully he slipped off the sack containing his duar and brought out the fragments one by one. Couvier Coulb examined each piece thoroughly, turning them over and over in his sensitive fingers. "How did you break this?"

"I fell on it."

"That was most clumsy of you. These are the components of a duar. One of a design unfamiliar to me, and quite unique. So you see, there is at least one other instrument maker in the world of a skill to match my own, for whoever fashioned this is no less a master. In the hands of a truly gifted spellsinger I can believe this would work great magic." He placed the pieces back in Jon-Tom's hands. "Alas, I fear that would not be enough to save me. I would be more than happy to repair your instrument, young human, but these days I cannot muster enough strength to climb out of bed. Even the thought of resetting strings that fade into another dimension tires me." He looked past his visitor.

"Amalm looks after me well and attends efficiently to my simple needs. But I am glad you came. It is pleasant to have guests even in one's last days." The delicate fingers patted the back of Jon-Tom's hand.

"Those demons who torment you so; Amalm could describe them to us only vaguely. Why should they pick on you?"

"I don't know." The kinkajou's breathing was labored. "They simply appeared one day and declared they had been assigned to my case—whatever that means. Demon lore. I thought perhaps they were talking of a case I had fashioned for a bass twiddle not long ago, but as it turned out they were talking of something else entirely. No doubt Amalm has told you we have tried everything. Wizards and magicians, doctors and physicians: None have been able to help me. I even went so far as to try to comply with their incessant demands, but these are so strange and incomprehensible I believe they invent them simply to torment me further. You can't fight them, young man. You can only try to mitigate the agony they inflict." Making a supreme effort, the kinkajou lifted his head off his oversized pillow.

"You should go. Go now, before they assign themselves to your case as well."

Jon-Tom rose, looked around the room. There was defiance in his tone. "I'm not afraid of demons, much less small ones. Neither are my friends. Are we, Mudge?" He peered into the darkness. "Mudge?"

"Went downstairs." That was Weegee's voice from near the head of the stairs. "Said he had to take a leak."

"He's had plenty of time. I'll go get him. I may need his help." He took a step toward the stairwell.

A faint glow appeared in the air between him and the exit. Weegee let out a gasp and Cautious a curse. Amalm rushed from her place to stand protectively close to the bed.

"Damn them," the kinkajou muttered weakly, "they're coming for me again." He raised his shaky voice. "Why can't you leave me alone? Why can't you suck at someone else? I'm not guilty of anything!"

"None are innocent; all are guilty," intoned a sepulchral voice. "Nor could we leave you if we wished to. We have been assigned to you—assigned to you—assigned to you." The words echoed through the room.

Jon-Tom held his ground. Shapes were beginning to form within the pale white mist that had filled the bedchamber. They were not the shapes he'd steeled himself to see. They took the form of words, quite indecipherable, that drifted hither and yon. Black letters that formed snakelike blobs and scorpion shapes. They danced and pirouetted and closed in on the bed and its helpless elderly occupant.

Poor Couvier Coulb sank deep into his pillow as the sheer force of the mysterious words pushed Jon-Tom aside. They did not try to injure him, but they did shunt him several steps backward as though he weighed nothing at all.

Then the words coalesced and shrank to create the figures Amalm had described. They accumulated on the headboard and the blankets in little knots of twos and threes, tiny faceless men some four inches tall. Each looked exactly like the one next to him, interchangeable and expressionless as they regarded the kinkajou stonily. Each wore a miniature three-piece gray pinstriped suit complete with matching gray tie and gray shoes. Now faces appeared, eyes and mouths and nostrils, and Jon-Tom saw that their eyes were as gray as their clothing. About half of them carried matchbook size gray briefcases.

"You haven't filed on time," declared one of the group gravely.

"But I told you," Coulb whined, "I don't know what it is you want filed, or how to go about filing it."

"That does not matter," said a second.

"Ignorance is no excuse," insisted a third.

"We have examined what you have returned." The first demon opened his tiny briefcase and portentously examined the contents. "You did not sign your form 1933-AB Supplement."

"Please, please, I don't know what a 1933-AB Supplement *is*."

The demon ignored this plea and continued relentlessly. "There is an error on Line 4, Subsection H of your 5550 Supplement."

The kinkajou moaned.

"Your 140 Depletion Allowance was filed incorrectly."

Couvier Coulb pulled his sheets over his head and whimpered. At the same time Jon-Tom noticed that each of the demons had a forked tail emerging from the seat of their perfectly pressed pants. The tip of each tail was darkly strained, possibly by ink.

"There is a mistake on your Form 440 which we have not be able to resolve with the current data." Tiny lines of type leaped from the open briefcase to stab at Couvier Coulb like so many micropoint hypodermics. He let out a yelp of pain.

"Now wait a minute!" Jon-Tom stepped forward and glared down at the tiny shapes. It seemed impossible anything so small and bland could be causing the kinkajou such agony.

A dozen tiny faces turned up at him and the power of those blank stares froze him in place. "Do not interfere," said the one Jon-Tom had come to think of as the leader. "You cannot help. No one can help. He did not file properly and must pay the penalty."

"Pay the penalty," echoed the whey-faced demonic chorus.

"Come to think of it," the leader continued, "have *you* filed?"

Jon-Tom stumbled backward. A huge, invisible fist had struck him in the gut. His breath came in short, painful gasps. Cautious started toward him but he waved the raccoon away.

"It's okay, I'm all right." He straightened, glaring down at the demon. "You still haven't explained why you're tormenting poor Couvier Coulb."

"Indeed we have. He did not file. Anyone who does not file is visited by representatives of the IRS—the Interdimensional Reliquary of Spirits. Us." Each word was uttered with utmost reverence by the demonic chorus.

"But he doesn't know how to file. Hell, he shouldn't *have* to file."

"Hell says otherwise. Everyone has to file. It is required. It is the Law."

"Not here it isn't. You boys not only have the wrong individual, you've got the wrong world."

"We do not have the wrong world. We cannot have the wrong world. We are infallible. We are always sent to the right place. He has not filed and therefore he must pay."

"How do you expect him to comply with rules and regulations he knows nothing about?"

"Ignorance is no excuse," the line of demons standing on the edge of the headboard intoned ritualistically. "He has been audited and found wanting. He must pay."

"All right." Jon-Tom reached toward his purse. "How much does he owe? I have some gold."

"Money?" The leader's lips formed a miniature bow of disapproval. "We do not accept money. We have come for his soul and we mean to have it and if you continue to interfere, man, we will take yours as well as interest earned. I Lescar, Agent-in-Charge, say this."

"Jon-Tom," whispered Weegee urgently, "the goblet's prediction!"

He stared at the tiny, threatening demon. Certainly his

expression was lugubrious enough. Wildly he wondered if the goblet was also right about IBM.

"It doesn't matter, Weegee. I have to get my duar fixed. Coulb's the only one who can do it, so I have to try to help him. I think I'd try anyway. I don't like these smartass bureaucratic types."

"No one likes us," the demons moaned. "We like no one. It does not matter. The end is never in doubt."

"We'll see about that." He began strumming the suar's strings, trying to think of an appropriate spellsong. What might have an effect on demons like these? Armies of the dead, skeletal apparitions, ogres and monsters of every description he could and had dealt with, but this was a different kind of evil, sly and subtle. It required spellsinging of equal cunning.

He started off with another bold rendition of Pink Floyd's "Money."

Though he was functioning without the power of the duar, the bedroom rang wih the sound of his voice. The house picked up on what he was trying to do and added a throbbing, contemporary backbeat. But no matter what song he tried or how well he played the demons simply ignored him as they concentrated their efforts on the rapidly weakening kinkajou.

Eventually Cautious put a gentle hand on Jon-Tom's arm. "Might as well save your breath. Ain't having no effect on them. Ain't nothing gonna have an effect on them, maybe."

Jon-Tom requested a glass of water, which Amalm readily provided. His throat was sore already. He'd been singing steadily for more than half an hour, with no visible effect on his opponents. Not one demon had disappeared. They continued their insidious harangue of Couvier Coulb.

"There's got to be a way," he mumbled. "There's got to be."

"Maybe spellsinging ain't it." Cautious looked thoughtful. "When I was a cub my grammam used to tell me 'bout magic, you bet. She always say you have to make the magic fit the subject. Doen look like you doing that, Jon-Tom.''

Was he going about it all wrong? But all he knew how to do was spellsing. He couldn't use potions and powders like Clothahump. What was it the wizard was always telling him? ''Always keep in mind that magic is a matter of specificity.''

Specifics. Instead of trying to adapt old songs to fit the situation, perhaps he should improvise new ones. He'd done that before. But what kind of lyrics would give such demons as these pause?

Fight fire with fire. Clothahump hadn't said that, but somebody had.

He considered carefully. A gleam appeared in his eyes. His hand swept down once more over the suar. Take equal parts Dire Straits, Ratt, X and Eurythmics. Mix Adam Smith with Adam Ant. Add readings from *The Economist* and Martin Greenspan. Mix well and you have one savage synoptic song.

Heavy metal economics.

Instead of singing of love and death, of peace and learning and compassion, Jon-Tom began to blast out raw-edged stanzas full of free trade, reduced tariffs, and an international standard of taxation based on ecus instead of the dollar.

It staggered the demons. They tried to fight back with talk of protectionism and deficit financing, but they were no match for Jon-Tom musically. He struck hard with a rhythmic little ditty proposing a simplified income tax and no deductions that sent half of them scurrying for shelter, moaning and covering their ears.

Those remaining countered with an accusation about an unqualified deduction retroactive to the first date of filing, a vicious low blow that cracked the front of the suar and nearly knocked him off his feet. He recouped the ground briefly lost and more with the ballad of unlimited textile imports and suggestions for a free market in autos. When he slammed them with a flat tax tune it was more than the strongest among them could bear. They began to vanish, holding their briefcases defensively in front of them, dissolving in a refulgent gray cloud of letters and incomprehensible forms.

Still he sang of banking and barter, of one page returns and other miracles, until the last of the cloud had dissipated. When he finally stopped it was as if the air in the room had been scoured clear of infection, every molecule handwashed and hung out to dry. He was hoarse and exhausted.

But Couvier Coulb was standing tall and straight by the side of his bed, assuring his sobbing housekeeper that if not completely cured he was surely on the way to total recovery.

At which point a fuzzy head popped into view atop the stairwell and declared at this solemn and joyful moment, "Damn, I thought I were goin' to piss for a week!"

"As always, your timing never ceases to amaze me." Jon-Tom had to struggle to form the words. His voice was a breathy rasping.

Mudge glanced rapidly around the bedchamber. "Timin'? Wot timin'? Now where are these 'ere demons everyone's so worried about? I'm ready for 'em, I am. Big demons, little demons, let me at 'em." He stode briskly into the room.

To her immense credit and Jon-Tom's everlasting appreciation Weegee booted the otter right in the rear.

As the two of them quarreled, Couvier Coulb led the rest of his guests downstairs. "Come, my friend. Amalm, I am sure our guests must be hungry." He put an affectionate arm and his prehensile tail around Jon-Tom's waist, which was as high as he could comfortably reach. "And I know this young man must be thirsty. I am going to fix your duar, Jon-Tom. Have no fear of that. If it is at all possible I will do it." He winked. "I may even do it if it is impossible. But first we must rest. You are tired from battling demons and I from a long illness. You must talk of your travels in distant lands and of the world you come from, and I would know more of this Clothahump who knew to send you to me."

"That's easy." Mudge and Weegee had rejoined them,

Mudge still rubbing his backside. "'E's a senile old faker with a 'ead as 'ard as 'is shell."

By nightfall Coulb had recovered much of his strength and led his guests into his workshop. The house was already perking up, having set aside its month-long funeral dirge in favor of some sprightly, cheerful tunes that would have done well on Broadway. It had a rejuvenating effect on Coulb and Jon-Tom. Mudge thought it spooky.

The kinkajou carefully laid out the shattered components of the duar on his workbench, a glistening long table made of pure white hardwood. When the last piece had been set down he turned the carrying sack inside out to check for dust and splinters. These were collected, placed in a jar, and added to the display. As he donned a pair of extra-thick work glasses Jon-Tom took a moment to examine the workshop.

Musical instruments in different stages of repair lay on other benches or hung from the walls. The air was thick with the rich smells of oil and varnish. Some of the tools meticulously arranged in boxes next to the workbench looked fine enough to do double duty in a surgery.

Coulb was muttering aloud. "Align these here, replace some wood there; that seam can be fixed, yes." He looked up, pushed the work glasses back on his forehead. "I can repair it—I think."

"You think?"

The kinkajou rubbed at his eyes. "As I said before, this instrument is unique. The most difficult part will be setting the strings. It is hard to achieve perfect pitch in two dimensions at once." He gestured toward the bench. "All the strings are there?" Jon-Tom nodded. "Good. I've never seen strings like these and I'd hate to have to try to replace them. Fortunately they are metal. But I will need help setting them properly."

Jon-Tom looked around the shop. "An apprentice?" Coulb just smiled.

Oil lamps, each in the shape of a different instrument, lined the walls. It was pitch dark outside. They were full of

Amalm's good cooking. Jon-Tom sensed he was in the presence of another master magician. What else could you call someone who took wood and glue and gut and created from such disparate elements the essence of music?

"Not an apprentice." The kinkajou was walking to another table. "Gneechees. A spellsinger should know gneechees."

"That I do, but I've never seen anyone except Clothahump and myself call them up."

"Not only must we call them up, young man, we must isolate those we need. In order to be able to do this I collaborated some years ago with Acrody, a master manufacturer of medical devices. Working together we built this."

Jon-Tom studied the contraption intently. It consisted of a series of transparent tubes, each stacked inside the other. Their sides were perforated by minute holes. The largest tube, which contained all the others, was nearly a foot in diameter, while the innermost was as narrow as a straw. This emerged from the middle of the stack and continued up and out until it entered a glass plate that was perhaps a quarter inch deep and some two feet wide by three long. It resembled a solar collector without the silicon cells. Coulb assured him it was covered with small holes but Jon-Tom could perceive them only as a roughness on the flat surface.

From the underside of the plate hung thin strips of metal, wood, glass, plastic—every imaginable substance. Coulb leaned over and blew on the plate. As the air passed through the glass the streamers began to vibrate, producing an infinity of musical tones.

Keys ran in a circle around the base of the big glass tube. They did not appear to be connected to anything but Jon-Tom knew better. Coulb hadn't placed them there for decoration.

"What is it?" Weegee finally asked.

"A gneechee sorter." Coulb looked proud. "Not an easy thing to build, I can tell you. I use it to isolate those gneechees who are musically inclined from those with other ethereal interests. It will help us to tune your duar, young man. *If* I can put it back together again. Which I cannot do if I stand here nattering away with you. Go on now, out, shoo, leave me to my work. Amalm will attend to your needs. It is late and you need your sleep while I am just waking up. I will see you again tomorrow night."

They filed out, Jon-Tom's gaze lingering long on the fragments of his duar. He felt as though he was abandoning his only child to another's care. *Better care than you gave it,* he reminded himself.

There was a large guest house out back. Amalm found beds for all of them and bid them a good night. They fell asleep instantly, lulled by the music of the house and the waterfall nearby which combined to sing them a liquid lullaby.

XVI

They spent several days as Coulb's guests, enjoying Amalm's cooking and exploring the village, regaining the strength they'd expended during the arduous journey to Strelakat Mews. Many times Jon-Tom was tempted to look in on Couvier Coulb. He did not, mindful of Amalm's admonition that the master worked best when he was not disturbed.

There came a day when Coulb interrupted their breakfast. He was tired from working through the night but quietly exultant. The right lens of his work glasses was almost obscured by varnish and he held a brush in his right paw as he looked straight at Jon-Tom and smiled.

"It's done. Come and see."

Though he wasn't finished eating, Jon-Tom pushed back his chair and moved to follow Coulb. So did Cautious. Weegee dragged a disgruntled Mudge away from the food.

Even Amalm put her apron aside and came to see what musical miracle the kinkajou had wrought.

Miracle was the only description that fit, Jon-Tom thought in wonder as Coulb proudly displayed the restored duar. At the very least he expected cracks and seams to show. After all, the duar had not merely been broken; it had been shattered.

It hung between padded metal clamps atop the workbench, and it glowed. Coulb had done more than restore it, he had improved on it. Those sections which had been irreparably damaged had been seamlessly replaced with jewel-like pieces of exotic woods. New wood and old had been polished to a mirror-like sheen. The tremble and mass controls sat flush with the resonating chamber.

"May I . . . ?"

"Of course you may, young man. It is your instrument, is it not?"

Holding the duar by its neck, Jon-Tom loosened the clamps and removed it from its mounting. He tried the controls. They turned with a fluid firmness. The old uncertain give and play was gone.

Even the feel of the wood was different. It was soft, almost malleable, the result of penetrating oils Coulb had worked into top, bottom and sides. Yet no matter how much he caressed it there was no lingering greasiness on his fingers.

The strings *looked* right. They gradually ran together over the openings in the resonator, vanishing into another dimension before reappearing on the other side. Yet when he ran his fingers lovingly over their taut surfaces the sounds they generated were unnaturally discordant.

"We still have to tune it." He was enjoying himself, Jon-Tom saw.

Taking the instrument, Coulb placed it between two braces beneath the strips of material that hung from the underside of the gneechee collector plate. Moving to the peculiar keyboard that encircled the concentric glass cylinders, he began to play.

Oddly clear, lilting notes filled the workshop. Slow Mahler on a glass harmonica. The chords deepened as Coulb leaned harder on the keys and picked up the beat. Sounds of several symphony orchestras mixed with synthesizers assailed the ears of the onlookers. Mudge put an arm around Weegee and pulled her close while Cautious closed his eyes. Amalm looked on and nodded knowingly, her face alight with pride.

The sonority brought forth a glow, one familiar to Jon-Tom and his companions. Gneechees, attracted by the thousands to the magic of the music. They clustered around old Couvier Coulb until he was encased in a luminescent blanket. More of them swirled around the glass columns. As Jon-Tom stared they began to filter through the minuscule perforations, filling one cylinder after another, until at last the most persistent of them reached the central and final tube.

It conveyed them up in a neon arc, up and around and into the collection plate as the cylinders separated out those gneechees whose especial affinity was for music. They filled the collector plate to overflowing, the glass growing so bright with the light of their concentrated bodies that Jon-Tom could hardly bear to look at it. Compacted within the plate they continued their joyous, celebratory dance, thereby agitating the tuning strips which hung from the underside of the glass. Jon-Tom began to cry from the sheer ecstasy the resultant music produced.

And as it poured into and through and around the duar that extraordinary instrument strained against its braces, bending slightly upward in the middle. But the clamps were strong and held it in place as it and everyone else in the room quivered in time to the rampaging music.

Then it was done. Couvier Coulb stepped away from his keyboard. The gneechees put forth a few final, questioning chords before they began to filter out of the collection plate and concentric cylinders. The music faded with them, back into the unreal realm from which the master instrument maker had summoned them forth.

Coulb took a deep breath and then, as if in intentional

contrast to the indescribable musical sweep they had just endured, cracked his knuckles. He walked over to the now transparent plate collector, reached beneath the motionless tuning strips, and removed the duar from its braces. In appearance it was unchanged, but when Jon-Tom took it from the kinkajou's grasp a subtle trembling ran from the instrument through his fingertips and up his arms, drifting away like a lost sigh.

Coulb looked up at him out of wise, gratified eyes. "Now try your instrument, young human."

Jon-Tom put the strap over his shoulder, let the duar rest against his chest. It felt familiar, comfortable, a part of him. The wood was golden and the strings gleamed like chrome. It had not been restored so much as resurrected.

The first sounds that issued from the resonating chamber when he passed his fingers across the double set of strings were exalted.

Couvier Coulb looked satisfied and found himself a chair. "Play something. Not for magic. For the music."

Jon-Tom nodded and smiled at the old craftsman. The bond between them transcended such insignificant differences as species. This was to be the kinkajou's reward. Play he would for the master, something high-spirited and full of life. A celebration.

Too much of a celebration for Mudge, who never had become a heavy metal fan. He ran from the workshop, his paws clapped over his ears. He was followed by a reluctant Weegee and an apologetic Cautious.

Though she winced a lot, Amalm stayed. As for Couvier Coulb, he seemed to drop twenty years. As the smile on his face grew broader he began snapping his fingers and tapping his feet, and his long prehensile tail twitched back and forth behind his chair like a furry metronome. The house went dead quiet for about five minutes before it began to join in, hesitantly at first, then with growing confidence.

Jon-Tom had never felt better in his life. Never played better either, he reflected happily. He bounced and pranced and leaped about the room, even managing an exuberant aerial split à la Pete Townshend. And when he concluded, the sweat pouring from his face and beneath his arms, the breath coming in long sweet sucks, it still was not silent in the workshop. Couvier Coulb was on his feet, applauding mightily.

"Such depth of feeling! Such insight and enthusiasm. Such wanton expression of personal karma."

"Say what?" Jon-Tom straightened.

"What do you call it?"

"A song for my lady love, who I wish was here to share this moment with me. It's called "The Lemon Song," by a quiet bunch of good-natured fellows who named themselves Led Zepplin. Very refined."

The kinkajou stored this information, then turned and walked toward the back of the workshop. "Come, young man. I have something else to show you." The twinkle was back in his eyes.

"Please, before I forget, let me pay you. My pack is out in our room."

"No money. You saved my life. Don't insult me by offering me money. And you have gifted me with this wonderfully sensitive music of yours as well." He grabbed Jon-Tom's hand and pulled him along.

The back wall was filled by a filing cabinet that ran from floor to ceiling. A rolling ladder provided access to the top drawers. Coulb climbed a few steps, halted to trace minuscule labels with one long finger, then opened one of the files. Jon-Tom could see that it was filled from side to side with five-inch-tall bottles of colored glass. They looked a lot like old-fashioned milk bottles except that their stoppers were made of some odoriferous golden-hued resin. The kinkajou removed one bottle and showed it to his young guest.

"The stopper is pure frankincense. I buy it from a trader who visits the Mews once a year from the desert lands. It is the only substance that seals."

The bottle appeared to be empty. Jon-Tom wasn't close

enough to read the stick-on label. He gestured at the filing cabinet. "What is all this?"

"Why, my music collection, of course. I am a maker of instruments. I can repair or design devices that will produce sounds imagined but not yet heard. I can play many of them passing well. But I cannot compose. I cannot create. So when I am tired or bored I go to my collection." He pointed toward the now empty gneechee collector.

"The music our little friends produce emerges through the tiny holes in the collector plate. When I am in the mood I place another filter atop it. This filter shrinks down to a tube which I then insert into one of these bottles. Thus do I collect music. Much of it I do not recognize, but that does not keep me from enjoying it. I have become something of an expert on the music of other worlds and dimensions. The gneechees move freely among many. Listen." He pulled the stopper.

The sound of a symphony orchestra again filled the workshop. Brass rumbled and strings queried. As Coulb began to close the stopper the music reversed itself, playing backward as it was drawn back into the bottle by some unimaginable suction.

"I have been able, by dint of hard work and much study, to identify music and composers." He squinted at the label. "That was part of the second movement of the Fourteenth Symphony by a gneechee who called himself Beethoven."

Jon-Tom could hardly breathe. "He wrote only nine symphonies."

"While he was alive, yes." Coulb wagged a finger at his guest. "In the gneechee form we all eventually come to inhabit he has continued to compose. Originally from your world, it seems. Let's see what else I have from the same plane." He chose another bottle and cracked the stopper.

An oceanic orchestral surge swamped Jon-Tom's senses. Coulb let him listen a little longer this time, until the last note of the overwhelming crescendo had receded into the far reaches of time and space. It continued to echo in Jon-Tom's brain.

The kinkajou checked his label. "This one must have been an interesting fellow. It took three bottles to hold all of this composition. Another of your symphonies, this one the Twelfth, by a Gustav Mahler." He climbed to the top row of drawers, examined the contents of another. "Here is one of my favorites: Prist'in'ikie's Tanglemorf for Gluzko and Eelmack."

The sounds that now assailed Jon-Tom's ears were utterly alien. Atonal without being disorganized, dissonant without being harsh, and extremely complex.

"I don't know that composer."

"Doesn't surprise me, young man. I'm not sure I know the dimension. Gneechees do get around."

"You've heard the kind of music I play. The Beethoven and the Mahler were wonderful but—don't you maybe have something a little lighter from my neck of the woods?"

"Lighter? Like your own music, you mean?" Jon-Tom nodded. Coulb descended the ladder, opened another new drawer and chose a bottle. The glass was a rich, dark purple.

It contained sounds that were as familiar as they were new and unmistakable. Only one man had ever been able to make such sounds with an electric guitar. It was full of raw, disciplined power.

"Let me guess," Jon-Tom whispered. "Jimi Hendrix?"

"Yes." Coulb peered through his thick glasses at the label. "From the *Snuff an' Stuff* double album. Bored yet?"

"I don't think new music could ever bore me, sir. I even liked that Pristinkeewinkie stuff." He stared silently at the cabinet. It must hold thousands of songs and symphonies and other posthumous unheard compositions by hundreds of long-deceased musicians.

"Call me Couvier. We have a lot to listen to."

The house shook all that day and on into the night as Coulb played for Jon-Tom pieces of Bartok's opera, *A Modern Salammbo*, selections from Wagner's second Ring cycle, and most of a heartrending album by Jim Morrison.

And when kinkajou and man fell asleep, it was to the haunting strains of Janis Joplin's "Texas Eulogy."

Both woke with the sun. Jon-Tom thanked the old kinkajou profusely. Coulb shrugged it off. "Any time you feel the need to refresh your soul with new music, come and visit. The enjoyment one gains from listening is doubled when shared."

"If I could get back home and then return here with a good cassette recorder and a crateful of blank tape I could set the music world on its ear forever."

"Ah, but you can't hear anything if you're standing on your ear." Coulb laughed softly. "Is there anything else I can do for you, Jon-Tom?" He blinked sleepily despite his recent rest. The sun was rising higher outside and the nocturnal craftsman would be wanting to retire, his guest knew.

"Just one thing. Can you recommend someone to guide us safely back to Chejiji? Preferably by a roundabout route? We had a minor altercation with some locals on our way here and I'd rather not have to deal with them again."

"Ah, the ogres. Yes, we can find someone to escort you around their territory. I wish you could stay longer. I have so much music to share with you."

"I'll be back, I promise. I've got to come back here with a tape recorder."

"I could loan you some bottles."

"I'd feel safer with a recorder. It won't break as easily if I fall on it." He grinned ruefully.

Together they exited the workshop. "What will you do once you get back to Chejiji?"

"Try to charter a boat to take my friends and I back to a certain section of the eastern Glittergeist. We found what I think is a permanent gate between our worlds. If it's still there I'm going back for that recorder—and other things."

"Then I hope I have the pleasure of seeing you again. *And* hearing you play." Man and kinkajou shook hands.

True to his word Coulb had Amalm locate someone to lead them safely through the Mews. There Weegee suggested they look up Teyva before bothering with an uncertain ship and unreliable crew.

They located the flying stallion in an aerial stable on the far side of town. He was delighted to see them again. With his fear of flying permanently cured, he readily agreed to carry them back to the eastern swamplands. Nor did he have to strain to transport them alone. Having won a substantial amount at cards, he called in his debts among his friends. So Jon-Tom and his companions each had their own mount.

From the air most forest looks alike, but eventually Mudge's sharp eyes spotted a certain tree, and from the tree they managed to locate the rocky ledge and the subterranean orifice it concealed. They landed, and while the flying horses chatted of alfalfa wine and cloud dancing Jon-Tom made his final preparations.

He was taking his duar and ramwood staff, neither of which should draw any unusual attention. His iridescent lizard-skin cape he would leave behind. As for the rest of his unusual clothing he had concocted various explanations with which to satisfy the curious until he could purchase sneakers, jeans and a shirt to match. It shouldn't take long to convert Clothahump's gold coins into ready cash at any pawn shop.

Cautious was regarding him fondly. "You be careful for sure now."

"You too. What are you going to do now?"

"I think maybe my hometown friends still pretty mad at me, you bet. So I think I go back with your otter fella and see what this Bellwood country is like."

"We'll be waiting for your return." Was Weegee crying? "I'll have a talk with your lady Talea, female to female, and explain what you're about. How will you make it home when you come back this way, Jon-Tom? You don't know how long you're going to be and Teyva can't wait here forever."

"I don't expect him to wait at all. Mudge and I have traveled a fair portion of the world. I'm not worried about getting home from here." He took a last look around, checked to make sure he had several torches handy. "I guess that's everything. Teyva and his friends will fly you back to the Bellwoods and. . . ."

A large furry mass struck him square in the chest. He staggered backward with Mudge clinging to him. The otter was sobbing uncontrollably.

"You ain't comin' back!" Black nose and whiskers were inches from his face and tears were pouring down fuzzy cheeks. "I know you ain't. Once you get back to your own world through that bloody 'ole in the ground you'll be back in familiar surroudin's, back among your own kind, an' you'll forget all about us. About poor ol' Mudge, an' Weegee, and that senile 'ardshell Clothahump who needs you to look after 'im in 'is old age, and even about Talea. You'll get back to where everythin's comfortable an' safe an' relaxin' an' you won't be comin' back 'ere." He grabbed the vee of Jon-Tom's indigo shirt and shook him. "Are you listenin' to me, you ugly, ignorant, naive bald-faced monkey? Wot am I goin' to do if I never see you again?"

"Take it easy, Mudge." Feeling a little teary-eyed himself, Jon-Tom disengaged the otter's fingers from his shirt. "I wouldn't run out permanent on my best friend, even if he is a liar, a cheat, a thief, a drunk and an incorrigible wencher."

Mudge wiped at his eyes and nose. "It does me 'eart good to 'ear you talk like that, mate." He stepped back. "Maybe you will come back, but I ain't goin' to 'old me breath. I've seen wot 'appens to folks when they gets back to where they belong. I sure as 'ell ain't goin' to take any bets on you returnin'."

"If for some reason I don't, I don't want you lying around moping and moaning about it all the time."

"Wot, me?" The otter forced a cheery smile. "Not a bleedin' chance!"

Jon-Tom looked at the entrance to the cave. "We had ourselves an interesting time, didn't we? Set some evil back on its heels, met some special folks, spread some goodwill and generally shook up the status quo. No reason for regrets." He dropped to his knees and lit the first torch, crawled toward the opening beneath the ledge.

"I'll be back, you'll see. Tell Talea not to fret. I'll be coming for her."

"Sure you will, mate." Mudge stood next to Weegee. Cautious waved farewell along with the otters while Teyva pawed the earth. The only thing absent from Mudge's goodbyes was a feeling of conviction.

Jon-Tom stumbled down the familiar tunnel until he could stand. Shouldering his backpack he held the torch close to the floor, following the damp footprints he and his friends had left on their previous subterranean excursion as well as those of the pirates who had pursued them. Within an hour he was following the crumbling wire back to the cleft in the rocks that led to his own world.

Halfway through the narrow passage he extinguished his torch. Light and voices reached him from the other side. He was able to use the distant glow to guide him the rest of the way through the defile.

Soon after he emerged, a voice yelled at him.

"Hey, you there!" He blinked as his eyes received the full force of a multicell flashlight, put up a hand to shield them as he tried to locate the speaker.

"What is it?"

The light was lowered along with the voice. "Don't lag back there. This cave's full of dangerous dropoffs and unexplored dead ends. We ain't lost anybody yet and I don't want to start today."

"Sorry." As his eyes adjusted he found a dozen people staring at him. A couple of families, some young couples, one or two younger people traveling on their own. One shouldered a backpack as grungy as his own.

The guide resumed his well-worn spiel. "Now over here, folks, we have a formation called the bashful elephant."

The faces turned away. Children oohed and aahed. No one questioned Jon-Tom's sudden appearance. Those in the front of the guided party assumed Jon-Tom had been in the back, and those in the back assumed he'd entered with the guide. He simply fell in step with the tour and followed it back out into the bright warm sunshine of a Texas afternoon. There was the old building where he and his companions had battled Kamaulk's pirates and then drug runners, behind him the stone entrance to the cavern below, at the end of the dirt road the sign identifying this as the location of the Cave-With-No-Name, and off in the distance the highway where a passing eighteen-wheeler had startled his friends. South of the highway lay San Antonio. Twelve hundred odd miles to the west was the megalopolis of Los Angeles, his home.

He turned to watch the old guide latch the gates which sealed the cave entry. Not too many yards below lay a small twist in space–time. Through that inexplicable, tenuous passage could be found a land where otters talked and a certain turtle practiced at sorcery, where he had battled armies of intelligent insects, ferocious ferrets and parrot pirates.

As Mudge would say, it was bloody unreal.

The tourists were filing back into their cars. Jon-Tom made several hopeful inquiries before one of the young couples agreed to give him a lift into San Antonio. Comfortably ensconced in the back seat of their Volvo he was removing his backpack when he happened to notice the elaborate digital clock set in the dash. In addition to the time of day it also provided full date information.

He knew he'd been gone more than a year, but it was one thing to view time in the abstract, quite something else to see it solid and irrefutable in the form of cool blue LED letters and numbers. How would his parents react when he turned up after a silence of more than a year? Fortunately he wasn't one of those clinging absentee college students who called in once a week. They were used to long silences from their distant, hard studying son. But a year?

What was his counselor at UCLA going to say? And his friends, and semi-regular dates like Suzanne and Mariel?

They and everyone else were going to have to buy the story he'd carefully worked out.

A unique opportunity had arisen (and that part of it was certainly no lie, he told himself) for him to go to work for the government. When the inevitable question arose as to what sort of work that entailed, he was going to smile knowingly and explain that he wasn't at liberty to go into details just now. Then his parents and friends and everyone else would (hopefully) nod knowingly in turn and let the matter drop.

It wouldn't go over as well with the university administration. There would be classes abruptly abandoned he would have to make up, professors to mollify. He was confident, though, that he could get his life back on track.

The Volvo had turned out onto the highway, heading southeast toward the interstate. Trucks and cars zipped past, belching fumes that reminded him of the swamplands. At first he thought there was a funny smell in the air. Then he realized it was the air itself. There were no industries, no internal combustion engines in the other world. The air there, if not the inhabitants, was pure.

Of course he was going back. Talea, the love of his life, was back there. The love of his life in that world, anyway. What *was* Mariel doing these days? And Suzanne? What would they think of his exotic gone-to-work-for-some-secret-government-agency story? Would it score points for him?

The young wife turned the radio to the local rock station and the Volvo was filled with the mellifluous sounds of a Ronald McDonald clone hawking the opening of three new San Antonio area burger Xanadus. Ads for Po Folks, underarm deodorant and used-cars-se-habla-espanol followed. The Cowboys were on their way to the playoffs again. Nothing had changed since he'd been gone.

Nothing much at all.

-A Great Deal Later-

The giant came trudging up the river road. He was impossibly tall and gaunt. A scraggly seaweed-like growth clung to his face and there was a wild gleam in his eyes.

The observer of this approaching apparition did not panic, did not flee. She stood her ground.

The giant saw her. Across his back was slung a thick wooden staff, knobbed at one end. Tied to and around it were a number of bulging sacks. Perhaps he was a pedlar, the observer thought.

"Hello there." The giant did not have a threatening voice. He sounded tired. "What have we here?"

By way of reply the observer darted forward and sank her teeth into the giant's leg midway between knee and ankle. Letting out a yelp of pain, he began hopping about on one leg, trying to balance his precarious load as he attempted to shake his attacker free. The third kick of that long limb sent her sprawling.

Rolling to her feet, she began spitting ostentatiously while rubbing at her mouth. "Phooey, phooey, phooey! Stink!"

Regaining his balance the giant felt of his not-too-severely injured leg and eyed the young otter warily, ready to dodge or defend against another attack.

"I can't say much for the resemblance, but the attitude is unmistakable. Will you go and tell your father that an old friend is here to see him?"

The young otter's brows drew together. She wore a frilly pair of short pants and a flowery necklace. "See Dada? Stinkman want to see Dada?"

"Yes." Jon-Tom couldn't repress a smile. When she wasn't trying to amputate his leg the little furball was damn cute. "See Dada."

The cub considered, then turned and scampered up the road. "Come wid me."

As he followed, Jon-Tom drank in his surroundings. The forest appeared unchanged, eternal. The belltrees tinkled melodiously at the merest hint of a breeze. Already the young otter was almost out of sight. She would stop and turn to wait impatiently for him to catch up, then take off with another burst of speed.

"Quick-quick, stinkman! You too slow."

He would smile and try to lengthen his stride.

She led him to the bank of a large stream. Several homes were built on the gentle slope and as many more in the sides of the banks themselves. His guide led him to one underground domicile which boasted broad windows looking out over the water and a large oval doorway. As they drew near another trio of youngsters materialized to cluster questioningly around him. Thankfully none of them decided to find out what he tasted like.

His guide vanished inside. While he waited for her to return he set his burden down one sack at a time. This did not allow him to relax, since he had to repeatedly but gently slap tiny paws away from straps and seals.

"You're your father's cubs, all right."

"Who's father's cubs?" snapped a demanding voice. Jon-Tom spun to confront the speaker. Eyes locked.

For a moment Mudge was speechless, in itself sufficient indication of the shock he felt. Then he rushed to greet his old friend. "'Tis a ghost." Hand met paw. "No, 'tis too solid to be a ghost. I never thought you'd come back, mate. We'd sort o' given up 'ope, wot?"

"It took longer than I thought to set my affairs in order, Mudge." Another figure emerged from the doorway. "Hi, Weegee." She wore an apron covered with appliqued flowers.

"I'm glad you came back Jon-Tom. We all worried about you, every day."

Insistent fingers were tugging at the bottom of Mudge's vest. "Dada know stinkman?" Mudge backhanded her across the face, sending her tumbling tail over head. In an instant she'd regained her feet and zipped around to stare at Jon-Tom while remaining out of her father's reach.

"This is the human I've told all o' you about."

"Jun-Tum?" Another of the otterlings had her finger in her mouth. "One dad have to save alla time?"

Mudge coughed self-consciously. "Well, once in a while, anyways."

The cub was not so easily silenced. "You say alla time, dada. Got to save mans alla . . . ."

"Shut up, sapling. Cubs should be fuzzy an' not 'eard." He smiled wanly at his friend. "You know kids; tend to misremember wotever they've been told."

"Yeah, I know."

"Well come on in then, mate! Tell us o' wot you been up to all this time in the other world."

He shrugged. "Not much to tell. It's the same dull, smelly, dangerous place you visited yourself." As he spoke he was staring upstream. Mudge noticed the direction of his gaze, grinned and nudged the tall man in the ribs.

"Now you wouldn't be worryin' about a certain red-'eaded 'uman, would you, mate? No need to. She'd been tendin' the 'ome fires, so to speak, ever since you left. I admit the rest o' us tended to give up 'ope from time to time, but she never did. Not that flame-'aired lass. Oh, she's 'ad one or two lengthy affairs, but aside from that . . . ."

"Mudge!"

He glanced back at the doorway. "Take it easy, luv. Old Jon-Tom knows when 'is mate is funnin' with 'im. Come on, you skinny sight for sore eyeballs. I'll run up with you."

"Me too, me too!" The girl cub who'd chomped Jon-Tom's leg ran up to join them. Mudge ruffled the fur between her ears fondly.

"This is Picket. Fancies 'erself the family lookout."

"Does she always look out for you by trying to take a bite out of every stranger who comes down the road?"

"Usually," said Mudge with exaggerated cheerfulness. "You'll get to like 'er. You'll get to like 'em all. 'Ave 'em callin' you Uncle before you know it." He yelled at another of his obstreperous offsping. " 'Ere you, Smidgen, put that down or I'll knock you in the creek!"

Together they shooed the other cubs away from Jon-Tom's packages. Mudge studied them with interest. "Wot you got 'ere? Stuff from your world?"

"Treasures, yes. But I'd rather reveal them to everyone at

once—if I can get home before your brood steals everything at that isn't tied down."

"Wot, me kids—steal?"

"Why not? They've got the most light-fingered instructor in this world."

Mudge put one paw in the air and the other over his heart. "Take me for a cookfire cinder if I ever teach one o' me own flesh an' blood to take wot ain't theirs." He looked apologetic. "I swear I ain't been teachin' 'em, mate. They seem to come by it naturally."

With the otter's assistance Jon-Tom shouldered his heavy load. Not much farther now. A long walk from Westwood. "If there's a gene for that I'm sure it runs in your family."

Mudge frowned as he scratched his head uncertainly. "Don't 'ave any relations name o' Jean. They'll turn out all right. Their mother's the civilizin' influence on 'em." He turned to his daughter. "Be a luv an' get dada 'is favorite 'at, that's a dear."

Picket rocketed back toward the house, re-emerged an instant later carrying a red felt cap with two long white and yellow feathers protruding from the crown. Mudge carefully placed it between his ears.

"What happened to the green one?"

Mudge nodded at the unkempt beard. "Wot 'appened to your face? Time takes all things, mate. Even green 'ats."

The trail led up the bank away from the stream and back into the woods. "Didn't throw it away, though," the otter continued. "Got it in a drawer somewheres. Sort o' a memento o' our former travels together. Each stain on it tells a story."

"So I come back to find an old married *Lutra* with a family and responsibilities, a pillar of his community. What do you do for a living these days, Mudge?"

"You asked me that strange question before. Me answer's still the same. I live. Still got your duar, I see." The familiar double-stringed instrument hung from Jon-Tom's right shoulder, as bright and shiny as the day they'd taken it from Couvier Coulb's skilled hands. The varnish the old kinkajou had rubbed into the instrument protected the wood like Lucite.

"Yep. Been doing a little singing here and there. Being a wandering minstrel grows on you."

They were in sight of the familiar grove. Little had changed in his absence. The ancient dimensionally-expanded oaks looked the same. There were more flowers, evidence of Talea's handiwork. A familiar figure let out a shout from the branch that hung over Clothahump's doorway. Sorbl yelled a greeting, then vanished through an upper floor window to convey the good news to the wizard.

Jon-Tom's attention was on the tree next door. Every limb, every leaf was engraved in his memory. Mudge saw the look on his friend's face and motioned for his noisy offspring to be silent. They were perceptive enough to sense that this was an important moment in adult lives.

The door opened and there was Talea. A little older and a little more beautiful. She'd been busy with housework and wore a bandana around her red hair and a large work apron over her shorts and halter. There was no wind to ruffle the vision she made.

He put down his oversized backpacks. "Hello, Talea."

She dropped her broom and stared back at him. "Jon-Tom." Slowly she walked up to him, stood there inspecting every line of his face, every hair, remembering. Then she kicked him in the shin, the same one that Picket had sampled. He yelled.

"Hello Talea, hello Talea—is that all you can say after years have gone by, you mindless son of a whore? Years! Not one letter, not one frigging postcard."

"But Talea my sweet, there's no mail service between worlds." She advanced on him and he backed up as best he could on one good leg.

"Don't give me any of your clever spellsinger excuses. Years I've been waiting for you, years hoping you *would* come back so I could tell you how angry I was that you went back without me."

Four otterlings sat politely nearby and paid rapt attention

to his unplanned lesson in adulthood. Mudge stood next to them, making salient points as Talea chased the apologetic Jon-Tom several times around their tree home.

"Now pay attention an' maybe you lot'll learn somethin'," daddy told his brood. " 'Umans do this sort o' thing all the time. This is 'ow they show affection for one another after they've been apart for a long time. 'Umans are like clocks that always need windin'. Soon these two'll run down. Then they'll strike love an' fall into each others arms."

Sure enough, Talea was running out of breath. Jon-Tom let her run down, just as Mudge said, and then swept her against him. She was too weak to do more than batter feebly at his chest. Before long the pounding ceased altogether and was replaced by a different kind of contact.

"Now lady crying," said Picket thoughtfully. "He hurting her?"

"No. They're just demonstrating their love for one another," Mudge explained.

"Humans are crazy," said Nickum, one of two boys.

"Absolutely. All 'umans are crazy. These two are crazier than most. But they can be fun. We'll give 'em another couple o' minutes to sweat against each other and then we'll see if we can't find out wot me old friend 'as brought back from 'is own world, wot?"

Before that happened Clothahump put in an appearance. Jon-Tom thought the ancient wizard moved a little more slowly, a little more hesitantly than before he'd left, but those wise old eyes missed nothing.

"It is good to have you back, my boy. I've always felt, since you first came among us and we dealt in summary fashion with the Plated Folk, that you belonged here. Let us go inside. It is hot in the sun."

Everyone moved into Clothahump's tree. The otterlings were on their best behavior and Mudge only had to cuff one every two minutes to keep them in line. Jon-Tom sat in his favorite chair sipping Selesass tea while Talea curled up on the floor next to him. Sorbl provided refreshments.

"It's funny, but while I was here all I could ever think

about was going home, and once I got home I couldn't stop thinking about coming back here.'' He smiled at the woman sitting beside him. She was resting her head against his arm. ''Of course, Talea's presence here made my return imperative.

''Once home I had a life I'd left behind to clean up. I told everyone that I'd been away on a secret mission for my government and that I was going to have go away again soon, probably for a longer period. They were puzzled and confused, especially my parents, but in the end they understood. As long as the money was good and I was happy, they said.''

''At least you'll be 'appy,'' Mudge chortled.

''While I was home I discovered that in my heart and maybe also in my mind I wasn't cut out to be a lawyer. A solicitor, you call it. I also found out that playing lead in a rock band was pretty dull stuff after spellsinging. I thought of trying my hand at spellsinging in my own world, but I'm afraid they don't take very kindly to magic over there unless its packaged in cellophane, advertised on TV, and equipped with a government sticker.

''But I wanted to be *sure*. The passageway between our worlds might close up some day and if it does I wanted make certain I ended up on the right side. So I took my time exploring my options and learning about myself. Then when I decided this was where I really belonged, I scoured my world in search of those truly important things I would want to bring back with me. Items of value and importance. I had to be very selective because I knew I could only bring what I could carry on my back.''

Rising from the chair and walking over to the pile of overstuffed backpacks, he began loosening straps and buckles. The otterlings stirred excitedly.

The first thing he extracted was a large tin containing twenty pounds of his world's finest chocolate chip cookies. ''Got the recipe, too,'' he declared proudly. Setting the tin aside, he wrestled free a small bucket with a crank attached to the top. ''Hand ice cream maker. All we need is rock salt, sugar, flavoring and the cooperation of a contented cow.''

The next sack disgorged several strange and wondrous objects. "Portable television, VCR, pedal-powered generator. Had to find the last in a surplus store." From a third pack came two cases filled with videotapes of classic cartoons: Disney, Warner Brothers, Fleischer and some new Japanese features. Sandwiched in among the tapes were music books full of songs old and new.

"For spellsinging," he told them.

Clothahump surveyed the bounty spread out on the floor before him. "I know of your world only what you have told me, my boy, but based on that little information I have I should say you have made excellent choices."

"I want you to be proud of me, Clothahump. Here, let's get the big stuff out of the way." He picked up the TV. Talea moved the VCR and Mudge fought with the generator.

As he was shoving it along the floor it caught a rising plank. Generator and wood collapsed and Mudge barely escaped tumbling down with them. Everyone moved to the edge of the unsuspected cavity.

The secret compartment Mudge had accidentally revealed was the size of several bath tubs. Reaching down, he brought up a handful of diamonds, rubies, emeralds, pearls and fireines. The compartment contained a hoard that would have to be measured in bushels instead of karats.

Years had passed but Jon-Tom had not forgotten. He turned furiously on the wizard.

"I knew I should have put in that extra closet last year," Clothahump murmured. "One can never have too much storage room in a tree."

Jon-Tom grabbed himself a handful and shook it in the wizard's face. Precious stones went bouncing across the floor as they slipped from between his fingers.

"Look at this! You lied to me. All the danger and pain, all the travails of that nearly fatal journey of years ago could have been avoided. Mudge and I nearly got killed a dozen times on that trek to Strelakat Mews, and for what?"

"Calm yourself, my boy. I honestly don't know what you're raving about."

"You don't, eh? Don't tell me you've forgotten about the night those thieves broke in here and I had come over to and rescue you, breaking my duar in the process."

"Of course I remember." Clothahump's expression was placid, his demeanor composed.

"All that risk to protect a few lousy jewels."

Mudge's eyes were popping out of his head as he stared at the treasure. "Let's not dismiss old 'ardhshell's motives out o' 'and, mate. 'Tain't like 'e didn't 'ave anythin' worth risking a life or two for."

"I did not lie. As you may recall, my nocturnal visitors specifically asked to be given gold. Not once did they demand gems. Only gold. If you will look carefully you will find no gold. If I'd had any I most assuredly would have given it to them. But surely you wouldn't expect me to volunteer information about what I did have, now would you? That wouldn't have been sensible.

"Now consider this: If you hadn't been forced to intervene on my behalf your duar would not have been damaged. Consequently you would never have been compelled to travel to Strelakat Mews. Mudge would never have encountered his Weegee. You would not have discovered the gate between your world and mine. You would not have been able to return to your home to learn where your true destiny lies. Consider."

Putting aside his initial anger, Jon-Tom did just that. It wasn't easy. He didn't want to consider the matter logically and dispassionately. He wanted to stomp about and yell and shout imprecations. Unfortunately he knew he was doomed to lose from the start. Not only was Clothahump right, the turtle had two hundred and fifty years of debating experience on him.

"I resent having to admit it, sir, but you're right."

"Of course I am," said Clothahump blandly. "You are a spellsinger; not a solicitor, not a 'rock singer', whatever that may be, not anything else. I am your teacher and you are my student. That is your fate and that is your mate." He nodded toward Talea, then gestured around the room.

"These are your friends."

Jon-Tom took a deep breath and returned their stares: Mudge and Weegee, the four otterlings, a sober Sorbl, and back again to Clothahump. Talea completed the circle. So many things seemed to have come full circle. He thought of all the delightful companions he and Mudge had encountered; of massive but ladylike Roseroar, of Teyva and Colin the koala, of Clothahump's first famulus Pog, the transmogrified bat.

For company they sure as hell beat hanging around the pre-yuppies at the student union.

"I guess you can't argue with the world's greatest wizard."

"Not advisable," said Clothahump.

He smiled down at Talea. "Will you have me back? If love can be magnified by traveling, then mine's big enough to encompass the whole world."

"Have you back? A big, ugly, clumsy catastrophe-prone freak like you? On one condition."

"Name it."

"That you shave that grotesque fuzz off your face as soon as we're back in our own tree. It makes you look like a damn otter."

He bent to kiss her but Wicket bit her on the leg.